THE

# DOLL FACTORY

# THE
# DOLL FACTORY

A NOVEL

## Elizabeth Macneal

**EMILY BESTLER BOOKS**
—
**ATRIA**
NEW YORK LONDON TORONTO SYDNEY NEW DELHI

An Imprint of Simon & Schuster, Inc.
1230 Avenue of the Americas
New York, NY 10020

First Emily Bestler Books/Atria Books hardcover edition August 2019

**EMILY BESTLER BOOKS / ATRIA** BOOKS and colophon are trademarks of Simon & Schuster, Inc.

For information about special discounts for bulk purchases, please contact Simon & Schuster Special Sales at 1-866-506-1949 or business@simonandschuster.com.

The Simon & Schuster Speakers Bureau can bring authors to your live event. For more information, or to book an event, contact the Simon & Schuster Speakers Bureau at 1-866-248-3049 or visit our website at www.simonspeakers.com.

Interior design by Kyoko Watanabe

Manufactured in the United States of America

10 9 8 7 6 5 4 3 2 1

Library of Congress Cataloging-in-Publication Data

Names: Macneal, Elizabeth, 1988– author.
Title: The doll factory : a novel / Elizabeth Macneal.
Description: First Emily Bestler books/Atria books hardcover edition. | New York : Emily Bestler Books/Atria, 2019.
Identifiers: LCCN 2018034029 (print) | LCCN 2018034690 (ebook) | ISBN 9781982106782 (Ebook) | ISBN 9781982106768 (hardcover) | ISBN 9781982106775 (trade pbk.)
Classification: LCC PR6113.A2728 (ebook) | LCC PR6113.A2728 D65 2019 (print) | DDC 823/.92—dc23
LC record available at https://lccn.loc.gov/2018034029

ISBN 978-1-9821-0676-8
ISBN 978-1-9821-0678-2 (ebook)

*For Enid and Arthur*

*London*
*November 1850*

# A PAINTING

When the streets are at their darkest and quietest, a girl settles at a small desk in the cellar of a dollmaker's shop. A bald china head sits in front of her and watches her with a vacant stare. She squeezes red and white watercolors onto an oyster shell, sucks the end of her brush, and adjusts the looking glass before her. The candle hisses. The girl narrows her eyes at the blank paper.

She adds water and mixes up fleshy colors. The first streak of paint on the page is as sharp as a slap. The paper is thick, cold-pressed, and it does not crinkle.

In the candlelight, the shadows magnify, and the edges of her hair are one with the blackness. She paints on, a single sweep for her chin, white for her cheekbones where the flame catches. She copies her faults faithfully: her widely spaced eyes, the deformed twist of her collarbone. Her sister and mistress are sleeping upstairs, and even the shushing of her paintbrush seems an intrusion, a deafening rally that will wake them.

She frowns. She has made her face too small. She meant to fill the page with it, but her head floats above a blank expanse. The paper, on which she spent a week's saved wages, is ruined. She should have sketched the outline first, been less hasty to begin.

She sits for a few moments with the light and her picture. Her heart skitters; the doll's face watches. She should return to bed before she is discovered.

But the girl leans forward without taking her eyes off the mirror and pulls the candle toward her. It is beeswax not tallow, pilfered from her mistress's secret supply. She dips her fingers into the hot wax and makes a thimble. Then she runs her hand through the flame, seeing how long she can bear the heat, until she hears the downy hairs on her finger sizzle.

*Part*
# ONE

Surely something resides in this heart that is not
perishable, and life is more than a dream.

—Mary Wollstonecraft, Letters Written During a
Short Residence in Sweden, Norway and Denmark (1796)

A thing of beauty is a joy for ever:
Its loveliness increases; it will never
Pass into nothingness; but still will keep
A bower quiet for us, and a sleep
Full of sweet dreams, and health, and quiet breathing.

—John Keats, "Endymion" (1818)

# Silas Reed's Shop of Curiosities
## Antique and New

Silas is sitting at his desk, a stuffed turtle dove in his palm. The cellar is as still and quiet as a tomb, aside from the slow gusts of his breath that ruffle the bird's plumage.

Silas puckers his lips as he works and, in the lamplight, he is not unhandsome. He has retained a full head of hair in his thirty-eighth year, and it shows no sign of silvering. He looks around him, at the glass jars that line the walls, each labeled and filled with the bloated hulks of pickled specimens. Swollen lambs, snakes, lizards, and kittens press against the edges of their confinement.

"Don't wriggle free of me now, you little rascal," he mutters, picking up the pliers and tightening the wire on the bird's claws.

He likes to talk to his creatures, to make up histories that have landed them on his slab. After considering many imagined scenarios for this dove—disrupting barges on the canal, nesting in a sail of *The Odyssey*—he has settled on one pretence he likes; and so he rebukes this companion often for its invented habit of attacking cress sellers. He releases his hold on the bird, and it sits stiffly on the wooden post.

"There!" he exclaims, leaning back and pushing his hair out of his eyes. "And perhaps this'll teach you a lesson for knocking that bunch of greens out of that little girl's arms."

Silas is satisfied with this commission, especially given that he rushed the final stages to have it ready by the morning. He is sure the artist will find the bird to his liking; as requested, it is frozen as if in midflight, its wings forming a perfect "V." What's more, Silas has skimmed further profit by adding another dove heart to one of the yellowed jars. Little brown orbs float in preserving fluid, ready to fetch a good price from quacks and apothecaries.

Silas tidies the workshop, wiping and straightening his tools. He is halfway up the ladder rungs, nudging the trapdoor with his shoulder as he cradles the dove, when the consumptive wheeze of the bell sounds below him.

*Albie*, he hopes, as it is early enough, and he abandons the bird on a cabinet and hurries through the shop, wondering what the child will bring him. The boy's recent hauls have been increasingly paltry—maggoty rats, aging cats with smashed skulls, even a half run-over pigeon with a stumpy claw. ("But if you knew, sir, how hard it is with the bone grubbers pinching the best of the trade—") If Silas's collection is to stand the test of time, he needs something truly exceptional to complete it. He thinks of the bakery nearby on the Strand, which made a poor living with its bulky wholemeal loaves, good only for doorstops. Then the baker, on the brink of debtors' prison, started to pickle strawberries in sugar and sell them by the jar. It transformed the shop, made it famous even in tourist pamphlets of the city.

The trouble is, Silas often thinks he has found his special, unique item, but then he finishes the work and finds himself hounded by doubts, by the ache for more. The pathologists and collectors he admires—men of learning and medicine like John Hunter and Astley Cooper—have no shortage of specimens. He has eavesdropped on the conversations of medical men, sat white with jealousy in drinking holes opposite University College London as they've discussed the morning's dissections. He might lack their connections, but surely, *surely*, one day Albie will bring him something—his hand trembles—*remarkable*. Then, his name will be etched on a museum entrance, and all of his work, all of his toil, will be recognized. He imagines climbing the stone steps with Flick, his dearest childhood friend, and pausing as they see "*Silas Reed*" engraved in marble. She, unable to contain her pride, her palm resting in the small of his back. He, explaining that he built it all for her.

But it is not Albie, and each knock and ring of the bell yields more disappointment. A maid calls on behalf of her mistress, who wants a stuffed hummingbird for her hat. A boy in a velvet jacket browses endlessly and finally buys a butterfly brooch, which Silas sells with a quiver of disdain. All the while, Silas moves only to place their coins in a dogskin purse. In the quiet between times, his thumb tracks a single sentence in *The Lancet*. "'Tu-mor separ-at-ing the os-oss-ossa navi.'" The ringing of the bell and the raps on the door are the only beats of his life. Upstairs, an attic bedroom; downstairs his dark cellar.

It is exasperating, Silas thinks as he stares around the pokey shop, that the dullest items are those that pay his rent. There is no accounting for the poor taste of the masses. Most of his customers will overlook the real marvels—the skull of a century-old lion, the fan made of a whale's lung tissue; the taxidermy monkey in a bell jar—and head straight for the Lepidoptera cabinet at the back. It contains vermilion butterfly wings, which he traps between two small panes of glass; some are necklace baubles, others for mere display. Foolish knick-knacks that they could make themselves if they had the imagination, he thinks. It is only the painters and the apothecaries who pay for his real interests.

And then, as the clock sings out the eleventh hour, he hears a light tapping, and the faint stutter of the bell in the cellar.

He hurries to the door. It will be a silly child with only tuppence to spend, or if it is Albie, he'll have another damned bat, a mangy dog good for nothing but a stew—and yet, Silas's heart quickens.

"Ah, Albie," Silas says, opening the door and trying to keep his voice steady. Thames fog snakes in.

The ten-year-old child grins back at him. ("Ten, I knows, sir, because I was born on the day the Queen married Albert.") A single yellow tooth is planted in the middle of his upper gums like a gallows.

"Got a fine fresh creature for you today," Albie says.

Silas glances down the dead-end alley, at its empty ramshackle houses like a row of drunks, each tottering further forward than the last.

"Out with it, child," he says, tweaking the boy under the chin to assert his superiority. "What is it, then? The foreleg of a Megalosaurus, or perhaps the head of a mermaid?"

"A bit chilly for mermaids in Regent Canal at this time of year, sir, but that other creature—Mega-what-sumfink—says he'll leave you a knee when he snuffs it."

"Kind of him."

Albie blows into his sleeve. "I got you a right jewel, which I won't part with for less than two bob. But I'm warning you now, it ain't red like you like 'em."

The boy unravels the cord of his sack. Silas's eyes follow his fingers. A pocket of air escapes, gamey, sweet and putrid, and Silas raises a hand to his nose. He can never stand the smells of the dead; the shop is as clean as a chemist's, and each day he battles the coal smoke, the fur-dust, and the *stink*. He would like to uncork the miniature glass bottle of lavender oil that he stores in his waistcoat, to dab it on his upper lip, but he does not want to distract the boy—Albie has the attention span of a shrew on his finest days.

The boy winks, grappling with the sack, pretending it is alive.

Silas summons a smirk that feels hollow on his lips. He hates to see this urchin, this bricky street brat, tease him. It makes him draw back into himself, to recall himself at Albie's age, running heavy sacks of wet porcelain across the pottery yard, his arms aching from his mother's fists. It makes him wonder if he's ever truly left that life—even now he'll let himself be taunted by a single-toothed imp.

But Silas says nothing. He feigns a yawn, but watches through a sideways crocodile eye that betrays his interest by not blinking.

Albie grins, and unmasks the sacking to present two dead puppies.

At least, Silas thinks it is two puppies, but when he grabs hold of the limbs, he notices only one scruff. One neck. One head. The skull is segmented.

Silas gasps, smiles. He runs his fingers along the seam of the crown to check it isn't a trick. He wouldn't put it past Albie to join two dogs with a needle and thread if it fetched him a few more pennies. He holds them up, sees their silhouette against his lamp, squeezes their eight legs, the stones of their vertebrae.

"This is more like it, eh," he breathes. "Oh, yes."

"Two bob for't," Albie says. "No less than that."

Silas laughs, pulls out his purse. "A shilling, that's all. And you can come in, visit my workshop." Albie shakes his head, steps farther into the alley, and looks around him. A look almost like fear passes over the boy's face, but it soon vanishes when Silas tips the coin into his palm. Albie hawks and spits his disdain on to the cobbles.

"A mere bob? Would you have a lad starve?"

But Silas closes the door, and ignores the hammering that follows.

He steadies himself on the cabinet. He glances down to check the pups are still there, and they are, clasped against his chest as a child would hold a doll. Their eight furred legs dangle, as soft as moles. They look like they did not even live to take their first breath.

He has it at last. His pickled strawberry.

# Boy

After Silas slams shut the door, Albie bites the shilling between his front tooth and gums, for no reason except that he has seen his sister do the same. He sucks on it. It tastes sweet. He is pleased; he never expected two bob. But if you ask for two bob and you get a bob, what happens if you ask for a bob? He shrugs, spits it out, and then tucks it into his pocket. He will buy a bowl of boiled pigs' ears for his lunch, and give his sister the rest. But first, he has another task to complete, and he's already late.

There is a second hemp sack next to his Dead Creatures bag, which contains tiny skirts he sewed through the night. He is careful never to mix the two. Sometimes, as he hands over the bag at the doll shop, he is convinced he has muddled them, and he feels an arrow-quiver in his heart. He would not like to see Mrs. Salter's sour face if she opened a bag of maggoty rats.

He blows on his little fists to warm them and takes off at a run. The boy zigzags through the streets, rickety legs bowed outward. He runs west, through the muck of Soho. Gaunt whores track his racing limbs with tatty eyes, just as worn-out cats watch a fly.

He emerges onto Regent Street, glances at the shop that sells sets of teeth for four guineas, taps his single tooth with his tongue, and then catapults into the path of a horse. It bucks and rears. He leaps back and masters his fear by bellowing at the coachman, "Watch it, cove!"

And before the man has had a chance to shout back at him or crack him with his whip, Albie has darted across the street, and crossed the threshold of Mrs. Salter's Doll Emporium.

# Mrs. Salter's Doll Emporium

Iris runs her thumbnail down the seams of the miniature skirts, poised to crack the shells of any fleas. She picks at a loose thread, then knots it.

Even though it is almost noon, her mistress Mrs. Salter is yet to rise for the day. Her twin sister sits behind her, head bowed over her sewing.

"Flea-less, at least. But do take more care with the threads," Iris says to Albie. "There's a whole city of seamstresses who'd sell their newborns to pinch the work off you."

"But, miss, my sister's got influenza and I nursed her through the night. I ain't even been able to go skating for days, and it ain't fair neither—"

"Poor thing." Iris looks around, but her sister Rose is preoccupied. She lowers her voice. "But you must remember you are dealing with a devil, not a woman, in Mrs. Salter, and fairness never has been a concern of hers. Have you ever seen her stick out her tongue?"

Albie shakes his head.

"It's forked."

Albie's smile is so open, so free of artifice, that Iris wants to embrace him. His mucky blond hair, his single fang, his soot-stained face: none of these things are his fault. In another world, he could have been born into their family in Hackney.

She tucks the next stack of fabric into his bag, checks again that Rose isn't looking, and then hands him sixpence. She planned to put it toward a new sheet of paper and a paintbrush. "To buy broth for your sister."

Albie stares at the coin, hesitant.

"It isn't a trick," she says.

"Thank you, miss," he says, his eyes as black as pin tops. He snatches it from her, as if afraid she'll change her mind, and scampers out of the shop, almost barreling into the Italian organ-grinder, who swats him with his cane.

Iris watches him go and allows herself to inhale. He may be a filthy little urchin, but even so she can never understand why he stinks quite so foully of decay.

The slender Regent Street shop is wedged between two rival confectioners. Due to slight fissures in the chimney, Mrs. Salter's Doll Emporium is perpetually filled with the smells of boiled sugar and burnt caramels. Sometimes, Iris dreams of eating bonbons and plum jellies, perfect little cakes with flared pastry and whipped cream, of riding gingerbread elephants down to Buckingham Palace. Other times, she dreams that she is drowning in boiling treacle.

When the Whittle sisters were first apprenticed to Mrs. Salter—whether she is, or ever was, married is a mystery to Iris—Iris was mesmerized by the salon. Given her twisted collarbone and Rose's smallpox scars, she expected they would be shut in the cellar storeroom. Instead, they were directed to a gilded bureau in the middle of the shop floor, where interested customers could observe their work. She was handed powdered paints and fox-hair brushes for decorating the dolls' feet and hands and faces. Of course, she knew that the days would be long, but she marveled over the ebony dressers that ran the length of the room, their shelves crammed with porcelain dolls. It was warm and light too; candles sizzled in gold brackets, and there was a fire in the corner.

But now, as she sits at the desk next to her sister, clasping a china doll and a scuffed brush, she is struggling to stifle a yawn. It is a weight of exhaustion she never could have imagined, a drudgery greater than if the shop were a factory. Her hands are red and cracked from the winter cold, but if she greases them with tallow, the paintbrush slips from her grasp and she botches the doll's lips and cheeks. She looks around her at the dressers which are not ebony but cheap oak painted black, at the gold varnish that peels from the brackets due to the heat of the candle flames, and her least favorite thing of all: the balding patch of carpet where Mrs. Salter paces daily, now worn thinner than her mistress's hair. The sickly smell of confectionery, the airlessness of the room, and the staring rows of dolls, make it seem more like a crypt than a shop. There are times when Iris struggles to catch her breath.

"Dead?" Iris whispers to her twin sister, nudging a daguerreotype toward her. It is a small sepia image of a little girl, her hands folded as neatly as doves in her lap. Iris glances up when Mrs. Salter enters the shop and sits by the door, the spine of her Bible crackling as she opens it.

Rose tries to silence her with a look.

It is one of Iris's few enjoyments, even if it does make her feel guilty: assessing whether the children in the daguerreotypes are dead. For a reason she can't explain, she likes to know whether she is making a mourning doll, to be placed on the grave of a deceased infant, or if she is painting a plaything for a bouncing, living child.

Mrs. Salter derives the bulk of her income from this custom doll service. It is winter now, and the cold and its sicknesses doubles their workload, often tipping their working hours from twelve to twenty. "It is understandable," Mrs. Salter will say in her customer-voice, "and indeed natural that you would want to commemorate a dear passed spirit. After all, as it is in Corinthians, 'We are confident, I say, and willing rather to be absent from the body, and to be present with the Lord.' Their soul is gone, and this doll is a symbol of the earthly vessel they left behind."

Deducing whether the children in the images are dead can be a subtle operation, but Iris has learned the clues. Sometimes it is easy. The child appears to be sleeping surrounded by flowers. There might be a clear prop behind the infant, even a person holding them who is hidden to look like upholstery; or if there are other people in the daguerreotype, the exposure will blur all but one child, who is picked out in perfect, unmoving clarity.

"Alive," Iris decides. "Her eyes are blurred."

"Silence! I will not tolerate chatter," Mrs. Salter barks, with the sudden flare of a lit match. Iris dips her head, then mixes a slightly deeper pink for the shadow between the doll's lips. She does not look up, dreads inviting one of Mrs. Salter's pinches, which are delivered to the soft inside of her elbow.

The girls sit side by side for the day, barely speaking, barely moving, pausing only for a meal of beef dripping and bread.

Iris paints the porcelain faces, threads the hair through the holes in the scalp, sometimes curls it with irons heated in the coals if the child has ringlets. Meanwhile, Rose's needle rises and falls like a violinist. Her job is to add the finer, more skilled detail to the rough skirts and bodices that the slop sewers make through the night. Seed pearls, ruched sleeves, passementerie trimmings, tiny velvet buttons as small as mouse noses.

Even though they are identical, the twins could not be less alike. As young girls, Rose was always singled out as the real beauty of the two, their parents' favorite, and she clutched this understanding like a treasure. Iris's warped collarbone, a birth defect that causes her left shoulder to hunch forward, invited a protective kindness from her sister that only occasionally irritated Iris. ("I'm not an invalid, you know," she would snap as Rose insisted on carrying any parcels, striding ahead as if expecting Iris to fall in line behind her.) They squabbled too, arguing over the largest roast potato at dinner, over who could skip the longest, write the neatest. They could deal blows of quick cruelty because they knew that with each fight, there would be a reconciliation: limbs overlapping as they sat by the fire, dreaming up details of their imaginary shop *Flora*, its shelves brimming with flower trinkets, wall brackets stuffed with irises and roses.

But when the sisters turned sixteen, Rose contracted smallpox, which nearly killed her. She said she wished it had when she saw the thick rash of boils covering her face and body, the cloudy roll of her blinded left eye. Her skin soon cratered and turned purplish, worsened by her endless scratching. Her legs dimpled with scars. "Why me? Why me?" she wailed, and then, only once, a hissed whisper that Iris wondered if she misheard: "It should have been you."

Now, at twenty-one, their hair is the same dark auburn, but Rose wears hers as a penance, draped forward to cover as much of her pocked cheeks as possible. Iris's is waist-length and gathered into a long, dense plait, her skin tauntingly smooth and white. They no longer laugh together, they no longer whisper secrets. They do not talk about the shop.

Some mornings, Iris will wake up and see her sister staring at her with an expression that is so blank and cold that it frightens her.

Iris feels her eyelids begin to sink, as heavy as if they had been sewn with lead weights. Mrs. Salter is attending to a customer, her voice a melodious hum.

"Most delicate care is taken with each commission—pure porcelain from the northern factories—we are a kind of family—indeed, such honest girls, so unlike those squawking bonnet touters on Cranbourne Alley—immoral, the lot of them—"

Iris digs her fingers into her thighs to stay awake. As she lolls forward, she wonders if a few moments of sleep would really be so terrible—

"Lawks, Rosie," she whispers, jolting upright and rubbing her arm. "I should wonder you require a needle with elbows like that."

"If Mrs. Salter had seen—"

"I can't bear it," Iris whispers. "I can't."

Rose is silent. She worries a scab on her hand.

"What would you do if we could escape here? If we didn't have to—"

"We are lucky," Rose murmurs. "And what else can you do? Abandon me here, become a mollysop?"

"Of course I should not," Iris hisses back. "I should like to paint real things, not these endless china eyes and lips and cheeks, and—ugh." Without realizing it, she is balling her fist. She unfurls it, tries to think of the pain she is causing her sister. But her illness was not Iris's fault, and yet she is punished for it every day, pushed out from any affection. "I can't stand it here, living in the den of Madame Satan."

Across the shop, Mrs. Salter's head revolves as sharply as an owl's. She frowns. Rose jumps and jabs herself with the needle.

The door slams in the wind. Iris strains her eyes through the grimy-paned windows. She sees the carriages rolling past and imagines the ladies cocooned inside.

She bites her lip, shakes out a little blue powder and dabs her paintbrush into the bottle of water once more.

# Pups

"Now, you naughty pups," Silas says, the black wing of his hair falling forward as he takes his seat at the cellar desk, "I'm sorry it's come to this. But if you hadn't helped yourselves to Cook's marzipan, things might have been different." He laughs, pleased with the history he has contrived, and lines up three knives of varying sizes. The conjoined puppies lie before him, bellies up.

He thought at first of pickling the beasts, but instead he will make two specimens out of the pair, by both stuffing and articulating them. When he builds his marble-walled museum, the taxidermy form and skeleton will sit side by side in the entrance hall, guarded by stucco columns.

He wipes his forehead, which sweats even in the November cold. He flexes his fingers. The largest knife chills his hand.

He makes a small incision in the left puppy's abdomen and tugs the fur with an even pressure. His breath is a thin whistle between his teeth. He is careful not to puncture the flesh and the organs nestling below it, all packed tight behind a purple membrane. He shifts an inch to the left so that the hounds fall into the lamplight, and then severs the pelt as far as he can, stopping short at the soft paw pads and the lozenge-shaped nose with four nostrils. The shadows make accuracy difficult, so he works more slowly, easing the smaller scalpel into the final cuts. As day turns to dusk outside, he detaches the fur in a single piece.

"All those guests, with no marzipan to go with their hothouse fruit and cream. Such mischievous pups," he says, picturing them pristinely stuffed. If Gideon were to see him now—how he has improved in the fifteen years that have elapsed—but Silas swallows the thought. He is determined to enjoy this part, when the potential of the corpse lies before him, before its promise sours. The thrill is as fresh as it was when he found his first skull.

"Walk with me," he said to Flick that day, as they left the pottery factory together, but for a reason he can't remember, he ended up alone in the countryside.

It was then that he happened on the decaying corpse of a fox. He was disgusted at first, and cupped his nose, but then he saw that its fur was as red as Flick's hair. The fox was perfect, fragile, each nugget of bone neater than a jigsaw. The creature had lived, breathed, and now existed in the curious liminality between beauty and horror. He touched its skull, and then his own.

He visited it each day, watching as maggots seized it, as its skin wasted and the intricacy of its white structure became apparent, like the slow bloom of a flower. He noticed new things each time: the surprising thinness of its thighbone, the laced webbing of the cranium. When he flicked it with his fingernail, it rang dully. Once the skull was entirely cleaned of meat, he wrapped it in cloth and took it for himself.

That summer, his skin coated in a thick paste of dust and sweat, he raked over each tuft of grass, each hillock, each copse and riverbank, until he had fifteen skulls. He set traps, whittled sticks into spears, and crept up on the old, slow rabbits, and pushed the air out of their throats with his fingers. They scrabbled and kicked for the first minute, and he often held his breath with them. Then they would limpen, and still he would cling on, just in case.

How neatly he arranged the skulls! He thought he would be content with five, ten, but he needed more. Each item made him happier and more anxious than the one before it. And now, he has this treasure. This furred, spidery beast, finer than anything he ever could have imagined as a boy, and he does not think he will ever want again.

His work is as complete as he can manage that day, and he has learned from experience that he will ruin the specimen if he continues without pause. It must be almost five o'clock; he yawns, decides to rest. He places the skinned pups into a tin bucket. Later, when he has boiled off the meat, he will assemble the skeleton with tweezers, glue, and wire as thin as thread.

He climbs the ladder to the shop, and then the stairs to his attic. As he pulls on his nightgown, he glimpses the shelf of stuffed mice next to his bed. Each is dressed in a tiny costume.

Silas picks up a brown mouse. He strokes its worsted skirts, the shawl he crocheted with the thinnest wool, the small round plate it grips in its paws. He places it back on the shelf and snuffs out the candle.

He is almost asleep when he hears a knocking.

He pulls a pillow over his head.

The knocking becomes a dull thunder.

"Silaaaas!"

He sighs. The impatience of the man! It's a blessing Silas has no neighbors to disturb, and can't he read the "Closed" sign?

"*Ouvrez la porte!*"

He groans, sits up, pulls on a jacket and trousers, lights a stuttering candle, and shoulders his way down the narrow staircase.

*"Je veux ma colombe!"*

"Mr. Frost," Silas says, opening the door. A tall, slender man in paint-spattered rags stares back at him. He has a kind of frenzied magnetism about him, an entitlement and self-belief that leaves Silas torn between wanting to please or despise him. Louis smiles.

"There! I knew you were in. I'm here for my dove, if I haven't frightened him off his perch." He doesn't wait for a reply, but bellows at a figure silhouetted in the alley entrance and beckons him over. "Here! Over here! Late, as ever."

It is almost nightfall, and at first Silas struggles to identify the skinny man trotting up the alley, swerving the fetid mounds of vegetable peelings and cinder dust. He comes closer; his face glints off Silas's lamp. Johnnie Millais.

"Goodness, Louis, what happened to your clothes? I wouldn't dress my dog in that shirt."

"A treat to see you, Millais, as always," Louis says, entering the shop without either being invited or cleaning his boots on the iron scraper.

"It's a bit of luck you're still open," Millais says, following him in, and Silas doesn't contradict him.

"Silas's arranged my dove. Where is he, then?" Louis lifts the lion's skull with both hands and pretends to throw it at Millais. "Rar!" he says, with a snort.

Silas tenses, wishing he had the courage to ask him to put it down; instead he busies himself retrieving the dove from the cabinet.

"Heavens! It's splendid. Just what I had in mind," the artist exclaims. He seizes it, strokes its head. "If only my models would sit as still as you." Louis presses a guinea into Silas's palm, double what they agreed. "And Millais, you must buy a mouse for the corner of your *Mariana*. To add movement to that bare patch of canvas." He lifts a stuffed brown mouse from a shelf by its tail and says, "I'll take this too."

"She's fragile—" Silas attempts, but Louis seems not to hear him, and crams the bird and the mouse into a satchel, head first.

Silas watches the two men run down the narrow passageway, Louis's hands on the back of Millais's shoulders, performing some kind of skip on each third step. His lamp picks out Louis's ankles, the white flash of his wrist. It reminds him of Flick, her touch that he has not felt in over twenty years.

When they vanish into the darkness, Silas looks around his little shop, at its low ceiling, its small chipped dressers, which he has done his best to paint, and the corners of his mouth press downward.

"No more attacking cress sellers, eh," he says. "Your new friend wouldn't like it."

# The Painter

Despite her drowsiness earlier, Iris cannot sleep. The smell of burnt sugar is making her head ache, and a whisker of horsehair pricks her thigh through the mattress. She shifts, casts a sticky arm outside the counterpane and lets it cool. She tries to concentrate on being still and peaceful, to time her breaths with her sister's. But her mind ticks. She wants to paint. She pictures the slim metal tubes of Winsor & Newton watercolors, the oyster shells on which she mixes them, and her own stock of sable-hair brushes, which she finally purchased after half a year of careful thrift.

She nudges her twin.

"But I haven't seen the parakeet," Rose mumbles, and Iris knows she will sleep soundly until St. George's tolls five. Through the wall, she hears the locomotive groan and whistle of Mrs. Salter's snores. She is as good as dead after her nightly swigs of laudanum.

When Iris can bear it no longer, she pulls herself free of the covers. The wooden boards squeak underfoot, and the latch of the bedroom door, which Iris keeps oiled, gives easily. She feels a strange compulsion to laugh, but stifles her rising giggle by clapping a hand over her mouth.

As she passes into the hallway, her nightgown whisked by a slight breeze, Mrs. Salter's door is ajar, the light from her lamp casting the floor with a jaundiced glow. There is a stench of stomach acid. Iris is sure Mrs. Salter's illness is caused, not eased, by her nightly battery of pills: "Mother's Friend" for her gastric aches, "Dr. Munro's Harmless Arsenic Complexion Wafers" to conceal her pimples. Iris tires of scrubbing the vomit-stiffened rug, her hands stinging with vinegar. Worse, of bearing Mrs. Salter's slaps on days when her hallucinations crystallize into certainty that she is sheltering twin harlots in her house, and that Iris is on the brink of being seduced by a green-skinned gentleman with tusks.

If only the apothecary would lace her medicine with rat poison, Iris thinks to herself, as she tiptoes down the edges of the stairs where the creak is quietest.

The cellar storeroom is small and cramped, damp staining the walls. The smell of moldy plaster blocks out even the slightest aroma of sugar.

Iris walks to the open dresser in the corner. It is stacked with baskets containing unpainted porcelain arms, feet, and heads. A cloth bag holds the bales of human hair, shorn off the scalps of South German peasants. Iris lifts this and takes out the top painting and her supplies, which are hidden below it. She carries them to the desk, sits.

The scale of her face is just as wrong as she remembered. At first Iris feels overwhelmed by a despair that she is not, and never will be, good enough. But when she peers closer, she finds a starkness that she likes, a brightness too. If only the head did not drift so absently at the top of the page, if only she could anchor it more. She is loath to cut up the paper; it is a small sheet already. Perhaps she can salvage it after all, find a way to fill the empty space.

The honest texture of her nightdress—white flannel with yellow stains under her armpits—scratches her neck. Before she thinks what she is doing, she stands and pulls it over her head. Her figure, on which the candlelight catches, is as pale and glossy as a minnow.

For a moment, she imagines her parents' disgust at what she is doing, their unswerving emphasis on morality. But there is no risk of them catching her here; more alarming is the thought of Rose's disappointment, or worse, Mrs. Salter stumbling into the room, her horror amplified by laudanum. The names she would call her ("whore," "strumpet"), the real possibility that Iris would lose her employment, and with it twenty pounds a year. But she does not dwell on this thought; she mixes her watercolors, the chair cold against her thighs.

She stares again in the mirror, but this time she lets her gaze travel down, to her small breasts with their hard nipples. She chews her lip. *Deformed.* And yet: she wonders if there are traces of beauty in her.

She used to hate that collarbone twist, the way the bone had healed at an outward angle after it broke when she was born. It only affected her gait a little, but she would catch the children on her street exaggerating it ("Here comes the hunchback"), her sister rebuking them with only a hint of pity, risking their vehemence too ("The twin giantesses"). But in recent years, she has come to accept it as a part of herself that she would not change even if she could. It certainly does not deter the shouts of the street boys. Occasionally, they try to grab her waist as she passes. "Fancy a brush?" or "I've got a hunch you're after a poke with my truncheon." She will set her face ("Got a case of the morbs, miss? Cheer up!"), push past them, ignore their whoops. Rose, unmocked, untouched, undesired, will look down, and Iris will place an arm around her shoulder and remind her sister how much she hates the whistles, in a tone that feels too insistent.

She supposes that one day she will have to encourage one of the boys who stands on the threshold of the shop, twisting his cap, because marriage is a way out, though to where she does not know. She is twenty-one, after all, and it is not long until her beauty tips like cream. Her parents have written to her with word of a porter who is keen to call on her, but she avoided him when he visited.

But. Rose. She will never find a match; the best Iris can hope is to marry adequately, and support her sister through it. To leave her sister—she does not know if she could do it. They are twins, bound together, and her sister's illness seemed both to tighten and unravel that knot. When they were children, and Iris sketched with a nub of coal on any paper she could find—butter wrappings, snippings of newspaper, offcuts of old wallpaper—her sister was fascinated by the way her pencil could echo the shapes in front of her. "Draw those scissors!" she would command, and Iris would oblige. "Draw me an elephant!" but she could never improvise. Now her sister turns from her when she tries to entertain her with a sketch.

Iris nudges away the thought, and mixes the right rosiness for the underside of her breast where the shadow falls. She runs the paintbrush along the page, watches the watercolor bloom on the sheet. She feels in control, as if her body is her own again, not a vessel for Mrs. Salter to use to scrub floors, not merely as a daily reminder to Rose of what she could have been. She feels a tremor of something that could be shame, could be satisfaction, could even be the cold.

She stares at her side. It is impossible to imagine a man's rough hand gripping it. She presses her palm there, moves it to her breast and clutches it. She flinches and returns to her painting.

She has never asked Rose about what she witnessed her doing with Charles, "her gentleman," as they called him. At the beginning, Rose chattered about little else, showing Iris with a blithe pride the gifts he sent: chocolate bonbons and a yellow canary (which flew up the chimney and died). They were fifteen, and he was supposed to rescue her from this grind of a life, pretty her up as his young wife in his modest townhouse in Marylebone. He befriended Iris too, and he told her he'd lend her some money to set up their shop when he and Rose were—he broke off at this hint of marriage. *Flora* would shimmer out of their imaginings and become real, and Iris turned to her sister to check that she didn't mind this attention, her gentleman including Iris in his and Rose's dreams.

He came to visit each Sunday when their parents were on their errands. Rose had always told Iris to stay in the upstairs room, but one afternoon the sisters had had a disagreement and Iris felt suddenly peevish at being shut away, kept apart from her sister's secrets. She settled outside the door and spied on them through the keyhole. She watched how he sat down, pulled her sister to him, teased up her skirts, and undid the buttons of his trousers. Iris barely had time to draw breath before Rose straddled him, rising and falling with a practiced rhythm. Iris was horrified, enthralled, unable to look away, mesmerized by the contortions of his face, his hands that gripped her sister's milky thighs. She wished for a moment that it was her with her petticoats hitched up, her twin who watched through the keyhole instead. It was all done so horribly easily, so simply, in the wooden chair that her grandfather had made.

Iris still does not know how Charles found out that Rose had contracted smallpox. The day after the boils pussed all over Rose's face and body, Iris admitted him into the hallway and took a letter from him. "She'll be so pleased to hear from you. It's just a rheum, and she'll be better in no time," she lied, but he said little and left abruptly. The letter was not a billet-doux, but ended everything, and with it her sister's boisterous laughter, her whispered confidences. When Rose screamed at Iris to be gone from the room, Iris took hold of the chair and drove it into the wall.

A sudden sound. Heavy footsteps.

Iris is so lost in the memory that she jumps, knocking the murky paint water over the desk.

She lunges for her painting, pulls it free before the liquid pools on to it. The footsteps have receded.

"Oh, heavens," she mutters, holding her hand over her chest, and she could laugh with relief. How foolish of her! But the noise *did* sound so close, and so loud that she was sure it was Mrs. Salter on the stairs. It was nothing more than the confectionery apprentices back from a late night at a penny gaff.

It is only when she starts to mop the water that she notices the doll's head. She curses. It must have been splashed by the jar as it fell. A gray watermark bruises its face.

"Oh, lawks," she mutters, picking up the head and wiping it against her nightgown. It took her hours to paint. She scrubs at the china harder and harder, spitting on each cheek, but it is no good. The porcelain is stained beyond repair.

She grits her teeth, releases a bestial growl. To think, it was just somebody passing outside. And now—she looks through the high barred window and decides it must be midnight at the earliest—she will have to work through the night to paint another face.

Iris pulls on her nightgown, suddenly aware of the cold of the small room. She will not look at her picture. *Obscene.*

She is struck by a familiar feeling that there is something wrong deep within herself, like a tumor that cannot be lanced. She should destroy her painting, catch the paper with the edge of the candle.

But she stands, tucks it under the basket, and picks out another blank china head.

# The Great Exhibition

It is Saturday morning and the bells are tolling. For the past fortnight, Silas has been so immersed in the construction of the puppies' pale skeleton that he has lived on nothing but stale cake and weak beer. He craves a buttered brandy at the Dolphin. He peers at the clock; it won't be open for several hours.

"Oh, hang it," he says, and resolves to fill the time by visiting the building site of the Great Exhibition. He is uncertain how he feels about it: how can his small shop ever compare to one of the largest museums ever built? Such a showy edifice seems designed merely to diminish his achievements, and yet he finds himself watching its assembly almost weekly, longing for it to be complete.

His alleyway is usually deserted, but a couple of men are sprawled in the gutter-muck, one smeared with his own vomit, his breeches damp with piss. Silas stares at them for a moment. The shape of the head and shoulder looks so like Gideon—but he knows he is mistaken. He holds his handkerchief to his nose and brushes the wall of the passage as he steps past them.

Silas met Gideon when he first arrived in London in 1835, when Silas was living in a cramped shared lodging in Holborn, his room stacked with stuffed creatures and skulls. He had moved to the city in the hope of expanding his reputation beyond the drawing rooms of Stoke; besides, there was little point in waiting around after Flick disappeared. He had heard talk of a coterie of surgeons, of medical men fascinated by dissection and preservation.

It was not difficult to find University College London, and each afternoon Silas would watch through the bars of the railings as surgeons of great renown criss-crossed the pristine green square, the heavy doors slamming shut behind them.

At night, he would loiter in the cloisters around the back, knowing that soon the bodies would be brought in, but from where he did not fully understand. Sure enough, after a little waiting, a movement across the quad, a whinny of a horse, and a scrabble with a blackened carriage, the bounty would be carried through on wooden boards, draped in cloth. He would inch forward, crane his neck, long to be part of the lesson that discussed them.

Gideon approached him one afternoon. He was a medical student, thickset and with a languid air of privilege. He told Silas of the specimens in the dissecting room: the tumorous lungs in jars, the rows of syphilitic skulls, a pickled brain severed from an axe wound, the blossoming nervous systems shot through with wax.

"Of course, we gather these samples to *understand* life, to see how it can be extended. Your interest in preserving the dead is different, though still quite fascinating—"

Silas puffed out his chest, and as the days passed, Gideon sought out his company more and more frequently. He coaxed specifics of Silas's collection out of him. Standing by the railings, Silas relayed details of his work on the sparrows and the rats and the field mice, confided his plans for a museum and the endurance of his name. He wondered at what point they had become friends; it seemed a moment that should have been accompanied by celebration, and yet it had happened without them realizing it.

"I think," Gideon said, when Silas brought in a stuffed robin after numerous entreaties, "that the wayward lean of its beak, a phenomenon I have never seen in the wild, is its most remarkable aspect." His mustache twitched, and he hid his admiration behind his hand. "A true scientific rarity. Indeed, I don't ever recall seeing a robin with such a lopsided gait. A marvel, a marvel."

Silas could have laughed. Gideon, a medical student, a *gentleman*, was impressed with his work. With *him*. And to have a friend like this, who chose to converse with him most afternoons, however briefly—it was an honor.

After that, he summoned the courage to ask Gideon for an "item for his collection," and Gideon intimated that he had an absolute treasure in mind for Silas, one that would be the making of him.

"It is a piece that even Frederik Ruysch would turn in his grave to possess," Gideon whispered, when at last he handed over a small cloth bag. His upper lip convulsed.

Silas took it with studied calm and started to unwrap it, imagining the subsequent discussions he would have with Gideon, their heads bowed in a tavern. From the weight of it, a heart maybe, or—

"No," Gideon said, stilling his hand. "Wait until you are home. It's too splendid a treasure. If my tutors were to discover I had given it—"

"How much? I can't afford a great sum."

"You mustn't think of it. After all of the"—Gideon paused—"pleasures I have received from your company."

"I cannot begin to thank you."

"You could acknowledge me in your famous museum? When it opens."

"Of course! Of course."

Silas nodded and smiled, and despite the tug of hunger to open the bag, he heeded Gideon's instructions and ran home, swerving carriages in his haste.

He slammed the door behind him, turned the key, and tore the cloth off the parcel.

A half-gnawed chicken leg lay inside, along with two overcooked carrots.

Silas bit his lip to prevent himself from crying, only then understanding the mockery that lay behind each remark, each twitch of the mustache.

Before he knows it, Silas is walking down a footpath in Hyde Park, his thigh cramping with fatigue. He casts back, and realizes that he remembers nothing of the walk, his mind empty after seeing the two drunk men. It is a familiar feeling; for as long as he can remember, he has swallowed occasional memories, like a daguerreotype before it is exposed to mercury fumes. He shakes himself, but no image appears.

But he should not worry. Here the air is less brackish, and a bird is singing. There is beauty. The skeletal trees are pretty, shedding the last of their summer greenings, and the dried twigs crunch like bones. A man elbows him, apologizes, and Silas moves on, following the crowd to the construction site of the Great Exhibition.

Silas has often visited to witness its assembly, paying the small fee to enter the confines of the wooden palisade. He cannot understand why the building will be dismantled from Hyde Park after a year. What is the point of a museum if not to preserve its objects forever? But as he stares up at the frame, at its cranes and pulleys silhouetted like vultures against the sky, he feels a shrinking within himself. It is *magnificent*. To capture and display so many products of industry, commerce, design, science—over a hundred thousand exhibits, he has read, and all under one huge glass roof—Silas does not know where to let his gaze settle. It is little surprise that *Punch* has nicknamed it the Crystal Palace.

All around him, activity bubbles. A foreman is bawling instructions as workmen in toppers haul on heavy ropes, while others whip the raw flanks of carthorses. Steam pants into the sky. The vast ribcage of the transept is winched up slowly, wavering in the breeze.

If only the organizers would ask him for a piece to add to the arts section. But nobody has approached him. Nobody has replied to his letters. And why not? Why is his collection not taken seriously?

He tries to brush away the webs of resentment, but his fists are tightly clenched. Low clouds gust across the sky. The black lungs of London fill and ebb. A horse bellows.

He will redouble his efforts. He will work harder, later, and perhaps one day he will open a museum even grander than this.

He sees a child dart forward and snatch a red handkerchief from a lady's purse. He peers closer, recognizing that scruff of pale hair. The familiarity is a balm, a reminder that he is not alone in this roiling mass of industry. Silas smiles, and calls out, "Albie!"

But the boy does not hear him. And then Silas understands: he has been caught. A woman's hand is on his wrist, the handkerchief a limp flag in his fist, and Silas slips on a piece of turf in his haste to hurry over, readying himself to play Albie's rescuer, to beg her not to notify the authorities—but then he sees that Albie is laughing.

Silas looks at the woman more closely. She is as tall as a man and has her red hair tidied into a long plait. She is—Flick? Grown up, womanly. But it cannot be. This woman has a slight stoop on her left side.

It is as if a bell has been rung in an old house. Silas has felt the tremor of the wire as it runs deeper into the building, through walls and floors. He stands transfixed, watching as the vibrations set a series of smaller bells ringing.

He could not say what it means.

# Pickpocket

Albie is hunkered down in a ditch in Hyde Park. As he strains on his haunches, his buttocks two grubby white moons, a group of men pass by. One of them stops, jeers, and throws a stick at him.

"Beat it, cur!" Albie yells, giving his cheeks a brief wipe with an oak leaf and pulling up his breeches. His shit steams in the air. He regards it with the same curiosity he reserves for all of his bodily waste. How do his ears know how to produce that sour-tasting orange gunk, and how does his nose know how to make that blackened gloop that he snorts into his sleeve?

He picks up the turd with two sticks and hurls it after the pack of retreating men, hiccups with laughter as they scatter, and then scampers off in the direction of the throng.

It is a fine day to pick up a treat or two, well worth the hassle of scaling the palisade to get inside. The crowds are distracted by the construction of the great palace, the straining ropes, the cheers and jostling. Albie does not know what the building is for, and does not particularly care, but he stares at the metal frame, so huge that it towers over elm trees. The surrounding ground is little more than a mud-tub, scrambled from the turning circles of carriages laden with iron and scaffolds. He pictures himself returning when the glass is installed and hurling a brick at it, just to see the shock of the wealthy men.

He ducks now here, now there, a little thread stitching the throng together. He has a false hand tucked into his sleeve, and he uses his real one to loosen silk handkerchiefs from pockets. He leaves the pearl bracelets and the glimmering silver chains. While he would not admit it, he is afraid of being sentenced to hard labor, or of being bundled on to a ship bound for the colonies and leaving his sister behind.

These people, with their gold brocading and cloistered houses, wouldn't even let him scrub their privies. And so, he grins as he un-burdens them. There is a pawnbroker on Duck Lane who will take the goods for a ha'penny each, no questions asked, and before long he'll have enough tin for a smart set of teeth. Sea-cow ivory—that's his dream.

He plucks a red spotted handkerchief from a woman's sleeve, and has just tucked it down his trousers when someone grips the plaster hand and shakes it free from his jacket.

"No—I didn't," he begins, but then he sees it is Iris. His relief comes as a throaty giggle, like a cat with a fur ball, and he throws her his most alluring smile.

"Hand it over, Albert," she commands.

"Hand over what, miss?" She frowns, and he sighs. "Aw, miss, it's just a thing, in't it? And it's a tough life. If you knew how hard—" But his line has lost its charm and he knows it. He gives the offending item to Iris, sees her return it ("Excuse me, ma'am, but I believe you dropped this—"), and avoids her eye. "You're a right old spoiler."

"Stealing things again, are you?" a man says, and Albie recognizes Silas, dressed in his neat blue cloak. "Thought you wouldn't need it after the two shillings I gave you."

Albie stiffens. He doesn't like the man creeping up on him. That clean, medicinal smell; it turns Albie's stomach. All the same, he decides not to correct the miser that it was only a bob he coughed up. "Iris thingummy," he says, attempting to feign an upper-class accent, but it sounds Irish. "This is, I mean, meet Silas. Dunno his surname either, as a matter of fact." Iris smiles curtly. "I sews slop for her at Salter's doll place."

"On Regent Street?" Silas asks, and Iris nods.

"And I bring Silas dead things." He considers strangling the air for dramatic effect, and thinks better of it, glancing back to where Iris stands. She looks faintly repulsed. He feels a sudden urge to laugh with her about Silas, but he can't catch her eye.

"Oh."

"My collection," Silas explains, "will be famous one day."

"Well, I look forward to visiting it," she says, but her voice is flat and almost mechanical, and Albie can tell she is barely listening. She is searching for somebody, and she waves her farewell. He watches the back of her bonnet disappear into the crowd.

Albie shrugs, and tips his cap at Silas. The man is looking into the distance, grasping his collarbone in the place where Iris's twists.

"Sir," Albie says to him, deciding that the man really does only have half his wits. "Her neck thing. It ain't a contagion."

# The Great Expense

Iris slips through the crowd, away from Albie and the man with him. She wishes she was shorter and could vanish beneath the toppers and the bonnets, that she wasn't so easy for Rose to pick out.

She looks about her for any sign of her sister. No. Good—she has escaped her.

Iris closes her eyes. When she opens them, she will see the scene afresh. She will imagine it is a wide canvas in front of her, each detail perfectly mapped, a study in perspective.

She looks up. The towering iron frame seems to touch the edges of clouds. The steam looks like the smoke of the Napoleonic battle scenes she has seen hanging in the National Gallery, but this is more vivid, so unlike the brownish pictures she remembers. She would like to paint with the colors she sees before her, to portray the world like a stained-glass window.

She imagines the frames of this museum filled with red and blue and green panes, like stepping into a vast kaleidoscope. But it would be too dazzling; already this has a grandeur unlike anything she could imagine. If men can make this, if they can encase elm trees and conquer nature on this scale, then what might she be capable of? There are times when she feels as unimportant as a louse, and then there are moments when she feels as if she could take off into the sky, and free herself from the trappings of home and the shop and even, she thinks with a sinking within her, her sister.

"Isn't it magnificent?" she says to a woman next to her.

"Quite marvelous," the stranger replies with unexpected warmth. Iris feels a rush of love for this unfamiliar human, and for all of the people pressed around her. Everyone, with their worries and their joys and their loves and their frustrations, their tears and dreams and laughter—they are all gloriously alike.

She starts to run. She dashes toward the open fields of the park, her red plait bouncing against her back. Her feet are kitten-light, the grass soft underfoot, but she has barely reached the first avenue of trees before she is forced to stand still, her breathing shallow. A shard of whalebone pierces her hip, her ribs packed tight by the frame of her corset. Her fingers sweat in their lace gloves.

She hears a sound behind her, a called-out name, and she knows who it is without turning around. She wonders why her sister insists on following her everywhere, what she could be hoping to find. Iris's life is duller than tarnished silver; besides, the hypocrisy rankles. Her sister would have accepted her gentleman, had he offered, without a backward glance at her *hunchback*.

"Oh," Iris says, pretending to see Rose for the first time. Her sister's hand is held out in agitation, dirt on the hem of her dress. She moves with the elegance of a lady, as if on castors, and from this distance Iris can almost believe she is as beautiful as she ever was. Iris thinks of her own gawky walk that she has caught in window reflections, the hunch of her shoulder. "Thank heavens, Rose! I've found you at last. We'll be late for dinner. Mama will be fretting."

"But you ran away from me. I saw you. I thought you'd left me—"

And her sister's face is so bereft, so lost, that Iris despises herself.

The clamor of the omnibus from Hyde Park to Bethnal Green; Iris's arm nudged away from Rose's. A brief tutting, a smell of sour laundry. They sit at the table. Iris's father coughs into his sleeve.

Iris tries to chew the suet pudding, but she swallows a lump of meat whole. She can hear the food turning over in her sister's mouth, the sift of her breath. When she can bear the sound no longer, she says, "I'm looking forward to seeing my favorite jolly minister tomorrow—"

"I am delighted you find his sermons so edifying," her mother interrupts, with a look of warning.

"Oh, indeed—" Iris pauses, her fork halfway to her mouth. The gristle on the kidney glints, the fat yellow. She tries to catch her sister's eye, to make up for earlier. "I have always felt that an over-indulgence in the communion wine is a clear sign of a strong religious bearing. The minister's desire for the blood of Christ cannot be sated."

She glances up, and Rose smiles for a moment, but then starts rubbing her hand against the pits of her chin. Iris stares instead at the polished china spaniel on the mantelpiece, a cheap gimcrack meant to ape the clutter of a higher-class household. It is just like her parents: their pathetic attempts to share the habits and morals of a society to which they don't belong. Other shop girls, she is sure, do not have parents this imposing, this concerned with moral ruin.

Her mother sighs. "Iris, please. I suppose you thought that was amusing?"

Iris sees her link her arm through Rose's, a battle formation that was drawn up on the day of the letter from Charles, the day of her sister's illness. Iris never could understand it. Her sister treated her as if it was she who wrote the letter, disappointed her prospects, ruined her face with those raised boils. After that, she could never fix matters, as if she had forgotten overnight how to console her sister, how to amuse her. She remembers how things were before, when they designed their imaginary shop with its flowered wallpaper and frames of pressed roses. She loves her sister; of course she does. And yet—

Iris tries again. "The Great Exhibition was quite splendid—"

"The Great Expense, more like," her father says, with a splutter of a laugh as if to encourage his audience to appreciate his wit. Iris smiles obligingly.

"Mrs. Salter says that the worshipping of commodities will be the downfall of society," Rose adds.

"She should know," Iris says before she can stop herself.

"And what, pray, does that mean?" her mother asks.

Iris does not reply. She dabs the napkin against her chin. Brown gravy on gray linen.

"Iris ran away from me," Rose blurts out. "I was so afraid. One moment she was there, and then I could not find her at all. She just vanished into the crowds. It is hard for me to see sometimes with my—" She does not finish the sentence, merely lowers her good eye. *Tattle.*

"Is this true, Iris? And why? You used to be so fond of your sister, and now—running off from her, abandoning her in a crowd—"

Iris still does not speak. She knows it was cruel of her, but it was not *her* who shut out Rose first of all. She tries to remember the sight of the transept as it hovered and swayed above the steel edges, the elation she felt. But the tightness in her chest refuses to lift.

She will never escape. She will never be free. She is destined to eke out this pitiful life, to suffer the slaps and insults of Mrs. Salter, to endure her sister's jealousy, until, at last, some scrawny boy fattens her with child after child, and she spends her days winching laundry through a mangle, swilling rotten offal into Sunday pies, all while tending to infants mewling with scarlatina and influenza and goodness knows what else, until she contracts it too—

Her mother sighs and Iris tries to ignore the scorch of her glare.

"More potatoes?" her father asks, patting his pocket subconsciously, as he always does once Iris and Rose have handed over the majority of their weekly wages. His head is bowed, his pate greasy.

"No, thank you," the others murmur.

Her mother coughs.

"Iris?" Her mother's voice is a thread, pulled taut. Her father looks up. The hairs on his forearm quiver. "Why can't you answer like your sister? Is it really so trying for you?"

Iris stares at the thick skin of gravy on her plate. It is an effort not to slam her fist onto the table, not to grab hold of the stained tablecloth, not to clatter everything onto the floor. She would like to see the china spaniel splinter into a hundred shards.

Iris smiles. "No, thank you." She takes another mouthful.

The clock chimes six.

# PRB

A tumbler of hot brandy," Silas says, placing a coin on the table as a church bell tolls lustily. Six o'clock evensong. He is sitting in the booth closest to the fire, his cheek pinked from the heat. The world glitters. The clam-shaped grate, the ceiling with its hanging silver tankards, the spat embers that glow and die on the rug at his feet. There is a plaque on the wall bearing the line *"What ales ye?"* and he makes a point of smiling at it each time, just to prove that he can read. His drink, when it arrives, is hot and spicy, and he skims off the layer of liquid butter with his first sip. He thinks again of the girl, of the winding of her collarbone, the green of her eyes.

"It's been a while since we've seen you here, mister," Madame says in a tone that appears friendly, but he is sure her expression shows discomfort, "though we see your artists often enough. Too often, it could be remarked."

"I've been busy," Silas replies, though he wonders why he has avoided the warmth and hum of the Dolphin for so long. He likes it here; the ale is sweet and eavesdropping sweeter.

44

A young girl in the booth opposite Silas, her dress pulled so low that the rosy crescents of her nipples show, roars with laughter and smacks a gray-haired man across the chest. She wears her usual ostrich feather in her hair, dyed pink. Madame hurries toward her. "Look here, Bluebell. I'll not have you disrespecting our esteemed customers—"

Silas clasps his drink, and even the foam of brandy reminds him of the color of her hair. Iris, Albie had called her. Her eyes, sockets slightly hollowed, contained a loneliness and longing that felt at once familiar. It was as if an invisible cord united them.

She reminded him so strongly of a grown-up version of Flick that he almost wondered if it could have been her. Flick, before she went missing from the factory when he was fifteen. He tried to show her his collection once, and she ran through the countryside beside him. He remembers the red flash of her hair, her bony-knuckled hands. He felt like a gentleman ushering a lady into his study for the first time: *This is my world.* He struggles to recall her expression as he brought out the skulls of the rabbit and the badger and the hare, and his treasure—the ram with the twisted horns.

His mind often winds back to her, and he was comforted by the vision of her as she might have been. Flick become Iris. Not the girl's imagined death in a Staffordshire river, or at the hand of the heir to the pottery factory, or under the wheels of a drunken coachman, but rather an escape, to London, to a doll-making shop and better prospects.

"Hop it, Louis," someone shouts, and Silas turns in his booth and recognizes three artists laughing on the boards by the bar. It is almost three weeks since Louis Frost and Johnnie Millais visited his shop, likely too soon to try and sell them another creature. The third man, Gabriel Rossetti, has linked arms with Millais and created a bridge at chest height. Louis stands a few paces back. His dark hair billows, as wild as a dandelion clock.

"Gentlemen! I beseech you—" Madame admonishes, but Louis has already taken a run-up and leaped over the outstretched arms. He lands with a thump on the floor. The ceiling rattles. He dusts his trousers, and grins at the customers. Some cheer, others scowl into their victuals.

"*Vive la PRB!*" Rossetti calls, and the shout irks Silas, not because the noise disturbs him, but because of the exclusion implicit in this secret set of initials they assign themselves. PRB? Something brigade?

"*Vive la PRB!*" Johnnie Millais and Louis Frost echo.

Louis leads the descent into the "Marseillaise." "*Allons enfants de la Patrie!*"

"*Le jour de gloire est arrivé!*"

"*Tais toi*—it has not arrived quite yet," Madame thunders over them, and they quieten. She flaps them into a wooden booth behind Silas. "Not arrived at all, in fact, if that scathing review of your work in *The Times* was an indication—"

"A low blow—"

"Most ungracious—"

"Our day will come, you'll see, dearest crone—"

A few patrons snicker. Silas is not one of them. He stares at the boys, ten years younger than him, but with a brimming energy and confidence he could never imagine inhabiting. He has seen them trawling for their so-called *stunners*, linking arms on a pavement and filtering each woman who passes them. Perhaps he could have found a friendship circle like theirs if he had been a medical student.

He catches fragments of their conversation.

"Tottenham Court Road—not a stunner in sight—how am I to finish *The Imprisonment of Guigemar's Queen* for the exhibition without a—"

"Better than scouring the rookeries for gypsies like Mad—"

"Says *the wry-necked, blubbering red-headed boy*—"

"Pray, do not remind me of that cretinous review—"

"Oh, Millais, everyone knows Dickens for what he is—" Louis's voice, consoling.

"A silly prick—"

The men laugh, and Silas wonders if he should lean over and talk to them, try to sell them a stuffed sparrow or a kitten or a skull as a backdrop for their paintings. He has immersed himself too much in the conjoined puppies lately, and not sold as many butterfly-wing necklaces as he would like.

"Look, it's the Cadaver!" Rossetti shouts, and Silas recognizes his nickname. The partition between the booths is slatted, and Silas turns, nods, raises his tumbler.

"Forgive his impertinence," Louis says, kneeling on the bench and leaning over so that his head seems to hover in midair above Silas. The artist looks even more vampiric than usual; his black hair is mussed, his skin so pale it is almost blue. "Gabriel, you rude pig. I'm sure you wouldn't like to be called that."

"Nonsense. It's an endearment," Rossetti replies, his face appearing alongside Louis's.

"I'm sure I've been called worse," Silas says.

Louis taps out an unknown rhythm on the banister of the booth, the paint banked in his nails.

"Silas, just the man I've been looking to see, in fact. You've saved me a trip to your shop."

*I will have a museum soon*, Silas thinks, *not a shop*. He takes another sip of brandy and says, "Oh? Is there another animal you'd like?"

Louis waves his hand. "No. And I'm sorry to say this, but it's that stuffed turtle dove you sold me—"

"Yes?" Silas asks. He thinks of the rascally attacker of cress sellers, the way he aligned its feathers in a perfect fan. It was one of his best-made pieces, a sublime example of craftsmanship.

Louis sighs. "Well, I'm afraid it—well, it moldered."

"Sorry?" Silas stammers.

"It rotted. I was away in Edinburgh for a mere week, and came back to find the house filled with bluebottles." He shudders, gesticulates as he speaks. "It was—oh, it was crawling with maggots. I came in the door and almost vomited. Heavens, Johnnie, remember the stink?"

"I could almost smell the thing in Gower Street."

"Are you sure it was the bird?" Silas asks, picking at the edge of the table. His stomach cools. "I am certain I dried it properly."

"Is he sure?" Rossetti bellows. "Is he sure? What else would it be? His paintbrushes sprouting fungus? You are only lucky it happened to Louis, and not to me. I don't have his equable temper—"

"Rossetti, please," Louis says, stilling his arm, and speaking more gently to Silas. "I hate to mention it, really I do, but it's just—well, it's made things rather tricky. My model—my Queen—she stormed out—she said she wouldn't be in the same house as a smell that putrid, and it's really quite an inconvenience at this stage of my painting—"

Silas grips his glass tighter. "I am sorry," he says. "I can't think what caused it. I will of course compensate you." Louis dismisses the idea with a waft of his hand, but his generosity only makes Silas more wretched. Could he have neglected to dry the bird properly, so absorbing was his work on another specimen—a bat, was it? He will give the bat to Louis to make up for it. Or he will insist on compensating him—he must, and he will not think of the money lost—though he does, and he kneads his brow. They will repay him with more custom in the future, he has a little saved to cover the rent—

"And now, courtesy of that rotten dove, your situation is dire," Rossetti says, turning away from Silas and speaking so loudly that even Bluebell frowns. Silas stares at his tankard, not daring to take in the disdain on the faces of other patrons. He is a failure, and Rossetti does not care who hears it.

"I would not say dire—" Louis begins.

"Your turtle dove is a maggoty disaster, slung somewhere in the depths of the Thames sewage."

"I'd almost finished painting it—"

"Your model, that fidgeting shop girl—"

"She only moved *some* of the time—"

"—has abandoned you, because your lodgings stink like a moldy crypt."

"I'm sure the Sid will oblige instead, or I'll dig out a rookery girl," Louis insists.

Rossetti snorts. "Lizzie Siddall? I should think not. Millais is using her. And your painting of a girl now has no girl in it, and no hope of one either. Currently, you have a blank outline and a small painted dove. Try entering *that* into the Royal Academy." Rossetti sits back, steeples his fingers. "And you say your situation is not dire."

Louis frowns. "But I have my vision, my idea is there. I can see it on the walls of the Academy. If only—" He falters. "If only, perhaps, with a girl in it."

"Your vision is what matters," Millais says, patting his arm. "These details can be resolved."

"And the Cadaver—" Rossetti continues, turning back to Silas. He flinches.

"Silas," Louis corrects.

"And Silas," Rossetti says with a sidelong look, "you've promised you'll make it up to Louis. How? Will you magic back the fidgety wench that your moldy specimen scared off? It is an outrage."

"It is not ideal, Silas," Millais adds, and Silas reddens. Even Millais is disappointed in him. "You should have seen Louis these past few days."

"His melancholia has been pitiful," Rossetti says. "As a professional, I thought better of you."

*I thought better of you. An outrage. Lopsided gait.* He wants to bury his face in his hands. *Lopsided gait.* The three men seem to leer as one with Gideon's face, their upper lips twitching with disguised mockery. Silas knows then that he is good for nothing, contemptible, talentless—

And then Louis says, "Really, gentlemen, it is not as bad as you make it sound. Silas, please forgive them. They are high-spirited tonight. I'm sure I'll find a way through it all. At least I managed to paint the dove before it rotted." He reaches out and Silas cowers, but Louis only pats his shoulder.

His touch is firm, comforting, and this abrupt kindness is too much after Rossetti's shouting. Silas cannot look up, cannot even steady his voice as he says, "I think I have a solution." His hand trembles as he downs his brandy, and he feels giddy. It tastes cloying. Too sweet. His emotions swim. He wants to please this man, to seize this bud of friendship, to make up for the dove—and before he can stop himself, he says, "I believe I have the model for you—it is a Queen you want, isn't it, somebody majestic? She works at Salter's."

"The doll shop?"

"I understand so, yes." He stops. He puts his hand to his face, covers his neck as if to pack the words back down his throat. She is too prized, she is *his*, and he can scarcely believe what he has done.

"She will not be right for you," he tries to say. "I spoke too hastily. She has a defect. Her collarbone, it would not please you."

"Well, I shall see for myself tomorrow." Louis takes out a leather notebook and pencil, and jots, "*Salter's.*"

It is too late.

# Quarrel

Iris is sitting with a doll's foot in her hand. She stretches, yawns with a pop, and then glances up. She jumps.

Staring back at her, through the circled mist of the windowpanes, are the faces of four men. They are youthful, handsome, and one of them—the man with curly dark hair—stares particularly intently. She flushes, looks down at herself, and feels a strange compulsion both to cover up her body, though she is fully dressed, and to let them keep watching her. Her insides twist, and she thinks again of the wrongness that lies within her: the urge that led her to paint herself so obscenely, to watch her sister through the keyhole and thrill at it.

Rose's head is bowed as she unpicks a minuscule lace collar.

Iris looks up again, intending to nudge her sister, but the man with the unruly hair raises a finger to his lips.

Iris starts. The impertinence of it! How dare they stare at her as if she is a strumpet in a shop, an exhibit in a museum! This man looks little more than a street seller. He doesn't even wear a hat. She sits up and touches her collarbone subconsciously.

"Look!" she says to her sister, checking first that Mrs. Salter is not in the room. "Look at those rude—"

But the men have ducked away, and she finds herself pointing at an empty window.

The sun filters weakly through the panes until darkness comes. The oil lamps and candles are lit, the fire given one last stoke until it is left to die. The girls eat their dinner, Mrs. Salter sucks on her laudanum bottle as if it were a teat, and they retreat to their respective rooms.

In bed, Rose tucks her knees into her sister's. Iris reaches for her hand, and Rose lets her hold it. "I'm sorry about running away from you."

"It doesn't matter."

"Do you remember our shop?" Rose's palm is hot in hers. "The biscuit tins I'd paint. The handkerchiefs you'd embroider."

"Mmm."

"What did I do wrong?"

Rose doesn't reply.

After a while, Iris realizes her sister has fallen asleep. She lies still for a while, Rose's hand limp in her own, and then she pulls herself free and pads out of the room, through the well-oiled door, down the stairs, and into the cellar. She undresses and settles to paint. The looking glass is in front of her, the painting flat on the desk.

With each stroke of the brush, with each arch of shadow, with each patch of light, the tightness in her throat begins to dissipate. She dips a hand onto her lower belly where she felt it flip earlier. Those men—such rudeness! But she remembers too the quiet approval of their gaze. She thinks of her sister asleep upstairs, the skim of her thighs against the rough wool of her gentleman's trousers, the bruises on her buttocks from his fingers.

Her hand is cold, and she dances it across her skin, trailing it below her belly button.

The door creaks open. Iris jumps and lunges for her nightgown, pressing it against herself.

"I—I—" she stammers, so confused that she does not turn around. Her heartbeat thrums in her ears. She is sure it is Mrs. Salter, and that her employment will be at an end. She will be forced to sew slop, to degrade herself, to explain her actions to her family. She should have known that she would be discovered, that her moral crime would be found out—

"What are you? What is—?" The voice, enraged, but it is not Mrs. Salter.

It is Rose.

And Iris cannot help it, though she shrugs off this feeling. She is disappointed.

Her sister is before her, holding up the picture to the candlelight. She peers with her good eye. "What are you doing? What—what is *this?*" Rose rattles the paper. Her cheeks are dimpled with two red blotches.

"Give me that." Iris snatches the painting out of her sister's hand. She is no longer sorry, no longer ashamed. "It has nothing to do with you."

"This—it's obscene! Without your nightdress—as if you're doing it just to taunt me. The vanity of it! And nothing to do with me? What if we were both cast out without a reference?" Rose raises her voice. "You know what Mrs. Salter would think of it! And what chance would we have, then? What mistress would have us?"

"I—I didn't think you would be blamed too—"

"Sister," Rose urges, taking hold of Iris's elbow, landing her fingers on the pale bruise where Mrs. Salter pinched her earlier, "you must promise not to do this painting—this picture—" She pauses, swallows a cry. "I know it, and Mama knows it too, that there is something wicked in you."

Iris feels Rose's eyes roving over her body. She gathers her nightgown closer to her, covering her breasts, and her sister looks away quickly, but it is enough for Iris to catch that expression which she knows well. Bitterness and jealousy.

"Promise me you'll never do this again," Rose urges.

Iris stands mute. In one hand, her portrait of herself, of how Rose looked too before her figure was pitted with smallpox. In the other hand, her nightdress. She cannot promise. She will not promise.

"Promise me," Rose repeats, her voice louder. "You must. I insist on it, or I'll tell Mama."

Iris says nothing, feels the pulse of her shock. She curls her toes against the wooden floor. Why did she and Rose become like this? They used to go everywhere together, willingly, their palms a puzzle that fitted only each other's, and now Rose's presence is suffocating.

"If you don't—"

"Then what?" Iris demands, and she hears herself as if it is the tantrum of a petulant child. "You will tell Mrs. Salter and Mama? Well, I hate them! I hate this waste of a life! You just want to trap me here, to make me as miserable as you are. And I won't promise. You don't care what I want and you never have since your illness—"

"Since my illness?" Rose says, and her voice breaks into a sob. "You—"

"I, what? I did nothing! Your illness wasn't my fault. I didn't want you to catch smallpox either, and yet you punish me for it! You lecture me on morality but you—" She searches for the right word as even in her anger she knows she cannot take it back. "But you were the one who erred. You think I don't know what you did with Charles?"

Iris hears the slap before she feels it. Her cheek reddens in a sharp crackle of pain. "How dare you!" she shouts, without a thought for

Mrs. Salter hearing. "I hate you!" She hurls her nightdress onto the floor, and forgets that she is naked, that she looks ridiculous.

Rose seems to unravel before her, and her cries are like those of a baby. Rasping, desperate. Her mouth is open, a thread of saliva hanging between her teeth, and her face is pinched with the pain of it.

"Don't—go—" Rose tries to say, but Iris cannot bear it. She will not let the sight of her sister soften her resolve. She clasps the picture to her chest and storms up the cold steps, back to her bed in the garret. She turns the key in the door, and realizes too late that her gown is downstairs. She will not go back. She cannot bear it.

She lies naked in bed, fizzing with rage.

Iris is woken by the bells of St. George's tolling five. The mattress beside her is empty. Patches of the night come back to her, and she pulls the counterpane over her head. She should not have spoken to her sister like that. She should not have lost her temper. She should have comforted her.

A knocking on the door and Iris unlocks it. Rose must have slept on the floor of the cellar.

Iris does not speak. Her mouth will not form an apology. *There is something wicked in you.* They dress quietly, coolly, interacting only to fasten each other's corsets.

"Please, sister," Rose whispers as she pulls the strings tighter.

Iris does not, will not promise, though she knows that her painting is at an end. Rose will never give her peace, will threaten and coax and goad—a small tear squeezes out of the corner of Iris's eye. She speaks at last. "I'm sorry for what I said. I didn't mean it."

Rose's voice is ice-water. "It's for your painting you must apologize."

"I'm sorry for how it made you feel."

"That is hardly the same thing," Rose says, and Iris does not reply.

When Rose turns away to use the chamber pot, Iris slips the picture from under the covers and hurries to tidy the cellar before Mrs. Salter wakes.

But the storeroom is immaculate. The cases of doll parts are back on the dresser, the bureau wiped clean. A thought occurs to her, and she searches under the basket.

Her sister stands by the door, skin pitted, her left eye milky and vacant.

"Where are my brushes? Where are the other—the other pictures I made?" Iris demands. "What've you done with them?"

Rose pulls a strand of hair, tightens it around her fingertip like a noose.

"Those paintings took me months! Where are they? If you have burnt them—and where are my paints?"

"Why does it matter? They are just things," Rose says, her voice quavering. "And you must understand I—I want the best for you. If we were to be thrown out, what would become of us? What—"

"Liar! You want me to be unhappy because you are," Iris snaps. "Those paints were mine. I bought them. I saved for them. It took me months."

"You should have given the money to our parents. It wasn't yours to spend."

"Bitch," Iris mutters, a word that she has never spoken aloud before. It lessens the sting of the wound. "Bitch."

They sit in mutinous silence for the rest of the day, Iris's body tilted away from her sister's. She confuses her blue and green paints, misses the lines of the lips.

At last, toward late afternoon, Mrs. Salter tells her to hand-deliver two dolls to a family on Berkeley Square. "I don't trust that fanged urchin with such an important commission."

The relief of escaping the shop is palpable, and Iris leaps up, pressing the dolls into the basket like a pair of herrings. "Do not dally," Mrs. Salter begins, but Iris is already out the door, the bell clanging behind her.

It is almost four o'clock, the street filled with shoppers and vendors. Everyone is buying, trading, bartering: soaps, gewgaws, sweets, a tup or a tug. A terrier seller holds a cage above his head, but his bellowed price and the dog's yaps are lost over the clatter of hooves and carriage wheels. Iris looks behind her at the green shopfront with its gilded lettering and wishes she had a flaming torch and a bottle of brandy.

"Excuse me," somebody says, touching Iris's sleeve.

She jumps back, about to raise an arm to slap off a pickpocket, but a woman with a long nose stands in front of her.

"I apologize for this direct approach—"

Iris wonders if she has mistaken her for someone else.

"I don't believe we have made one another's acquaintance. You work in the doll shop. My name is Clarissa Frost—" Iris struggles to hear her over the grinding of carriage wheels. "And you are?"

"I'm sorry?" Iris lowers her head to hear her words.

"Your name?"

"Iris."

"Miss Iris—?"

She flushes at her lack of etiquette. "Whittle. "But why—"

"I hope you will forgive the impertinence of my approach, Miss Whittle. It must seem quite out of nowhere."

Iris looks behind the woman and sees the nervous face of one of the men who had watched her through the window yesterday. She scowls. He is still hatless.

"You again," she says. The pique of the morning has soured her, and she finds herself unable to curb her annoyance.

"Oh," Clarissa says, turning to the man with a frown. "I understood you hadn't been introduced?"

"Introduced? Oh, no. He should learn not to stare through windows at shop girls."

He laughs, an unabashed bark.

"It isn't funny," she says. "I am a woman, not an exhibit."

"He is my brother," the lady says, silencing him with her hand as he looks about to speak.

"Brother?" she repeats. He looks like a rag-and-bone man in his too-short trousers and white-flecked shirt. His blue jacket is coming loose around the seams. The idea that he might be related to this elegant woman in a silk dress is almost laughable.

"I'll be the first to admit his sartorial style is different from mine," Clarissa says, then as Iris jolts from a passer-by's elbow, she adds, "Perhaps we could talk more amenably in here? The din of the horses. It is abhorrent."

She steers Iris into a smart cake shop, its ceiling vaulted, white tablecloths neatly ironed, silver tea sets gleaming. Iris forgets about the basket in her hand. Her mind runs over the possibilities, but nothing is satisfactory. Why is she worth such extravagance? Her old poke bonnet is hopelessly outmoded compared to Miss Frost's *petit bord*, and Iris tries to ignore the sneer of the porter. The woman seems not to notice: she clicks her fingers, orders a plate of sandwiches and tea. "Do not scrimp on the cucumber this time, and I know thinned cream when I taste it."

It is only then that she realizes this woman is a bawd, and the man is a pimp, sent to scour the streets for naïve young girls to hoodwink.

"I must be going," she says, moving to leave. "I'm not some silly green goose. I understand it all now. Good day—"

"Wait—please," the woman says. "My brother is a painter."

"A painter?" Iris repeats.

"He is Louis Frost."

He looks up hopefully. She shakes her head.

"Well, then—perhaps—he is part of a brotherhood, a group of

painters. The PRB. That is the Pre-Raphaelite Brotherhood? Holman Hunt—John Millais—Gabriel Rossetti?" Clarissa raises her voice with the same expectation.

"I don't—I haven't heard of them."

"Oh, but you will, and soon," she says, pressing forward earnestly. She gestures at the chair, and Iris lowers herself into it. "Louis trained at the Royal Academy. He had two paintings in their last Summer Exhibition. He is on the brink of great things, I am sure." Her voice falters. "Albeit, the critics need some convincing."

Royal Academy, exhibition, critics. Iris repeats these words in her head. They sound delicious, as ripe as cherries. To pluck such words out of the air, frame such sounds! Perhaps they have found some way of seeing her paintings, and they want her to join them in the Brotherhood—but already, she knows from the name that this is a group only for men.

"And me?" she asks. The man is staring at her. He does not snap his head away when she catches him looking. His eyes are so dark that they are almost black. In the middles, they are gold. If she were asked to paint a doll with those eyes, she would not have the color.

"It sounds indelicate, but I assure you that everything would be done with the utmost propriety." Clarissa coughs. "He is looking for a model."

"A model?" Iris tries to keep her expression fixed. She picks at a thread on her sleeve. Even she knows that modeling is only half a step above prostitution. Her sister would never forgive her. She would read her flaunting of her body, her face, as a personal slight. Her parents would not let her set foot in the house again. She would lose her position at the doll shop.

"Is something the matter? I admit that it can sound—"

"No. It is nothing," she says.

"Here, just here," Clarissa says to a girl who places a gold-fringed plate on the table. It is heaped with white de-crusted sandwiches.

Clarissa chews thoughtfully, gestures to Iris. "If Louis achieves the fame that he deserves, don't forget that you will be immortalized on his canvas. Just think of it! To be admired a hundred, two hundred years from now." She takes a sip of tea, her little finger pointed outward. "Besides, you would be paid a shilling an hour, which I imagine far exceeds your current salary."

"A bob—I should say, a shilling—an hour?"

"Yes."

Iris tries to swallow. She has forgotten how. She pushes the food into her cheek. "And I would be, well, how to say it—"

"I assure you it is respectable," Clarissa replies briskly, and Louis looks at her in a way that implies it is quite the opposite. "I myself have sat for him. And if you wanted to bring a chaperone—"

*Rose.* She remembers flashes of their argument. The stolen paints, the burnt pictures, the slap. Iris's mouth tightens.

"I see that perhaps there is nobody suitable? If you wanted me to be present, I would gladly oblige."

"Is it because—I—" She gestures at her collarbone. She bows her head. "Do you want to paint this?"

"What?" Louis says, speaking at last. His voice is educated, deep, syrupy. "No! It's because you are interesting. You have a certain majesty. Your face—half beautiful, half bewildering. And your hair! A forest of pins couldn't tame it, I'm sure. So *extraordinary.*"

She feels a tremor, and doesn't know if she should be flattered or insulted. She tries to focus on the sandwiches.

"Besides, I fancy you are the perfect Queen. No, you *are* Regina herself."

Clarissa cuts in. "You see, he's working on a painting. *The Imprisonment of Guigemar's Queen.* Louis can be a little obsessive. He forgets that the rest of us do not always share his enthusiasm for medieval lays. In brief"—she looks up, and her voice takes on a dull intonation from repeating well-worn lines—"a Queen is imprisoned by her jealous husband. A chap called Guigemar finds his ship is wrecked nearby, and they fall in love. But of course it can't endure, and they're discovered by the King, and cast out—but she knots his shirt in a way only she can untie, and he does likewise with her dress—is that correct?"

Louis nods through a mouthful.

"And then she escapes the husband, and finds herself at the castle of King Mériaduc, who tries to seduce her but she refuses. Then she meets Guigemar by chance at a tournament and proves who she is by untying Guigemar's shirt—at least, I think—and then he besieges King Mériaduc and rescues her. How was that summary, Louis?"

"It will do," Louis says, rapping out the syllables with his fingernails. "And we are here to rescue you from King Mériaduc."

"Who?"

He snorts. "That gray-haired crone, with the mouth as pinched as a dog's hindquarters."

"Oh! Mrs. Salter." Iris conceals her laugh as a cough. She glances at Louis and then says so quietly that it comes out as a whisper, "Can you teach me to paint?"

"Teach you?"

His incredulity pricks at every insecurity. She rises. "I should be going. I'm late on my errand, after all. Thank you for the tea—"

"Do stay a little," he says, reaching out. His fingers settle on the soft inside of her wrist where her sleeve meets her glove.

The license of it stuns her. She pulls her arm away.

"Look, I'm sorry for this, but it is quite simple. You must be my Queen."

"*Must* be *your* Queen?"

He ignores her. "I knew it the moment I saw you."

She feels her irritation rise. "Well, I knew the moment I saw you that you are very impolite." He laughs, and she remembers her sister's words. *There is something wicked in you.* She raises her chin. "I'm sorry you think it so amusing that I'd like to learn to paint—"

He straightens his face. "Forgive my impertinence. I hadn't expected it, though I suppose that Miss Siddall, one of our other models, paints too. Very well. A shilling an hour to be my model, and I'll teach you to paint for an hour a week."

"But I'd like to learn properly, not just as a pastime—"

He laughs again. "Quite the woman of business. So be it. Tuition for half an hour a day. And you can use my paints when you aren't modeling." He looks at her askance, and adds, "Oh, Miss Whittle—*do* agree to it."

Iris steadies herself on the table. She wants it more than any-thing—and yet she does not know Mr. Frost or Clarissa. She has been brought up on tales of innocent girls lured in by promises that are not kept, warned of all the dangers that lie in wait like a wolf in the shadows—seamstresses offered well-paid roles in shady establishments, maidservants hired by ill-reputed rakes who are then subjected to all sorts of horrifying abuse—but then, painting, education, escape—if it is true—

Clarissa pats her hand. "Listen. My brother can be a little enthu-siastic. A bit of a pup. Why don't you visit the studio, just to see it first of all? Surely, nobody can object to any impropriety there. And then you can decide."

Iris pauses, sets her bonnet straight on her head. She is trembling as she gathers up her basket.

"When can I come?" she asks.

*Part*

# TWO

Lizzie, Lizzie, have you tasted
For my sake the fruit forbidden?
Must your light like mine be hidden,
Your young life like mine be wasted,
Undone in mine undoing,
And ruin'd in my ruin,
Thirsty, canker'd, goblin-ridden?

—CHRISTINA ROSSETTI, "GOBLIN MARKET" (1859)


Gather ye Rosebuds while ye may,
Old Time is still a-flying;
And this same flower that smiles today
Tomorrow will be dying.

—ROBERT HERRICK, "TO THE VIRGINS, TO
MAKE MUCH OF TIME" (1648)

# Megalosaurus

Albie is on a tea clipper. It is tilting and grinding in the breeze, its sails the pulses of a heartbeat. Its chambers are coffered, hammocks slung out. His sister is with him, her hand in his, and he's got new teeth in his mouth. If he closes his eyes, he can feel the gnawing of wind and sea on his cheeks, can race from prow to stern, try out the words that a seaman once taught him—*Clew up courses! Spanker to windward! Lee ho! Helm's a-lee!* All around him, the horizon hums without end, a blue line of sea meeting sky meeting cloud.

The ship growls more violently, and his sister whimpers a little. The smack of the sails grows louder and more percussive, a *slap-slap-slap* in the wind. He is on a ship. He is on a ship. His sister clasps his hand more tightly.

Now he is below deck—in his hammock, with another just above it. In the storm, the ricochet of the wind causes the bed—no, the hammock—above him to press down on his nose with each gust. He is on a ship. He *is*.

The storm passes with a final roar, a digging-in of his sister's fingernails, and he would like to kill the wind, to strangle it in its tracks, to beat the last puffs and pants out of it.

When the door slams, he crawls out from underneath the bed. His hand aches. There are four red half-moons dug into the back of it.

His sister flinches when he reaches out his hand to tuck her pale hair behind her ear.

"He weren't violent this time," Albie says. "Was he?"

She shakes her head, counting the grubby coins on to the pillow. She bites them. He counts too. Sixpence. She'll make at least five times that when the night's over. She'll be busy what with her influenza, Albie knows: she's passed it off as consumption and put her rates up by a penny. Dying girls are the most treasured of them all. At the thought, he squirms closer to her and buries his face in her hair. "Much better'n factory work."

She stands, and he stays on the bed, picks up a needle and thread, and sings to himself. The old coal room is as small as a snuffbox, and from where he is sitting on the bed, Albie can touch all four walls and, if he kneels on the narrow mattress, the ceiling too.

> *"The first I met a cornet was*
> *In a regiment of dragoons,*
> *I give him what he didn't like,*
> *And stole his silver spoons."*

Out of the sliver of his eye, he watches his sister, crouched over the basin of vinegar, a plunger in hand, her pubic hair a greasy whorl. He longs to say to her, "Let's leave! Let's sneak on a ship, let's go—" but won't it always be the same? Wherever they are, it will be the same. He hates it. He hates it in sudden, unexamined flashes, though he accepts it too, and does not think of his life in terms of happiness or unhappiness, just as survival, a keeping-out of the way of the workhouses or coffins—he feels an urge to run, to sprint, to escape it all with each pounding footfall.

"Is you being strangled?"

"It's called singing," he says, in a matter-of-fact voice, wielding his sewing needle. "'Sides, I'm armed. I'll prick any attacker's eyeballs as easy as piercing a gooseberry."

He returns to his stitching. He is making a rosette as a Christmas gift for Iris out of the offcuts of slop, but he daren't tell his sister for fear she'll call him a petal. He has thought often of that coin which Iris pressed into his palm, and it only confirms his belief that she is a sort of queen. He recalls her other kindnesses: a loaf sneaked into his sewing bag, a spinning top that she said was hers as a child.

His sister tucks herself under the cover. "I'm going to sleep, afore more of them come," she says.

"Oi!" A clattering on the window grate above them. "Oi, Alb—there's a dog—"

"Don't even think about bringing its stinking corpse back here again," his sister says, but he is running, through the curtain that stands for their door, up the stairs, and over the rotten step into the street, an empty Dead Creatures bag in his hand.

"How bad? How old?"

"Dunno. But the cart got it," the boy says.

"Dead?"

"Oh, no. Howling fit to wake the corpses in St. Anne's. Better be quick."

The sun is dipping, a faint yolk filtering through the coal dust and the smoke. The two boys rocket off, catapulting along the skinny streets—Old Compton, Frith, and Romilly—until they hear the dog's whine. As they run, they negotiate—a sweet, a bag of scratchings—and Albie settles on buying his friend a bag of candied ginger for the tip-off.

The dog's hind leg is trapped under the wheel of a cart, mangled and fleshy, the bone showing. The hound squirms to free itself, but each time it moves, its wails become more pitiful. Blood seeps into the gutter.

"Someone put the bitch out of its misery," a man says. "A few kicks'd soon do it."

"Leave her to me," Albie says, and he approaches the dog carefully. "Hush, hush." He fears a bite that will make him go mad and froth at the mouth. The leg is ruined; the dog can only die. It's as raw as the butcher's cuts he's seen the beggar boys tuck up their sleeves for sympathy pennies.

"You're a pretty little thing, ain't'ya?" he says, and he strokes its back. The dog quietens, its eyeball white with fear. It trembles. "Hush, hush, princess."

He signals to his friend, who hands him a cobblestone. Albie closes his eyes. It is better this way, better than leaving the animal to die slowly in pain, or to be beaten by a group of boys for a lark. And besides, this way he might squeeze another shilling out of Silas, one step closer to his new teeth. He would be better off strangling the dog, and he'd fetch more money as the skull would be in a single piece. But he couldn't bear to scare the hound like that, to watch the scrambling panic as its pulse faded.

A thump, a crack, and silence from the dog. Albie sits on his haunches, panting. The hound's eyelid flickers, but he knows it is dead. He wipes his face with his hand, his fingers shaking as he frees the dog's mashed leg from the cart's wheel.

"I'm sorry, princess," he says, and he means it, too.

*Megalosaurus, Megalosaurus, Megalosaurus.*

Albie can't remember where he heard the word or what it means, but it gives a rhythm to his paces. He repeats it under his breath as he dashes and weaves, hurtling to Silas's shop in Covent Garden. The dog in his sack is still warm—poor beast. One day he'll wind up like it, his body laid out in one of the charnel houses, good for nothing but the surgeon's slab. He shudders. His sister is always telling him to slow down, not to dance in and out of the jams of carriages, the rearing horses, the coachmen with their silver whips. It was how he lost most of his teeth; whacked sideways by a cart when he was four, and his new ones never came in. He flicks his lone fang with his tongue.

*Megalosaurus, Megalosaurus, Megalosaurus.*

Down the sweeping boulevard of the Strand, through the ant trail of hurrying clerks, and into a dead-end alley, barely a shoulder's width—he takes a breath, as the smell is abominable—and he trots to Silas's shop. There is a small sign next to the door. When Silas first put it up, he instructed Albie that it informed customers that they should knock and ring, and so Albie pulls the bell and pounds the door. It is coal black, no candles in the windows, no wretches in the passageway. A cat is crying, scraping at a wall.

"What is it?" Silas demands. He looks even more gaunt than usual, his eyes unable to settle. They scan Albie, then the alley, back again. He fidgets with a thread of hair.

"I've got a right jewel," Albie says, though he knows that this haul isn't his finest. "Or at least I had a diamond, 'cept I had to throw it at a cur what chased me down."

"What was it?"

Albie scratches his head. "If I remember rightly, it was a Megalosaurus, just a small one, but s'pose you'll have to do without it now." He shrugs, but it seems Silas has not heard him. "But wait till you see this, sir—"

He pauses, fearing the dog will be met with scorn—he can already see that Silas's attention is fraying. All the same, he grips the dog with both hands, pulls it out, and looks up with hope in his eyes. The ivory teeth are four guineas and he only has twelve shillings saved. At this rate, he'll be all gum until he's thirty.

Silas says nothing. He seems to stare through him. Albie continues, but his sing-song voice has dulled a little. "Sir—a most fresh specimen, just dead, not even stiffened—think yourself of the skeleton of it—all laid out, sir—skin turned to gloves, fur to trimmings. And the bones—you could whittle 'em, sir, make whistles and combs and whatnot—or dog-bone pian-ner keys—or—"

"That girl," Silas cuts in, batting Albie's hand.

The dog falls to the ground, and Albie picks it up. He strokes its crown absentmindedly. "What girl?"

"You know." He touches his collarbone, and Albie tries to arrange his face into confusion, though he understands at once.

"I don't know who you mean, sir."

"The one from Mrs. Salter's. Iris."

Albie wrinkles his nose and pretends to scratch it. "Don't say I recall nobody of that name, sir. Nope."

"At the Great Exhibition site. You introduced us, for heaven's sake."

"No—you must've imagined it," he insists, hoping he can prey on the man's distorted way of seeing the world, his delusion. "Sir, I didn't introduce you to nobody. You must've dreamed it. Nobody of that name. I know nobody."

But Silas looks past him, pulling his hair, chewing his already torn lips.

"Please, sir, you didn't see no girl."

There is no reply.

And Albie knows it is no good.

# Correspondence

The Factory, 6 Colville Place

*January 2nd*

*To nobody's Queen,*

*I apologize: it has been more than a month since we met. I have been called to Edinburgh twice in that time, and was most grievously unwell. But fear ye not: you can recall your summons for a black ostrich feather and full mourning garb, for my darling Guinevere has nursed me back to rosy health. My sister was most unkind & said I suffered from a rheum particular only to gentlemen hypochondriacs. If you had heard the bone-breaking coughs which racked my feeble frame, I am sure you would not have been so cruel.*

*I write only to say, flee King Mériaduc, your captor, at once! I have never been one to observe the Sabbath (by no means the least of my many vices), so if you can do without your genuflections & whatnot, I will await your presence on the twelfth of this month.*

*Bring a sample of your drawings etc. and I will assist with some brief lesson.*

*I shall ask Clarissa to be present.*

*I remain &c. &c.*
*Louis Frost PRB*

———————————

*Mrs. Salter's Doll Emporium, Regent Street*
*January 2nd*

*Dear Mr. Frost,*

*I am glad to hear you are recovered.* ~~Who is Guinevere?~~
*I can take an hour on Sunday after church, no later than 3 o'clock. As we discussed over tea, I will attend only for interest etc. I cannot be your model. My mistress and parents would not allow it, so I beg you not to rest your hopes on it.*

*Respectfully,*
*Iris Whittle*

# The Factory

The house is both shabbier and finer than Iris imagined; tall, narrow, and brick, with the look of a rake gone to seed. Its windows stare. One is broken. Ferns and palms froth out of every orifice; over window boxes, out of terracotta pots and planters, around the sides of hanging baskets. The straw-strewn lane is barely passable when a horse and cart trots by, and Iris almost has to crouch in a plant pot, a fern tickling her face.

Once the cart has rounded the corner, she clears her throat and looks down at her dress. She wears a small silk rosette on her chest, a Christmas gift from Albie, and she smooths its ragged edges. She picks at a soup stain on the sleeve of her gown. It is her finest outfit, grayed cotton that was once blue. She used to like the way it pulled in her waist, the pert sleeves that made her arms look slender. But now, she thinks she looks like a poor maiden aunt, not the sort of person likely to indulge in perfect triangles of cucumber sandwiches or cream so rich it gave her a stomachache.

She hovers her hand over the doorbell, and then reads the plaque beneath it.

*"The Factory. PRB. (Please Ring Bell.)"*

She smiles at it, a sly drawing of a line separating those who know the initials' true meaning, and the uninitiated who do not. *Pre-Raphaelite Brotherhood.* She feels a brief pride over her inclusion in that inner circle. *She* knows because Clarissa told her. Her sister does not. Only those who season their speech with phrases like "critics," "Royal Academy," and "exhibition" would know it. But then, she has no claim to any of that. The paper painting in her hand, tucked into a sleeve of fabric pinched from Mrs. Salter, crumples in the wind.

"Are you going to ring the bell, or would you prefer to have your lesson on the street?"

Iris leaps back, trips over a pot, and stubs her toe. The pain is searing. She looks about her.

"Up here, Miss Whittle," he calls. Louis salutes her from the second-floor window.

"I—I was just about to ring the bell—"

"And have been for the last five minutes? I must admit I nearly gave myself away when that cart burst past. It looked like you were grazing on the potted plant."

"You've been watching me?" She reddens.

"I would say *observing*. It's an important skill for an artist. I'll attend you now."

She has her words prepared. *I am not your model yet—somebody you can stare at unannounced for five minutes!* But when the door opens, Louis smiles at her and her outrage falls away. She breathes in the scent of turpentine and wax and linseed oil. The carpets are threadbare, the chandelier missing most of its shards, but the walls are thick with paintings—some finished, some barely begun. The hallway is painted a startling swampy blue, and peacock feathers are arranged in a neat row between the dado rail and the ceiling. There is gilding everywhere—the skirting boards, the door frames, the banisters and newel posts.

She wants to take her time, but Louis hurries her along.

"Is your sister here, Mr. Frost?"

"Clarissa? Oh, no. She has her fallen women causes. The Marylebone Society. Some mite needed tending to. And please, call me by my Christian name. I can't stand all this mannerly nonsense."

"But—"

"I know, I know. I did ask her to chaperone. But I can promise that you will leave here entirely *unsacrificed to Venus*."

Her chest constricts. She would like to find a way to tell him, delicately, that he should desist from such flirtation—she is here to learn to paint, and for nothing else. Other models may comport themselves like prostitutes, but *she* is different; she will grip tight the jewel of her respectability. And then she realizes she is already thinking as if she has agreed to model. She has not. She will not. Or *may* not.

"Are your servants present?"

"Servants?" Louis wafts his hand. "I couldn't bear to have anyone fussing like that. A weekly charwoman is all a gentleman should need in these modern times." He gestures at the narrow staircase. "Come, I'll give you a grand tour of the studio."

She has never met anybody like him. It is either very liberating or very intimidating, and she is not sure which. She can see that he is the kind of person used to getting his own way, who makes a virtue of shocking with his views, and it gives her a perverse sense of delight: *she* won't humor him by being outraged. *She* will take pleasure in thwarting him, and feign complete composure at his remarks.

"I note, at least, that you're no longer at death's door," she says.

"I must assign the credit for my hasty recovery to the nursing skills of Guinevere."

"She sounds very generous," Iris says, and she finds herself pleased that he is married. It removes any complexity.

"She is. But she ate all of my Christmas pudding so she is far from being a model woman. In fact, you will meet her shortly."

"Oh?"

Louis leads her up the stairs and through a door. "The studio, ma'am. I tidied especially."

"Tidied?" Iris steps on a mussel shell and flinches. It is as if the room has been spun like a globe until the contents of every drawer, every bookshelf, have been hurled up. A stuffed bear cub lies in the corner, blanketed by newspapers. There are a pair of convex mirrors on the wall. The studio is brimful with clutter.

"Of course, Mother and I could never agree on a definition for the word, either. Ti-dy. What a dull sound it makes! But there is such mediocrity, when everything is arranged as it should be. Don't you find that? I've never believed in cataloguing things—of putting books here, and cutlery there, and whatnot. It shows such a want of taste and imagination."

As he speaks, she tries to take it all in. She looks at his easel, streaked with color.

"Such a dismal mechanical mind which tidies. A factory mind—"

A movement in the corner, and she screams. "What is—the bear is alive! Good God—"

Louis starts to laugh. He laughs until he is holding on to the edge of the door, his mouth open in a silent howl, eyes pinched closed. "A—a—a bear—"

"It really isn't funny," Iris begins, trying not to flinch as the creature ambles toward them. She does not want to provoke his mockery further, but she worries it will attack. He looks just the sort of person who would buy a dangerous animal for a jape, and then find himself killed by it. She moves back. "Have you had its teeth and claws pulled?"

It is enough for Louis to straighten, wiping away the tears from his eyes. "No! How could I? That would be cruel. This is Guinevere, a wombat, and she is in mourning."

"Oh. Ah—I see," Iris says. "And she is not your—" She almost says *wife*, but stops herself. She tests the unfamiliar word. "A *wombat*. In mourning." Iris notes the small black handkerchief fastened around the beast's neck, and tries to hide her amusement behind her hand.

"I see nothing humorous in it," Louis says. "She lost Lancelot over Christmas, although admittedly they were not friends. He roamed upstairs and she lived down here. I was quite bereft."

"Was he very old?"

"If only." Louis looks down. "Rossetti thought it would be entertaining to have him smoke a cigar, but Lancelot gobbled the whole box, a slab of chocolate besides, and snuffed it the next day. Rossetti and I are no longer on speaking terms."

"I'm sorry to hear that." She extends a half-hearted pat in the direction of the wombat, which fails to make contact with its fur. Guinevere is built with the heft of a brown, hairy cannonball. "Is she friendly?"

In response, Louis bundles the creature into his arms, groans at her weight, and tickles her under the chin.

While Louis strokes his pet, Iris wanders the studio, trying to commit every detail to memory. His easel sits in the far corner, a huge paint-spattered structure, so unlike the small desk she paints at. She longs to see what he is working on, but does not dare intrude. To have a room like this, a space in which to paint! But if her family could see her now, alone with an unmarried artist, considering becoming his model. Her reflection tracks her, and it makes her feel as if she is being watched, or—for a fraction of a second—that Rose is here too.

She inspects the dressers more closely, their shelves crammed with all sorts of curiosities. She wants to pick them all up, to feel their weight in her hand, to discover all the treasures that lie behind them. Pearly shells, skulls, blown eggs, a bird's nest, and then the larger things: a knight's armor and chain mail, a stone gargoyle, and vast plaster torsos and busts. She runs her finger along the fine nose of a Roman senator, and then picks up a marble hand.

"Oh! You'd better put that down," Louis says, taking it from her.

"Is it very fragile?"

"Not at all—but it *is* exceedingly valuable. You see, I borrowed it from the British Museum."

"I didn't know you could."

Louis fidgets. "Well, I didn't exactly ask them."

"You stole it? What if you'd been caught?"

"I'm sure I wouldn't have been. I'd make an excellent professional thief, if I wanted. I had Rossetti create a diversion. Millais would never have consented to it." He gestures expansively as he talks. "And it isn't theft if I return it."

"What a fascinating logician you are," she says, picking up a silky peacock feather and staring at the blues and greens and purples in the fronds. The black and gold remind her of Louis's eyes.

"I can see you disapprove."

"Me? No—"

"You wouldn't steal a thing."

"How do you know?" she says, but she does not meet his eye.

"Prove it." He takes a step closer.

"Why?"

"Well, then, that just confirms it. How prim you are!"

"I'm not!" She folds her arms. Yet she can feel the closeness of him, smell the oil on his clothes. She feels a fluttering: she cannot tell if it is panic or excitement.

"Well, until you're able to show me otherwise, I'm afraid I've formed the view that you're an unthieving, delicate little thing."

"Delicate little thing? You scarcely know me," she says, trying not to rise to the bait.

"Some ladies may find that a compliment."

"I am not *some ladies*," she says. He is so close to her that she thinks for a moment that he is about to kiss her. She would turn away if he tried, though her chest patters. But he merely sucks in his lip, and walks to the window.

"Can I see your painting?" he asks, and he pulls out two chairs at a desk in the corner. "Come, sit."

"It isn't that good," she says, hesitant. She takes the paper out of the sleeve of fabric and flattens it on the desk before them.

It was the only picture that survived her sister's outburst—the one that she hid under the bed—and she has cut off the paper just below the chin. She looks at it through fresh eyes, and decides she is pleased with it: she hopes he will be impressed.

She waits.

"Hmm," he says, peering closer. "It is certainly primitive."

"Primitive?" She snatches it back.

"Oh, hush. It isn't an insult—though I admit there's limited grasp of anatomy, proportion, perspective, chiaroscuro, or composition—"

Iris doesn't know if she wants to scream, cry, or slap him. She flares so quickly that she cannot stop herself. "I expect I wouldn't find your work to my liking either."

"That may be so, and you wouldn't be the first. I believe Dickens drew attention to my"—he uses a familiar lilt, as if used to trotting out the review by heart—"'odious slime-merchant of a Romeo, with the fragrant Juliet having much in common with the corpse of a workhouse hag.' There. That is my work. If you want *praise*, then my suggestion is to return to the doll shop."

"I haven't left the doll shop, and I have no intention of doing so," she says, but her voice falters. "And the critic—he said that? I think I'd hit him for that, if I were a man."

"Well, I did sulk for a few days. But we are doing something new in art, and it takes time. He likes the old stalwarts, the dullards, with no imagination, no spark at all."

79

He picks up her painting once more.

"I did say this is primitive, and I meant it. But I don't necessarily consider the term an abuse. In fact," he says, peering closer at the small portrait, "there is some promise here, which I must say I didn't expect. I expected wishy-washy flowers, not something so natural. It certainly lacks skill and mastery, but you've had no tuition—and what matters more is that it is *honest.*" His gestures grow in energy. "See, how you have painted the shape of your face as it is, not in an idealized oval—admittedly, your nose does have the same contours as a marrow, which undoes the beauty found in the original. But your use of color—why, it has the look of an illuminated manuscript. It is *alive.*"

Iris sits on her hands to stop them from shaking. He motions to her. "Come, pull in your chair. You must return to your beloved factory soon, but I promised you a quick lesson." He lifts one of the convex looking glasses off the wall and places it in front of her. It reflects the room in its glorious cluttered entirety, like the portrait of a perfectly formed new life. "I hate these mirrors sometimes—it makes me feel like I have a distorted double. But when I'm painting, I can see an object in multiple dimensions. It can make it feel magical too."

"Oh."

His voice softens. She glimpses a gentleness to him that she hadn't noticed before. "See under your nose, you've made the first mistake of amateur painters. You have the shadow here as a darker pink." She blushes to see her reflection. Their eyes meet in the mirror. "Look at it. It isn't a dark flesh color—there is blue in there too, a little red, some yellow. And your eyes—they are not merely green—look at the depth of color in them. They are shadowed by your eyelids as well as rich in their own hue." She blinks. "Do you mind if I improve this?"

She shakes her head, and he mixes up a pale blue and dabs it under her nose and chin. He intensifies the green of her eyes, corrects the swell of her nose in a few simple strokes.

"How can you do that?" she asks, and she can scarcely believe it is the same painting. It looks so much more real, so much more like her. It is as if he has performed a magic trick.

"Practice. And that's what you'll have time to do if you agree to model for me. When I'm not painting or sketching you, you can sit at this desk and work by yourself. You can borrow my paints and canvases. I'll give you a lesson at the end of each day."

She says nothing.

"And I can teach you how to use oils, and perhaps next year you can enter a canvas into the Royal Academy Summer Exhibition. You might be rejected, of course." He shrugs. "I live for painting. If I couldn't paint, I don't know what I'd do. You either feel this way about art, or you don't. And I see something in you akin to our principles—but no matter. The decision is yours entirely."

Iris looks around her, determined to delay the moment when she must refuse him. "Could you tell me about you—about the PRB?"

He nods and stands, and walks behind his easel to where the canvas sits. She follows. The weave is so fine it looks like wood. It is painted all white, with small thimbles of rough color built up in patches on the background—the russet leaves of Virginia creeper, the yellow of the stone. The only part that is finished is a dove, which flies past a sketched window: the beak and feathers are painted in intense detail, its eye catches the light with minute touches of pale blue, of white. It grasps a silvery olive branch in its bill.

The blank outline of a woman and man are drawn in graphite: she stands as he kneels at her feet and kisses her hand. "Millais will pose as Guigemar," he explains. "It will show the moment when he rescues the Queen from King Mériaduc."

It could be Iris's face that will complete it.

"Our technique is different from that taught at the Academy— we use vivid colors on a wet white ground," he says, and he talks and talks, and Iris listens. She listens harder than she has ever done in her life. No man has ever spoken to her this frankly, this intelligently. He speaks as if he believes she will understand him, not as if he were addressing a child or a pet. She wishes that there was some way of saving his words so she could hear them later, to mull over everything that he has to share with her.

He tells her how their brotherhood wants to represent nature as it really is, how Johnnie Millais, the youngest ever member of the Royal Academy, is now slighted by the institution, but he does not care, because he believes in their painting movement. He tells her about the importance of the Royal Academy Summer Exhibition and how much rests on where a picture is hung—on the line, which is within the viewer's eyeline—and how dull they all found their studies at the Academy and the endless drawing of plaster casts and sculptures. He makes her laugh by telling her how Millais was despised by the other students for his talent, and how he was once suspended from the window by a pair of silk stockings tied around his ankles, rescued only because Louis happened to be walking past. He draws out a book of engravings from Pisa's Campo Santo, and talks about the beauty in them, before art became dishonest and idealized after Raphael. "It's all a pack of lies now. We want to paint Jesus with dirty feet, Joseph with a wart on his chin—that is *real*—not this wishy-washy dullness with dark backgrounds. We will bring our pieces to life."

"But if you want to make things lifelike, if you paint with this detailed—this exact—reality, why do you choose these idealistic scenes?"

"I'm afraid I don't follow," he says.

She points at a painting of a knight holding a bouquet to a simpering barefooted maid. "Well, a knight and this sort of perfect love—shouldn't you be painting real scenes to match your style? Real love—poor girls left abandoned by their lovers" (against her will, she thinks of Rose) "or starving children in the street. There's enough *reality* in London—enough life and honesty—"

She sees Louis regarding her differently, his chin raised. "Hmm," he says, and Iris feels her neck redden. "Hunt is trying to do more of that. But I suppose I see it." He looks at her. "Will you sit for me?"

She chews her lips, wishes they would form the words she wants of their own accord, that the decision could be taken out of her hands. She imagines Rose and her parents are standing behind her, urging her toward it. Instead, she says, "I'm not sure. I would like to, but—"

"Are you certain you can't model *and* work for Mrs. Salter? The Sid—Lizzie, that is, who often models for Rossetti—she continued to work, and her family don't mind it."

"I know Mrs. Salter wouldn't allow it. And my family would never forgive me."

"Fine." He brushes a curl from his forehead. "In that case, you would have enough tin for an attic of your own. There's a place on Charlotte Street for women, quite respectable, for two shillings a week. You'd make that in two hours. In time, you might make more money through your own art. But perhaps you won't do it."

Her thoughts flash—Rose and the burnt paintings, the china spaniel, the sound of her sister's piss hitting the basin.

And then she pictures a small attic room, her own chamber pot. A little piece of privacy. More: painting every day, surrounded by artists. Her own picture hanging in the Royal Academy. She takes a feather off a shelf and toys with it.

"I understand," Louis says at last. "Not everyone cares enough for art to make sacrifices for it. I can hardly blame you for that. I'll find another Queen, though I do find it a shame for the sake of your painting."

"No—" Iris bursts out, and everything in her, everything yearns to stay in this room. It is as if there is an anchor within her that holds her in place, that makes her want to plead, *Do not let me go! Not now, not ever! Just let me stay here—*

"You will do it?"

She has never had the luxury of choice before, never felt she has had a right to steer her own life. It makes her feel bilious. She thinks of the oily porter, the future stews, red-cracked hands from labor, and then *this*. Another life. Painting. And Louis.

She nods so slightly it is almost imperceptible, and then presses her hands together. "Yes, yes, I will. And you *will* teach me to paint?"

"I promise."

They discuss the finer details: her resignation, how Clarissa will make inquiries at the women's boardinghouse, a tentative start date in a week. He helps her gather up her shawl and bonnet, and her fingers will not make sense of the buttons of her gloves.

When she steps out of the front door, the air is cold and her breath plumes. She hears a window opening, and she looks up.

"Farewell, dear Queenie!" Louis calls, and Iris laughs.

As she walks down the street, she tries to disguise her stoop. It is difficult to move without bending her figure to one side because the marble hand is heavy. At least he won't consider her a *delicate little thing* any longer. She suppresses a smile.

"*À bientôt!*"

Iris waves.

"Oh, beg pardon," she says, knocking into a passer-by.

Iris's joy, that warmth within her, curdles.

"Rose—I—"

Anger has stiffened her sister, made her lift her chin when usually she keeps it bowed and furtive. Her hands are white, her nose red from the chill of waiting outside.

"I hope *your gentleman* paid you well," she says, and her voice is a knife.

# A Pair of Letters

*32 Belgrave Square, London*
*Fifth January 1851*

*Dear Mr. Reed,*

*I write on behalf of the Great Exhibition Commission, London Local Committee, with particular regards to your correspondence both to us and Stoke-on-Trent Local Committee on 16th June, 27th July, 18th August, 8th September, 29th September—&c. &c. Forgive the delay in this reply; as I am sure you must appreciate, we have received several thousand applications, particularly considering the scale of our ever-expanding metropolis, and Stoke-on-Trent's position as a fine manufacturing capital.*

*We are interested in displaying your "Lepidoptera Window" in Class XIX, "Tapestry, Lace and Embroidery," provided you can confirm you are its Inventor and Manufacturer, and are willing to loan your work for the duration of the Exhibition. To confirm its suitability, it will be necessary for you to bring your product to my residence, as a member of the London Local Committee, on the forenoon of the 8th of the month at 32 Belgrave Square, London. This urgent availability has arisen due to a number of inventors being unable to complete their works to schedule.*

*In addition to a sample of your product, please also bring a brief makers' statement which should summarize the labor involved and any thematic intent. For example, item number 218 is described as follows: "Table-cover, consisting of 2,000 pieces of cloth, arranged into 23 historical and imagined characters. The design and execution is the sole work of the exhibitor, and has occupied his leisure hours for 18 years."*

*Respectfully,*
*Thomas Filigree*
*Committee Member of London Local Committee, Great Exhibition of the Works of Industry of All Nations Commission*

---

*Seabright Street*
*January 7th*

*Dear Iris,*

*We were most upset following your visit yesterday, and your resolve to leave your satisfactory position at Mrs. Salter's. Indeed, we rue your choice and beg you (in the strongest possible terms) to reconsider. It is not too late. We believe you have been hideously misled, tricked into a course that you cannot wish to take.*

*We remain firm in our decision. We have done all we can for you, provided education beyond the station of your life, assisted you in your apprenticeship, and paid the fee for this with no complaint, brought you up honest and with a strong Christian bearing, introduced a possible match in a most respectable profession (whose advances we needlessly say will cease on discovering your voluntary ruin), and are injured by the way in which you repay such kindnesses.*

*We ask you, when you are ruined, to whom will you turn? We mourn it. We mourn for your sister, whose own chances will be lowered more than ever by your disgrace. At least consider her, she who has already suffered so much.*

*If you alter your course before the morrow, we say, we will forgive all, and we vow never to discuss it, never to remind you of how close you came to imperiling yourself & your reputation & future. But if you choose otherwise, you leave your place in this family and may never resume it.*

*We return the advance payment received from your new "employer." You may keep these tainted coins.*

*"For this my son was dead, and is alive again; he was lost, and is found."*

*We pray you will find your way and become our daughter once more.*

*Your loving,*
*Father and Mother*

# Robin

P lease, sister," Rose says. It is the evening before Iris has to leave, and Rose's face trembles with the effort not to cry. Iris's few clothes are folded in a small bag in the corner, a chill reminder that this is their last night together.

"Please," she says again.

As Iris's resolve has hardened, Rose's haughtiness has given way, finally, to this pleading. *Stop it*, Iris wants to say, and she longs to provoke an argument that would ease the parting and the guilt that has even muted her appetite. She notices her sister's fingernails, bitten until they've bled. Rose is staring at the bag as if willing it to unpack itself, for Iris's spare petticoat to tuck itself into the chest of drawers, her gray linen dress to drape itself onto its hook by the door, next to Rose's own.

"I'll buy you new paints, if only—"

Iris says nothing, just fastens the last turn of her plait and climbs into bed beside her twin. The horsehair scratches her leg. She runs her palms over the mattress. "Where's that—" she says, her agitation rising. "That damned hair—it scratches me every night. Every night! Where *is* it?" and she pummels the bedding, surprised to find herself so close to tears.

Rose leans over, grips a small black speck and pulls it out.

"Oh, thank you," Iris says, embarrassed, but her outburst has had the effect of making anger permissible, and Rose speaks so suddenly, so passionately that Iris knows how long she must have been stalling her words.

"You don't understand," Rose says.

"Don't understand what?" Iris says, with the same quick vehemence, and she finds herself relishing this final confrontation, needling it.

"I wish I could make you see it—" Rose speaks fiercely, but underneath it, there is still that pleading edge, that sadness, and Iris realizes—too late—that the argument will have the opposite effect, that it will magnify not lessen her self-reproach. "You don't know what it's like to be *ruined*, to have your life wasted, to give yourself utterly to something and lose it. To wish, even now that he"—her voice breaks—"I just know—I know that he'll destroy you, just like—"

"He won't," Iris said, cutting across her, and she can't understand how her sister doesn't see how simple her desire is. "I just want to paint."

"But he *will*. And then you'll become like me, and—"

"Oh, Rose," Iris says, extending her hand, under the covers, and her sister takes it this time, clasps it to her, and scorches kisses on it, again and again and again. It is such an abrupt, ferocious show of affection, so unlike anything she has experienced from her sister in years, that Iris finds herself cringing from her touch, dreading those kisses that land on her knuckles. She pulls her hand away. "It will be different. It's because of painting, not because of him."

"You're lying," Rose says, turning on to her side, away from Iris. "You're lying, just like you were when you said you couldn't find me at the Great Exhibition, when I *know* you ran from me. I saw you looking over your shoulder, trying to get away from me, like you are now—"

"But I'm not lying," Iris insists. "I wish you could understand, that you could see what this means to me. You know how I've always wanted to paint."

Rose scrubs at her purpled cheeks. "It means more than me. You've made that *quite* clear."

"No," Iris said, trying to frame the words she wants to say, but she finds herself gabbling. "It doesn't have to change anything. We can take walks, and look into the windows of the smart shops in Mayfair, and maybe it will be more like it was before, if we don't see each other every day—oh, Rose, remember how it was?"

A sharp sucking of breath. Rose moves her thumb to her mouth, and shreds the skin with her teeth, and Iris wants to tell her to stop it, that she can't bear it.

"I've thought on this. And you can't choose both. You can't. You leave me—and—I won't ever see you again."

"You can't mean that."

Rose makes a choking sound, and opens her mouth as if to speak, then closes it again.

There is nothing left to say.

Iris stares at the ceiling, at the pattern in the plastering that looks like a shell. The silence stretches; ten minutes, thirty. At last, she hears Rose's breath steady as she falls asleep. The candle is still lit but Iris does not blow it out. She turns onto her side, gazes at her sister's shut eyelids, the downward tug of her lips.

Twice in the night she climbs out of bed and picks up a pen and begins a letter to Louis. *I beg you to forgive my change of heart.* But each time, she pauses, recalling the studio with its chemist-like smell of oil paints and varnish, and the convex mirrors like portholes to a new life—and she crumples the paper.

As sunrise starts to lighten the room, Iris kisses her sister's cheek. She can't wake her. She might change her mind. She dresses quietly, stealthily, her fingers slipping on the strings of her corset, missing the buttons of her dress. She checks for the marble hand.

She shoulders the bag, and allows herself one final glance at Rose. She catches the quick closing of her sister's eye. Awake, then. Iris wavers on the threshold, inhaling that sickly sugary smell for the last time, and then she closes the door behind her.

By the time Iris reaches the perimeter of the British Museum, her back is aching from the weight of the hand. She curses her foolishness in stealing it from Louis in the first place. The trick seems to belong to a different life, to a levity she has forgotten how to inhabit. She is no longer certain what to do with it. She pictured herself returning it to a porter, but what if he questions her, assumes it was she who stole it?

The railings are thick, ornate, three times her height and tipped with gold. They look as if God himself could not shake them. They tell her that this is a place of private study, of intellect, of money, of men. But more than that: they look like the bars of a prison.

She imagines a cry of *Thief! Catch that girl!*, a constable's rattle, a cell in Newgate. She would accept jail as a just punishment for the betrayal she has committed. She has devastated her parents and abandoned her sister.

Suddenly ashamed of the dramatic turn of her thoughts, Iris takes out the cloth-wrapped hand. She slips it between the railings and pushes it as far into the courtyard as she can. She hopes it won't be cast away as rubbish; was it safer left with Louis? She knows he would have had the courage to return it properly.

Nobody notices a thing.

As she walks away, Iris opens her mother's letter once more, a pinch she cannot resist delivering to herself. *Ruined, injured, imperiling*—the words waft free of the page, mingling with the smoke and the hot fat of frying whitebait—and she tears the paper with an abrupt violence, scattering the pieces into the street. She watches as a carriage rolls over the muddied fragments, and tries to swallow a rush of delight. She is *free*, and she is doing what she wants. Her sister was right: she has been given a choice, and she has snatched it, clutched it to her. She darts past a fish seller and, laughing, runs toward Louis's house, *her* attic, her bag bouncing against her back. For the first time in months, years, maybe ever, her chest no longer feels bound.

A robin is singing in a heap of splintered chicken bones, his wings oily. She reaches out a hand but he hops away.

# Coffin

A man dressed in navy livery holds open the door for Silas. He has the smug, puffed chest of a robin.

"Good afternoon," the butler says, and then pauses deliberately, "sir."

Silas touches the lapels of his own blue coat, the fabric cheap but neatly sewn, and thinks of some petty remark or action he can take—but nothing comes to mind, and he ducks out of the entrance into the cool green of the square. Fresh white stucco, neat railings, clipped trees: it is so pristine that it feels like a row of doll's houses. Silas prefers this area of town with the clean geometry of its terraces. He loathes the frayed alleys of Spitalfields and Soho, where nature is left to run its course, where the men and women are not buffed and folded and pressed, where cracks of reflected light come from piss-soaked puddles not polished doorbells.

The taxidermy puppies and their carefully assembled skeleton are in a wooden box in his arms—he made a rehearsed joke about excavating the creature from its coffin when he met Thomas Filigree, but the man did not laugh—and the butterfly-wing bauble is in his pocket. The Great Exhibition will feature all three items. Silas's footsteps grow more bounding as he thinks of it. He expected resistance from Mr. Filigree when he brought the puppies, a last-ditch chance that the Committee might display them too.

But Mr. Filigree admired the specimen, singling out the fineness of its minuscule skeleton, the spidery intricacy of ribcages, spines and pelvises, its match-sized legs. He sucked on his pipe and said, "Yes, I can see it will do quite well in the zoological section. There is some talk—just rumblings, I should add—of moving the exhibition to a new location when the six months are spent, and I can assure you I'll be pushing for a dedicated palaeontology section. To think of this, and other specimens of yours besides, next to iguanodons and pterodactyl remains."

Silas tamped down his heart.

They discussed the Lepidoptera window, of which the bauble is a small example. It will be two foot tall and wide. Silas will trap butterfly wings between two sheets of glass so that they create a beautiful pattern, almost like stained glass. He will need a hundred and fifty butterflies, maybe more, in different varieties—peacocks, red admirals, and tortoiseshells. He will be rushed to complete it by the start of May, not least because it is too cold for butterflies until April, but he can prepare the frame and he'll send Albie out to the parks with a net as soon as the weather turns. How pleased the brat will be for more work from him, his kindly patron!

As he walks down the wide boulevards, past shining carriages, polished horses, bewigged roués, and fat dogs being walked by powdered servants, his success reminds him of the first recognition he received, the first guinea in his hand. The finest thing of all is that it was his mother at the heart of it: if only she knew what she had done to help him escape, when she wanted nothing more than to grind his face into the dust.

Gin-soaked and lurching, she had found Silas's collection one evening, sequestered in a linen bag behind the cottage that they shared with three other families. And when she shook the sack at him and demanded what was wrong with him—what this kind of witchcraft meant—Silas was afraid. The skulls jangled, a sharp chime, and he snatched the bag from her, outran her easily as his footsteps did not pitch with spirits, and hid it. He returned to the cottage, late and with the shrinking gait of a puppy that knows it has been wicked. He hoped his mother would be asleep.

The next day, his cheek bruised, he sat next to Flick and watched as she sanded the hot plates. He would run away with her, if only he had money. His mother, in her voice as deep as a man's, had already regaled the yard hands with the story of his collection—bellowing about the skulls and how her youngest son was wrong in the head, and she was such a raconteur that the men had recoiled and laughed.

"A bag of 'em. Skulls all yellow and grinning. Like some kind of grim reaper, he is. Must've been his father's influence, I always said he'd dropped him on his noggin that first summer—"

When Silas felt the factory owner's hand on his shoulder, he cowered. He had only seen him from a distance—him and his fussy wife and his six stamping children.

"Are you the boy with the skulls?" the man asked, and Silas's eyes ricocheted from the brickwork of the kiln, to the soft dustiness of the unfired plates in front of him, to Flick and the basket of glaze brushes.

He did not know what it meant to say yes.

"Are you Mo Reed's youngest?"

"I—"

"Come with me," he said, taking Silas into a cluttered office with a leather-topped table.

The owner told him how he had heard Silas's mother talking

about his skull collection. His wife had a curiosity cabinet, see, and it had a butterfly in it and a stuffed robin and a dung beetle and other nonsense besides. He didn't understand, preferred her needlework to this *morbid* and unsettling collecting urge—there was something wrong with the female condition, he was sure, but it seemed quite in vogue now, didn't it—and the ladies with whom she spent so much time had advanced collections—a mermaid from the Indian colonies, though any fool could see it was just a monkey sewn onto a dried fish tail—but that was beside the point, wasn't it, and would he consider bringing a couple of his skulls to show his wife, and she would pay him if they were to her liking?

He would, but the owner was not to tell a soul. Not his mother, not anyone.

The day that fifteen-year-old Silas sold his first skull was the hardest and best day of his life. He regretted each sale he made thereafter, each parting with a yellowed companion he had grown to love. But with every coin that slid into his pocket, he came a little closer to easing free of the factory, taking Flick with him. His family did not know that gawky Silas was the darling of the Stoke-on-Trent drawing rooms, fluffed, preened, and fussed over, his blackened cheeks wiped by the servants each time he appeared at the door, as he made a sweet trade in skeletons and prepared for his escape.

And now, as a red-breeched flunky elbows past him, he pictures how Iris will react when he tells her the news about the Great Exhibition. He converses with her often in his head, and he imagines her face creasing with delight, her hand warming the crook of his elbow. As usual, she does and says very little; he orchestrates their conversations with curated precision, and she sits or stands in awed rapture.

"Tell me again what he said," she says to him. "Thomas Filigree!

A man of Belgrave Square. Describe it all so I can picture myself there."

And he tells her, and her eyes widen, and she tips back her head and laughs at his joke about the coffin and the puppies, and he can see the pink inside of her mouth. He takes her arm, steers her through his shop, explaining the specimens to her, and she pauses over them, picking up each item as if testing its weight.

She says, "Silas, I've thought of you often—so fondly—since Albie introduced us, and now your friendship" (she dabs at her eye) "means everything to me, more than life itself" (no, that is excessive, he scraps that sentence and her tearfulness) "means everything to me, as dear as if you were my own brother." (There, better.)

Silas blinks, looking around him, surprised to realize he is at the crossroads of Piccadilly. He is about to continue east to his shop, when he finds himself sloping west instead, onto Regent Street. If he is good enough for the Great Exhibition Commission, then surely he is good enough for her too? He is certain she is waiting for him, always hoping that he will appear.

He will speak to Iris. He will share his news. Didn't they meet at the site after all, so his mentioning his inclusion in the exhibition is not at all untoward, and she herself had said she wanted to visit his collection? His heart is a drum. He will show her the puppies, give her the butterfly-wing bauble. "Oh, Silas, I've often wondered where to find you," she will say.

He walks down the half-crown side of the street, the hubbub a pulse in his ears. ("Oh, what a pleasant surprise!"—and she will tease a frond of hair behind her ear, look at him admiringly.)

He has passed her shop many times in the past few weeks, each diversion built on the shallowest pretext. Each time he has resisted glancing in, kept his eyes on the pavement.

He enters.

He sees Iris at her desk, bent over a piece of fabric. How prettily she sews! A miniature lace bobbin is unspooled on the bureau in front of her. He creeps closer, willing her to look up, waiting for the moment of recognition. A glance, a smile—

She lifts her head, and he almost trips. Her face is horribly scarred. It cannot be her—she could not have become so disfigured in so short a time—but the hair, figure, everything—how can it be? Her left eye is blank and gleams whitely, the other bloodshot as if she has been crying. She has a look of intense sadness.

"Iris—what has—"

The girl's mouth pinches.

"I am not Iris," she says, with the coolness of syllabub. "If you're looking for my sister, she no longer works here. She left this morning."

"What? Where is she?"

"What is it to me? Or to *you*?"

Silas puts down his puppy box, trying not to prickle at her manners. So unlike her sister! "I need to find her. It's very important. She was a good friend of mine."

The girl scoffs. "That comes as no surprise. It seems she made a number of *acquaintances* without my knowledge."

He does not know what she means. "Do you have an address? Anywhere I can find her? I must, you see."

"Why should I tell you?"

"I mean no harm," Silas says, but then he catches a shift in the sister's expression. He understands by her disgusted squint that she thinks that he and her sister were lovers. It thrills him, and he does not correct her. "I *knew* her well. She absconded from me without a backward glance, and now I need to see her."

"I knew it," the girl says, twisting a piece of fabric between her fingers, and he delights at her misunderstanding. "Interrupt her, for all I care. Give her a fright. Surprise her latest *inamorato*."

Silas does not know what the word means, and he stares at the pile of doll's hair on the desk in front of her, willing her to yield the information he needs. "And where—"

"Six Colville Place," she says. "You can find her there."

Silas picks up his box. "Thank you—?"

"Rose."

"Rose. Thank you."

Colville Place is narrow, the houses hunched into each other. The buildings are tall—four floors—but each looks no more than a room wide. Several of the houses on the terrace are shopfronts; a chandler's and a carpenter's.

He considers knocking at the door, but thinks better of it. He assumes Iris is a scullery maid or similar in this residence, watched over by an elderly widow, and she may not be permitted visitors. "The Fact-ory. PRB. Please—ring—bell," he reads carefully. So *that* is what the initials stood for, when he heard the artists shouting them in the Dolphin. But why were they bellowing about ringing bells? It must be some sort of street slang that young swells use.

Silas sits and waits on a step outside a deserted shopfront, knees together, his box perched on his lap, his hand playing with a button. He is almost directly opposite the house where Iris is working. To distract himself, he inspects the broken glass of the shop window. He practices his introduction. She will be impressed that he managed to find her, of that he is sure.

Somebody starts to play the piano. It is a mournful tune. Sometimes Silas has slipped into churches, listened to the thunder of organs, the hum of violins, of choirs. He imagines Iris is the kind of person who could be stirred by a requiem—a tender, feminine soul. He wonders if it could even be her playing. He thinks of her slender fingers racing up and down cool ivory, the swaying of her spine.

He waits and he waits and he waits, fumbling and standing each time he hears footsteps on the street. It is never her. But at last, just when he is becoming so cold and hungry that he thinks he will leave to buy a baked potato or a pudding, she is there, turning the corner into Colville Place, taller than he remembered, less waif-like. He is surprised by the strength in her shoulders.

Silas pats his box and stands. She walks right past him. He calls out.

"Miss—Iris?"

She turns. There is no smile, no flicker. He wets his lips, swallows.

"Yes?" she asks, but she looks about her. ("Silas—you have come at last.") "I'm terribly sorry. I don't recall—"

Of all her responses, he did not imagine this. He was so sure that she thought of him too. "I—my name is Silas." Still her brow is furrowed. She will laugh soon, pretend it is a jest. But he continues, just in case. "We met at the Great Exhibition. My friend Albie—"

A slight frown. It was, he thinks with a downward glance at his dog box, no jest.

"Yes. Of course. Now I remember." She waits. He says nothing. At last she says, "Well, can I help you at all? Has Albie been taken ill?"

"Oh no, it's—I've just been accepted for the Great Exhibition." He nods at the box. "Or at least I haven't, but a skeleton and a stuffed puppy and a window have been—I mean, a window made of butter-flies. The puppies are here, conjoined." He clears his throat. "In their coffin, as I call this box. And when I open it, it's like they are being excavated."

She looks perplexed.

"That is just a—a small joke of mine. Well," he carries on, his voice only wavering a little.

"I must be going," she says, nodding at number six. "I only came out briefly for a candle. It was a pleasure—"

He says, too quickly, "When we met, you said you wanted to see my collection, and I wondered when might be convenient for you to visit?"

She looks around her, and then speaks slowly. She is polite. She is unfailingly polite, and now he knows that she barely remembers him, it occurs to him that she may not want to come at all, that she may just agree to spare his feelings. And what then? A thought passes across his brain, as clear as glass. Well, then, the voice says, you must kill her. He almost laughs at himself—how ludicrous of him.

"Well, if I happen to be passing—" She touches a rosette on her dress.

He fidgets. "Will you come tomorrow?"

"Tomorrow?"

"Come at five o'clock." He reaches into his pocket, draws out the butterfly-wing pendant and hands it to her. "You can have this. It's for you."

She looks at the blue wing, at its brown-white eye. "You made this?"

"Yes."

"Oh." She does not say anything else, does not seem to mind if empty expanses of conversation linger. She is stroking the butterfly glass with her thumb, but does not seem to be aware of it. He can see the shape of her clavicle through her dress. He would like to know how the bone feels under her skin.

"I can show you how I make the butterflies, if you like, but my other exhibits are much more impressive. My shop—it's called *Silas Reed's Shop of Curiosities Antique and New*. It's at the end of a quiet passage leading from the Strand. Ask any of the clerks or letter-writing boys for directions."

She nods, but doesn't appear to be concentrating. "And you are Mr. Reed?"

"You can call me by my Christian name. Silas."

"Silas?"

"Yes," he says, trying to swallow the bitterness. Albie *had* introduced them, after all, and he mentioned his name again in the conversation earlier, and she has remembered nothing of him.

"*Silas's Shop of Curiosities*, tomorrow at five," he repeats.

"Very good. Thank you for the gift."

"It's nothing," he says, but she has already turned away, and it is as if the ground roils under Silas, as if he is adrift on black waves.

# Gamboge and Madder

"Do try not to move," Louis says, tapping his pencil against his teeth.

"I *am* trying," she says. She holds her pose, one arm raised, the other cradled before her. She is wearing a long green dress, a belt tied loosely around her waist. "If my image were taken, I wouldn't even blur. I could be mistaken for a memento-mori daguerreotype."

"Dearest corpse, please—your chin—there—better."

His easel is little more than two paces from where she stands. He has a small freckle on his cheekbone, which she mistook for a fleck of paint before. His eyelashes are dark against his pale skin, and his lips are as plump as a girl's.

Looking at him distracts her from the torment in her arms. Nobody told her that modeling would be this long, this dull, this uncomfortable, this profoundly *physical*. It is as if her legs have been pierced by a thousand of Mrs. Salter's needles. She pictured herself sprawled on a chaise longue, propped up by cushions, not standing endlessly until her limbs mottled.

And Louis is looking at her. He is *really* looking, as if she is something to be studied, treasured, appreciated. His eye is focused on a small square of her cheek, his pencil held still against the paper. His gaze is as strong as touch.

Does he think she is beautiful? Is he critical of the slightly uneven geometry of her nose, the spot on her forehead? Or does he merely take in contours and shadows? He told her earlier that a true painter sees the world like a tableau; a series of angles and shapes, a movement that could be paused and captured. There are so many questions she would like to ask, and she feels like a little girl again, tugging her mother's hand, asking why pigeons have wings and why sugar is grated from cones. And her mother's rebuke: *Sit, quiet, be still, talk less, be more like Rose.* Always a battening-down, and no answers given.

It is easier to think of Louis than her family, so she redirects her mind to him. She wonders if he always looks at his models the same way, with that softness in his expression as if he is halfway through a joke. Has he pulled women to him, unbuckled himself, gripped their thighs, twisted his mouth in ecstasy, just as her sister's gentleman did? She imagines Louis kissing her hand, his lips against her fingers. She blinks the thought away. Instead she envisages the critics pausing over her paintings, her family's scorn turned to pride: "A picture by *our Iris* in the Royal Academy! Sold for—" (How much do paintings sell for? Twenty pounds? She isn't sure. She must remember to ask Louis, but perhaps it is a vulgar question.)

Louis's pencil strokes the paper. Across the room, she can hear the *scrape, scrape, scrape* of Mr. Millais's palette knife, a reminder that he is here too. Out of the blurred corner of her eye, she glimpses the white shape of the human skull he is painting. When she first saw it, she thought of the face that was once papered onto it, the jaws that hinged open over dinner, the teeth bared in a laugh. She shudders. And now that person's skull is just an object to be painted.

Outside, carriage wheels grind on Charlotte Street, churning the slush to mud. Snow sits on the edgings of windowpanes. A man is singing, a woman calling out, "Lemons a penny, lemons a penny." Her sister will be in the shop, tugging her needle through stiff velvet. Everyone is going about their lives, and she is in here. She is with artists, and she doesn't regret it a jot.

After returning the marble hand to the British Museum yesterday, she went straight to the garret on Charlotte Street that Louis's sister had arranged for her, just around the corner from Colville Place. The matron opened the door to her chamber, handed her a key, and it dawned on Iris anew that she had her own bed in her own room with her own washstand and dresser.

She visited Louis to borrow two candles, and Clarissa returned with her, bringing coal and kindling for the tiny iron fireplace. Together they scrubbed the grimed panes, mopped the wooden floor, polished the brass bed frame with spit and a cloth. Clarissa said she was used to maid's work, and she talked without pause: about Louis and his art, about her mother, about her charity work where she teaches former *disgraced women* sewing and household management. When Clarissa left, Iris tried not think of herself as a kept woman, tried to shut out her sister's scorn if she could see her. *Little more than a whore's attic.* She dusted her hands against her dress, crossed the room in a pace and a half, and stood by the window. She watched a young girl lead a frock-coated man down an alleyway. What even *was* respectability? The landlady was firm—no gentlemen visitors—so she is hardly living in a brothel. She has never even kissed a man, while her sister and her gentleman—

The anger at Rose's hypocrisy edged away her guilt, and Iris fell back on to the bed, waking only when it was dark.

"Much better," Louis says, picking up a stick of charcoal. "I know these are only preparatory sketches, but you stand so still."

Iris says, with the innocence of a child, "I was doing my best to imitate your marble hand."

He does not reply.

"Is the marble hand larger than mine or smaller?"

Still silence.

"Perhaps we should measure my palm against it?"

"Why don't you see for yourself?" Louis says, from behind the canvas. "It's there, on the shelf."

Iris turns, and there it is—the clawed hand looking as if it might scuttle away.

"What—"

"It was a good trick," Louis says. "At first I searched the house in a frenzy. I credit you—I enjoyed it when the truth dawned on me. Very sly. But I knew you'd return it, yesterday morning most likely, and I waited for you by the museum. Once you'd finished hurling papers into the street, I fished it back through the railings."

"You—" she begins, but Louis is hidden behind his easel and she cannot catch his expression.

By three o'clock, the light is fading and the studio is lit mainly by the fire. Louis puts down his pencil for the day and Iris revolves her shoulders, her limbs stiff and aching from standing so still. Millais is sprawled on a tapestried cushion, and he uses Guinevere as a bolster.

"Shall we have your lesson now?" Louis asks Iris, and he ushers her to the desk in the corner. He places the marble hand in front of her, scrabbles for a sheet of paper and a pencil, and says, "Draw the hand. Draw it as you see it." Then he leans back and thumbs through a journal. *The Germ*, Iris reads along the spine.

Iris makes a few lines on the paper—a semicircle for the fingertip, a line for the edge of the palm.

"Millais, this poem of Christina's—"

Iris watches the snow turn to hail outside. She puts down her pencil and cups her chin in her hands.

"What's the matter?" Louis asks. "Why've you stopped?"

"I thought you were going to teach me."

"How can I, when you've just put two marks on a page?"

"You aren't even looking."

"Well, what would you like me to teach you?"

Iris looks at the easel, thickly textured with paint. "Can you teach me how to use oils?"

"You should learn to crawl first—"

Millais snorts. "That's exactly what our old tutor used to say. *Learn to crawl first!* How you hated it, Louis. Don't you remember how you railed against him? Louis Frost, a tutor cast from the same mold as old Perky. I never thought I'd see the day—"

Louis stands and brushes down his trousers. "Oh, very well. I'll give you a lesson in oils, if just to quiet *him*. But I warn you, tomorrow you must return to sketching."

Millais nods at Iris and she smiles.

"A look between conspirators," Louis says, and he sits beside her at the easel, squeezes an oil-paint bladder onto a porcelain palette. "Our trick is to prime the canvas with zinc white. We barely mix our colors, and use them quite transparently so that the white background gleams through. It makes it so much more vivid."

She glances at the colors before her—emerald green, ultramarine, madder, and gamboge. It is like being handed a toffee pudding after months of gruel. "Here," Louis says, handing her a sable brush. "Practice with it."

Iris dips it in the crimson. "How?"

"Anyhow you please."

"But what should I paint?"

When she doesn't move her hand, he adds gently, "Just make a mistake. See how it feels. Lord knows, I've put myself in the way of enough failures."

Iris grips the brush and scores it downward in a single, triumphant streak. She dabs at the canvas again, making marks little better than a child would, but there is something boisterous and euphoric about it. She is allowed to make a mess. She sneaks small glances at Louis, at his dark curls that gleam auburn in the firelight. His finger, paler than the marble hand, is pointing at something on the canvas, and she should listen to him, but she doesn't. She remembers how he held her wrist on that first day in the vaulted tea shop, and she brushes her palm against her cheek to feel the memory of it.

The bell rings and Louis stands to answer it. He returns holding a crumpled letter.

"Who was it?" Millais asks.

"Nothing of any import," Louis says, and he throws the paper into the fire. Iris watches its edges catch, the looping hand consumed by flame. *Dear Iris*, she remembers. *We were most upset—*

"Will you paint another self-portrait?" Louis asks.

"My first painting will be of the marble hand."

"Ah, the stolen antiquity. Why?"

It reminds her of the doll shop, of Albie's plaster hand for pickpocketing, of a time that makes her chest constrict. But she doesn't want to forget it either; the hand feels like a bridge between her two lives, though she just shrugs and says, "No particular reason."

Iris draws her brush across the canvas, and the colors leap and soar. The silence in the room is counterpane soft, just the sound of sable on cloth, of the spit and crackle of the fire. Louis yawns and stretches with the dexterity of a cat. The hail turns to rain. A belly growl of thunder. And they are safe inside, three painters. She remembers briefly the man who approached her yesterday afternoon and invited her to his shop—Elias? Cecil?—and she wonders what he was trying to sell her.

She hears a whistle and a snort, and Millais is asleep. He lies back, his mouth open, his nose upward like a pig's. Louis and Iris start to laugh, silently, until they forget what amused them in the first place. She closes her eyes and thinks, *I do not want this to end.*

If Iris were back at the doll shop, would still be painting mouths and boots and fingernails, and the pale insides of her arms would ache from the pinches of Mrs. Salter.

Rose—

No.

In the corner of the room, the grandfather clock strikes half past four.

# Lion

Silas tracks the ticking of the clock with his finger. In thirty minutes, at five o'clock, she will be here. He will be sitting in the armchair as he is now, next to the Lepidoptera cabinet, with an expression of rehearsed study and learning on his face. The door will click, and he will look up, adjust his pince-nez, and close and fold his copy of *The Lancet* as if interrupted. He has rearranged his posture twice, three times. He has slicked back his dark hair, buffed his pallor with soaps and oils. His nose, with its senatorial curve, is his favorite feature, and he has lit the candles rather than oil lamps as it looks best in shadowed light.

"Iris," he will say, "what a pleasure. Indeed, I was so transported by *The Lancet* that I scarcely noticed the time." She will hold out her gloveless hand (the same poached pink as the salmon he has seen dandies eating in restaurants), and he will lock the door behind her to ensure that no customers disturb them.

"Now you have my full attention," he will say, and she will laugh fondly, her eyes sparkling as she admires his treasures. She will pick up the lion's skull—perhaps he will help her as it is heavy—and run her hands over the snagging texture of its cranium.

"I had always thought that bones would feel so smooth," she will say. "I did not picture them this way. It is too ghastly for the likes of me."

She will giggle behind her hand, and tell him that she has a secret to impart. He will look troubled, say he hopes that she is well.

"Oh, yes," she will insist, before revealing that she pretended not to recognize him the day before just for a lark. "It did, I confess, pain me to witness your disappointment," she will say. "Could you not tell by the arch of my eyebrow that I was jesting?"

"Most cruel friend," he will sigh, and then wag his finger at her.

She will settle on the stool at his feet, and spear a pickled strawberry that he bought from the baker on the Strand. She will hover it in front of her mouth, the flesh red and wet, and then chew it slowly. Pushing the fruit into her cheek, she will beg him to tell her how he made the puppies' skeleton ("the butterfly bauble, now my most treasured possession. Such generosity I see in you, such a good soul. If only I had the talents to make something for you of equal worth!"), and he will glimpse the strawberry meat as she speaks. Her teeth will be as white as thrown porcelain, as small as a cat's.

He contrives her history, decides that her parents were doting, but they perished when she was eight years old, and she and her maimed (though loving) sister were forced to rely on a benevolent aunt.

She will confess she has also been lonely, in want of a friend. He will tell her that he has been unable to work since he last saw her, so immediate and intense was the bond of friendship between them. He will talk about his childhood, about the beatings and the smoke and the heat and the pain in his fingers and his neck, about how he wondered if he would ever escape it. And the sprawling, boundless loneliness; the children who despised him. He will tell her about Flick, how she went missing one morning after they went blackberrying, and how nobody found her. How he imagines her lying dead in a river, her red hair about her like the corpse of a fox, how he has always suspected it was her father who killed her, but of course she may not even have died, yet he just *knows* she did, though he cannot say why.

The clock ticks on. Quarter to five. He should have asked her to come earlier. Then she would be here now. Each second chimes with the beating of Silas's heart.

*Chck.*

*Chck.*

*Chck.*

He stands, stretches, and moves a candle from one side of the dresser to the other, assesses it, and then decides the original place was best. He studies himself in the mirror. Its frame is made of the fanned bones of tiny trout ribs, which Silas glued only a month before. He cannot imagine having the patience for it now, the steadiness of hand. His reflection is trembling very slightly. He runs his fingers through his hair, then wipes the oil on his shirt.

The clock has barely moved.

Ten to.

He watches the hand judder.

Five to.

He sits again, careful to place his knee in a way that makes him look severe yet approachable. Any moment now, she will breeze through the door.

He picks up *The Lancet* again.

"Sev-ere double tal-tali-talipes," he mutters, "resulting from long dis-use and fal-faul-ty pos-ittiron—position—of the feet; ten-o-t-omy and rup-ture—"

The words swim, and he cannot make sense of them. He flings the journal to the floor, then checks she has not arrived, and gathers it back up, ironing the pages with his hands. He pretends to read. He can feel his pulse in his ears and in his throat.

Five o'clock.

She will be teasing him, making him wait a little. His body twitches with the effort of holding his stance, and he finds himself staring at the door. It is raining harder, sluicing the windows. Thunder snarls. She will be wet when she arrives, dripping. He will wring her out like a cloth.

"What a storm!" she will say. "But one worth battling to be here."

Five past.

She will be sheltering from the rain, biding her time for a pause to run. "I could not arrive here sodden! Would you have a lady ruin her dress?"

Ten past.

The rain has stopped, but she will not want to dampen her shoes. She will be sidestepping puddles as if they are rabbit holes, secretly pleased that he is waiting.

Quarter past.

She had to stop on an urgent mission. A child fell off a pony, a kitten required rescuing from a high window. It will be something mildly heroic, enough that she retains her daintiness but that squares away her absence. She will be hurrying now, anxious that he is waiting.

Half past.

Something has befallen her. She has been knocked down by a cart. As she lies bleeding in the street, she sends an urgent message to him to come to her.

He waits and waits and waits, as stagnant as a shadow.

The clock strikes six, seven, eight o'clock, and still he does not move. He sits as if in a trance. She is coming. She will send a note. Perhaps she is dead. At the very least, she is playing a game to see how much he truly cares.

It is dark and the hubbub of the Strand has passed away. And

Silas knows, though he pretends he does not, that she is not coming, that no accident has befallen her. She did not recognize him yesterday, and she has forgotten today. It is no jest; she merely does not particularly care for him.

He flexes his fingers, stands. He crosses the room to where the lion's skull is balanced on the dresser (*I had always thought that bones would feel so smooth*—you fool, you imbecile—she is laughing like Gideon) and cradles it in his arms like a swaddled infant.

He unlatches the door—the clicking sound he has been waiting to hear all day is a cruel taunt—and steps out, breathing hard. The edges of the buildings are thick with drifts of slush, the cobbles glossy with light reflected from the candle in his shop. He catches his face in a puddle, grotesquely distorted. He holds the skull above his head, and wavers for a moment, before heaving it onto the ground. It cracks into three: jaw, and the seam of the skull neatly halved. It is as easily broken as bone-dry clay.

He picks up half of the cranium and presses the splintered edge against his neck. The pain is warm. He pushes harder, feeling the elastic give of his skin. His breathing steadies. It will not take much more pressure to pierce his throat.

He hurls the segment onto the cobbles, and then lifts each fragment in turn and flings them downward, again and again and again, until the lion's skull is fractured into pieces no bigger than fingernails and he is panting, sweat rivering down his back.

# Bauble

A loud crack wakes Iris. Her garret is cold, the fire long dead, and she puffs on her hands to warm them. She looks out of the window, at the white blanket of snow. New flakes are falling, rubbing out footprints and carriage churnings as efficiently as the swish of a broom. From her attic room, the world has shrunk to miniature. The horses tripping through the slush are as plump as sugared mice, and the costermongers look like wind-up tin toys. She sees a man splitting open kindling, his axe little bigger than a matchstick.

"Honest folks is trying to sleep," a woman shouts from a house across the way.

"Honest as this snow, with a dozen men's dirty footsteps through it," the man bellows back, before raising his axe once more.

She starts to dress, muscles stiff from standing endlessly, keen to see Louis and to continue her sketch of the hand. Over the last week, she has drawn it once a day, each picture an improvement on the one before it. In her haste, she knocks something off the shelf. She picks it up. It is a butterfly wing, pretty enough, trapped between two small circles of glass. She remembers the peculiar man and how he pressed it into her hand.

When she is smoothing the sheets, she drops it again. This time, she doesn't bother to retrieve it. It isn't that she doesn't like it, but it makes her uneasy—he must have given it to her as a sales ploy to convince her to visit his shop. It was something, at least, that he mistook her for the kind of lady who had tin to spare on such trinkets.

It reminds her of her and Rose's imaginary shop, *Flora*. Its blue awning and the galaxy of gas lamps. It would appear through the London fog like some sort of magical cave. Of course it was always a dream that would never happen, of course it was just a way of whiling away the hours, and of course they'd never have the ready money to escape the Doll Emporium. Iris wonders if, now she is earning more, she could put a little aside and give her sister the money for an establishment of her own—if Rose would accept it.

Every day, Rose sews on and on and on, her chances narrowing with every stitch, as she pitches closer to becoming an old maid, a drain, a dependent. Iris will write soon, now that Rose has had a week to adjust to her absence. She walked to Regent Street yesterday evening and stood on the pavement opposite the shop for fifteen minutes or more. The candle was burning in her old garret.

Iris shivers. It is not worth lighting a new fire; best to be out as quick as she can. Louis keeps his house as hot as an oven, and he rises early.

But when she rings the bell, a girl in a tawdry pinny answers the door.

"Is Mr. Frost here?" Iris asks as the charwoman curtseys.

"Who should I say is calling, miss?"

"Ir—. . . Miss Whittle."

"A relative, miss? Shall I take your card?"

"No. I'm his model and—"

A sneer appears on the maid's face. "Fetch him yourself," she says, and she bends over and tugs a cloud of laundry into a basket.

Iris stares. For a maid, a charwoman, to snub her, to show her the same disgust she would to a bedbug—she sidles past the girl, who makes a sound like *tchah*—and takes the stairs to the studio. She keeps her back erect, her chin raised. She won't tell Louis, won't give the girl the satisfaction of seeing how well the blow landed.

Louis bows briefly. "Ah! Queenie." He stands in front of his painting, amidst his clutter and treasures, rubbing his face. She imagines that it is her hand stroking his cheek.

"Is something the matter?"

"It's no good," he says. "I can't work. Why wasn't I a clerk or a lawyer or any of those black-hatted professionals? Even an undertaker. Why did I choose to *torture* myself in this way?"

"What on earth is wrong, dear princeling?"

"It isn't funny—" Though he smiles. "I can't get him right. Guigemar. It feels too idealized, too—I don't know. Typical? What you said about the *reality* of painting—it struck me. I want it to be interesting, different. And it's just a man kneeling at a woman's feet and—"

She stares at the figures in the little cell, one of Guigemar's hands holding the unraveled knot of the Queen's dress, the other kissing her knuckle.

"Perhaps you should just paint the Queen. Without Guigemar."

"What?" Louis says, and she realizes she has interrupted him. "But how would we know she is rescued?"

"Why is it important?" Iris says. "You can show suffering and hope, and the love she has in her desperation—isn't that more interesting? And the dove"—she points at it, flying past the window with its olive branch—"that symbolizes redemption and escape. Isn't it too much to have that *and* Guigemar?"

Louis frowns.

"You could frame her differently—have her palm reaching for

the bird? It could be her imprisoned by her jealous husband, after Guigemar has been cast out, before she breaks free by herself. Not the later rescue by Guigemar, when she's held by King Mériaduc."

"I'd need to start again."

"You have time. And you wouldn't—you'd just need to paint over where Guigemar kneels." She almost touches the canvas.

Louis barks, "Stop! The paint is wet," and she retracts her hand. His expression starts to change.

"I was hardly going to—"

"Yes, I believe that's it," he says. He stares at her. "You're right. I could position a looking glass just behind her, which shows the viewer that the door of her jail is ajar. Perhaps she hasn't noticed it." He pulls on a moth-eaten cape and throws Iris's cloak at her. She follows him downstairs. "Come, I can't stay in this cell a moment longer. We will walk—"

She laughs. "Have you gone quite mad?"

"I believe I have. My malady is a grave one."

"Is there any hope of recovery?"

"The apothecary assures me," he says, pulling her palm into the crook of his elbow as they step into the street, past the pinched face of the charwoman, "that the company of a kindly friend is my only chance."

She smiles. She enjoys the placement of her hand on his arm, and wonders at how quickly they have fallen into this easiness around each other. It is normal, respectable, for a woman to walk arm in arm with a gentleman. Has she not walked to church like this with her own father? She can feel nothing through her gloves except a faint pressure, the occasional brush of his trousers against her skirts.

They walk through the muffled streets, their footsteps creaking in the snow. He squares his fingers, tells her how she should look at the world as an artist would. "See those icicles hanging off that house? You could think how you would compose them, what they could indicate. Peril, perhaps, and you could also use them as a mirror, to reflect back something outside the scope of the painting. See the flicker of that girl's dress in them"—he points to a child shaking small vials of white powder—"look at the angle of her arm, how it forms a triangle, how that could lead the eye into something more important in the painting."

"Rat poison a penny," the child calls out. "Secret recipe—a penny, a penny."

"You could send your dear Mrs. Salter a gift," Louis suggests. "To add to her medicine collection."

"You are wicked."

"Ah, now, this is more like it," and he stops a little boy with an armful of hothouse flowers when they are outside Regent's Park. "I'll take one of those blue primroses."

"A shilling, sir."

Iris is about to tug his arm—a shilling for a single flower! But he pushes the coin into the boy's fist. She remembers saving tuppence a week for her paints, and there is something about his extravagance that unsettles her just as much as it thrills her.

"It isn't quite an iris, but it will do," he says. "May I?"

She nods, and he tucks it into her hair, his finger brushing her ear. This is all too much—it is too fast, too enchanting, and she wants everything to slow down. She does not have time to drink it all in, to adjust, to reflect on what is right or wrong in what she is doing. It feels so easy that it must be a trick. Just a week ago she was at the doll shop. *We believe you have been hideously misled, tricked into a course that you cannot wish to take.*

Her throat feels oily, dense, as if she has just eaten a spoonful of dripping. She and Rose used to eat it for lunch each day, and she remembers the white viscosity of it, the cooled fat that they would scoop out and spread on their bread. It used to stick to the roof of her mouth in a thick film, and all through the day she could taste it.

"You're dreadfully quiet," he says, but she just tells him that she is tired.

As they walk through Regent's Park, Louis talks with an openness that surprises her. He tells her about his French mother, recently deceased ("She was a widow for all of my life, and comfortable too—she felt no need to remarry after Father died, and why should she? I felt no want of a stepfather"), and he tries to coax details of her own life out of her. But she is as closed as an oyster. It isn't that she wants to be secretive, but how can her history begin to compare to his? It seems as if her life was charcoal before, and now it takes on the vividness of oil paint. How can she tell him that she has seen little but the inside of a shop, done nothing except rise at five each morning and pass through each of her duties as if sleepwalking? She is sure that he has never smelled the vinegar of washing or turned the wheel of a mangle. And through all this, she considered herself fortunate.

"What is your mother like?"

"Let's not talk of her," Iris says, because it feels as if a vise has closed around her throat. She opens her mouth, and a snowflake fizzes on her tongue. "See if you can catch that one," she says, seeing a flake as large as a dandelion puff.

He runs under it, snaps at it like a terrier. "What do I win?"

"Eternal glory."

"Eternal, eh," he says. "I had no idea it was so simple."

They stroll to the edge of the frozen lake and stand next to the huts of the icemen. She watches the skaters, and they race as fast as her thoughts.

# Pond Skater

Albie spins a long pirouette, the hem of his coat fanning into the ice. He comes here most mornings after dropping the sewn outfits at Mrs. Salter's, but today the pond is busy, wealthy children in billowing silks skating alongside the bakers' and butchers' apprentices. He looks around him, at the small shacks of the icemen, at the low boil of the winter sun, and at the mounds of browned slush. The ice snickers. Albie links in with the long line of boys "doing the train," and they whizz around the lake together, blowing their *choo-choo*s into the air.

When his feet are wet and start to bite with the cold, Albie teeters to the edge and unties his borrowed skates. He thinks of buying his sister some gin-laced furmity.

"Albie!" somebody says, and Albie turns and grins. "I thought you might be here. I've been waving like a madwoman."

Iris holds out her arms and he bounds into them.

"Tell me," she says at once. "How was Rose this morning?"

"She don't like me much. Always holding her nose around me, and saying I smell." He sniffs.

"Could you—could you tell her I miss her?"

Albie shrugs, then points at the rosette on her chest. "You're wearing that thing I gave you."

He thinks for a moment of telling her about Silas and the odd way he inquired after her. Albie saw him once with a woman pinned to the wall by her throat, but he knew nothing of how it came about, if she'd tried to swindle him. Would a warning to Iris be strange, extreme? Surely she'd just laugh if he said, "There's a man who asked about you"?

But before he has made up his mind, Iris severs his thoughts. "Albie, you must meet Mr. Frost."

"How do you do," the man says, and then peers closer when Albie smiles at him. "Goodness, whatever happened to your teeth?"

Albie places his fist over his mouth. "Big ones never growed, sir. I want 'em false."

"Those'll cost you a pretty penny."

"Four guineas a set," Albie says, and then he notices the man's gaze sharpening, and Albie feels like he is being peeled. He shrinks back in the way his sister does when a certain bloat-faced spotty man visits her. The potato, Albie calls him, on account of his crusted boils like starchy black eyes.

"Damn it, Queenie, he's perfect," Louis says.

"Perfect for what?" Iris asks, and Albie has a mind to query the same, as well as who Queenie is, but his tongue is busy exploring the roof of his mouth from where he burnt it on a pie earlier.

"For my shepherd picture, which I'll start soon," the man says. "Can't you see it?"

"I s'pose," Albie says. "If there was tin in it, there ain't much in the skill of herding sheep. I'm a quick learner. For Spitalfields Market, sir?"

# The Queen

The months turn.

In the remaining half of January, Louis completes his preparatory sketches and pins down the outline of Iris as the Queen, and he begins to shade her copperish hair.

Iris learns how to stand still ("I am now a model woman," she says to Louis, archly), and how to paint too: how to build up the colors and depth of oils, how to add increasingly fine detail with a sable brush so that no strokes are apparent, how to discern the geometry and perspective in a face or a hand. She washes down the paints with so much linseed oil that her pictures almost have the transparency of watercolor. ("Close to Rossetti's style," Louis says, and Iris wants to ask if she shows any of his talent, but she leaves the question unspoken.) She paints over all of these, and finds a delight in how temporary they are, how her early mistakes do not matter. Her sketches stack up, one a day, and she allows only Louis to see them, shielding her work from Holman Hunt or Millais. She draws the marble hand more often than anything else, observing the slant of the fingers, the little chip in the heel of the palm.

At night, she sews dresses for Clarissa's *reformed women*, snipping the reams of thick navy cotton into waists and skirts, backs that the girls can button themselves, arms loose enough to permit household work. She imagines these girls starting their lives afresh like her, even if polite society may think that she has done the reverse of these rescued women and chosen degradation.

Hunt and Louis argue briefly when Hunt says that *The Imprisonment of Guigemar's Queen* is too similar to the prison cell in the painting he has recently finished, *Claudio and Isabella*, and the rescue is an imitation of his *Valentine Rescuing Sylvia from Proteus*, but they reconcile when Louis points out that, if anything, he may as well accuse Millais of copying him with his *Mariana* wistfully awaiting her lover in her chamber, and he buys Hunt a box of his favorite boiled sweets. Hunt laughs at last, and agrees that as their paintings all seem to touch on imprisonment, rescue, and the agony of waiting, they may as well embrace it as a PRB motif for 1851.

Each night, Louis escorts Iris around the corner to her boarding house, and their farewells on the street are restrained, quiet. When she cannot sleep, she traces the pattern of the wallpaper with her fingertip and thinks, *I am alive—my life did not truly begin until now.* She feels as if her blood is threaded with a new capacity for happiness and for love and for laughter. For the first time, she is afraid of death. She stares at her hand, unable to believe that her spirit will one day leave it, that her spark will depart. Her painted face will outlive her, preserving her as she is now.

She is so full of joy that it seems as though it can never be extinguished.

In February, the charwoman's sneer at her lowered state is as pronounced as ever, and her parents refuse to open their door to her. Iris minds it less, but she feels differently about Rose, who is still not answering her letters. She remembers Rose gazing at her sketch of their father's snuffbox when they were thirteen, enraptured, saying, "You really drew this? You aren't lying to me?" and then insisting on taking her to the National Gallery, spreading out her hands and telling her she'd be better than any of them. "Once we have our shop, you can be a shop girl *and* a famous artist. And that will pull in the trade, won't it?" Another memory lands on top of this, and grief saws at her: her sister's anguished expression that evening in the cellar.

She thinks of Rose whenever she squeezes paint onto porcelain, whenever her pencil touches the paper. But the thoughts brush past her quickly, and then the slow joy of building colors or copying shapes will take over, and she will sit in contented, suspended concentration for hours. She draws the hand from all angles, and then maps the outline she will use when she is ready to paint it properly. She buys a tiny, fine-weave canvas from Brown of High Holborn, so smooth that it looks like a primed mahogany panel. Louis gives her a thin brush and she has to hold it to the light to see the bristles.

She practices painting on small, stamp-sized areas. Louis allows her to work on the background to *The Imprisonment of Guigemar's Queen*. She paints two bricks of the cell, five leaves of ivy that link their tendrils through the barred window, two rubies set into the Queen's crown. He completes the food placed at her feet on a silver tray: ripe plums gorged on by a wasp ("To hint that her beauty is wasting while she waits," Millais explains), a loaf of bread, a goblet of wine. Louis uses copal resin to heighten the gloss further, to make the Queen's green, fur-trimmed dress shine like stained glass. "If this is imprisonment, I'd delight in it," Iris says, plucking a grape from the bunch. But Louis cannot get the Queen's expression right: it is too wan, too simpering. He decides to leave the face for a month or so.

And still Louis and Iris talk, about poetry and ambition and Millais and spring and family and Iris begins to wonder if he sees her as a sister. She is surprised by his thoughtfulness: if she mentions a pigment she wants, she finds it on her desk the next morning. If she talks about a delicious suet pudding she smelled when walking to the park, he will return from a PRB meeting with a treacle cake wrapped in paper. He will wave away her thanks, say it is nothing more than he would do for Clarissa, and she feels sure that if he wanted her, he would have tried to seduce her by now. Even if she would have had to turn him down.

She hears talk of the love between Ford Madox Brown and his model Emma Hill, and their illegitimate baby Catherine; and Millais gossips about the attraction he has observed between Gabriel Rossetti and Lizzie Siddall, though Rossetti denies it. And Iris makes tentative inquiries of Millais (no longer Mr. Millais to her) that are so muted that he does not understand what she is asking—yes, he assures her with a frown, of course Louis has painted other models before. And Iris does not know how to sharpen her questions.

One afternoon, Louis asks Iris if he can show Millais her sketches. She agrees, and sits in the corner, stroking the sleeping head of Guinevere, straining to hear every word. "By Jove, what a secret you've kept her," Millais says, peering closer. "There's a dignified simplicity here."

"Now do you see what I meant?"

And Iris realizes, suddenly, that Louis has talked about her art with Millais. She wishes she knew what he had said, so scant are his compliments about her work. He tells her only how she can improve.

"I thought they were just silly girlish sketches. And all these weeks, I was wondering over the time you wasted, tutoring her."

Louis nods. "See how she has drawn the fingers here. Of course it isn't masterly, but there's such promise, don't you think?"

Millais turns to the next sheet. "Quite. She'll be snapping at our heels if we aren't careful."

And it is an effort for Iris to stop herself from picking up Guinevere by the paws and waltzing the room with her.

In March, Louis and Iris take long walks. She has to skip every few paces to keep up with him. His strides are even longer than hers. He picks a bunch of bluebells, and it is difficult for her to throw away the bouquet when it wilts and dies. She begins to see the world as a canvas: the swift fingers of a fishwife gutting herrings could be stilled on her page. The way her knife, dented a little, glints off the coal fire behind her. A dab of madder mixed with gamboge for it, a hint of ultramarine too to show the silver metal, and her fingernails, white at the quick, five scuffed mirrors—the possibility of movement shown in the strain of her arm, her hair lifted in the breeze. And yet, Iris is afraid to paint something so *real*, so alive, so she draws the marble hand again and again and again.

She and Louis walk through Regent's Park and Green Park, and to Highgate Cemetery, where they sit side by side and sketch a stone archangel, and it seems to her that each day she moves further from her role as his student and model to become that of a co-painter, a friend. She treasures each of his touches—when he puts his hand over hers to help guide her pencil, when their fingers accidentally brush as they walk through the cemetery gates.

She wears a looser corset with simpler dresses, leaves her hair unplaited, and she greets any disapproving leer with cold nonchalance. Once, she smokes Louis's pipe.

"My," Louis says when she scowls at a sour glance from a gentleman as they descend the steep hill from Highgate, "you have mastered the withering glare. I hope never to receive such a look—it would smite me dead. Not a delicate thing at all."

He assists her with her painting of the marble hand, as she traces the composition in graphite and adds the first layer of white and a speck of emerald and ultramarine, drawing out the finer lines of the palm. She works on it late into the night, and whenever she is modeling, she mulls over the adjustments she will make to it that evening, the edges she will draw out, the shadows she will extend. The painting consists only of the hand resting on a wooden surface, the background behind it a smooth reddish pink.

When it is finished, it is far from perfect, but she is proud of it, and wonders about submitting it to the Royal Academy Summer Exhibition. Louis tells her it is unlikely to be accepted and urges her to wait for another year. "Think of the improvement you'll make in that time! You have so many years ahead of you." But she is impatient for success.

They visit the site of the Great Exhibition and watch the glazing wagons running along the gutters, as hundreds of panes of glass are melted into place.

And all the way they talk. He tells her about his own travels— Ostend and Paris, and Venice, where the fat gondolier almost sank the boat, where they danced through the night at balls and there was the most magnificent Gothic architecture. He tells her about the energy and inspiration he found in the city, how he read *The Stones of Venice* and how Ruskin values artistic freedom and truth in a way that Louis feels is akin to the principles of the PRB, how he wishes the critic would notice his work.

He tells her about the Georgian squares of Edinburgh, where Clarissa will be living for the next half-year to nurse a sickly friend, and he leaves for a week to accompany his sister on the journey.

In his absence, she borrows some of his brushes and paints, and for the first two days she enjoys the seclusion of working alone in her attic bedroom, the time she can dedicate to painting and drawing. She has never encountered such peace, just her and her work. On the third day, she craves company, longs for the hours to pass, to have somebody she can talk to about her painting, who will entertain her with an anecdote. On the fourth day, she writes to her sister, and watches for a letter in return with a fretfulness she has never felt before. There is no response. Her solitude strikes her anew; her absolute reliance on Louis frightens her. He is all she has. She thinks of him constantly, reimagines their conversations, remembers how his hand grazed hers. She must put him from her mind. But the more she tells herself this, the more he occupies her thoughts.

When he returns, she finds herself curiously awkward around him. She is quiet, as is he. Their acquaintance seems to have lost its ease.

He sketches her for *The Shepherdess*, and she has pins and needles each day from having her legs tucked underneath her. He asks her if she is comfortable, and she lies that she is. When he teaches her in the evening, he has the coldness of a professional, and she wonders if something happened or was said in Edinburgh that has forced this distance. He keeps their conversation on art, away from any mention of Clarissa, or home, or feeling.

"No," he says, tapping her drawing. "That disobeys the fundamentals of perspective. Draw it as you see it. I know you can do better than this."

Iris takes the paper from him, answers his questions in monosyllables, and he does not try to snap her out of her sulk.

And before long it is early April, and the deadline for the Summer Exhibition. *The Imprisonment of Guigemar's Queen* is wedged in the easel, the paint dry except for the Queen's face, which Louis is doing his best to perfect.

"Must you, Queenie?" Louis says, when Iris yawns, and she sees the first glimmer of affection in him since he returned from Edinburgh. "Please—there—now, do not move."

It has been dark for hours, the carriage waiting outside the door for the finished picture. Iris can hear the snort and whinny of the horse, the pawed clip of its hoof on the cobbles.

"Always at the final hour. Burning the midnight oil," Millais says.

"Such a helpful contribution," Louis says. "I'm sure you sent off your canvases weeks ago, and varnished too. We can't all work with your speed."

"They barely accepted me last year, don't forget."

"If *Mariana* is rejected, I'll torch the place for you." Louis frowns. "Or eat Guinevere. Pray, do not distract me."

Iris feels the rise of another yawn, but she swallows it. The clock strikes eleven. Louis is chewing his lip, his hair fluffed and wild. Every so often he paces, holding up a hand if Millais tries to speak.

"Are you sure it's a wise idea to work on it now? The paint will be wet and could smudge—"

Louis hisses at Millais in response.

As Louis works on, sometimes smiling, sometimes growling at his easel—"It's all wrong! I'm sure they will reject it"—Iris thinks of her own painting, the small marble hand, the rose madder she used for the background. She knows that she could improve it, that it is unlikely to be accepted, and not just because the thumb is a little out of proportion. The committee does not view women artists generously. But hasn't Mary Thornycroft exhibited several times previously, and might Iris at least enter? She will wait until the final moment to decide if she will cram her picture into the carriage next to Louis's canvas. Guinevere nudges her leg and she resists reaching out a hand to stroke the wombat.

When Louis slams down his paintbrush at last and says, "I am finished," she walks over to his easel and looks at it afresh. "What do you think?" he asks her, tapping his palette knife against his wrist. "It isn't too—garish?" He has painted the cavity where her lips part in unmixed emerald. "Too trite—too—oh, I don't know. I doubt they'll accept it."

She intended to say something mocking, perhaps, "At least it shows promise," but she does not speak at all.

Part of her is pleased for him. But another part of her is jealous.

The brush-strokes are invisible, so precise that she feels she can smell the dampness of the prison walls, touch the vein on an ivy leaf, feel the wrapped silk of the spider's prey. The Queen stands, almost as real as she is, reaching toward a dove flying past a barred window, an olive branch in its beak. A silken ribbon is knotted around her waist, lavish food littered about her feet. Her face is in profile but tilted toward the observer, a half-smile on her lips, color on her cheeks, and Louis has managed to capture her as if she is poised, about to run free. It is a moment of redemption.

It is intended as an echo of Millais's *Mariana*, and Louis has inscribed an identical quotation underneath it, *"My life is dreary, / He cometh not,"* as well as three lines from the *Lai de Guigemar* in medieval French.

"Well?" Louis demands, drumming the paintbrush on the palette. "Well?"

"It is quite—it is perfect," she says.

"Remarkable," Millais says. "By deuce, if that isn't hung on the line, nothing will be."

"Fine," Louis says, and then he whisks it off the easel and packs it into a wooden crate. He has written *WET PAINT* and *TAKE CARE* on the lid, and Iris decides then that she will enter the Summer Exhibition. They may reject her, but at least she will try.

"Where's my painting?"

"Come down to the carriage with me, then I'll walk you home," Louis says.

"But where's my painting? You said you'd have it framed for me."

Louis looks at Millais. They stop in the doorway, the crate held between the men like pallbearers with a coffin.

"Iris—" he begins.

"What? You don't think I should enter." She bites down on her lip. "I know it isn't as good as yours, that I can improve. But—"

Louis looks at Millais again.

"Well, I shan't tell her," Millais says.

"I should have mentioned—"

She feels a pain in her throat. "You think," she says bitterly, "that I don't show promise after all."

"Oh, Iris," Louis says. "Don't be so hard—it isn't that." He does not meet her eye. "It's—Guinevere. It was my fault entirely. I left it on the sideboard in the drawing room. Hunt was round, you understand, and I wanted him to see it. But I didn't notice she was in the room—I should have checked, I know—and she must have got hold of it. And you know how sharp her claws are and she—well, it's quite ruined."

# Rookery

ilas has forgotten Iris. He tells himself this as he wakes up each morning. It has been two and a half months since the afternoon she failed to come to his shop. He knows that she isn't dead because the next day he went to Colville Place and waited until she appeared. No missive arrived explaining her absence, and she did not visit at five o'clock the next day, or the day after that.

And so, he has forgotten her.

If he were to encounter her on the street, her hand would fly to her face. She would apologize for having missed their engagement, and he would try to remember who she was. "Oh," he would say at last. "You were the girl who was supposed to call on me. I'm afraid I can't recall your name," and he would have the pleasure of rejecting her beseechings to visit his shop another time.

Or, he would be observing his works in the Great Exhibition, and see a vaguely familiar form next to his Lepidoptera window, neatly silhouetted. She would hurry to him, her shoes clacking on the tiled floor, clasping her butterfly bauble, and he would not care.

"If only I had come," she would say. "I was afraid to." Or, "I forgot your address." And he would reply, "Oh—Isobel, was it?—you need not worry about that, but I am far too busy now to show you my small museum."

He works on his exhibits tirelessly. The puppies are packaged in padded boxes (marked *VERRY FRAJILL*) and hand-delivered to the Committee. The Lepidoptera window is almost complete. Albie has caught more than sixty butterflies and he brings the creatures trapped in clay bottles, still alive because the boy is so soft he says he can't bear to kill something that pretty. Silas wonders whether the urchin was always this sentimental; it seems new, and it tires him.

Silas takes the jars from him, pays Albie a farthing or a ha'penny depending on how many he has gathered, and uncorks the insects in the cellar. He has lost one or two butterflies that fluttered out before he could catch them. Now he is more careful. On one occasion he pulled a single wing off a brimstone so that it crawled in flightless circles, its body like a slender Havana. He watched it for a while before he grew bored and crushed it with the clip of his pince-nez.

Once he has the wings, Silas arranges them by color, and they look like autumn leaves spread out on the floor of the cellar: blues and cabbage whites and tortoiseshells. He glues them in symmetrical patterns to the panes of glass, the window divided into nine neat squares. When he has finished a square, he places another frame of glass on top. The work soothes him in a way he did not expect.

But as the month progresses, and Silas has filled only five of the nine panes, he realizes that he will have to fill the empty spaces with moths. When it is dark, he sets a lamp in his shop and opens the door. They flutter in, their movements almost drunken, knocking against the ceiling and the cabinets. Silas traps them in a net, carefully, for it takes only a slight knock for their wings to crumble to dust.

One afternoon, once Silas has attached the wings of six fritillaries in an orange-speckled arc, he feels in need of a drink. He kneads his shoulders. They ache from being hunched all day.

"The usual buttered brandy?" Madame at the Dolphin asks when he arrives. She wipes a smear of rouged salve from the rim of a glass.

"Two," Silas says, sliding the coins toward her. The tavern is quiet for a Thursday afternoon. It is one of the first hot days of the year and all the sots must be clogging up the parks.

"Got company, sir?"

"No."

"Lawks, well, two brandies, sir. Spoil yourself, that's what I always says—spoil yourself as if you was brought up on candied ginger and turtle soup." She laughs, but he has heard her trot out this line before and his smile in return is more of a grimace.

He takes his two hot drinks and knocks a glass back in one. The liquid sears his belly. He winces, but it feels good. He *has* been busy—he has been living in a kind of frenzy. His clothes hang off his bones, and at night, he can run his hands over the gutters of his ribs. He has forgotten to eat; he needs a female touch. Perhaps, if he achieves renown at the Great Exhibition, and is commissioned to open a *real* museum, he will be able to afford a maid. He pictures a young girl fussing about his collar, scooping bone marrow onto his plate, plying him with steaming mounds of beef pudding. She would listen to him, wonder at his ingenuity and his skill, call him "the greatest mind of his generation."

Silas glances across the table to where Bluebell is pawing the chest of an elderly lawyer, fingering the chain of his fob watch. She winds it around her finger, and then winches the gentleman nearer as if he were a fish on a line. The lawyer's wrinkled face is flushed from her kisses, his eyes half-closed. The pink ostrich feather in her hat trembles in the heat from the fire.

The gentleman stands, and Bluebell bellows, "Madame, fetch the gentleman a bucket to piss in."

When the man has gone, Bluebell leans closer to Silas. He blushes, longs to feel her touch. He thinks if she holds him, he will weep.

She whispers something.

"Sorry?" he says.

"I said to shove your filthy tongue back in your mouth. You're like a bitch in heat. It makes me sick."

"Me?"

"Yes, you. You ain't called Starey Silas for nothing."

"St-Starey Silas?"

"Oh, just crawl back to the vile pond you sprung from, would you?"

He smarts, stares down at the swirl of his drink. His reflection bobs back at him. He feels a redness creep up his neck, and the world swims as he downs his second glass. He slams it onto the table, then stands. "You should learn some manners," he says. "I'll be a fine gentleman one day, and you'll wish you hadn't spoken to me like that."

She shrugs, pouting into a brass pocket mirror as she applies another layer of rouge.

Silas slouches to the bar, trying to keep his footsteps even. The room blurs. He really should eat. "That harlot," he says, pointing a finger at Bluebell, "you'd better teach her some graces."

Madame leans forward, anchoring herself on her elbows. "Teach her?" she demands. "After what you did to her? It's little surprise—"

"After what *I* did? I've never spoken to that *slattern* in my life—"

"As innocent as a lamb new born," Madame says, before swiveling to serve another customer.

Silas's footsteps hammer the pavement. He does not dodge street hawkers, does not edge out of the way of children or dames or frock-coated gentlemen with their varnished boots. *They* should respect *him*, for a change. He walks fast, unstoppable, as straight as a hem.

He stands at the crossroads of Oxford Circus, watching the horses as they thunder past—some silver-bridled, others gaunt and foaming—and imagines throwing himself into their tracks, the churn of their hooves, the iron scrape of a barouche wheel—annihilation. His body would be little more than a carcass, split open on the road.

He rocks on his heels, and memories crackle at the corners of his eyes. *Starey Silas*, *lopsided gait*, the hiss of Bluebell's scalp as he pulled back her hair, the nought of Flick's mouth, and Iris—Iris who did not come. He shuts his eyes, tipping a little further, a little closer to the racket of carriages.

He starts, pulls himself back. He won't give them the satisfaction. He will be a success. He *will* be. And hasn't he almost achieved all he wanted? Wasn't this everything he dreamed of? He tries to picture his Lepidoptera window, his puppies' skeleton next to their stuffed pelt, on display at the Great Exhibition. The finest spectacle of the age, and *he* is included. The organizers estimate that at least five million people will visit in six months alone. Five million people will cast an eye over his work, admire his skill.

But all he can see is Iris's face.

He tugs at the skin of his cheeks, and then sets off in the direction of St. Giles. And when a white-blond girl takes his hand (he is only a brief walk from Colville Place), he allows himself to go with her.

"Is it far?" he asks, and she distracts him with her prattling.

"Our 'stablishment's a fine one"—they turn into a grimed alley, a cesspit of rat-picked waste, which smells worse than the tanneries of the South Bank—"don't let the street deceive you, sir"—he sidesteps drifts of horse dung—"us girls are young, innocent as doves"—and she pauses outside a tottering rookery, propped up by a wooden beam like a gouty limb—"cheap, sir, but honest—mind the step"—he winces, sees a window weeping as a woman empties a metal bucket, and steps inside.

She takes him downstairs to a tiny room, the roof so low that he cannot stand upright. It smells vinegary, sweaty, of the grassiness of ejaculate. The ceiling is swollen and smoke-stained like a black lung, damp pressing it downward. But the walls are dark too, and he realizes that this used to be where the coal chute went.

The girl lifts her soiled nightdress to reveal dugs no larger than puffy flea bites. He stares into her face for the first time. There is something so childlike about her, something so—

"No," he says, his voice a choke. "You will not do—I want a redhead."

"Oh, sir, give me a try. I'm sure I'll be just up your alley—or maybe you'll be just up mine, sir?" She cackles, and he stares at her blackened teeth. He cannot meet her eye. He sees a cap in the corner, and recognizes it at once. *Albie.*

"No," he says, and he turns from her.

"Wait—" the girl croaks.

"Is there a redhead here?"

The girl looks down, the flirtation gone from her voice. She says, quite dully, "Moll. Room above this one."

Silas takes the steps, two at a time. He feels a pull in his trousers, a tingling at what will be awaiting him. He enters without knocking.

A red-headed girl sits on a single bed. Her nightgown is less discolored, her eyes less young, her *frontage* more than adequate. The room is taller; it has a small window though the bottom pane is broken, and embers smolder in the grate. It smells better than the last room—cheap perfume and old alcohol masking the sour aromas beneath.

"Ah, at last," Silas says. "This is altogether finer." He stares at the yellowed bandage of the bed. "When were the bedclothes last cleaned?"

"You get what you pay for," the vixen croaks, her voice low and cracked. "You want a *grande horizontale*, go to Haymarket, and you can have 'em for guineas and guineas. But ye'll pay up a sixpence according, dearie, pr'vided you want it usual." She taps the bulge in his trousers. "And I can tell that our humble surroundings don't put you off, sir, not really."

"Indeed," he murmurs. "Your hair—so *red*."

She starts to rub his crotch, and he closes his eyes, handing over the coins. He sits down on the bed next to her. The springs scream. Even in the dim candlelight, he can see specks of blood on the sheets, a maggot-shaped indentation in the mattress where the girl must curl up each night. He sees himself through her eyes: his benevolence in visiting her, a far better prospect than the factory scabs she must service. He even took the care to wash two days ago.

"You like us rascally women, sir," she says, "I can tell you do, sir." He wants her to stop talking, to shove his hand over her mouth until she quietens. He hates the deep rasp of her voice, the lilting intimacy that sounds forced and tired. Her red hair—he concentrates on that at least.

She starts to scratch her elbow, and flakes of dried skin catch and dance in the candlelight. He tries not to think that he is breathing in this girl, breathing in her skin and grime and sickness, and, as she eases open his trousers, taking him in her hand ("What a fine truncheon, sir, you do know how to spoil us naughty girls"), he wants nothing more than for darkness to take over. He wants to hurl himself into her, to fuck every part of her until he feels nothing—until all of his shame and sadness and anger and loneliness are void. He wants to fuck away every thought of Iris. *Iris*.

He knocks her fist away and grabs hold of her hair, pushing her onto her back. She lets out a brisk cry, "Oh!" and he tears her nightdress in a swift movement, his fingernails snagging on her chest and scratching it. The fabric splits easily and she hisses, "You'll be paying for that," but he wrenches her hair again, ignoring her cry. He readies himself, one hand on her throat, the other pinning down her drumstick arms. He takes a quick glance at her flea-bitten body, and her pubic hair is black.

"What—false—" he cries, pushing her away from him. His prick softens, and he notices the tincture of her hair, its deceit. She gasps free, scrambling away from him. Her pillow is red from seeped dye. There is a low pain in his stomach, an ache in his testicles, and he fumbles for the buttons of his trousers. He wants to be away from her, to be on his own once more, and he stumbles out of the room and down the stairs, ignoring the moans he hears from behind each door, the mewl of a baby. This place—it is repulsive! A cradle of vice—

He runs into the street, his palm over his mouth, and finds himself retracing his earlier footsteps, to Soho and the Dolphin, and as he sits outside waiting, waiting, waiting, the tremor in his hand steadies and he feels a calmness pass over him.

# Sea-Cow Ivory

The shelves are stacked with glass jars brimming with teeth as yellow as stained pearls. Display cabinets show them in plaster sets with two hinged gold springs. Albie wonders who they all belonged to, remembering a girl in his rookery having hers pulled the day she died of consumption. Waterloo teeth, plucked from the soldiers, isn't that what they say?

He pictures them nestled in his own mouth; the grins he would flash, the gristle he could eat. He lives on pap: soft potatoes, boiled pigs' ears, dripping. He could crack walnuts between his molars like his sister can, and chew an onion like an apple.

The proprietor and his apprentice haven't seen him yet, and Albie ducks below the counter, smearing his grubby finger against the glass case. The apprentice has his back turned and is wielding a ferocious set of pliers, a child pinned to the chair. The boy squeals like a blood-let pig, and Albie feels a hot rush of jealousy: what's a bit of pain when the swine'll get a set of ivories out of it, all paid for by his careless mama? Albie'd knock out his last tooth with his own fist if he knew a set of falsies would come hot on it.

The proprietor is talking to an old dandy. "Four guineas for a set of the sea-cow ivory," he says. "They discolor less than Waterloo teeth—but my, those brave soldiers were devilish careful of their pearls, weren't they? And only three guineas for the porcelain, but it's worth spending a little more—they can be frightfully prone to cracking—"

Four guineas! Hearing the sum spoken rekindles his distance from them. He'll have his gummy mouth forever, his lone tooth like that of an imbecilic rabbit. His sister says there's bigger things to worry about, that he's as vain as any swell.

He considers smashing the glass and grabbing a pair, or slitting the man's pocket for the tin—or he could make his fortune as a drag sneak pinching luggage at the stations and buy a dozen sets if he cared to—but he knows it's nothing but a far-off dream. Stealing handkerchiefs is as daring as he'll get. He couldn't bear to be parted from his sister if he was rumbled, couldn't bear leaving her to suffer through the men on her own.

The owner catches sight of him: "Oi! You! I've told you before not to hang around here—begone, I tell you!"

The man starts toward him, making to grab his jacket, and Albie cries, "Gerroff, you infernal hyena, you pickled sow!" and he leaps up and away down the street, swerving into Mrs. Salter's Doll Emporium.

Rose is waiting, her ugly eye white and rolling. He wonders if she knows she could get a glass eye for a pound, and hang it if anyone could tell the difference.

He hands over the bag, and she thumbs through the tiny velvet skirts and bodices. She counts aloud.

"Three bodices, four skirts, four bodices, five skirts—"

Albie gnaws on a loose fingernail.

"Iris says—"

"Please don't," Rose says.

"She says—"

"Please—" Albie hears the quiver in her voice, catches her expression of resigned sadness as she glances around the shop. "I asked you not to mention her—"

"Do you miss her?"

"That's none of your business," she snaps.

"She says to say she misses you."

"Will you—"

"She says you're her sister and she never wanted to leave you, miss," Albie says, before he can help it. "And she's happy, she really is, and she says you could escape too—"

He expects a fight from her; a spider-fast pinch delivered to the inside of his elbow, a particular speciality of Mrs. Salter. Or at the very least hissed words: *I told you to shut your trap!*

But Rose says nothing, and there is such a downturned sadness in her purplish face that Albie has to look away.

Albie's footsteps drag, like a locomotive that has run out of steam. He has no energy for a lark, and he heads home, longing to see his sister, to make her laugh and to fall asleep next to her.

He is outside his house when Silas runs past him. Albie is confused—the rookeries of St. Giles may be close to the man's shop, but they are a world away in every other sense. Could he have been looking for him? But then he notices Silas's half-done trousers, the expression on his face—hand over his mouth—and Albie drops his Dead Creatures bag and races inside, the rotten step splintering underfoot. *No,* he thinks. *No, no, no, please not—*

He barges past the women in the hall ("What fire's caught his breeches?") and past red-headed Moll in tears on the bottom stair, Nancy's hand locked on hers ("There's no harm done, is there, my sweet. Just had a fright—we all have 'em"), and he leaps over them, and almost falls down the stairs. He pushes aside the stained old theater curtain, and his sister is sitting on the bed, staring at the wall. A candle is drowning in its own fat.

"Oh! You're fine—I thought—" He sits next to her and takes her hand. "There's a man—a wicked man—and if he comes in here, you can't see him, not at all, you've got to shout and say no. I don't care if Nancy don't like it—"

"What you talking about?" his sister says, ruffling his hair. "Who? Who's wicked?"

Albie takes a breath. "A man was here just before. He's got black hair and he smells so strange, and you ain't to see him, not at all. I got a bad feeling about him—"

"He came," his sister says, in her dull monotone. "I saw him."

"You didn't—"

She shakes her head. "Said I weren't to his liking. That he wanted a redhead. Nancy weren't happy, says she's sick to her back teeth of the men not liking me—that my debt's gone up to two pounds. But the Exhibition should pull in the punters, shouldn't it?" She tugs at her hair. "Alb, sometimes it's worse if they doesn't want me than when they does."

# The Wombat's Lament

*The Factory*

*April 9th*

Dearest Queen,

*Thank you for visiting briefly earlier, and it certainly is no inconvenience for you not to come today. I am glad you will still attend dinner with us tonight. I am sorry for what happened to your painting. I know you have been gracious about it, but it was careless of me. I will make good on it, to say nothing of the lengths our disgraced friend will have to go to in order to redeem herself.*

*In fact, that is the principal purpose of this missive. Just after breakfast, I happened upon this poem, accompanied by an ink-stained paw-print bearing a striking resemblance to that of your repentant nemesis. Could she be the author of this work? I admit her style is lacking but she is a fat quadruped who prefers snoozing to any form of intellectual fulfilment, so we can hardly blame the naughty beast for it.*

*Yours,*
*Louis*

———————————

**The Wombat's Lament**

*CANTO I*

*Ah, me! What tragic happ'ning could divide*
*A muse and wombat? May this poor poem guide*
*A reconciling, 'twixt two gentle souls*
*Oh, Goddess, pray! inspire me in this goal.*
*To trace the source of this most somber tale*
*Turn to Colville Place, a girl outside, milk-pale*
*Dare she enter, low abode of this poet*
*Or flee, return to life as she knows it?*

*CANTO II*

*And lo! ere the sun barely seem'd to rise*
*Three months departed, our goddess sighs,*
*And three could not live in much greater bliss*
*Than poor artist, wombat, most dear mistress.*
*Each morn, the sun would light its tender rays*
*On her sweet locks, e'en clouds avert their gaze.*
*And wombat Guinevere, no servant more devoted,*

*Her mourning of Lancelot 'came less noted.*
*But oh! Great doom and tempests loom ahead,*
*Because the naughty beast was left unfed.*

*CANTO III*

*For wombat, from true hunger almost fainting*
*Seized 'pon a morsel—but 'twas a painting!*
*She lick'd her lips, ignorant of the feud*
*Just then a-brewing: she meant nothing rude.*
*But darling Iris—sweet flower, bloss'ming blue,*
*Rail'd and wept, howl'd and scream'd, "Vile wombat, SHOO!"*
*Cursing painting, artist, wombat, enrag'd hops,*
*Weeping, howling, her tears she mops.*
*And what of wombat? I hear you sigh*
*No creature ever lived who louder cry'd.*

*CANTO IV*

*Poor wombat in t'studio slaved away*
*Till her face grew lined and fur turn'd gray.*
*While the shadow o'er her life forever loomed:*
*"It's me, Iris!" her cruel voice boomed.*
*But slave she did, and a palace built*
*To show her mistress th'extent of guilt.*
*No finer temple ever was created*
*Than that made by wombat, so deeply hated.*

*CANTO V*

*And, after such cruelty, will she be forgiv'n?*
*We leave our tale here—the break unriven.*

# Moonlight

I ris," Louis says, opening the door. He half-smiles at her, but she does not return it. Over the course of the day she has wandered to the site of the Crystal Palace, visited her favorite painting, *The Arnolfini Portrait*, at the National Gallery, and taken a secret pleasure in missing Louis's call, the invitation unanswered for her to accompany him to Brown's to pick out a new canvas.

She thinks of the painting that she labored over, the way she'd thinned the oils so that the white background shone through behind the hand. When Louis showed it to her after he'd put his painting into the carriage, she struggled not to cry. The threads of the canvas were torn, the paint chipped and flaking—she knew there was no repairing it. She hurled it into the grate before he could stop her. The flames blackened and smoked and Louis had to wrap the poker in a blanket to swat out the fire.

He draws a hand across his face. "Come in, come in. Look, Iris, I'm sorry—"

There is a noise behind them, and Guinevere ambles into the hallway.

"Avaunt, beastly creature," Louis says, flapping his hands. The wombat looks at him with sad eyes and then waddles upstairs. "You aren't welcome here—if you stay, she may challenge you, and what good are your soft claws against her sharpened wits?"

"It's just a diverting joke for you, isn't it?" Iris says, following him into the sitting room. She has borrowed a blue silk dress from one of the girls in the lodging house to wear to the dinner Millais is holding, and it is as tight as swaddling. The discomfort heightens her irritation. "You wouldn't have found it so amusing if it'd been your painting. If you cared for my work, you wouldn't have discarded it on the side table like a piece of rubbish. I left it on the easel, out of her reach. I know you don't think much of it—"

"I *do*. I wanted to show it off to Hunt—"

"But you needn't make fun."

Louis looks at her. "I'm sorry. I am, truly. I only make light of things because—well, I don't know what else to say. It is vexing." He tucks his hair behind his ear. "I really am sorry."

He is so close that she can smell the mint tea on his breath and the cigar smoke in his clothes, and she feels her anger fade to nothing.

"Will you ever forgive me?"

"Oh, I should think not. You'll still be repenting in half a century's time."

"I'll ask them to inscribe a final apology on my tomb."

"Died of remorse." She looks at him anew, takes in the tight floral waistcoat, the fob watch, his hair oiled into a sharp crease. "And what in heaven's name are you wearing?"

"Millais's cast-offs, as if I'm his butler." Louis tugs at his sleeve. "Now. Guinevere—I trust you received her poem?"

"I did. It was good of her."

"Don't you want to see the palace she built you?"

"What are you talking about?"

"The poem," Louis says. "Honestly, to think she went to all that effort, curling her fat paw around a quill. It wasn't easy for her, I'll wager. And you paid it no heed, not a jot, when she went to such lengths to demonstrate her repentance."

"Do you have a fever?"

"Come. I think we should investigate," Louis says, and he pinches his earlobe twice, one of his nervous tics.

She follows him to the studio, feeling as stiff as a dressed-up doll in her borrowed outfit.

"Tell me, disgraced creature," Louis says, approaching Guinevere, who is sleeping on a bolster. He crooks his ear toward the wombat's mouth. The animal's fur is greasy, heavily pomaded with Macassar oil. "Where is this promised palace? Where have you built it?"

"It had better not be one of her mud nests or I'm afraid our friendship is quite ruined."

Louis lifts Guinevere's paw and points up the staircase. He shrugs. "I suppose we'd better follow where she directs."

Iris does not know what to think. She wonders if he has bought her something—a matchstick house, or a snow globe, perhaps. She follows him past the floor where his bedroom must be, up to the maid's attic at the top. She has never been this far.

"Not much of a palace," Louis sniffs, and he smiles at her, artless and brimming. "I hope you won't be disappointed."

A sign on the door reads *"Beware: Artist Toiling."*

"What is this?" Iris asks.

He pushes open the door, and she stares.

The garret has been turned into a studio—there is an easel in the corner with a stretched canvas the color of bandages, and neatly shelved bottles of paints and brushes. The little window faces west, and the sun is setting over hundreds of London steeples. It has the pristine look of a painted biscuit box. In the evening light, Louis's face is golden when he turns to her.

"Guinevere appears to think this is for you. Though how she got the money for the paints is anybody's guess. Perhaps she has been doubling as a chimney sweep's brush." He laughs slightly, but it is uncomfortable, and his eyes do not smile. He watches her.

"For me?" she asks. She crosses the room and picks up a jar. Louis has glued a label to it which reads *Iris's Brushes*. She rubs her finger over it.

"Do you like it?" he asks. "I know it isn't much, but I felt so wretched about the painting—"

"Like it?" she repeats.

He touches a brass hook. "This is where your first painting can hang. You can work here whenever you aren't standing for me—I won't disturb you—and now you don't need to draw at that little desk in the corner downstairs and tolerate my insufferable prattling." He looks at her, and she can't read his expression. "I'm sorry again about the painting. I really am. You can submit next year—and think what a debut you'll be then! The critics will run out of ink." He adds hastily, "In their praise."

He is barely a palm's width from her. She could reach out and pull him to her, feel his weight against her. She feels suddenly uncertain, and says lightly, "Oh, Guinevere—she is too naughty arranging all of this."

"And you are pleased?" he asks again.

"I am," she says, and she is glad too, when he closes the door, and leaves her all alone. She stands by the window, her hands clasped in front of her, and she starts to laugh. She spins round—the room is just big enough, though the dress is too tight for her to raise her arms. This is hers! This is for her—*her* studio to paint in—she is so happy that she balls her fists and hammers them in the air. What will she paint? The canvas is huge compared to the little painting she worked on before—three foot high at least. She grips the edge of it until she feels the fabric give under her hand. It is all she can do to prevent herself from tearing it into strips, from hurling the glass bottles at the wall, from destroying the room in her glee.

She hears a knock on the door and Louis says that they must go.

"Millais will be expecting us," he says. "And they will need rescuing from the insufferable Mr. Rossetti."

She composes herself, smoothing her hair with the flat of her hand, resisting the urge to let out a burst of laughter. She doesn't want to go to the dinner any longer. She just wants to stay in her studio by herself. "I'm looking forward to meeting him."

"I'm sure he is looking forward to meeting *you* more."

"What do you mean?"

Louis shrugs, and he takes the stairs before her.

"Besides, Millais and Hunt like him," Iris says, trying to keep her mind on the thread of their conversation, but it loops back, stitching its way into the room and the easel and the brushes.

"He didn't poison their pet with a box of cigars. Poor, dear Lancelot."

"A day ago, I wished he'd poisoned Guinevere too. I was close to having her skinned for my next canvas to make up for it."

"You don't mean that," he says, and he corners the wombat in the hallway where she is pawing at the rug, her nails as round as almonds. He picks her up with a *ngh* and sings behind her bulk, his hands flinging out her paws in expressive melancholy:

*"Voi che sapete che cosa è amor,*
*Donne, vedete s'io l'ho nel cor,*
*Donne, vedete s'io l'ho nel cor!*
*Quello ch'io provo vi ridirò,*
*È per me nuovo, capir nol so.*

*Sento un affetto pien di desir,*
*Ch'ora è diletto, ch'ora è martir."*

Iris has no idea what he is singing, whether it is in French or—or any of the other continental languages.

"Mozart," he says. *"Le Nozze di Figaro."*

"I know," she lies.

"Have you ever been to the opera?"

"I—"

"Then I will take you."

There are times when she wishes she knew more, that she could impress him with a knowledge of travel, of poetry, of art and architecture, but without money or privilege the only things in which she has superior understanding are in fabrics and low trade: the difference between needlepoint and bobbin lace, or the importance of display in a shop window. She feels she has seen nothing except the tired tread of the streets between Bethnal Green and Regent Street, the eroded gilding of the doll shop, the decaying walls of her garret and basement room. Her life was a cell before, but now the freedom terrifies her. There are times when she longs for the enclosed familiarity of her previous life, because this expansive liberty seems like it will engulf her. What is she to make of it all? Two attics of her own—one in which to sleep and one in which to paint. And is it wrong of her to treasure them, to want to press them tight to her chest and not let go? And while she feasts on all this, she has left her sister to suffer in that dreary fleapit of a shop.

She brushes wombat hairs from her dress. "Come, let's go."

"Quite honestly, I don't know why you waste your time with the Royal Academy," Rossetti says, through a forkful of quail. He is handsome, his neatly curated hair loose about his shoulders, though he is shorter than Iris expected. When they were introduced, the crown of his head reached her brow and made her feel as if she had to stoop. "The critics have made their stance *more* than clear—if they won't accept us, then I don't give a fig for any of them. I didn't enter a canvas this year."

"But don't you think we should attack the institution from within?" Millais suggests.

"Pah! The trouble is you think you are a Trojan horse, when in fact you are a child's hobby horse and all the critics are laughing."

Hunt snorts, but Louis exchanges a look with Iris as if to say, *I told you so*, but in truth, she finds Rossetti's frankness quite charming.

She looks around her, at the dining room with its long windows overlooking Gower Street, at the plaster rose of the ceiling and its elaborate cornicing. Even though it is April, a fire thunders in the grate.

There are six of them at the polished table: William Holman Hunt, Johnnie Millais, Gabriel Rossetti, Lizzie Siddall, and Iris and Louis. The other members of the PRB—William Rossetti, Thomas Woolner, and Frederick Stephens—are busy. ("Shunning us," Rossetti remarked, "except my brother, who must bring home the tin and is working late.")

Lizzie sits opposite Iris, and she is as beautiful as Iris imagined. Her skin looks so smooth that it could shatter, her auburn hair is loose, and her face has a doll-like perfection. She has an expression of such quiet concentration that Iris is sure that she, like her, is drinking everything in. Iris can scarcely picture her among the milliners of Cranbourne Alley where she used to work (she remembers Mrs. Salter briefly, *squawking bonnet touters, immoral, the lot of them*), so dignified does she appear. Iris is not wholly sure why they were invited: the dinners are usually gentlemen-only affairs, and she thought at first it was because she and Lizzie both want to paint. But when

Rossetti passed on his landlord's concerns about his profession with a guffaw ("He advised me that my models must be kept under gentlemanly restraint, as some artists sacrifice the dignity of art to the baseness of passion"), she wondered if it was just because the painters' other models are whores, and she and Lizzie were being paraded because they are more respectable.

After all, Lizzie seems perfectly controlled, perfectly muted: she barely eats. She merely stirred the Julienne soup, turned away from the fish, and now she slices off a sliver of quail and nibbles it. It brings to mind Iris's mother's instruction on manners ("In polite company, eat little and daintily"), but she cannot help it—the food is so delicious that she finds herself scanning the bird carcass for any edible traces, and heaping buttery mounds of mashed potato onto her fork. If she could lick the plate clean, she would.

"These fussy creatures," Rossetti says of the quail. "I've a mind to gobble it up whole." He tears off a wing and pops it into his mouth, crunching the bones and grimacing.

"That will be a painful rupture when you evacuate tomorrow," Hunt says. "Better summon the physician."

"Ladies present," Millais says, but Iris catches Lizzie's eye and sees she is stifling a smile.

"Our delicate sex," Rossetti says. "Do excuse me."

Rossetti slides a hand to Lizzie underneath the table and holds it, and Iris has to look away. They are whispering, only a thread's distance between their foreheads. And they claim not to be courting. She hears scraps of their whispered words: *my dear petticoated philosopher, sweet Sid.* She senses Louis is concentrating a little too hard on his plate.

"What are you working on next?" Louis asks, clattering his cutlery.

Hunt talks about his idea for either pastoral drawings of a shepherd and shepherdess, or a painting he has decided to call *The Light of the World*, which he has been mulling for a while; Millais speaks of his plans for *Ophelia*, of the look of quiet melancholy he wants to paint on the face of the drowned girl, of the symbolic profusion of flowers that will surround her—forget-me-nots, poppies, and fritillaries. "By Jove, I'll need a stupendously beautiful creature for it," he says.

"You must use Lizzie," Rossetti says.

"Of course," Lizzie says. "It's my favorite of his plays."

"There! I knew the education I've been giving her would prove effective. We are moving on to Shakespeare's histories next," Rossetti says, and Hunt nods approvingly.

"Very good," Millais says. "I'll need you to lie in a bathtub, but I'll heat it with oil lamps."

"I'm not quite ready to perish of the cold for art's sake yet," Lizzie says.

"As for me," Rossetti says, lighting a fat Havana off the chandelier. "I haven't decided what's next. I know I would like to paint Dante and Beatrice. Perhaps Dante being consoled a year after Beatrice died."

Louis sniffs. "I don't much care for that story. How can Dante love a woman for the rest of his life—nay, even neglect his wife for her—when he has glimpsed her only twice? Courtly love—it's begun to tire me." He turns to the butler, who is clearing the plates: "Thank you, Smith."

"How can it tire you?" Millais asks. "Isn't it beautiful, real, where true emotions reveal themselves honestly? Not stifled by convention, but rather expressing passion, heroism, spiritual awakening—"

"But that's quite it," Louis says. "These feelings are *not* real. Iris first drew this to my attention, and I've thought of it ever since. All those romances—they idealize love when it really is nothing at all like it."

Iris leans forward. She says, "What *is it* like?" and almost adds *to you*, but her words are drowned out by a snort from Rossetti as he swats away the idea with a wave of his napkin.

"I *want* to believe in the love that we paint," Louis continues. "But these past months, I've begun to wonder—well, if love isn't something quite different from all of that. If we confuse this foolish rapid infatuation—Dante glimpsing Beatrice twice—with the truth of love, its endurance, admiration, of actually *knowing* somebody."

"You cannot possibly be serious," Rossetti says, blowing a plume toward the ceiling. "Your latest painting—Johnnie told me all about it—if Guigemar's rescue isn't courtly love, I don't know what is."

"But I'm *not* painting the Queen's rescue any longer. I painted her escape after Guigemar was cast out. And don't forget that Guigemar and his Queen were lovers for a year and a half. Not a mere glimpse like Beatrice and Dante."

"Pah," Rossetti says, "the truth is, Guigemar rescued his Queen later, and *that's* the heart of it. Don't we want to rescue women, and don't women want to be rescued in turn? We rescued Miss Siddall and Miss Whittle, after all." He waves his hand at Iris and Lizzie, and Iris remembers the snooty frown of the charwoman; her parents and sister would certainly say she had been ensnared, not rescued. "I see how you've railed against marriage, Louis, and how you've said it's stifling to love, that it causes only trouble, and I heed your warning."

Iris catches a look between them; a knowingness from Rossetti, a warning from Louis.

"Who wants the expense of acquiring and keeping an old wife when there is the thrill, the joy of sweet love?" Rossetti kisses his fingers in turn. *Puck, puck, puck, puck.*

Iris cannot look at Louis; she inspects the prongs of her fork and says in a voice that tries to be neutral but betrays itself by a strange crackling quality, "You do not agree with marriage, Mr. Frost?"

"I—admit that, no, I see many reasons why it is a stifling state," Louis says, with another frown at Rossetti. "Why must there be a legal document declaring you love one another—why witnesses to see it—when, if you love each other, isn't that enough? Why parade it, why entangle yourself? What if you make a mistake? And I'm a heathen, after all, and the union of flesh in God's eyes means little to me."

Iris stares.

"I bow to your superior knowledge of the matrimonial condition," Rossetti muses. "No marriage, no passionate love either. Poor Sylvia, your first courtly maiden. But surely your *latest* paramour has not soured all your hopes of love?"

"Watch your tongue, sir," Louis says, flushing. "Insult me if you will, but I won't have you disrespecting Miss Whittle—"

Rossetti flings his cigar onto his plate. "Egad—these damned Havanas are damp—there's no lighting them," and he dabs his fingers into the rose-scented fingerbowl. "Fine—enough."

And the conversation moves on, to an attack on Joshua Reynolds.

Iris stops listening. She does not know how to sift through her thoughts. *Is* she seen as his paramour? And who is Sylvia? And is Iris a fool for caring for Louis? He will never marry her, not least because he doesn't believe in it; but also because she is only his model and he has given her little encouragement. He has not written her billet-doux, taken her hand, made her promises of any kind except for contracted payments and painting lessons. His generosity has sprung from friendship, from a brotherly sense of duty. She half-listens to the conversation—Sir Sloshua, Chaucer, Eastlake, Shakespeare—names she only just recognizes from her recent months with Louis.

When the butler brings in a large treacle pudding, spined like a hedgehog with set caramel threads, Iris feels her stomach turn. She thinks for a moment she is going to be sick. She is back in her narrow garret bed, Rose's thigh warm against hers, the smells of burnt sugar creeping through the chimney. Her sister is there, and she is here, trotted out like a whore, Louis's *paramour* with whom he is not even infatuated, never mind willing to marry. She turns over the sponge with her spoon, and will not meet Louis's eye.

"I told you he was insufferable," Louis says. "The way he did his best to humiliate us, the things he implied—I can't understand it. And what for? Spiteful fun, like a kitten toying with a mouse. But I ought to have bitten back properly, shown him I have claws and teeth too—"

As they cross into Colville Place, Louis talks on, and Iris quickens her pace. She wants to be back in her boardinghouse in Charlotte Street, a space that is hers and where she can sift through the evening, weigh up what she has heard.

"Queenie—you move faster than a firework—"

"My name is Iris," she snaps at him, louder than she intended. The wine has given her a headache, and she feels a little giddy. She steadies herself by looking at the sky. The horizon yawns. Through the drifts of smoke, she can see the fat coin of the moon.

"Iris, then," Louis says, and he stands in front of her, stopping her from moving any further.

It is dark, and the street is empty except for a hunched vagrant.

"You are upset. Do try and ignore—"

"I'm not."

"Come, I always know something is the matter with ladies when they answer so abruptly. It was Rossetti, wasn't it, ruining—"

"Well, perhaps I'm different. Perhaps I'm not like all the ladies who you seem so—" She nearly says *familiar with*, but even through the fog of tipsiness she draws back. She has never drunk anything except watered beer or communion wine, and the feeling is quite new to her. She wonders again who Sylvia is.

"All of the other ladies who I seem so—what?"

"Nothing," she says. "I meant nothing by it."

He pauses, toying with the silver chain of his fob watch. The smartness doesn't suit him.

"I want to walk," she says.

"Walk? Walk where?"

"I haven't decided."

They strike north up Charlotte Street, away from her garret. His footsteps chime. "Well, I have resolved to be undecided in my destination too. If you prefer, I can trail behind you, like an obedient dog."

"If you must," she says, and she smiles a little despite herself. He is beside her, their paces falling into a pattern with each other, and she begins to forget why she was upset. They whisk around corners and across squares and crescents. Bitterness still sits at the back of her throat, but there is a different feeling too—an edge of transgression that makes her heart beat faster. Here she is, doing exactly what she has been warned against. Unmarried, unbetrothed, walking the streets of London after midnight with a man who is not a relative, a man who is no innocent. She can see the bounce of his hair out of the corner of her eye, as soft as the wood shavings on the floor of Millais's painting. His breathing has fallen into rhythm with hers.

"I've always found London quite romantic after nightfall," he says, breaking the silence. Her pulse quickens. "Despite the thieves and the"—he steers away from a woman who reaches out to him—"solicitations. I think, Iris, it is the risk of what *could* happen."

"What do you mean?"

He points at a pocket of gloom behind a stairwell. "Isn't it thrilling to think that a man may be hiding there with a knife, ready to spring out and accost us? Or there—behind those railings—" He looks across at her. "I hope I haven't scared you."

She snorts. "I'm more robust than that. I'm not one of those fainting girls."

"What—you mean you are out without your smelling salts again? Really, Miss Whittle." She smiles. "Well, it's a damned shame. I would rather have liked to prove my clout against a brigand, to take a fist on the chin to defend you." He shrugs. "But perhaps I'm beginning to sound a little like Rossetti." He looks about him. "Where are we?"

"I don't know. I was following you."

"Well, *I* was following *you*." He cranes at a street sign. "The trouble is that we both walk with such authority that we assume the other knows where we're going. We're a terrible pair." He nods at a black expanse in front of them, where there is no glimpse of streetlamp, no flicker of a candle. "I suppose that must be Regent's Park. To think, we've crossed the whole of Fitzrovia and Marylebone without noticing."

"I thought artists noticed everything."

They cross the street and stand next to the dark speared railings of the park. Louis runs his finger over the tip of a spike. "I once knew a man who, out of his wits on opium, fell from a window and impaled himself on one of these. He looked like a fish on the deck of a ship, flopping around. It was ghastly."

"How horrid!"

"It was." His eyes are so black that she can't tell where he is looking. "Sometimes I can hardly believe that we will die. That I won't exist any longer, and the world will just keep turning as it always did, with my paintings the only sign I ever lived. When Mother died—it sounds foolish, I know it does—but I remember being surprised that the sun rose that morning. It seemed as though everything should halt, that the sun should stop shining when she couldn't be there to see it. Am I talking nonsense?"

Iris shakes her head, thinking of the webbing of her fingers as she spread her palm against the wallpaper, the blue veins like those on the butterfly wing. "Do you miss her?"

"Every hour," Louis says. "She was quite magnificent."

"Oh."

"She would have liked you, I think. She liked spirit. She was always excited about things, whether it was teaching us French, or one of my drawings, or the cherry blossom each spring." He looks down. "Heavens, I miss her."

"I don't think I'd miss my mother a jot if she died."

"You might," Louis says but Iris shakes her head.

"She never liked me. I could never please her. Even when I was little. There was some, I don't know"—she lowers her voice—"*complaint* that occurred as a consequence of my arrival, and she was often in pain and unable to have more children, and it made her angry at me. That was what happened with my collarbone. Her lying-in was difficult and it broke when I was born, and never healed right. I was naughty too—I always did wrong."

"I can't imagine being angry at you," Louis says. "Just like I can't imagine growing old."

"You'll be wrinkled like an old boot one day," she says, and then walks through the gate, into the gloom. She spreads out her hands. The wine warms her now; her head no longer pounds.

"Iris, where are you going? The park is dangerous—"

"I thought you wanted to fight off the brigands?"

"Yes, well, there might be *actual* brigands here."

And, with a laugh, Iris starts to run. She runs into the blackness, into the coolness of the April night, the grass whispering against her shoes. She quickens her pace, hare-fast. Her chest heaves against the straitjacket of her dress. She has never done anything so freeing in her life. If her sister could see her now! In Regent's Park, after dark, with Louis racing beside her, trying to stop her—and she does not care. Because she *can*. Because she never could before. She stumbles slightly on a rabbit hole. The black is graying—she can pick out the shapes of the trees, the gravel paths, and the lake.

She stops at the brink of the water, clutching her side and panting. Louis is here; he has outrun her, and he is smiling too.

"Oh, Iris—" he says, staring at the pond. "It is beautiful."

They stand and gaze at it, at the brimming silver of the moon, its twin reflected in the lake, the mists that rise like steam. It is as if the world has been assembled just for them.

"I want to paint it. I don't want to forget this. It is just—*perfect.*"

"It is," she says.

He takes a step forward, tugging his laces. "I'm going to swim."

"Don't be absurd," she says. Unbidden, a thought rises: Louis, pale and nude in the moonlight. She frowns, and then adds, "It's better if you go in first, so then I can rescue you."

"Rescue me? Not a chance—I'd have to save *you.*"

Part of her is warmed by the hint of seduction in what he says, but she also registers slight disappointment. She expected more imagination from him, words that were less worn.

"Ladies first," he says, and he puts his arm around her waist and pretends to throw her into the lake. She stumbles, trips, falls against him, grabs his side. The water laps her feet; her shoes might be ruined.

He does not move his hand, and she does not move hers either.

They stand there in the silt, the water gaspingly cold, side by side, neither speaking. She does not look at him. She is afraid he will kiss her if she does, and if he kisses her, then what is next?

She can feel each finger as it grips her waist. He holds her tighter and she could die. Her hand rests under his ribs. He is strong, slim, and she can feel him shiver a little. It makes her body hot, as if all of her energy is channeled to the places where they touch. She wants it to stop, and she does not want it to stop.

His hand is on her waist. His hand is on her waist. This moment will pass, but she wants to stay here with the mists and the darkness and him. Right now, she is his.

# Kindred

Silas is standing outside Iris's lodging on Charlotte Street, his feet blistered from walking. He stares up at a streetlamp, at the gas orbs that stutter and flicker, and he does not even blink.

Like an opium addict who has managed to be dry for weeks, who feels his footsteps winding him toward the soiled dens of Shadwell to breathe in the poppy vapors, he knew he could not resist finding her. His creature.

He can remember little of his evening, and he longs to shake free the dregs of memories that still linger: wandering the streets in a daze after lingering outside the Dolphin, his eyes flitting over ladies in silk, in rags, in cotton frocks—sitting outside Colville Place, waiting, waiting, waiting, convinced she was a maidservant in that house—but then the reeling shock, the first sight of *him*—bad enough in itself, but more, far more terrible—by the lake—

It was worse than when he saw Flick with the factory owner's son, her coy wriggle as he planted kisses on her neck.

The streetlamp putters, gasps, shines again.

Within him, there is turmoil; red-hot anger, a ferocious, crashing desire. But he does not show this. He is as motionless as stone, gazing at the faltering lamp with his lips slightly parted. His feet and hands prickle from his stillness, but he enjoys this reminder that he is alive, breathing. He concentrates on what he can feel, see, and smell. His fingernails, digging sickles into his palm. The dancing light. The smell of cheap perfume, Bluebell's. She must have rubbed up against him in the tavern.

The lamp ticks and fizzles out. Silas blinks. The light next to it extinguishes itself; and he turns stiffly, slowly, and sees dawn spreading like a bruise across the horizon. The urge to sleep hampers him, and he feels thinned by the sadness of his night.

He turns the corner to Colville Place, his limbs aching. He sits on the same step as before, leaning against the wooden door of the empty shop. He rests his head on the blistering paint.

An idea comes to him, and he presses the door. It creaks a little. The shop is clearly deserted; if he broke in, he could be safe, hidden, and he could slumber for as long as he wanted. He looks about him, waits for a girl with a pail of milk to pass. He squares his shoulder to the wood, and it takes only a few shoves until the flimsy lock splinters, and he half-falls into the hallway.

It is dark at first, but his eyes adjust quickly. The plaster on the walls is cracked, the stone floor dusty. He balls his coat into a pillow, and sleep comes almost immediately.

When he wakes, he doesn't know where he is. He grapples about him, the flagstones grimy under his hands, searching for his shelf of mice, for his stack of periodicals. Nothing. Then he remembers, and he recalls too the embrace, Louis's hand on Iris's waist. He shields his face.

He walks to the broad shop window. From this angle, he can see into the second-floor room, where Louis paces and eats and sleeps and lurks—the creeping devil! Louis in the Dolphin, with his arm wrapped around a stream of women, pulling them onto his lap—the way Silas handed her to Louis as if trussed up on a platter—

He waits. She will come soon, with her vixen ways. She was *his*, and she betrayed him.

It isn't long—a few tolls of the half-hour bell, perhaps—until she arrives, with her endearing gait. He feels a jolt at the sight of her, a tug of longing from deep within him. She has a magnetism that he finds impossible to deny, a string that links his heart to hers. It is disarming how quickly he can forgive her. She is wearing his favorite dress—the one she wore when they first met—the clavicle exposed in all its beauty. The pale skin, the way it bows outward. If only he could forget her—if only she had not cast this spell on him.

She stops outside the shop, and he reaches out a hand as if winding her in.

*If you look inside*, he tells her, *I will understand that you are mine. I will understand your message, that he means nothing to you, that you want me to keep watch over you.*

He doesn't dare breathe, and he pushes his fingers against his throat where his pulse swells. It calms him a little, though it frightens him too, that she has this power over his body, that he responds in such a potent way to her.

She steps closer and circles the pane with her sleeve to clear the dust, and then—he can scarcely believe it—cups her hands around the window and looks in.

Silas is still, his back pressed to the wall, as her breath fogs the glass.

A moment later, she has turned to the house opposite. The sun is joyous, beaming through the fumes and turning the buildings to ghost-shapes.

He sees her stand outside Louis's door, fidgeting as she waits for him. The things that a crueler mind than his might conjecture! But he would suspect no such baseness, not since her clear sign.

When he watched Flick's cottage, all of Stoke was sleeping except the men who shoveled coal into the hot mouths of the kilns through the night. He always hid himself well. He learned her by rote: the way she walked with a slight flexing out of her foot. He loved her—oh, how he loved her! He knew that the factory owner's son was only exploiting her, a napkin in which to frig, a trial ahead of the wealthier ladies he would meet in time. Silas nursed his love for years, until he could wait no longer. Her hair was like a flame as she raced across the countryside. He showed her the spot for blackberries, and she crammed them into her mouth greedily, and he saw the fruit glistening between her teeth.

And when he laid her out on the grass, she was so thin that he could see her skeleton beneath her skin, the rung of each rib.

# Blossom

Iris adjusts her plait while she waits for Louis to answer the door-bell. Her skin prickles. In the cool light of morning, what they did feels both shocking and precious. It was nothing, and it was something. She wonders what they will say, how much has changed. She once stood at this door on a different day, and was nervous then too. It is as if she could reach out and catch her shadow, see her old self reflected in the windowpane.

He is before her, his hair crumpled, a slight frown. He smiles briefly, and then waves her in. There is a torn letter on the dresser.

She wonders who will speak first.

She follows him upstairs. The house breathes, its pictures crooked.

"I've been thinking about my new painting," he says at last, when they are in his studio. He walks to the window and stands with his back to her, his forehead pressed against one of the panes.

"Oh?"

"My shepherdess one, which we did the sketches for. I want it to be three foot by two foot. I might even start the painting today, if I can track down that boy with no teeth."

"Albie." She stares out the window at a hunched figure sitting on the step opposite. He wasn't there a moment ago when she looked through the glass of the empty shop.

"Shall we send for him?"

"We might as well. I need something to absorb me." He rubs his neck. "I shouldn't have drunk so much wine."

She looks down, wondering if he means he regrets it. "I shouldn't have either."

"We aren't known for being in our cups. But," he says, "I enjoyed myself yesterday evening."

"I did—I did too." She looks up at him, and he meets her eye, and they both look away.

"Do you think I would have died if I'd swum in that pond? Of the cold?"

She laughs, partly as the suggestion is self-indulgent, and partly in relief that he has acknowledged that the night happened and she did not imagine it. "I should think not."

"I'd have been written off as a suicide. No irises for me. No plot in the churchyard at all." He plays with a hole in his shirt, winding the thread around his finger, and she is comforted to see that he is nervous too. But there is something in his eye that unsettles her—something ashamed that she cannot place. After all, she tells herself, nothing really happened last night. He made no promises, no avowals, he did not kiss her. He has had a previous lover, serious enough that Rossetti knows of her—Sylvia—and her chest kicks with jealousy.

She distracts herself by looking again at the deserted shop, and imagines her sister running it. It was difficult to see inside, but she could tell it was deep, with enough room for two tables and three long shelves on each wall. It would be perfect for *Flora*. The dusty panes polished like mirrors, stacked with perfume bottles, embroidered cushions, soaps with pink petals.

"We'd better begin our day's work," Louis says. "I thought we could work in the garden, if Guinevere will admit us into her lair."

They send word to Albie through a runner who knows him, and then settle in the overgrown garden. It is a mine of holes dug by the wombat, and Louis has to take a walking stick to the nettles to clear a pathway to the mossy fountain and gargoyle. Iris arranges herself on the edge.

Louis sets up a stool and an easel beside her and starts to sketch her. He works quickly, broad strokes.

*Glance*, stroke, *glance,* stroke.

Iris tries not to mind the stiffness in her legs. But today, sitting still is a kind of torture. She wants to throw off all her nerves and excitement. She feels a pulling low within her.

Louis pauses, and beckons her over.

She stretches, her shoulder crackling.

"See, Queenie," he says, pointing at the sketch in line and stump, though it isn't his best and the marks are wavering. "How I haven't drawn your shape in a single line—though Rossetti and the others might favor this method—but as light and dark, your neck picked out by its shadows." He touches his finger to her throat in the drawing.

"I see," she says.

"Now," he says, giving her a sheet of paper. "Your turn."

"What shall I draw?"

"Whatever you choose."

He doesn't offer himself, so she sits in the chair while he hovers behind her. She sketches the gargoyle, trying to see the shapes in its pout and horns. It is a relief to be free of the stillness of the house, to study how the breeze sieves light through the trees.

Her drawing is more confident and accurate than it was a few months ago, less linear, more an exploration of darkness. She turns the pencil on its side and cross-hatches the shadow, and out of the corner of her eye, she sees a bird settle on a branch. She painted a marble hand before, and now she is drawing a stone statue. All she has done is doggedly replicate the forms, produce something not quite achieving the detail of a daguerreotype. She is glad, for the first time, that the painting of the hand will not be her debut. She can do better. Her pictures have had no narrative, unlike Louis's, no sense of a moment paused in time, of a life continuing outside the canvas. She is suddenly tired of the stasis of her work, and she turns her eye to the robin, trying to convey the energy in its plumage, the dart of its beak. Millais and Louis do not even paint from live animals but buy stuffed creatures. It feels like a deceit.

She makes mistakes, sighs. "I want to draw his wings, the way they flutter when he preens himself."

"Then I'm afraid you're fighting a losing battle. Art is about *stopping* movement."

She stares at her sketch. "I'm not any good."

"Is that truly what you think?"

"I'm *not*."

He never responds to her promptings for praise, and she finds herself growing irrationally vexed by it.

"I should stop painting," she says, wanting him to contradict her. "I'm really no good at all."

But he just pulls a branch of blossom from the tree and the petals are whipped away in the breeze like limp confetti.

# Shepherd

Albie is wearing a sheepskin jerkin as he lies on an assortment of cushions in Louis's studio. He pictures the heaven that the do-gooders rant on about as a nest in the clouds, and this sheepskin must be how they feel. How he'd love to bounce up and down on the clouds! He strokes the fluffed edge of the jacket and hears a growl across the room. He remembers he is meant to be lying still, and returns his hand to his hip.

"When'll I get the payment?" Albie lisps. And then, as he is a working man now, he announces in the brusque tone he has heard his sister use, "Ye'll pay up two bob according, dearie, I ain't seeing you scarper when it's all over."

"What?" Louis says. "I'm not scarpering anywhere—this is my house. Hold *still*."

"'Pologies," Albie says, but his nose itches and before he knows it, his hand is on his face.

The man growls again.

"I ain't a fool, sir, no, if you don't hand me a pretty silver piece I ain't handing you my cunny."

"What?" Louis says again. "What in heaven's name are you talking about—" He slams down the pencil. "You'll be lucky if I pay you a damned thing. By God, will you *lie still*."

The threat of no payment is enough to curb Albie's fidgeting for at least a minute and a half. He's going to be paid two bob a day. He'll almost be as rich as the swells in the circle. If he knew his adding, he could work out how many days' work it would be before he could fit his teeth.

"Are there fleas in that sofa?"

"Sorry, sir," he says, and he tries his best to be good.

He remembers again the cloaked body of Silas, snoozing on the step outside the empty shop, and he shivers. He saw him on the way to Louis's door and thought at first that he was a vagrant. But that chemical smell, even from a few paces off—he knew who it was. He wondered if Silas had found out where Iris lived and was watching her.

He sucks on his tooth and thinks of what to say to Louis. *I think a man might be taken with Iris.* But he frets Louis'll laugh at him. He doesn't know for certain there's anything to it, after all. He could tell Iris herself, but she's in the garden sketching birds around an old rotten fountain and he doesn't want to scare her. He remembers the red marks on Moll's neck the day before. Isn't it better that he lets Iris know to keep her wits about her?

"There's a man," Albie begins.

Louis frowns, a look that says, *Shut your trap*, but Albie has started now, and like a horse running full gallop, he can't be easily stopped.

"I saw him outside, sir. He can be quite wicked and you should be minded to keep an eye."

"For the love of God, child, hold still!"

"But sir, I think he might be watching Iris."

Louis looks at him. "Who's watching Iris?"

"The man, sir. He was outside just now, on the step opposite. He saw Iris at the Exhibition and he asked me about her and—"

Louis stands and walks to the window. "There's nobody there. See for yourself—wait, no, no, don't move—"

"He was there before, I swear it, sir. He's called Silas, he's got a shop stuffed full of the strangest things."

"Ah," Louis says, laughing a little as he picks up his pencil. "*Silas.* I know exactly who he is. He's a harmless fool. He couldn't hurt a fly, even if he wanted to. I'll wager it was me he was seeking, not Iris— wherever could you have got that idea? He pesters Millais on Gower Street all the time, but he must have found out my address too. He probably just wants to sell me a dead dove or a spaniel."

And Albie blushes, wishing he hadn't said anything at all. He knew it was silly. So why, then, does his mind still fuss? He recalls the woman pinned to the wall by her neck, the distracted way Silas had asked about Iris. He tries to quell his fears, but they only rear back at him, more violently than ever before.

# A Child

Two weeks have passed since the night by the lake, and they have not spoken of it again. Iris begins to wonder if Louis regrets it, or if he simply never thinks of it. She remembers the pressure of his fingers against her side every evening as she undresses, and sometimes the surprise of a recollection is enough to make her body fold over, her thighs pressed tight at the ricochet of desire. She could not name it: she does not know where her feelings lead, except a longing to feel the weight of his body against hers, his hands *there*, cooling the heat or inflaming it—she could not say. Sometimes she catches him looking at her, and then glancing away.

She watches him turn over the envelope, the paper caught in a slant of midday sun. The Royal Academy stamp is on the back: a metal brand sunk into hot wax.

"Oh, do open it," Iris says.

He plays with the edge, bites his lip, puts it down on the sideboard, and then picks it up again.

They both stare at it.

"I'm certain you've been accepted," Iris says.

"But after last year—the critics—perhaps even because I signed it 'PRB' that will be enough to irk them—"

"Then I will," Iris says, and seizes the envelope.

"Private correspondence of a gentleman!" Louis says, but he does not stop her. "Oh, put me out of my misery. What does it say?"

Iris slits it with a knife, the paper creasing in her hand. "Dear Mr. Frost," she reads falteringly.

"Oh, for heaven's sake, give it here," Louis says, snatching it. His eyes knock from line to line.

"Well?"

"They've accepted it."

"Then why do you look so miserable?"

"I don't know. So much still rests on where it's hung. And the critics—"

"I thought you said you didn't care a fig for their opinion."

"Well," Louis says, folding the paper, "I may say I don't, but show me an artist who doesn't mind if horrid things are said about his work." He starts to smile. "I suppose it *is* good news."

"You suppose? Oh, to think of your painting in the Royal Academy!"

"You'll be on display too. You'll be famous—you'll throw me over for next season's Turner or Constable."

"Without question." She picks up the letter. "But I *will* be there, won't I? It will be me—heavens, to think of everyone visiting me in my prison." Centuries from now, when she is long gone, the painting could still exist. Next year she will make her entrance, and be the creator not the muse behind the work that might endure. She only needs to find an idea, and then she can begin.

There is a rap on the door, and Louis runs for it. "Millais—have you heard?"

Millais has had all three of his paintings accepted—*The Woodman's*

*Daughter, The Return of the Dove to the Ark,* and *Mariana*. Louis pulls him into an embrace. "I feel sure that this is the year when the establishment will recognize us—when we will become lauded, when Dickens will be forced to gorge on his own vitriol—*Le jour de gloire est arrivé!* Perhaps even Ruskin will take note."

Louis leads them into the sitting room and takes a bottle of green chartreuse and three plump cigars from the sideboard. Millais attempts to decline, but Louis forces a glass into his hand, pours three generous measures, and knocks his against Iris's. "To the day of our glory," he says, and Iris coughs a little on the sweetness.

It reminds her of the last time she drank with Louis. It does not take much to bring back that night—just the sight of his hands, his waist.

"We must go to the Dolphin," Louis says.

"I'll stand you a drain of pale," Millais says.

"I'll stand *you* a drain of pale." He turns to Iris. "You must join us."

"I can't."

"Why not?" Louis says, reaching for her gloves and bonnet. "Do you have better things to do? A soirée to prepare for, or the opera—"

Iris stares at him. How easy it must be to be a man, not to think of these things. "To a tavern with two unmarried—"

"Nonsense. Besides, we are your chaperones."

"You? You aren't married and—nor am I. I would be considered a—" And she wonders if she is of the class where such things should even be a concern. A shop girl turned model. What is enough to be ruined?

"I didn't think you cared for the sensibility of prigs."

"I appreciate her concerns," Millais says.

"Thank you," Iris says, and she clutches the glass so tightly that she thinks it might crack. Then she adds, as if trying to gather in the respectability that seems to slip further from her grasp each day, "Mr. Millais."

Louis frowns. "Am I to be Mr. Frost too, now?"

"You must go without me."

"Don't be absurd," Louis says, and he looks at her askance. "I shouldn't have pressed it. I'm perfectly content to stay here, and stare at the dado."

There is another knock on the door. "That must be Hunt," Louis says. "I feel sure that *Valentine's Rescue* will be accepted, and yours, Millais—all three will be on the line."

Iris is standing closest to the door, and she says, "I'll play butler."

The babble of their talk drifts through the sitting-room door as she unfastens the latch.

But she does not find Hunt on the threshold.

A child blinks at her. He has a cowlick of blond hair, his large eyes as round as plums. He wears a rumpled sailor suit, his face held in the remarkably adult expression that she recognizes from other wealthy children. She almost laughs—he looks as stern as a schoolmaster.

"Good morning," she says, bending down so that their eyes are level. "How can I help you, little gentleman?"

"Where the ship came in"—he wrinkles his forehead—"the docks, that is, they said they'd send my trunk here. But is—is my father here? Mama is sick. She sent me on the steamer with Aunt Jane and I didn't like it a jot. My aunt is paying for the cab and she walks inter-intermin-ably slow—"

"Your father?"

"Yes," he says, and she hears the hallway door open behind her.

"Papa!" the child shouts, and all the gravity on his little face vanishes as he pushes past her and hurls himself at Louis.

# Inquiries

*7 Gower Street*
*April 12th*

Dear Mr. Reed,

I have attempted to visit you in your premises on several occasions
but have been unable to determine your visiting hours.

I am looking for a lapdog as a prop for a painting, much like
the pair of greyhounds with which you furnished me for "Isabella."
Ideally a Blenheim, Yorkshire, or similar. I wonder if you have
anything suitable either currently, or if you could secure a specimen
within the month? Would two guineas suffice?

Do write to me at your earliest opportunity.

Yours,
J. E. Millais

---

*The Factory*
*April 17th*

*Iris,*

*I was sorry to see you depart in such a hurry—I would be grateful
for a chance to explain my situation etc.*

*Yours,*
*L.*

---

*The Factory*
*April 18th*

*Iris,*

*I trust you received my last missive, and that you are in good spirits.
I must admit to some concern that I have not had a response from
you or that you did not attend your painting this morning—will
you be up to a sitting tomorrow as planned? There is a matter that
I would like to discuss with you, of some import. I would also like to
apologize if I have caused harm in any way.*

*Yours,*
*L.*

_____

*Briefly—*

*Your landlady says you are taking a walk but I can see your candle is burning. I do not like to accuse a matron of dishonesty, so I will allow her the benefit of my doubt, and would like you to be aware of the hazards of lit candles left unattended etc. etc.*

*You were missed in the studio today—Guinevere is barely surviving without the fodder of your discarded pictures.*

_____

*6 Colville Place*
*April 19th*

*Iris,*

*Your silence alarms me.*

*I would be grateful for the opportunity to speak to you and address a pressing situation.*

*I hope you will enjoy the bag of your favorite caramel truffles.*

*Yours,*
*L.*

# Claude

Silas has learned Iris. He has learned her habits: the sucking of the end of her hair, the smoothing of a ragged rosette on her chest. She sleeps in a women's boardinghouse, and her chamber is the top-left window. He knows this because he sees the candlelight pour from those panes a few moments after she enters the building every evening.

She enjoys toffee truffles, which she buys from a vendor on Tottenham Court Road. He eats them too in order to feel closer to her, even though the sweetness is sickly and furs his teeth. Until today, she has spent entire days in Colville Place, and he tries to swallow any thoughts of what she is doing. Occasionally an image will force its way past his filter, and he pictures Louis thrusting himself into her white body, the chime of her laughter, her hot panting. But he puts these thoughts aside because they are lies. He knows that she will be his, that she *is* his.

He remembers when he thought the same of Flick; now she seems little more than a lark, a distraction from the real beauty that lay in wait for him years later. He was so kind to that girl, and she so ungrateful! He put aside pounds and pounds given by those wealthy Stoke hags in exchange for his skulls; every companion he parted with was for her. It was so that they could escape it all together, make their way to London. He forgave her dalliance with the heir to the pottery factory. But she scorned him, railed at him when he showed her his collection.

With Iris, he will master himself better. There are days when he feels a sapping of control, when he thinks that his love is a madness, that Iris does not love him, not really. But an emotion this strong can only be reciprocated. He must wait silent, quiet, hidden, until she is ready to come to him. He does not yet have a plan, but it doesn't worry him: his plot for Flick hatched so naturally and unexpectedly that he is sure one will occur to him soon.

And in all this time, he has been too busy looking after Iris to spend long in his curiosity shop. He has not been into his cellar for over two weeks. It all feels so hollow, so meaningless—what is the point of a Lepidoptera window? It has never been where his interest lies, so why should he care about it? And so he has discarded it, the wings Albie collected turning to dust. A few months previously, if he was away, the urchin would leave him markers that he had been there, that he had a treasure. But there is nothing now. He wonders if the boy has grown bored of this work too.

The only communication he has received is from Millais, a letter that Silas scanned slowly, spelling out the words, and then crumpled into the grate. He could have laughed at Millais's naïveté—as if he has the patience to make him knick-knacks for his paintings at a time like this!

And then—another sign from Iris.

She is in Regent's Park, a few flaking daffodils still out in the meadows. Silas can see her sitting by the lake. He prefers her seated: she looks more fragile, less tall. It is only a shame that she is wearing a high-necked dress that conceals her collarbone.

For the first time, she did not visit Louis this morning and he can tell from the drift of her shoulders that she is sad. It makes him ache to see her shedding blossoms one by one from a fallen branch, the pink oval petals falling about her. She sits there for over an hour, her head bowed, and he longs to approach her, to touch her back and comfort her, to taste the little tears that drip from her pretty chin.

"You will look after me, won't you? You, who is so caring," she will say.

The wind teases a curl loose from her bonnet. Every so often, she raises her hand to tuck it back in, but a few moments later it falls free. She stares downward, and her face is pale, her eyes lacking their usual liveliness. He wonders what saddens her. Perhaps Rose has fallen ill. He should watch the doll shop to check.

A spaniel bounds across to her. Silas usually hates lapdogs. He has heard of the way these pampered rats are treated—meals of boiled liver, sponge baths of egg yolk, satin-lined baskets to sleep in, velvet mittens to protect their paws. Their owners show more compassion to these beasts than to men on the street—was he not raised on hunger and fists? While the factory owner's daughters dressed up their ratty hounds and wheeled them through the yard in prams!

But he shrugs off these thoughts when he sees the look on Iris's face. She holds out her hand to the dog, and it is the first time today that he has seen her smile. The dog licks her, noses her wrist, and she tickles his white belly.

There is no misunderstanding this signal. It is as clear as if she bellowed it. *Do not neglect your work!* she says, with each stroke of her hand on its fluffed pelt. *This is the hound for Millais.*

And he is touched by her consideration for his trade; another way they are akin. Kindness matching kindness.

*Are you sure?* he asks her in his head. *Are you sure it is this one?*

And she answers by laughing as the dog dances on its hind legs.

Back at his house, Silas reads snippets of *The Lancet* for advice on chloroform. This is his chance to experiment. For the last five years, he has cut out each mention of the sedative from the periodical with slender silver scissors, never knowing when he might need them. He opens his drawer, takes out the ragged stack of paper, and studies them carefully. He lifts the wick of his candle.

Volume 51, 1848: "Chloroform—its ben-e-fits and its dang-dang-gers—dangers."

When he tried to purchase the chemical two years previously, it was new and difficult to source. Now he is more hopeful. He visits a chemist he has not called on before, catching an omnibus to Farringdon. He feels a strange security in these establishments: he usually loves marveling over the china jars stuffed with rattling pills, the drawers of powders with metal shovels, the wooden skeletons in the corner, and the neat rows of boxes and tins and bottles behind the counter. Today, however, he barely looks around. His manner is brusque, businesslike.

"I'm here for a bottle of chloroform," he says to the chemist. "The doctor sent me. My wife will soon be ready for her lying-in."

"Very good, sir," the chemist says. "The popularity of the drug—it is said that even the Queen might try it with her next child. Mrs. Dickens was all praise for the method. Hoping for a son, I take it, sir?"

"What?" Silas blinks. "Oh, no. A girl."

The chemist turns, scanning the shelves with his finger. Silas raps the counter with his nails, a sharp tattoo. "Here we are, sir. You'll only need a small bottle, I would have thought. Just the one dose?"

"I'll take two bottles," Silas says.

The chemist pauses. "Do be mindful, sir. There are still dangers. I would not want your wife to encounter any ill effects."

"I'm quite sure. I'll be careful. But there's no telling if there'll be further complications after her lying-in. I'm sure you understand."

"Very good, sir. Despite our advanced age, there can always be difficulties," the chemist says, and hands Silas two little glass bottles, their mouths stoppered with cork.

And the rest is easy. He just needs to watch, to wait. The spaniel slips in the same puddle every morning, coating its shanks and pink collar in muck, to the vexation of the maidservant. Its name is Claude. It lives at 160 Gloucester Place, and has a squashed, piggy face. The creature is white except for mackerel stripes on its legs and a liver-colored patch on its back. It yaps at spiders. A careless scullery maid walks it at dawn on a velvet ribbon—she yawns loudly, chatters with other maids in the park, and does not clean up after its messes, but leaves them for the pure collectors to gather up.

After three days, he knows he is ready. The footsteps of the languid maidservant are plodding next to the ratty scuttle of the dog at her feet. He waits beside the trees. He has brought meat scraps as an additional lure.

The sun is up and the dew sparkles like mouse eyes. There are no swells in the park this early, just servants congregating in groups, picking fatigue out of their eyes and keeping a vague watch over their mistresses' lapdogs.

The servant unties the ribbon, and the dog runs free, snorting around the undergrowth. It sniffs the backside of a greyhound—he laughs to think of its spoilt owner kissing the beast on the nose after that—and then the spaniel begins its laps. It totters down to the brink of the lake, dips a paw into the water, and then scurries back. It weaves behind a tree, barks at nothing, and then trots into the woods. Silas finds it on its haunches, its turd smoking in the cool morning air.

"Here, precious," he whispers, holding out the scraps.

Its snout twitches. It is young, little more than a puppy; it will be just what Millais wants. Iris chose it well. It starts to feast on the meat, its docked tail wagging from side to side like the pendulum of a machine.

It is the work of a moment. Silas takes the vial from his pocket, seeps the liquid on to his handkerchief, and clamps it over the dog's face. He adds more drops, one every five seconds. The experiment takes longer than he thought it would, perhaps a couple of minutes. Silas worries over this. The dog whines a little, then is drowsy and limp.

Now that the dog is sedated, he smothers it. He can only tell it is dead because of the muting of its pulse, the cessation of the rasping breath from its squashed nose.

He tucks the little beast into his coat and leaves the park. He has done it for Iris, and she ought to be pleased.

# Taint

*The Factory*
*April 20th*

*Iris,*

*I beg a moment of your time. I know that the arrival of my son will have come as a surprise, even a fright, to you. I am sorry. At the time, I did not see a matter of such privacy and delicacy either to be of great import, or to be an appropriate topic to raise. I was mistaken.*

*I would like to explain myself, imperfectly, and to reassure you that this does not affect your position as my model and "apprentice," if you will. I am married in name alone; Sylvia and I have lived apart for a number of years. My name does not carry any taint; indeed, nobody in London (aside from the brotherhood) is aware I am anything other than a rather shabby bachelor. I will understand if, following an explanation of my situation, you decide to quit my employ (though the art world of 1852 onward will be the lesser for it, and Guinevere may never recover her wits); but I beg you not to reach a decision before I have had the chance to speak with you.*

*Yours,*
*L.*

———————————

*6 Colville Place*
*April 20th*

*Dear Iris,*

*I spoke with your matron, who informed me that you are seeking a position in a shop in Covent Garden.*

*From a selfless perspective, I beg you to reconsider: your painting abilities are fine, and I am of the persuasion that you would be making a grave error in quitting this so soon, when a promising career is within reach.*

*From an entirely selfish perspective: you are missed.*

*I will be taking a walk in Regent's Park at four o'clock and beg you to meet me at the south gates—I can explain my situation.*

*Yours,*
*L.*

———————————

6 Colville Place
April 20th

Dear Iris,

I was disappointed not to have the opportunity to walk with you this afternoon and to offer an explanation in person.

I will set out my situation here, because it is important to me that you understand the truth of matters. It is difficult to know where to begin. It feels strange, as if you should be here before me, not as the distant reader of words on a page. I've never liked letters for that reason; such scant compensation for real company!

But perhaps it is easier if I don't imagine you here; if I write this as if narrating the history of some other person.

It began, I suppose, because of our fathers, that is Sylvia's and mine. They were friends at school and later Oxford; Clarissa and Sylvia were of the exact age and were sweet companions; as children we spent our summers together.

Sylvia's family had always intended her for me, and she told me later how her mother weaned her on stories of me: from the age of ten, her mother would buy her a new ribbon for her dress, or force her to sit for hours with hot irons in her hair if there was a chance of encountering me. I returned from school one summer when I was fifteen, and I saw Sylvia as if for the first time. I believed myself to be struck by Cupid's bow: instantly and deeply in love.

Her family invited me and Clarissa to stay with them in the Trossachs, and I took my sketchbook and a few cakes of watercolor paint. Sylvia and I were allowed the freedom usually granted to children; we walked alone by the lochs, dammed streams—I digress. The point is, we became infatuated with one another. It was all quite idealistic, all quite naïve. I fed my love like a poisonous *bonfire, nourishing it with poetry, music, art—all insufferable, but these were the only lessons I had on love. I ask you to remember my age at this time. I believed that love was supposed to consume me, conquer me. It would crush me in its great maw and make me miserable, and I could only succumb.*

*Sylvia's feelings mirrored my own: we exchanged terrible poetry, wrote gushing letters to one another late at night, which we would press into each other's hands the next day. We pictured ourselves as figures in a painting, each gesture carefully considered.*

*Of course, our parents thought it was a childish passion that would pass and hopefully develop into something more substantial & lasting, and my mother in particular urged me to postpone the match for several years so that I could travel to the Continent and secure an independent source of income. We dismissed their concerns. After all, we reasoned, how could her parents, with their pitiful damp tenderness for each other, or my mother, privately joyful after my father's death, grasp a love deeper than anything that had been felt for centuries?*

*We decided to elope, a selfish plan from the beginning. We married secretly at night, even though our parents would likely have consented had they been consulted. This was the ridiculous fact of it: we wanted to create a notion that it was a forbidden, undying love, when it was all a creation.*

*We were unhappy almost immediately. Our ideals quickly crumbled when we were faced with the reality of little money, the irritation of each other's company. She was not what I thought she was—I had built her in my mind, and she me. We disappointed each other. Because what disappointment is flesh and blood when pitted against romantic legends? In hindsight, I can see I was difficult, far from an idyllic companion. I was scarcely seventeen—what hope did I have? I wanted to spend my time painting, or reading, or traveling, not tending to her every whim. As it turned out, we* had little in common, and when the infatuation passed, we realized there was nothing left beneath it.

The disappointment caused an illness in her, one where the melancholia of the mind infected the body. She lay in bed all day. Small things angered her. She would scream if I read a newspaper as she believed it carried a contagion, and any smells would cause her to sicken. She would sooner burn damp towels than move them, and she expected me to sit for days at her bedside, comforting her and cradling her.

I spent money on doctors, we journeyed to Venice, to the Alps, and she could not bear me. We had nothing left to say to each other. I reread her early letters to me, and I realized I could see nothing of myself in them. I wasn't real. Ultimately, she insisted she could not live in the same house as me, and frankly it was a blessed relief: within two years, she had returned to her family in Edinburgh, and our son went with her. I have never felt a desire to divorce her, to accuse her so openly of wrongdoing, and contaminate both our names. Indeed, I will never. Now it seems her illness is no feint, or so the doctors say. She has a growth, or a swelling in her. They say it is a cancer. Clarissa is in Edinburgh, nursing her old friend. Sylvia writes to me incessantly—demanding I attend her, saying she's dying. But whenever I visit, I find her a little peevish, propped up in bed making demands for watered broth and sweetmeats. And she storms at me and I can't bear it.

What more is there to say? These are the salient facts: a wife, living apart from me. Little scandal, as we have lived apart for five years, before anybody had heard my name. I regret it all immensely.

And why do I tell you this? Because I hope that you will return as my model and as a painter in your own right. I hope we will take walks in the park, laugh at the priggishness of Millais, and have our paintings hung side by side. I hope you will accept my imperfect situation and realize that you are in no way stained by association *with me. That this changes little. That our friendship must be based on truth.*

*Please, I beg you to visit me tomorrow.*

*Sincerely,*
*Louis Frost*

———————————

*Charlotte Street*
*April 21st*

*Dear Mr. Frost,*

*I will visit you tomorrow forenoon. I thank you for setting out your situation in such detail, and I am grateful to you for sparing me the time to reflect on my position. However, I must ask you to provide me with a reference.*

*Sincerely,*
*Iris Whittle*

# Sylvia

Louis has tidied the sitting room, even by Iris's definition of the word. The logs are stacked in the basket, the coal in the scuttle, and the periodicals and books indexed on the shelves.

Louis is sitting opposite her in an armchair. Less than a week has passed since his son appeared at the door, and yet he seems almost as skinny as Millais. His eyes are ringed, his skin whiter than china. He does not sprawl, does not fill the room with his gestures and laughter. He sits as stiffly as a match in a box: ankles tucked together, hands in his lap.

"I bought your favorite toffees. I'll fetch them from the scullery," he says, moving to stand, and shifting his gaze from the ceiling to the door.

Even now, she thinks he is handsome—his tight curls, the quiet strength in his forearms—and she feels a sudden racketing of desire. He is so close to her; she could hold him. Where did wanting to paint end and wanting Louis begin?

She waves her hand to dismiss his offer.

"How are you?" he asks.

"Quite well, thank you," she says, addressing the mantelpiece. She feels suddenly alone, and she realizes that she wants her sister, that she misses her so intensely that it is a struggle not to cry.

She has written to Rose, but received no reply. She remembers when they made flags out of wallpaper, and pushed through the crowds at St. James for a glimpse of the little Queen after her marriage to Albert. When they would confide everything to each other in whispers, sucking the rich truffles given to her by her gentleman and giggling over Rose's report of his declarations.

*We believe you have been hideously misled, tricked into a course that you cannot wish to take.*

"You read my letter," Louis says. Out of the corner of her eye, she sees him crane forward, and she feels a flush of rage, at Louis, at Sylvia, at her own stupidity in nursing so many foolish hopes. "Will you allow me to explain more?"

"Really, I see no need. Indeed, you owe me nothing except my drawings and a letter of recommendation. That's why I've come."

He scoffs. "You can't possibly mean that."

"Of course I do," she snaps. "Do you have them?"

"I meant that I owed you an explanation."

The air is thick. Woodsmoke and damp wool.

"There is a position I have applied for—at a milliner's in Covent Garden."

"You might as well work in a factory," he says.

"Who are you to tell me—"

"You'll hate it. You'll hate the monotony. You'll have no creative freedom, you realize. You'll be entirely unremarkable, just a factory hand, referred to by nothing except the function of one of your limbs, as if you're a cog."

"What do you know of it?" she says, her voice lifting a pitch. "I came for my reference. If you won't give it to me, then I'll leave now—"

"You're right. I won't."

"You won't provide me with a reference?" She is aghast.

"If it makes you stay, then no, I shan't."

"But you can't do that," she says, and she bites back her anger. She won't rise to it; she will thwart him by remaining calm.

"There's really no need for you to leave. I don't see why—"

"I have to."

"But why?"

"Because—" She wants to say, *Because you are married and I am frightened.*

"You're afraid," he says.

"Why would I be afraid?" She tries to keep her voice steady, but her temper breaks away from her. "And I wish you would stop trying to tell me how I feel. You don't know anything about me."

"You're right," he says, with sudden vehemence. "You give away so little—you are so closed, so difficult for me to understand—"

"*I* am closed?" she snarls back, and her words spill out, more forceful than she can believe. "While you have a wife—a *wife*—who is kept out of the way in Edinburgh so you can undertake flirtations with your models. You talk about honesty in art, and truthfulness, but you're a fraud, a hypocrite—and"—she remembers Rossetti's snide remarks about Louis's knowledge of the *matrimonial condition*—"and I'm just a toy you can pick up." He tries to seize her wrist. "No! Do not—don't insult me with your ministrations—your advances—"

"My advances? I've done my best to hide my feelings. I could easily have seduced you—"

"You could not!" she fires back, and she wants to smash the smug vase of flowers on the table. "How dare you! I care nothing for you—and I've told you before, I'm not like your *other girls*."

"I know you aren't! They meant nothing—mere rookery girls—"

"How can you speak of them like that? They are people too—"

"You think they cared for me in any way? At least now I know where you stand." She can see his hands outspread, shaking, out of the corner of her eye. "You care nothing for me—fine, fine. Well, I'm sorry for liking you—I'm sorry for thinking you were different. I've been a fool all of this time, to think that there was even a slight chance—no—*you care nothing for me!*"

She stares at him, and her limbs are treacle-slow. His hair is ruffled, and he rubs at his eyes. His words echo. *A slight chance—*

He is turned away from her, and she could press him to her, kiss him, if she didn't detest him so much.

She pulls her shawl about her, readying herself to leave, but he risks a slight glance at her, and she cannot stop herself. She cannot let him go—she cannot. It feels, in that moment, that she must have all of him or nothing at all, and she cannot bear to lose him and all that she associates with him: his hand over hers, guiding her pencil across the page. A slash of bright red on a canvas. A painted strawberry, perfectly ripe, the gleam of its catchpoint.

She moves toward him, and her lips are on his. She can taste his mouth, its pipe smoke, and she feels a creep of shame, of desire. She always told herself that she would resist this, that she would hold up her hand and remind him of her respectability, her honor. And yet, when his kisses slide down her neck, and she slips her hand under his vest and maps the smooth warmth of his chest—she cannot stop herself.

"Iris—" he says, but she kisses his mouth quiet, and pulls him onto the sofa, on top of her. She feels a prickle of delight when he pulls up her skirt and petticoats, and slips his hand between her legs. She cries out, reaching for him in turn. The armchair rasps against her thighs. She wants all of him. She wants to be as close as she can to him, to be a part of him—to give herself to exquisite disgrace.

# Butterfly

Dear Mr. Reed,

I do hope you are in good health.

I have attempted to correspond with you on several occasions and have also sent a footman to your residence. It would be appreciated if you could acknowledge receipt of this.

We have not yet received the completed "Lepidoptera Window," Item 297, Class XIX. The receiving date has passed, but we would be content to extend it until the 25th of this month. As I am sure you can appreciate, we have a great deal of curatorial work in compiling the works before our opening day on 1st May. If there is anything hindering the timely completion of the product, it is important that we are notified. We may be able to provide assistance in its assembly or transport.

*We have received Item 106, Class XXX (conjoined hound, articulated and stuffed).*

*I urge you to write to me at your earliest availability.*

*Yours,*
*T. Filigree*
*Secretary of London Local Committee, Great Exhibition of the Works of Industry of All Nations Commission*

# Bone

I ris is lying on the floor of Silas's cellar, and Silas reaches out to her. She edges her high-necked dress down and smiles at him, softly so that her teeth don't show. There it is, just as he saw it on the day when they watched the Great Exhibition being built. A twist of skin over bone. She nods to say, *Yes, you can touch it.* He reaches out. He grasps her clavicle, and it comes loose like a butcher's cut, and he holds it in his hand. She places her fingers on top of his.

"Now you have escaped him," he says.

"Thank you," she replies. "If only I could see your work in the Crystal Palace, I think I should always be content. The finest of minds," and she looks around her at a hammering sound.

"Don't go," he urges, but already he feels himself being pulled away from her, sees Iris begin to dissolve, and the bone in his hand vanishes. The knocking again—and she shimmers into nothing.

Silas closes his eyes, luxuriating in the heat of the vision. It was so vivid that he was sure she was in front of him, that it was *real.* Her mention of the Great Exhibition gives him an idea; he will arrange a ticket for her.

The knocking continues and a shouting follows, but he holds the pillow over his head, recalls the texture of bone.

"Silas! I know you're in there—open this door, you coward."

He recognizes the voice of Madame from the Dolphin, using the same tone as when she hurls vomiting sots out of the tavern at midnight.

Silas frowns, closes his eyes, and tries to imagine the continuation of the dream. Iris's hand on his—that is where he was—and what will she do after? She leans closer to him and says—

"Open this blasted door, you bastard!"

But Silas does not care.

He has heard other customers ring and knock on his door, more than ever now that the season is almost upon them and the Great Exhibition crowds are starting to swell the city, but when he doesn't answer, they eventually step back down the narrow alley with their noses pinched against the stink. The lapdog is rotting out there. He has lost interest in it.

The house shakes with another kick of the door. Whatever can she want that provokes this violent a reaction? He won't open the shop for her or for anyone. He has barely even thought of the rent for weeks. He smiles. Iris believes—

"What did you do to her?" Madame shouts. "I know you had something to do with it—you don't fool me! Dead in a ditch the evening of your quarrel—a slip on the cobbles, my arse. You won't be getting away with it neither. Bluebell was like a daughter to me—"

And then with an animal cry, and a whack of her boot against the door, he hears her footsteps retreat down the passageway.

Really, he has no idea what the woman is bleating about. She must be half-soused on gin. And if Bluebell has dropped it like

Madame claims, well, she was a sour-tongued wench, and he feels nothing for her. He scratches his chest and climbs out of bed.

He walks over to the wall with its shelf of mice, all frozen as if in fright. He thinks the tableau looks like a daguerreotype: he has stopped time, stilled each creature forever. These beasts will not molder and decay. They will endure.

The mice were an early obsession of his. He dressed them up in little clothes and made or bought dollhouse props for them. There are about a dozen of them in various guises—a mill worker in skirts, a bonneted sweet vendor with a sugar cane that she holds like a staff, the prostitute in a silk dress—and they stand there gathering dust.

He has not looked at them for a while, and he starts at the end of the row. There is little Flick in rodent form, holding a minuscule porcelain plate. He has snipped strands of red fur from a cat and glued it to her mouse head.

He remembers the thick pads of her tiny fingers toughened from the heat of the pottery—their friendship—is that not how it went, even though they never said a word to one another? And he remembers more: the bruises on her face and legs that bloomed yellow and purple and black. The way her father grabbed hold of her arm as if she were little more than a doll, the sounds that came from the cottage—how Silas trembled for her. They were alike in their beatings, in the way that many of the other children were, but to him it felt significant. A connection. Silas and his mother; Flick and her father. Everything in her sad, shattered body said, *Save me. My life is nothing more than a spit in a fire.*

And he did save her. He made it easier for her. He helped her escape.

# Gentleman

Albie has fled the rookery before Nancy can catch him to clean the bedclothes. He's been enlisted as a kind of washerwoman lately, scrubbing the sheets with their dried snail-like slime. The vinegar and the rough brushes sting his fingers. It isn't fair, after all, and yesterday he told the old sow he's a fine *model* now and daren't degrade himself, but she just laughed and handed him a brush.

He's wearing a pair of blue chammy breeches, fresh from a barrow off Petticoat Lane, which the hawker gave him in exchange for attracting customers with his acrobatics and somersaults. They have patched holes in the knees, and little horn buttons to fasten at the tops of his calves, and they befit his new station perfectly. He struts like a swell, doffing his billycock hat at the costermonger with a mock hauteur.

"Din't I tell you I'd be a fine man?" he says to the lemon seller, but the lemon seller only scoffs.

"Closest you'll get to a gentleman is stood outside the hotels," he sneers back, but Albie taps his feet together and leaps into the air. "What with your raw gums."

"I'll have fine ivories soon, you'll see if I don't." He consults his fob watch—a round card on a short rope—and announces, "Punctuality for a gentleman is important, to be neither early nor tardy, and I'll take my leave of you, you poxed old coxcomb."

The lemon seller shrinks his head into his neck.

Albie swerves into Colville Place, taking up more of the pavement than he needs, his arms spread like wings, and a man raps his wrist with the silver end of his cane—"Watch it, brat"—and Albie sticks out his tongue. Nothing can sour his mood, not even the whistle of the wind between the gaps of his jacket, or the fact that the stray cat he enlisted to walk on a grubby piece of string in the manner of a gentleman's spaniel bolted off on Oxford Street. Trade is good too: the Great Exhibition crowds will bring more rural folk for his sister.

He is early, and a gentleman is punctual. Arriving early is as rude as tardiness. (He has begged Louis to tell him some traits of a gentleman, and this is one he can remember. He has demanded the meanings of the words as if they hold the clue to life—"tardy" means "late," and "punctual" means "on time.") He whispers under his breath, *Punctual, punctual, punctual.* The bell tolls out its hour, and he counts out the rings on his fingers. "Ten o'clock, egad!" he whispers to himself. "'Twas not invited until the half past of the hour."

He notices the step outside the closed shop where he saw Silas before, and he decides to sit there until the single toll of the bell, criss-crossing his legs like a flunkey, his chin raised.

He feels unsettled, as if the dusty panes of glass are watching him. He turns, and it is dark inside the shop and hard to see, a few old cobwebs hanging from the edges of the window frames. He catches his reflection, and he grins, but remembers his gums and puts his hand to his mouth. Then he smells it: a chemical scent.

He swallows, and stands to peer through the glass more closely. A pair of eyes, and the man's mouth curls in recognition.

Albie tries the door, and it opens easily. He enters the old shop. Empty candle brackets sit on the wall.

"Silas, sir," Albie says, and the man flinches. He is crouched next to the window. Usually he is so clean, so neat, but his cheeks are downy and his blue coat is torn and dirty.

Albie looks around him, wraps his jacket tighter. "What's you doing here?" and then, longing for Louis to have been right about Silas, asks, "Is you here to sell Mr. Frost some of your animals?"

Silas says nothing but taps his collarbone three times. It makes a horrid knocking sound, and Albie does not know what to make of it.

"Sir?" Albie asks. "Is you in your cups?"

"Begone," Silas hisses. "If she is to come—"

Albie swallows, and he knows that he should have fought Louis harder, that his instincts were right. "Leave off her."

"Leave what?"

"Her," Albie says, and the *tap-tap-tap* cuts through him, as if the man were rapping out the rhythm on his skull. "Iris. I knows what you're about, sir, I does—"

Silas waves a hand, and Albie follows the line of his gaze to Louis's studio. "You know nothing, Alb—you know nothing of the suffering she endures."

Albie looks around him. "Sir, please. Leave off her. She does not want it. You *must* leave her." He puffs out his chest to make himself bigger, remembering Silas's hands on the neck of that girl, the quilt of bruises on red-headed Moll. He feels a rush of anger, of protection for Iris. She doesn't deserve it—and isn't it all his fault? He introduced them, didn't he? Now he must set it right and warn her. He pulls himself taller. "I am telling you to leave her!" He is so close to the man that he can smell him. Underneath the chemical scent, there is a foul, more bestial stench.

Silas does not shift his gaze. He swats Albie as if he is nothing more than a fly. His arm is stronger than Albie expected, and the boy tumbles backward, landing with a square thud on the flagstones. His new breeches are coated in dust. He feels a flush of hatred so pure that he is shaking. He stands and tugs on the sleeve of Silas's coat.

"You must stop it! You must—you must forget her!"

Silas's mouth is a thin line.

"Please," Albie says. "Leave her—I begs you—not her."

The more Silas ignores him, the greater Albie's agitation. He shoves Silas to little effect, so Albie slaps him across the jowls.

Silas snaps his eyes onto the boy and grabs hold of the scruff of his jacket, the fabric screaming. Albie feels the force of the man's hands, the reek of his breath, the sourness of grubby breeches.

Albie tries to pound his fists, to dig his nails into the man's back, but he has no momentum, nowhere to grapple. He is held tight in an embrace, Silas's arm a manacle. A wave of pain as his head ricochets against the wall behind him—his mouth a hot red sting—the crack of bone. And his nose is wet, running—he pants through the bubble of blood.

"If you," Silas says, his breath hot, "interfere. If you do *anything*—meddle, breathe a word—I will find that rat of your sister. I know it was her, in that old coal room. I know exactly where to find her, that cheap whore." Silas shakes him, and Albie whimpers, trying to summon a ball of phlegm to hurl in the man's face, but there is nothing left in him.

Silas lets him go, and Albie can do nothing but sink to the floor. He coughs something hard into his hand—it is his last tooth—and blood drips off his cupped palm like water. He tries to ram the tooth back into his gum, but it is no good.

When he looks up, Silas has gone.

Albie pushes himself upright. He won't give up. He won't. He'll protect Iris. She's the kindest, the best-hearted soul.

He leaves the shop and knocks on Louis's door, twenty minutes early. *Punctual*, he thinks, and his legs tremble.

But there is no answer, though he knows they are in.

He feels detached from himself, light and shimmering, his rickety legs liquid. The pain in his head is ferocious, and he touches his nose where he heard it crunch. He lets out a cry, his fingers quivering.

He knocks again and again, and the ache comes thicker, like the beat of a butterfly wing against his face. "Please," he tries, and he can hardly speak without his last tooth. *Peath.*

His new breeches are dappled with blood, and more rolls off his chin, down his shirt, into the dust. It reminds him of the slime on the bedsheets that he scrubbed yesterday morning, his sister's chipped grin, her palm in his as the bed rocked above him. He knows Silas meant his threat.

His legs are shaking less, the surge of panic is subsiding. As the pain intensifies, he imagines his sister beaten, discarded on the street like an old rag. Just another whore in the gutter. Nobody would care; nobody would listen to him.

Stooping at a sharp needling in his side, he starts to walk away from the door. He can't risk his sister. He can't.

He isn't fit for anything, not for the life of a model, not as a friend to Iris. He's just a brawling street-dog, yellow, a coward. A fat tear rolls down his cheek, stopping at the dent of his mouth. He doesn't wipe it away. He licks it with his tongue. Salt and iron.

# Gaze

They ignore the knocking at the door. Nobody will impinge on their perfect little world. Iris rocks the heavy chintz hangings of the bed with her toe, and then glances back at Louis. His eyes are closed.

She could stay here forever, making love again and again and again. She can feel the stickiness of his seed on her belly, where it has dried and cracked like egg white. He told her he must not leave anything inside her. She lays her cheek in the dent of Louis's chest, just below his shoulder, and listens to his heart beating.

"My head fits here perfectly," she says. "It's as if your chest were carved out especially for me."

"Perhaps it was," he says, and he plays his fingers up and down her spine as if it were a pianoforte. "Are you content?"

"Entirely," she says, and she closes her eyes. She shuts out the fears that lurk at the edges of her mind, and just concentrates on *here*, *now*. I am here now, she thinks, and Louis is here now, and things are perfect. Or perfectly imperfect. She is perfectly ruined. His chest is hairless, soft, and she runs her hand along the curve of his hip. She feels an ache, a bruising within her, her nipples tender from his fingers. Their kisses were not rosebud pecks, but thirsty, urgent, and twice he pulled her lip between his teeth and bit it.

She always imagined that any form of *venereal matters*, as her mother once termed it, before covering her mouth, was about suffering, pain, endurance. She once saw a man in rags pushing the head of a street seller into his crotch at little past eleven in the morning, his hand rough against the tangle of her hair, the sound of her gagging like the retching of a cat. Even her sister and her gentleman—she shrank at the sight of his groping hands, the force in his arms, the bruises he inflicted on Rose. Iris wanted it for herself, and she did not. She learned to regard her own *parts* with shame, a secret, raw piece of herself to keep hidden. But now it feels like a conspiracy: nobody told her that the trap she was threatened with would be so enticing. Louis gazed at her naked, laughing as she squirmed, and then kissed her *there*. He called *it* beautiful. She was horrified at first, but then—

"If you keep doing that, I'll have to break my word as a gentleman and sacrifice you to Venus once more," he says.

"What I'm interested to know," she says, kissing his earlobe, "is whether it was worth sacrificing the dignity of art to the baseness of passion?"

"Oh, certainly not."

"Spoken like a true painter. Besides, this is little more than an anatomy lesson."

"It's crucial that I study your form carefully." He picks up her arm and kisses it. "I must note each inflection, the tension of each joint, and search for dramatic truth within it all." He moves his hand across her shoulder and traces a finger over her breast. "And here, I am really just striving for purity of feeling. I must gaze on this for days until I've learned it by rote."

She grips him tighter. She sees a flash of dark, the crook of his—what to call it?—and she clenches with desire. When she saw it first of all, she felt a strange conflict between awe and disappointment at its ugliness. She had no idea that men shielded these stiffened parts behind their trousers (or behind their "unmentionables," as her mother would call them).

She lets her mind wander, to the blank canvas in her studio. She feels a surge of energy, as the picture assembles before her eyes: she will fill every inch with detail and color and vibrancy. Louis and Albie will be at the center of it—but what if she were to be in it too? Rather than taking her cue from Shakespeare or medieval romance, she could mimic the simplicity of her favorite Van Eyck painting. She can see the triangle formed by their bodies—she and Louis hand in hand, with Albie sitting at a table hulling strawberries, the quick slice of the knife catching a shard of sky. His hand poised with still concentration, the fruit ripe but not turning.

Their postures will be relaxed, not drawn with the china-doll stiffness that the brotherhood is known for; rather, this will be a scene interrupted, as if the viewer has peered through a window. There will be no passive sourness in their expressions; she will have Louis look as if he is about to break into a laugh. It will be a celebration of life as it is, each object indicating joy. If only she could convince her sister to model too, but of course she never would. Instead, she will have a rose in a vase to indicate her.

She remembers a poem Louis read to her about beauty and loveliness, and she will inscribe an extract from it in the frame. *A thing of beauty is a joy for ever*—and then something about a bower and dreams.

"Have the goblins snatched you?" Louis asks, and she blinks.

"I was just thinking that I'm going to paint you," she says.

"Is that so? And how?"

Her idea feels fragile. The slightest touch could break it.

"I'm not sure," she says. "I *do* want to be taken seriously as a painter, you know. Do you think a woman can be?"

"Well, you're fortunate, because you have talent. And a model of your own who generously allows you access to his figure, purely for the purposes of perspective."

She props herself up on the bolster. "Talent? Do I?"

"You know you do."

"You've never said that before. You said *promise* in a sniffy kind of way as though you had a nasty smell under your nose."

"Did I? Have I really never told you that?" He winds a ringlet around his finger. "We could pretend you're a man. Your paintings will sell far better. Other artists have done it and tricked them all."

She shakes her head. "It won't feel like me if I'm—Ivan or—or Isaac."

"Miss Whittle, the famous painter! Living proof that women can create finer things than tapestries and washy flowers." He looks across the room, and she follows his eye to a miniature framed on the wall. "My mother would have loved you, you know."

"Would she?" she asks. "Even though I was a shop girl?"

"She would have forgotten it as quickly as I did. You have the stature of a queen."

"Oh, Guigemar." She strokes her favorite part of him, a rough patch of skin on the edge of his hip.

"I warned you," he says, lifting her chin, and she kisses him and kisses him and kisses him until she thinks she will drown.

# Ticket

Iris,

*I inclose a ticket for the Grayt Exhibishon opening day tomorow as you asked.*

*Yours—*

# Crystal Palace

It is all noise, confusion, and pressing crowds. A vast fountain spurts glittering jets of water into the sky, and a sea of women thrust through the turnstiles, grasp one another in a kind of ecstasy, and heap cloaks and bags over their male chaperones. The colors are as overwhelming as a high-class brothel—nests of tangled feathers, obscenely swollen hats, raised parasols, and acres of stiffened crinoline. Crystal chandeliers drip among the elm trees and the sculptures and the thick-veined potted palms. It is a turning kaleidoscope, impossible to pin down, impossible to contain. Silas tries to calm himself by picturing the exhibition at night, empty of crowds. Silence reigning over rows of artifacts. *This time will pass.*

"As bad as the parties at court."

"That gown of Lady Charlemont—so *gilded*—what was she thinking—"

"And the ladies-in-waiting—"

A coarser voice: "Flushing privies too here—I'll be first to christen 'em."

Silas is whacked by a fan; he is hot, and he loosens the neck of his shirt. The building is a hothouse, and he is a moldering fruit. He looks everywhere for Iris, picturing her plain dress among these squawking peacocks. He knew the Crystal Palace would be large—how couldn't he, having watched its progress so carefully?—but its enormousness strikes him afresh. The curved glass ceiling seems as distant as the dome of the sky. It could take him weeks to view each exhibit, to roam the floors and aisles and galleries. He thinks of his own little palace in which he has taken such pride: its dark corners, the enveloping warmth of it. His packed shop, with the tiny attic bedroom above it, and the thick-walled tomb of the cellar below it—he could fit them into this space thousands, tens of thousands of times over. And the work: how could he, with only the lifespan of a single human, ever make enough exhibits to rival this edifice?

Iris will remind him of his greatness. Her presence will make up for a lifetime of disappointments. She will be his greatest achievement, his jewel, the most delightful of creatures. It does not occur to him that she may struggle to find him in the crush. She will find a way to his puppies and meet him there.

When the organ crescendo sounds and the Queen shuffles her way up the nave, Silas would not care if a cannonball destroyed these gaudy crowds, if there were nobody but him and Iris left in the world.

Silas roams the aisles of whirring steam presses, mesmerized by the rhythmic champing of their jaws, the slam of the anvils, just like the black machines of the pottery factory. As a child he longed to jam a stick into their filthy mouths. What place can such mechanisms have here? They may show the advance of industrialization, but what is advancement if they churn out only identical typeset journals, identical heraldic china, identical bobbins of cotton, neat and symmetrical though they are? If this is the modern age, he wants nothing to do with it. At least, he reassures himself, a machine could never inhabit his particular skill, could never gut and stitch and articulate or stuff a creature.

As he hurries to see his puppies, he passes along the lurid galleries—blue and yellow and green girders—stacked with cabinets of creatures. Taxidermy elks, a sleeping orangutan, a pair of stuffed Impeyan pheasants entitled *Courtship*. (He could lead Iris to this, ask her which pair it reminds *her* of; she would giggle, touch his arm, and call him a wicked thing.)

He scans up and down, worrying that perhaps his companions have been lost, damaged, forgotten—but then he lights on them. There they are: tiny, intricate, *perfect*. He is seized by a hot wave of pride. He remembers the ring of the bell all those months ago, Albie holding the conjoined pups out to him, how he pictured them in his museum—and now here they are, just as he imagined, pelt and skeleton displayed side by side in glass cages, raised on stone plinths. He made them. He glued each carpal, each vertebra together. He stuffed the skin, tended carefully to each stage as to a suckling infant. This is all he has dreamed of—hundreds and thousands of people admiring the skill of his labor. He stands between the cabinets, watching as the crowds stop, pause, stare at his work. He can scarcely resist nudging them and telling them that he is the great mind behind it all.

"Remarkable," a man in a silk tailcoat says to a female companion. "Quite remarkable. Perhaps he could make you a little something for your cabinet."

Silas wishes Iris were here to witness it all. Without her approval, his success feels unreal. He cranes into the crowd, hoping that she will appear soon and forge her way to him. She will be a little flustered, but when she sees him she will smile, perhaps dip a curtsy (is that what respectable ladies do? Or is it only the upper classes? He should take closer note), and then he will read to her with impressive fluency from the printed card underneath his specimens, to prove his education.

"*Conjoined puppies, articulated and stuffed. The design and execution are the sole work of the exhibitor, Mr. Silas Reed, and form part of an extensive collection of curiosities developed by Mr. Reed over a period of twenty-three years.*"

But as the day ticks on, as morning turns to afternoon, and the building grows hotter and hotter, the quiverings of doubt intensify. He should have learned from last time—she will not come to him, even if she claims that she is interested. His achievements will never be enough for her. He does not impress her. She keeps herself cool, detached, at a distance from him. He has waited for more than five hours for her.

She has not come.

He steadies his breath, trying to remain calm. He knits his hands together to avoid smashing the glass case of his puppies, to keep from tearing the pelt, crushing the tiny skeleton. They mean nothing—little more than foolish knick-knacks. What are they compared to her? Could she not even have been courteous enough to reply to his correspondence, to return the ticket that cost him so dear? She is a lying, ungrateful bitch of a woman.

This was her last chance, and she has not come.

# Rose

"I received the most peculiar letter yesterday," Iris shouts to Louis, over the roar of coaches. It is the afternoon of the opening of the Great Exhibition, and the traffic is a jam. Rows of broughams are at a standstill, horses stamping and whinnying, coachmen yawning and flicking their whips. Wheels creak. Two men are bellowing, their sleeves rolled up as a prelude to fisticuffs, but Louis hurries Iris past the fray, crossing to the west pavement of Regent Street. Her hand rests in the nook of his elbow. "It arrived when you were at Millais's—I meant to say, but I forgot all about it."

"Forgot what?" he asks.

"The letter." She sighs. "Occasionally I like to talk of things other than the Academy." Louis is all nerves; tomorrow is the private view at the Royal Academy Summer Exhibition, and they will see where his painting is hung and hear the first rumblings of critics.

"Sorry," he says, and he squeezes her hand. "Who was it from?"

"I really couldn't say. It had a ticket in it."

"For what?"

"The Great Exhibition." She shrugs. "It must have cost a bit. But it said that I'd asked for a ticket when I've done no such thing." She realizes she is rambling, that Louis is looking at her strangely. "Oh, ignore me. I'm sure it's quite harmless."

"Is this your way of telling me I have a rival? Should I dig out my dueling pistol?"

"Oh, certainly," she says. "He talks far less about the Academy, I'm sure."

It is enough of a prompt to start Louis back on his favorite topic. "I would be surprised if it's on the line, but maybe a little above it, or below—and the chances of it being in a decent room—"

But she isn't paying attention. Because they are walking closer, ever closer to Mrs. Salter's Doll Emporium. She flinches at the staring eyes of the dolls in the window, recollects painting most of them. This is where she suffocated for years, a spider trapped in amber. Her world has changed so much that it feels strange to see that there is no difference in the shop. The green paint is perhaps a little more blistering, one of the dolls is new, but apart from that it is exactly as it was, a perfectly preserved relic.

Through the paned windows, she can see her sister's bent head, the copper curl of her hair.

"I have to go in. I have to see her."

"Are you sure? She's ignored all of your letters, after all," Louis says. "Perhaps—"

"She mustn't see you—it will only aggravate her." Iris hands Louis her parasol, and pauses for a moment, conscious of her lack of corset, her loose hair about her shoulders. The bell on the door clatters as she walks in. Mrs. Salter is not there.

Her sister looks up. Iris stands with the sun behind her, the rays lighting the dust motes, and she can see Rose perfectly. She doesn't realize at first that Rose is blinded by the light, that she does not recognize her.

"Can I help you, ma'am?"

"I—I—" Then Iris catches the blank roll of her sister's left eye, the other struggling to adjust in the dim candlelight. "Rose?" Iris says, and her sister's face changes.

"Why are you here?"

"Please, sister," she says, and she walks toward her, her feet catching on the worn ply of the carpet.

"Well, have you come to torment me? Have your laugh—see if I care."

"What? No—I wouldn't dream of it," Iris says.

"Why can't you leave me alone?"

"I miss you." She takes a seat beside Rose, where she used to sit. Her dress snags on the familiar splinter, her back resting into the chair that almost seemed molded for her. It is as if time has creaked to a standstill, and she feels the skeins of the old web constrict around her. She tries to breathe more deeply.

"What are you sewing? Dead or alive?"

Her sister does not reply, but Iris notes that her hands shake with each stitch.

"Where's Mrs. Salter?"

"On an errand. She's looking for a new apprentice. The one after you didn't last."

"I—I think of you often, Rose."

Her sister is silent, and then bursts out, "How could you do it?"

"Do what?"

Rose puts down her sewing. "How could you do it to Mama and Father, to me?"

"You know it wasn't like that—"

"How was it, then? I should be used to being abandoned by now."

Her laugh is a hollow cough. "And this artist—this man. I imagine that he fucks you—"

"Rose!" Iris says, and she could not picture her sister saying such words, did not even know she had the vocabulary.

"Well? Does he?"

Iris looks down. "Please—"

Rose laughs. "I knew it. He will discard you, you know, once he's had his fill—"

"He will not," Iris snaps. "He loves me."

Neither speaks, and Iris traces the spiral on a knot of wood. She tries again. "I want you to know, I didn't leave to hurt you. I love you."

"Don't be absurd."

"Of course I do! Can you doubt it? You are my *sister*. I think of you all the time."

"Stuck here."

"Yes, stuck here," Iris says. "You want the truth? You don't need to be here. There are other ways, other means."

"Disgrace, you mean? I am far too *pocked* for that."

"Not disgrace," Iris says, and she has to link her hands to avoid embracing her sister. "I can help you—"

"Save your charity," Rose says. It is only then that Iris realizes what the smell in the room is, beneath the must of wallpaper and the scent of sugar: disappointment. The air is sour with it. Mrs. Salter hiding behind pills and potions in an attempt to heal her own misery. And Rose. Bitterness that gnaws at her, bitterness at her heartbreak of losing her gentleman, bitterness at her dreams being snatched away in a single letter, bitterness at her loss of beauty and prospects. And every day, Iris's face shining back at her as a mirror of who she once was, or could have been. Iris feels such a tenderness for her sister that she has to grip the edge of the table.

"I know you hate me for it," Iris says, and Rose looks away. "But I didn't leave you—I left this life. I left this grind, this misery, Salter—

the drudgery of it. I left it to paint. Don't you remember how much I wanted to be an artist, how you wanted it for me too? Remember when we visited the National Gallery?"

Rose's hair is draped forward and Iris can't read her expression. She hears her own voice echo in her head, whiny and insistent, but the questions spill out, questions she has tamped down for years. "Why did everything change? What did I do wrong? I know you had your illness, and your—your disappointment—but it wasn't my fault. I would have helped you, been a friend, but you shut me out and—"

Rose turns to her, her good eye flaring. "Oh, very good, Iris. Very well performed."

Iris stares. "What do you mean?"

"You were always jealous of me. Always comparing yourself to me."

"I wasn't! You—"

"And in the moments you weren't envious, you saw me as pitiful, pathetic—"

"No," Iris says, though she feels a queasiness within her.

"And to say it wasn't your fault! After you ruined *everything* for me—"

"How? I don't know—"

"Don't lie to me."

"Really, Rose, I have no idea—"

"You wrote to him."

"Wrote to whom?"

"Charles."

It takes Iris a moment to remember that Charles was the name of her gentleman. "What can you mean? When?"

Rose gestures at her ravaged face. "When I sickened. You told him of it. There you were, jealous, jealous, jealous! Worming your way in, befriending him, and how else did he hear it? You told him about my illness. And you even had the nerve to hand me his letter!

You destroyed my one chance of happiness. If I could only have told him, perhaps he would have—"

Iris cuts her off. "But I never wrote to him. I swear it—I thought it was a billet-doux. I had no idea—"

"How else did he discover it?"

"I—I couldn't say." She presses closer. "I don't know. But you must believe me." She frowns. "How long have you thought this of me? Why did you say nothing?"

Rose is silent.

"I would swear all I own on it. Can you really believe it of me? I wept too, remember."

Rose keeps her eye on the little corset in front of her. "But I thought—I always thought—"

"No." Iris shakes her head. "No. If anyone wrote to him, it wasn't me. He just gave me the letter and left. I said you were suffering from a rheum, nothing more."

"I—I see." Rose jabs herself with the needle and puts down her work. "Please, I need a little time. To think."

"Let me help. I can help all today, Mrs. Salter will not mind it—" Iris cannot bear it; she jabbers on. "Do you remember our plans for the shop? When I drew the brooches we would make, and it was going to have a blue awning and hundreds of lamps—"

Her sister's head is lowered. Iris can't see her face, and she longs to stroke her hair—her hair that she brushed each morning with the badger brush, the tangles that she teased out.

"We were going to be mistresses of it together. We said we didn't want any dreadful husbands. Do you remember?"

Iris rubs Rose's tear, which has dropped onto the desk.

"We had such plans, the two of us."

"I'm sorry," Rose says.

"I am too. Can't I stay?"

Rose shakes her head. "Not now."

Iris stands, and starts to walk to the door. She can't stop talking, can't stand the silence that yawns between them. "I'll leave in a moment—but first, just know that I'm saving for your shop, and I can help you with it. I know you don't want *his* money, but I'll make it from selling my own paintings. We can set it up together, but you can be mistress of it—I'll be a mere shop girl. I'm better at drawing than ever I was, and I can make all sorts of little portraits in oils—" She is about to turn the handle when she looks back, and her sister's eye is on her. She has a look of such anguish that Iris feels it like a fist in her chest.

Rose murmurs something.

"Sorry?"

"Will you meet me sometime?"

And Iris nods.

# Blade

The top-hatted men nod their greetings to each other, and for once, Albie does not note their behavior to imitate later. He's used to feeling as though he can bob up against anything that pushes him down, like a piece of flotsam in the churn behind a river wherry, but now he is sinking. He runs less. He sings less. He's always tired.

He is sporting two purple eyes and a nose the color of jaundice, and he's slept badly ever since Silas appeared at his and his sister's window and rapped it twice. Just a warning, just a gesture to say his threat was true. It's been enough to stifle Albie's conscience, and any dreams he has of cautioning Iris are undercut by the thought of his sister, her throat slit like a pig's. He thinks of her, naked on her bed counting out pennies from her night's work, her crooked smile, the way she tucks her legs into his when her labor's over and they can sleep at last.

He's settled on the next best thing: he'll track Silas like a shadow, watch every interaction with the utmost care. He's following a man who's following someone else in turn—it almost feels like a jest, as if the whole of London is involved in a ludicrous spying chain. But this is no tomfoolery, and if Silas tries to hurt Iris, he'll have Albie to reckon with. He's learned from his childish attack on the man, and he dipped into his teeth fund to purchase a blade in the rag-and-bone shop. It lies tight in his pocket, wrapped in cotton like a bandaged limb.

"The Academy's finest show yet," someone says, but Albie has no idea what the great stone building in front of him stands for, and frankly doesn't care. He sees the streets as dangers and shapes to be dodged—as falling masonry or thrashing carts or whips waiting to lick his cheek.

His eyes follow Silas as he elbows through the crowds, holding out a piece of paper. Albie runs his tongue over his smooth gums. It soothes the fear that sits in his chest, that tightens his throat.

He knows that the paper means the same as the ticket at the Great Exhibition yesterday: that Albie can go no further. He's just a snivel of a wretch with a bruised-up face. He hopes, at least, that if Iris arrives too, she is safe in that fine society, that Silas wouldn't harm her before all these swells.

He rubs his forehead. Surely Silas will be in there for hours, as he was yesterday at the Great Exhibition? Hours and hours Albie had waited, and he'd almost missed him in the fray. It means—it means this might be the moment he was too scared to snatch yesterday. Albie's got time, and if he finds something wrong in the man's shop, a sign that he's planning to hurt Iris, then he can lead the constable right there, and Silas'll be hanged for it. Then his sister will be safe, and Iris too. He's sure Silas has been hiding things—bad things, evil things—and it's only in the last two weeks that he has opened the lid of fast-boiled panic.

He scampers off, away from the grand pillars of Trafalgar Square. His left leg still hurts from when Silas shoved him, so he runs like a wonky tin toy, his ankle bowing outward.

*Academy, academy, academy,* he repeats, dancing out of the way of an omnibus piled high with clerks, ignoring the cry of the coachman.

*Academy, academy, academy.*

He glances about him, a quick left and a right, and then ducks into Silas's alleyway. The buildings around him are as tall as ships, their windows broken. Smoke buffets from one of them. The alley is dense with cinder heaps and dust, a paste that thickens against Albie's feet. Silas's shop is at the end, leaning into the street, two floors high and as rickety as an aged sot.

Albie chokes a little as the smell of decay hits his nose. He sees a moldy creature, the flesh pulsing with wasps and maggots as they work the meat down to the skeleton. The jaw looks like that of a fox. He must get inside, away from it. He breathes through his sleeve. And he must be quick too—what might Silas do if he found him?

He shakes the door, but of course it is locked. He looks up, notices that Silas has left the top window ajar. It is little bigger than a chimney pot, but Albie's used to scaling walls, to squeezing through the narrowest of gaps if it means a jape or a shortcut. He can climb better than a cat, even with the pain in his limbs. His feet are as tough as paws. His sister used to joke that his bones were made of folding card, that he'd be the best housebreaker in the metropolis if only he were less honest.

He glances about him, rubs his hands together, and starts to scale the side of the building.

# The Private View

The black-coated men draw to one side, their faces turned in raven sneers. Silas thought that they might not admit him even with his ticket, which he has paid vastly over the odds for, but after a little wrangling, they let him pass.

In previous years, he has waited outside and drummed up trade with the painters, several specimens with him to prove his abilities. He doesn't doubt that Louis will be here today; the artists always are, and he is sure he will want to show Iris his work.

He walks through the cavernous rooms. The disorder is unnerving—he wants the pictures neatly laid out, their frames uniform and precisely measured, but instead they form a monstrous, ornate wallpaper. The ceiling, at least, is molded into symmetrical scrolls, and he looks at it to calm the whirlpool of his mind. He knocks into a whiskered gentleman who regards him as if he is a mere fart lurking under his nose—*Gideon, Gideon*—and Silas feels again that he does not belong. He was never accepted in Stoke—even his mother loathed him—and yet the society to which he aspires treats him like either a stray dog or a jester. He tries to focus on the thought that soon Iris will be here, that he will see her. He craves just a glimpse of her, an understanding to pass across her face that he is part of the establishment, that he too can secure tickets for this private view.

What a start it will give her, to see him surrounded by this crowd! Silas wanders through the clouds of pipe and tobacco smoke, barely looking at the paintings. He wonders what he will say, whether he dare approach her. Should he rebuke her for her failure to visit his shop, to attend his exhibition yesterday? It was unfair of her, heartless even. "I am sorry," she will say, bowing her head, "I could not come unchaperoned."

He casts a glance around the room, and then—he can hardly believe it—she is here, on the wall. He pushes through the throng, elbowing a man who barrels round and scolds, "Excuse *you*, sir," but he is set on his course.

It is Iris. Lifelike, perfect, stilled. The exactness of it astonishes him. He feels as if he could climb in and join her in the painting, feel the warm pulse of her throat, the cool silk of her hand against his chest. Her look—so afraid, yet so hopeful—seems directed only at him. She wears a gold coronet in her hair. A Queen, then, as Louis said all those months ago in the Dolphin. Silas notices a group of men admiring the painting, but they must not gaze on her. He does not want these impostors absorbing the puck of her lip, the twist of her collarbone, the wide spacing of her eyes. She is *his* Queen.

When the gentlemen have moved on, he looks more closely at the scene that surrounds her. He notes the bars of the cell, her expression of longing. And the bird that flutters past—isn't it *his* dove that she cranes toward? Each feather is so perfectly rendered that it does not seem far-fetched to imagine the creature sweeping free of its painted cage.

He reads the inscription below it. "My life is dre-dreary—he com-eth-not," and then something more that he tries and fails to decipher.

All his imaginings crystallize. He realizes shakily, gratefully, what he must do. How he can earn that look, how he can have her all to himself. How he can delight her, scrub away her sadness.

Joy flushes through him, a trembling, hesitant thrill that he cannot name and would bottle if he could. This is greater even than racing across the meadowland of Staffordshire, the ecstasy of seeing the curled skull of a ram, of having Flick all to himself at last, her mouth his alone.

She will be his.

# On the Line

My darling," Iris says, pulling Louis's arm. "You lumber slower than Guinevere. There are more important things to discover, after all, like whether I'm on the line."

"Come, be dignified," Louis says, but he laughs, and turns his walk into a skip. "I'm sure it won't be—that it'll be shut off in a corner like Hunt's *Rienzi* last year—"

The Royal Academy is before them, a huge edifice of smoke-blackened stone. Men in dark top hats congregate, pipe fumes ribboning in the breeze. They stand square, firmly planted, their confidence echoed in the squat solidity of the building and its pillars. It looks as if an earthquake could not rattle it, the windows as impermeable as rock. Iris thinks for a moment of her chewed canvas, but again she is glad it isn't on display. Next year she will make her entrance. Her painting will be flawless, ambitious—five foot tall at least. She will not be afraid to take up space.

A porter holds open the door, nods his greeting, and they are waved past the waiting queue. There is a tenseness in the way Louis grips her arm as they climb the marble steps, and she feels a swell of desire. An image flits: her lips tight against his prick, his mouth parted as she rises and falls above him—she blushes, stifles a laugh.

He doffs his hat at various people whom Iris does not recognize—or doffs Millais's hat rather, another of his cast-offs—and she notices that there is a dab of blue paint in his hair. He whispers their names under his breath—"That is Brown, I have heard mighty things of his *Chaucer,* oh—Eastlake—and Lady Eastlake with him—and over there Reynolds—Leighton—"

There is a roar of chatter, a thick haze of billowing smoke. Louis delves into his pocket for his pipe and chews the end. They enter the first room. Louis glances around him, first scanning at eye level, and then above and below it. And Iris tries to join him, but her eyes cannot settle. She has imagined this day for so long, picturing a neat row of pictures. But this—it is chaos, beautiful chaos. The walls are a patchwork of gilded frames from floor to ceiling. She can scarcely comprehend all the toil and labor that went into this room—tens, hundreds of years when all stacked in a single place. She tries to take in a picture of a Scottish burn, and she imagines each mix of pigment, each dab of the paintbrush. This is a room hiding careful consideration and ticking minds, all of which exist beneath these paintings like the machinations of a clock behind its plain face.

"It isn't here," Louis says, pulling her into the next gallery. Her skirts sweep the parquet, and they edge through the crowds. Some stare at the art, others point and laugh. All of London seems to have gathered in these rooms to chatter.

"How many paintings do you think there must be?" she asks Louis.

"What?" he says, and she repeats her question. "Oh, over a thousand, at least. But where is it?"

She pulls on his sleeve. "There, *there,*" she says, and he marches toward it.

It is on the line. Perfectly, squarely on the line, in the center of the West Room. Its colors gleam amongst the brownish paintings around it.

*She* is on display to the world. He has pinned her down in paint, hemmed her in with the four edges of the golden frame. She is there—life-size, stilled in a fleeting moment.

And how beautifully he has captured her!

It has been a month since she last saw it. The Queen, *she*, stands in the cell, her face half in profile, one hand by her side and the other reaching out to the dove that flies past the barred window.

She wonders how she could ever have questioned whether Louis loved her, now she realizes the tenderness with which she is painted, the affection of each brush-stroke. It is a love letter.

"I should have done more with the ivy," Louis says, frowning. He takes a step back.

"It's on the line," she whispers to him. The room feels reverent, despite its noise, and she wants to preserve this moment between them.

"Yes," he says. "Yes, it is. And look—" He points. "There is *The Return of the Dove to the Ark*, on the line too, and *Mariana*, a little below it."

She imagines her own painting hanging here, next to Louis's. She has only just begun it, traced the contours of shade and light onto the hard white canvas: the curve of a bowl of strawberries, the vase bursting with flowers. This afternoon, she will add the first dabs of paint, and she longs to return to her studio.

"Mr. Frost," a man says, tapping him on the shoulder, and Louis turns and bows, introduces Iris, and the man says with a chuckle, "What a majestic creature she is! So tall! There's really no mistaking her—but is she for sale too?" and Louis does not smile. They make small talk for a moment, discussing how Ruskin has already visited, how marvelous it is for London to usher in two exhibitions within two days.

"Though ours is the *greater*," the man says, "but the Great Exhibition has pinched most of our crowd."

Louis scoffs. "Such a want of individuality, I have heard, such a gorged medley of designs. And did you hear, that there is no space for fine art unless a painting is submitted to illustrate improvements of colors—imagine, recognized not by artistic skill but as a mere preparer of paints!"

Iris has listened to his complaints before, and after a while, she stops listening and merely watches their mouths. The man has a maggot-shaped scar on his cheek that twitches when he speaks. He taps Louis's elbow, screening Iris out of the conversation, and says, "May I introduce Mr. Boddington—who has already expressed an interest in purchasing your *Imprisonment of Guigemar's Queen*."

The men bow, and Iris turns away, blinking. "Please excuse me," she says, but nobody seems to have heard her.

She gazes at the canvas again, at the tenderness in her expression, the passivity of her unsmiling face. She feels a weight within her, a flattening. She starts to see it not as a celebration, but as a trap that has snapped around her. The woman in the painting has become her twin, like her and yet nothing like her. She has suffocated her, until Iris does not know where she ends and this image begins. She has escaped one half of herself for another.

She wonders how it did not occur to her that *Guigemar's Queen* would be for sale. She imagined, somehow, that Louis would want to keep her, that the picture came with too many memories to part with, that she would not be sold. But it is *not* her, she reminds herself, and yet it is, too.

"Of course, it is not to everybody's taste. I understand some of the critics have been rather relentless in their abuse of your sweet sugarplum already. But I admire it intensely, and wondered the price?"

Out of the corner of her eye, she sees Louis smile, nod, and he says, "Not that I wish to be a tradesman here, but I would not part with it for less than four hundred."

Four hundred pounds! That is her worth. She stares again at the painting, at the paintings of other women about it—their images, too, will be preserved for hundreds of years, there for anybody to criticize or gaze at—and they all have a price. This is little more than a prettied-up shop, where rows and rows of wan, painted women are for sale. And she is among them.

She drifts away and sees a Frenchman scoffing at Millais's *Mariana* and she does not care. Mariana—for sale, too. She tries to control herself, to consider that Louis is an artist, that it is a trade and he must make a living, that he transacts for models just as he transacts for paintings. But there had been a way that he intellectualized his work and made her forget it was rooted in commerce. She recollects Millais's words: *By Jove, I'll need to find a stupendously beautiful creature for it!* And now: *What a fine creature she is!*

She feels a hand on her arm, and she jumps. It is a hard grip, the fingers pressing into her elbow, and she thinks of Mrs. Salter. A smell hits her—sour, unwashed—and she cannot bear the touch.

"I understand it all," the man says, and she stares at him. His breath is putrid, his lips purple and glistening. The intrusion is as sharp as a bite, so unexpected that for a few seconds she can do nothing. She feels that he could lead her from this gallery as mutely as a child going with its mama, so shocked is she, so taken aback. She stares at the room as if through a veil, opens her mouth but no sound comes out. She is a fly, paralyzed by the wrapped thread of a spider. "You must be my Queen—"

It is only now that she recognizes him; the man from the shop who gave her that bauble so strangely—Elias? Cecil? Silas, that was it—and she tries to bend her arm away, but he will not release her. The harder she thinks of escape, the tighter he clings. She cannot breathe, cannot bear his cold, clammy grip. She needs to steady herself: her vision swims, and she chokes at his stench.

His fingernails dig in, and the shock of the pain causes her to recall herself, that she has strength, too. "Let me *go*," she says, and she tears back her arm with an abrupt violence, unsettling a group of gentlemen behind her. They sigh and tut, and Iris blushes. She has ruffled the polite waters of this occasion.

As she turns away, she half-expects him to follow her, to clutch her tighter. But he is motionless against the braying crowds, and his face is snarled with pain, as if her touch has scorched him.

# Mice

The room is dark, and Albie blinks. Yellow shapes float across his vision, and his knee aches from where he knocked it on the ledge when he thrashed his way through the window.

He takes in Silas's old metal bed frame, the sheets surprisingly clean. The far wall is lined with little balls of fluff, and Albie peers closer.

It is only when his eyes have adjusted that he realizes the baubles are stuffed mice, some white, some brown. They are almost all dressed in skirts and corsets and bonnets. They remind him of the rows of frilly, passive-faced dolls at Mrs. Salter's. He picks up the smallest specimen. The mouse wears a knee-length dress, its claws closed around a small circle. There is a dab of red fur glued to its head.

Albie shudders, though a part of him also admires the mice, and at any other time, he would imagine setting up a street scene and playing with them. A clock chimes and he jumps; he takes a breath and descends the stairs to the shop below.

The room is quiet. He can hear little from the Strand. The eyes of the stuffed creatures follow him around the shop. The skulls bare their teeth at him. He realizes he has no idea what he is supposed to be looking for; it feels laughable that he imagined Silas might have a murdered woman in this room, or have sketched plans for an attack on Iris. But the silence chills the boy, and he feels the texture of a huge yellowed bone with his fingertips. A sparrow is trapped in midflight, its needling beak poised. It is as if the wheel of time has ground to a halt, stopping these creatures as they fly or settle or sleep.

He must keep his mind on the task at hand: he scrabbles through the drawers of the dresser, finding nothing but odd pieces of paper, fragments of pottery. Even if there were some incriminating note, Albie wouldn't be able to understand it. Hand-penned squiggles fade in and out of focus.

It is so still, so eerie. At the back of the shop, he notices a deer-skin rug on the floor, its nose flat and shiny. He wonders where Silas makes his specimens—surely not in this cramped shop? There were no tools in the bedroom either. He looks about him for another room, but the far window abuts a courtyard, and there are no doors except the one facing the street.

He coughs from the dust. The chemical smell makes his head ache. He should leave. He imagines again what Silas might do if he found him, and he pats his pocket. Good; the knife is still there. He recalls the man's surprising strength, the shock of the punch and his lost tooth, his head that hummed for over a day. What is he playing at? Dicing with a madman, breaking into his house? He tries the door, but it is locked, and he takes the stairs two at a time, his feet slipping. He is sweating, his shirt dampening under him. He has to escape.

But as he hurries across the floorboards—they creak with the mew of a kitten in pain—he catches sight of a pink feather under Silas's bed. He doesn't know why it unsettles him, but he crouches and dusts it against his finger. There's nothing wrong with keeping such a thing—the man collects enough clutter, most of it far stranger—and yet, Albie feels a crawling sensation, as if Silas were running his fingernails up and down his spine.

It reminds him of somebody who wore a pink feather in her hair. She once had the room next to his sister, and was famed for the false trill of her *satisfaction*. But she left, became a finer lady, pegged her way up from the St. Giles rookeries to the better part of Soho. Bluebell; that was her name. Hundreds of girls pass through his brothel, and he hasn't thought or heard from her in years. He wonders if Silas bought the feather from the same street vendor, a little girl with a grubby face who cried out the colored plumes.

He thinks again of his sister, counting the greasy coins, and he pushes the feather back under the bed and stands. Albie is in such a hurry to contort his little figure through the window frame that he half tumbles to the ground, landing on his bad foot. Even the stench of the dead animal in the alley is a blessed relief.

# Rooftops

And tell me again what he said?" Louis reaches for the decanter as they lie in a little dip in the roof. They climbed out of the attic window, skittling tiles down the edge of the building, and Louis insisted on bringing his port, leaving only one hand free to grab hold of the parapet. From the rooftop hollow, they can see nothing of London except the tips of steeples pressed down by fog and smoke.

"I can't remember exactly," Iris says, and she looks at her arm. Four red spots where his fingers dug in. "Something about understanding me—or maybe understanding something, and about being his Queen—oh, I don't know. It was peculiar."

"And this man—he grabbed hold of your arm?" Louis swigs from the decanter, and then Iris pouts and he tips the port into her mouth. "He sounds as though he's quite mad. Did he approach anyone else?"

"Not that I saw," Iris says. It really doesn't seem much, and yet it unnerved her, made her feel vulnerable. "But he came here once before—he asked me to visit his shop." A thought occurs to her. "Do you think it can have been him who wrote to me with that ticket?"

"Wrote to you?"

Iris sighs. "You don't listen—"

"Oh, that letter. Of course I listen," Louis says. He traces the marks on her arm. "But it does rather sound as though the man who caught hold of you merely recognized you from the painting and was struck by the likeness. You are very captivating."

"It isn't like that," Iris says. How can she explain how she feels? How naked, how afraid all of a sudden? How all her life she has been careful not to encourage men, but not to slight them either, always a little fearful of them. She is seen as an object to be gazed at or touched at leisure: an arm around her waist is nothing more than friendly, a whisper in her ear and a forced kiss on the cheek is flattering, something for which she should be grateful. She should appreciate the attentions of men more, but she should resist them too, subtly, in a way both to encourage and discourage, so as not to lead to doubts of her purity and goodness but not to make the men feel snubbed—she is tired, her limbs heavy. She tries once more. "I know it sounds like nothing—"

"It doesn't at all," Louis says. "Look at your arm—the bruises he made. If I knew who he was—"

"But what if he's—" She almost says *obsessed* or *besotted*, but it feels arrogant. "I don't know. It's as if he's singled me out. What if he's out there now, watching me? It just makes me"—she shudders—"uneasy."

"What do you know of him?"

"I know his name—he's called Silas, and he gave me a bauble. It had a butterfly wing—"

"The Cadaver!" Louis says, sitting up. "What a beast."

"You know him?"

"Of course I know him. He makes us the creatures for our paintings. Well, he *is* an odd sort, but you needn't worry about him, not really." Louis looks thoughtful for a moment. "Somebody told me that—Albie it was—yes, Albie. He said he thought he was loitering outside, that—" Louis shakes his head. "No matter."

"What did Albie say?"

"I can scarcely recall. I just remember he was afraid of him. I was absorbed in my sketching." He pauses. "But truly, I think it's nothing. If you knew the Cadaver like I did, you'd know what a pitiful soul he is. He always used to loiter around Gower Street, trying to sell me and Millais dead whatnots for our paintings. He's known for it. He flocks to any places where painters might be, peddling his creatures and bones. That will be why he was at the Academy too." Louis's face is triumphant, as if he has solved a riddle. "*Now* it all makes sense. He's quite harmless, I assure you, not as talented as he seems to think. He's rather deluded." Louis shrugs. "I can go to his shop if you like, have a word. Ask him what he was doing, frightening you like that."

For a moment, Iris wavers. She pictures the scene: Louis playing her rescuer, elbowing his way in, raised voices, coaxings, threats, Silas recoiling. But she wants to forget this man, and she worries that Louis will provoke Silas, or magnify a cinder heap to a slag pit. Even now, he occupies the air between them. She shakes her head. "No. I'm sure you're right. He's just a fool. And it was mere chance."

Louis settles back. "Only if you're certain—and if he bothers you again, you must tell me."

They take alternate drinks of port, and Louis's hand is in hers. She traces her shoe along a roof tile. It is the kind of quiet love that she has always wished for, and she lays her cheek on his shoulder. He strokes her hair. Silas feels absurd, irrelevant, when she is this happy. Louis has reassured her that the man is just strange and lonely, and there was nothing premeditated in it. He merely held her wrist a little too tightly.

"You know, a chap wanted to buy my painting."

"I couldn't help overhearing."

"Well, I've decided not to sell it."

"Why?"

"Because—" he says. "Oh, you'll think me sentimental."

"I won't."

"You will," he says, and he starts to tickle her.

"Fine!" she gasps. "I will."

He sits back, his lips port-bruised. "I don't know. It feels as though the painting is you. Isn't that odd of me?"

"But I'm *me*. I'm not a piece of canvas—I'm a real woman."

"Don't remind me," he says, and he nuzzles against her neck. "It isn't for sale. Not even if Ruskin himself were to ask. I did offer Mr. Boddington *The Shepherdess* when it's finished, and he's taking it for three hundred."

"Three hundred pounds!" She thinks of all the hours in the doll shop. It would take her fifteen years to earn that, hundreds of thousands of pink-lipped dolls. In that time, her sister would be worn away to nothing.

"I'm going to give you fifty of it."

"What? You can't."

"Why can't I?"

"But all I did was stand—"

Louis scoffs. "I'm not paying you for *that*. No, you painted the meadow, the sky, those blasted buttercups. Dozens of them. It was a simple commission, and I won't allow you to do it for free."

"I can't accept it," she says, but when he puts up his hand to stop her resistance, she does not try again.

She imagines Rose, mistress of her own shop, piles of fabric stacked like boxes of sweetmeats. Iris could accept it for her sister. And Albie with his blackened gums. She could give him three pounds toward his new teeth—an absurdly generous sum, she knows, but why shouldn't she? She touches the rosette on her breast. Apart from Louis, he's been the only friend to her in the last few months, and she sees how he suffers even if he doesn't utter a syllable of it. He spoke to Rose, tried to coax a resolution between them, ran letters for her for nothing. And that would leave thirty-five pounds for Rose; she'll keep twelve for herself.

He kisses her on the forehead. "I don't want to be apart from you, ever."

"You *are* sentimental," she says, though her chest feels expansive and sore at the same time. "What's in your port? I worry I'll have to carry you off to Bedlam soon."

"Very well. Carry me to bed."

"To Bed*lam*, you fool."

His words are as hot as wine. She sips from the decanter, and leans over and kisses him, hard. She passes the drink into his mouth, and he splutters and tells her that she is beastly, but she can tell he is aroused, too. He tastes sweet, of cinnamon and pipe tobacco. Aren't they as good as married? She nudges her hand down his chest.

"Should we climb back inside?" he asks.

"Should we?" she asks, and there is nobody to see except the pigeons and the gulls as she tugs the studs free of his shirt. She does not worry over Silas any longer.

Later that afternoon, Louis and Iris sit in her studio. The sun is ticking down for the day, and Louis is feasting on a bowl of peeled pears and chocolate.

"Some gamboge, please," Iris says, and he drinks the last dregs of syrup.

"You need some ultramarine too, to draw out the shadows." He picks up two oil-paint bladders and squeezes yellow and blue onto her palette.

In her painting, behind the sketched outline of the man and woman arm in arm, there is a vase filled with irises and roses. She has drawn each petal, each stem. Now she needs to fill in their colors, breathe life into them with each turn of the brush. The bunch of irises that Louis bought her is browning fast, the petals crisping, but they will do. She sucks the sable to a point, then adds a thin wash of ultramarine watered down with linseed oil, but she leaves the canvas clear where the petal is milky and where the light lies. Louis says she is moving too fast, that she should do more preparatory sketches before committing to paint, but she ignores him.

As she works, she makes demands like a pompous customer. "More blue. A little emerald—no, more—yes, and oil too—" and he cleans the brushes she has finished with, splaying their soft fur.

"Iris," Louis says, interrupting her steady, abstract concentration.

"Mmm."

"Do you mind that we won't ever be married?"

She wipes her hand on the turpentine cloth and doesn't reply. It feels too loaded a question for her to answer. She knows that he would like her to ease his concern, but she can't. Because she *does* mind it, though she would rather have this than nothing.

"I really do love you," he says.

"I'm trying to paint."

"My cold-hearted Queen." He pauses. "Is that the bell? I'll answer it. I wouldn't want your masterpiece to be disturbed for a moment."

When the door closes behind him, she stares out of the window at the angles and pitches of London's skyline. The city looks as small as a picture, conquerable, within reach, as if she could prize off all the roofs and play with the figurines inside them. Albie and his sister, Rose in the shop, her parents sitting at supper with their Bible.

"Who was it?" she asks.

"You'd better go down." Louis pulls a face. "It's your sister."

Iris stands, upsetting the palette. "Oh, and for you to answer the door—"

She hurries downstairs, and catches her appearance in a looking glass. Her hair is loose and untidy, the dress she wears for painting crumpled and paint-stained, her fingernails thick with pigment. "Rose," she says. "I wasn't expecting you. I'm sorry—I—"

"I should have written. It was rude of me to turn up like this. But when Mrs. Salter sent me on an errand, I had to come, after yesterday."

Her sister stands in the hallway, wearing her usual wide-brimmed bonnet, which shadows her face and its scars. She holds out a single iris. "They are only just blooming," she says.

Iris takes it, and says fondly, "You were always so scornful of such extravagances. Did you know, I was painting one just now, but it was half-dead, and this will be perfect—oh, we don't have any tea, and our biscuits are gone—Guinevere, who is a wombat, she broke into the tin—"

She realizes how mad she must sound, and stops talking. Her sister follows her into the sitting room, and Iris winces at the mess. She clears a tortoiseshell comb (Guinevere's) and a dirty brandy glass from the sofa, smooths the cushion, and Rose sits down.

"How different you look! You always were wilder than me," Rose says, but she smiles when she says it.

"Oh," Iris says, determining not to catch her reflection again. "I just look like this when I'm painting."

Rose looks at her, and her voice breaks. "I missed you. I was so— so jealous."

"Oh, I was awful too." She remembers running from her sister at the Exhibition, leaving her panicking in the crowd. Rose opens her mouth as if to apologize further, but Iris cannot bear it. There is something grotesque about seeing her sister humble herself with an apology (*You saw me as pitiful, pathetic*, she remembers, realizing again the truth of it), and the unkindness of this thought makes Iris want to cough, as if her throat is thick and oily.

"I am so very—"

"Please don't," Iris says, interrupting her. She realizes how abrupt she sounds, and she sits on the sofa next to her. "What I mean is, there's no need."

Iris reaches over, and they curl their fingers together. The feeling is as familiar as if Iris were holding her own hand. She stares at the small craters denting Rose's knuckles. "Is Mrs. Salter still half-human, half-pill?"

"Her laudanum fits are worse than ever. She berated me for having a love affair with a china doll this morning."

Iris laughs, though it isn't funny, and she imagines her old mistress in a pique of rage, twisting the soft skin of her sister's elbow. "What if"—Iris leans forward—"you were to set up a shop of your own?"

"And shake a thousand silver pieces from a money tree—"

"No," Iris says. "If I were to lend you the money for it."

Rose scoffs. "You'd never have enough. Think of it—rent, and the stock too. I'd need—I don't know—maybe fifty pounds!"

"You could borrow for the stock, with thirty-five pounds capital."

"But I don't—"

"I have it."

Rose stares at her. "How? How on earth—"

"From painting."

"Thirty-five pounds? Thirty-five *pounds*?"

"I helped Louis with the background to his painting, and then he sold it."

"How much for?"

"Oh, I don't know. He didn't say," Iris lies.

"I couldn't take it. It's *your* money."

"We could call it a loan at first, if you wanted—"

"I'll consider it," Rose says, cutting her off, and Iris worries she has been too hasty, too extravagant, that Rose might think she is lauding her new wealth and opportunities over her. No sooner has she got her sister back than she frightens her off again. She looks around this cluttered room, remembering how impressed she was at the beginning: the gold-framed paintings, the thick blue wallpaper, the peacock feathers, the volumes of periodicals and novels, the Oriental cut of the cornicing. Rose must feel as she once did.

"What are you painting?" Rose asks.

"I've just started something new. It isn't very good, yet. It's only a few shapes."

"Can I see it?"

"Oh. I suppose you can, but—"

"Louis is upstairs."

"Yes," Iris says.

"Well," Rose says, pulling down her sleeves to hide the bruises on her arms. "Well, we met just before—and if he doesn't object, of course."

"Come," Iris says, and Rose tucks her arm into hers as they take the stairs to Iris's little studio.

# The Cellar

Silas twists his sleeve. He is unaware that his hand is trembling, and he stops only when he hears the rip of fabric. He does not recognize the man he has become—agitated, untidy, unable to find joy in the simple pleasures that amused him before. She has done this to him—she and her trickery. He thinks of the painting, of the sweet look of adoration on her face, and he does not know why she will not love him. How can she fail to understand how deeply he adores her, how kind his interest has been, how much he has given her, the time and money he has spent on their friendship? She inflicts these wounds on him with such careless abandon—what for her may seem like a thoughtless scratch scores a deep ravine into his chest.

If she hates him, he hates her even more. When she pulled her arm from him, his rage giddied him, and he could scarcely hold back from hurling himself at her, from throttling the life out of her pathetic wiry neck, from smashing her head against a gold frame, again and again and again. She deserves it—she has scorned him, rejected him, over and over, and he has given her more chances than he can count. Each time, she has flung back his kindness with a mounting rudeness.

He falls to the floor. He gives way to grief, to anger, to loneliness, to jealousy, to feelings that he cannot name. And then, at last, he rubs his cheek and his expression stills. No, he thinks, he will not let this break him. He must have her. He *will* have her. He has been too hasty, made himself too vulnerable.

He stands, climbs down to the basement where the walls are as dense as rock, where the only sound is the hum in his own ears, and he begins to plan.

Over the next two weeks, he works relentlessly, harder even than he worked on the conjoined pups. He stitches the tears in his clothes, washes himself and dabs on his scent. Slowly, carefully, he moves his cellar specimens up to the shop, draining the fluid of the larger bottles jug by jug, and then transporting the wet creatures. It tires him, but he takes a satisfaction in the detail of it, the curated minutiae of his work. The excavation of each bottle yields a thrill, because it brings him closer to the time when everything will be ready. He fingers the shelves that he has emptied, proud of the labor that he undertook to clear them. No bridegroom was more scrupulous in his arrangements for his beloved, no lover more thoughtful. He has considered everything.

It is different from his preparations in the countryside—that small green world, the sky little more than a blue bead. The bushes thick with blackberries—he whispered to Flick about them. She looked surprised, and arched her lip because he was speaking to her and that was what people always did when he addressed them, and she checked over her shoulder to see if any of the other boys or girls were watching. He told her there was so much fruit in this place he'd found: the ground was carpeted with wild strawberries and there were plum trees, and apples so plentiful that the earth was soft with their pulp. He knew she was hungry from the way her bones poked through her clothes. She tucked her hair behind her ear and regarded him with a sly frown. He could see that she wasn't sure if she believed him, and again that quick glance to check that nobody saw them speaking, that nobody would mock her for the association.

The next day, with money from his London fund, he went to the markets and he bought fine fruits and told her he had picked them, and if she came with him, he could show her where. She took the harvest from him hastily, a snatch that nobody else saw. Her wrists were as thin as twigs, there was nothing but dusty, stale bread soaked in water for her noontime meal, and she devoured those fruits as if she had never been fed before.

When the cellar is emptied of all but a wooden chair, it looks nothing more than a cave. A nest. He would like to make it homely for her like the cell in her painting—he is generous that way—to hang paintings, to add an armchair, bowls of rich food—but first he will have to trust her.

He sits and imagines how he would escape if he had to. He stares at the damp stone walls, the way they bow over him like the roof of a mouth. He touches the rock. It is wet but it does not crumble. The floor is flat earth, polished and compacted from years of his foot-treads. The only light is from his lamp, which he places on the ground—all brackets are gone, all fixtures removed. There can be no shard of glass, no possible weapon remaining. He has even taken the shelves away, though he dithered over removing the bell and decided to leave it, as that way he will be able to hear the arrival of customers when he is with her.

He tries to pull a stone free from the ceiling. He tugs with all his strength, but he only grazes his knuckles and chips a nail. No, she will stay safe here. He will let her back into the world when she proves that she loves him. That it will happen, he does not doubt.

He climbs back up to the shop, arranges his tools neatly. The bindings are made of a thick, dense fabric and he will loop her hands as tightly as a surgeon's bandage. There is a gag, and most important a handkerchief and the glass vials of chloroform he has traveled all over London to obtain from different chemists. He counts them out, wagging his finger over them. Twenty-eight. Twenty-eight bottles! He remembers the foolish lapdog, its brimming eyes, the fading thrum of its heart as he smothered it.

All he has to do is wait for the time when she will not be missed, when she is alone. His shop has been ready for a week. It feels as if he has been ready his whole life.

# Teeth

Albie has begun to smell that chemical scent of Silas every-where, even finds it embedded in his grimy palms. There have been moments when he's begun walking to Iris's door, convinced he will warn her, but every time, he pictures his sister with her throat cut, and him, mourning her alone.

He notes the shift in Silas's mood; the hazy stumbling replaced by a more alarming attentiveness. Silas watches Iris from the stroke of eleven until four o'clock, and then he hurries back to his shop. He has left his window locked, not that Albie would dare to climb in again. Albie remembers the pink-dyed ostrich feather tucked under the bed, and when he asked after Bluebell, he was told that a few weeks ago she'd slipped and fallen and died in a gutter—and Albie had choked back a cry.

His sister has teased him about his endless fidgeting, his inability to concentrate, to entertain her with his street ditties as he once did. "What's wrong, my buttercup?" she asked. "If you're fretting you'll be given to the men too, you needn't worry—Moll's brother needed the tin more'n I do. *You're* to go to the Ragged Schools and get an ed-cashun." But he wriggled free of her and wouldn't tell her a thing.

It is five o'clock now. He knows Silas won't move from his shop until the morrow, and he tries to relax, to snatch these precious hours of sleep before he's booted out at eight o'clock and not allowed to return until his sister's night labor is over.

He stares at her, with her white hair splayed against the pillow, mouth slack. She lies so still with her limbs at such an awkward angle that he is gripped by a fear that she is dead. He touches her cheek. Her breath steams his hand.

There is a rap at the window, and Albie jumps—it will be Silas again.

"Alb," someone calls, but it is the boy who used to lead him to the dead creatures.

"Shhh," he whispers back, "sister's trying to sleep."

"Can't hear you," the boy bellows back. "Meet me outside."

Albie casts off the gray blanket and plods up the stairs.

"There's that woman again what wants to see you," the boy says. "Gave me a penny if I found you."

Albie shakes his head. "Tell her you couldn't."

He shrugs. "Tough. She's down there."

Albie turns, and Iris waves. Her red hair is crinkled and she picks her way through the rivulets of piss and vinegar and horse and human shit, and Albie holds up his hand.

"Miss—wait—this ain't a fit place for the likes of you."

She points at the stained building, its walls crooked. "You live here?"

"I do, miss," he says. He won't look at her.

"I have something for you." She opens her arms to embrace him, but he stays where he is. "You're harder to track than a ghost these days. Come—I've got tea and a surprise—"

He follows her through the streets, with all the enthusiasm of a miserable lapdog being dragged by a capricious owner.

But when they get to Louis's door, he shakes his head. "I ain't got time to come in."

"I bought cold custard especially," she says. "Easy to eat with your tooth—"

"Ain't hungry, miss," he says, just as his stomach defies him by growling, and he wonders that she hasn't noticed his missing fang. He pulls his lip lower. "Got a sickness."

"Won't you step in?"

"I've errands to run." He speaks churlishly, forcing a distance between them.

He won't look at her. He won't. All the same, he reads the surprise, the disappointment in her voice.

*Coward.*

"At least come for your surprise," she says, and he has no option but to step inside.

He sees her shoes turn toward him. They are grimed like the braiding of her skirt, a sticky brown stain caused by his street.

"Well, if you don't have long—" She clears her throat. "Louis sold the painting of *The Shepherdess*, the one he was painting you for, and I—he, rather, gave some of the proceeds to me."

Albie is barely listening. He stares at the patterned carpet, thinking of the rotten steps in his rookery. His sister, the way she slept so peaceably—

"The thing is," she continues, "I wanted to give you three pounds toward your teeth."

"What?" his head snaps up, and he makes the error of looking in her face, at her kindly eyes. He glances away, resuming his study of the rug.

"For your teeth. I know it's a significant sum, and some might think it foolish, but you're as good as a brother to me." She pauses.

"I didn't know that—do you really live in that rookery? Does your sister—?"

Albie says nothing.

*Warn her, you lily-livered pup—you selfish wretch—you milksop!*

He starts to scratch his arms. Little bubbles of blood form, as shiny as paste diamonds, and still he gouges with his nails.

He sees her reach into her pocket, and he wishes she wouldn't, that she'd leave him be. He deserves nothing.

*Tell her, you blasted fool!*

And before he can stop himself, he seizes the money from her hand as fast as a thief, and starts to run.

"Albie—" she calls after him, and she sounds shocked, wounded by his rudeness.

*Good*, he thinks, because he didn't ask for the money—he didn't—and he wants to slam himself on to the pavement, to hurt himself against the wheels of a cart.

*Megalosaurus, Megalosaurus, Megalosaurus—*

He tries to concentrate on the words, but they twist.

*Megalosiris, Megalosiris, Iris, Iris, Iris, Iris—*

He can't run for long, not when his chest is gasping and his nose is blocked.

Albie arrives at the shop, snot on his upper lip, the whites of his eyes as pink as sherbet. He scrubs at the wetness on his cheek with one hand, the other clamped around the notes. He daren't let go, not even for a moment.

"Scram!" the proprietor bellows, shielding his jars of teeth from Albie's reach.

"I got the tin, don't I?" Albie insists, but he won't make a show of it, not when he's seen a costermonger knifed for two guineas.

"Show me."

"I ain't going to, not till you've showed me a set of fine ivories."

"Who you gulled for it? Pinched it, I'spect—"

"What's it to you? Ain't nothing to you *where* I got it, even if it was from honest means."

The proprietor sighs and lets him in, though he keeps a hand on the scruff of Albie's jacket.

The teeth are laid out in pearly splendor, as valuable as silver lockets. Hard pink gums, white polished teeth.

"Got three pounds, sir—will you take that for the sea-cow—only three shillings short I am, what with your Exhibition sale on, and those are the ones I want, sir, won't crack like the porcelains or stain yellow like them Waterloos—"

He checks the notes, a surreptitious glance, and is horrified to see that he holds five curled bills for a pound each.

Was it the lowness of his rookery that made her give him more on a whim? Hearing about his sister?

*You're as good as a brother to me.*

"Ain't enough," the man says.

"I got enough." Albie says. "I was mistaken."

"And don't even think of running off with them in your filthy maw, or I'll box them so far down your throat they'll stick in your stomach." The man unlocks the glass cabinet, and hands Albie the teeth.

The gold hinge is handsome, like a coiled lock of hair, and the teeth—why, he's never seen a sight like them. He shakes a little as he forces them into his mouth.

They feel obscenely large, swollen, and he tries to speak but just says *ghrggghhh*.

"Takes a time to get used to," the man says, handing him a mirror.

Albie smiles, and clasps his jaw. They are beautiful. *He* is beautiful. It is all he's wanted, all he's yearned for. His face with a normal grin on it. Smooth, straight rows. He flicks his tongue over the back of them. Why, they're better than his sister's—

His sister, sprawled on the bed. His sister, for whom the men will come soon—what five pounds would mean for her, how it could pay off her debts and untether her from the rookery, while he fritters it away on a mere vanity—

He spits out the teeth, and before he can stop himself, he's wriggled free of the man and left the sea-cow ivories on the counter.

# A Review and a Reply

Excerpt from "Exhibition of the Royal Academy, second notice" printed in *The Times of London*, 7 May 1851:

We cannot censure at present as amply or as strongly as we desire to do, that strange disorder of the mind or the eyes which continues to rage with unabated absurdity among a class of juvenile artists who style themselves PRB, which, being interpreted, means Pre-Raphæl-brethren. Their faith seems to consist in an absolute contempt for perspective and the known laws of light and shade, an aversion to beauty in every shape, and a singular devotion to the minute accidents of their subjects, including, or rather seeking out, every excess of sharpness and deformity. [. . .]

These young artists have unfortunately become notorious by addicting themselves to an antiquated style, and an affected simplicity in painting, which is to genuine art what the mediæval ballads and designs in Punch are to Chaucer and Giotto. With the utmost readiness to humor even the caprices of art, when they bear the stamp of originality and genius, we can extend no toleration to a mere servile imitation of the cramped style, false perspective, and crude color of remote antiquity. We want not to see what Fuseli termed drapery "snapped instead of folded," faces bloated into apoplexy, or extenuated to skeletons, color borrowed from the jars in a druggist's shop, and expression forced into caricature. [. . .]

That morbid infatuation which sacrifices truth, beauty, and genuine feeling to mere eccentricity, deserves no quarter at the hands of the public.

————————

Excerpt from John Ruskin's letter to the editor, printed in *The Times of London*, 12 May 1851:

*Sir,*

*Your usual liberality will, I trust, give a place in your columns to this expression of my regret that the tone of the critique which appeared in* The Times *of Wednesday last on the works of Mr. Millais, [Mr. Frost,] and Mr. Hunt, now in the Royal Academy, should have been scornful as well as severe.*

*I regret it, first, because the mere labor bestowed on those works, and their fidelity to a certain order of truth (labor and fidelity which are altogether indisputable) ought at once to have placed them above the level of mere contempt; and, secondly, because I believe these young artists to be at a most critical period of their career—at a turning point, from which they may either sink into nothingness or rise to very great greatness; and I believe also, that whether they choose the upward or downward path may in no small degree depend upon the character of the criticism which their works have to sustain. [. . .] I must take leave to remonstrate with you when you say sweepingly, that these men "sacrifice truth, as well as feeling to eccentricity." [. . .]*

*But, before entering into such particulars, let me correct an impression which your article is likely to induce in most minds, and which is altogether false. These pre-Raphaelites (I cannot compliment them on common sense in choice of a nom de guerre) do not desire nor pretend in any way to imitate antique painting, as such. They know little of ancient painting who suppose the works of these young artists to resemble them. [. . .] They intend to return to early days in this one point only—that, as far as in them lies, they will draw either what they see, or what they suppose might have been the actual facts of the scene they desire to represent, irrespective of any conventional rules of picture making.*

*[. . .]*

*I have the honor to be, Sir, your obedient servant,*
*THE AUTHOR OF MODERN PAINTERS.*
*Denmark-hill, May 9*

# Malady

*62 Great King Street, Edinburgh*
*May 11th*

*My love, my strong knight, my Valentine,*

*My malady worsens; I grieve that you have ignored my previous letters—how can you care so little for me?*

*The doctors say it is hopeless. Clarissa has nursed me through the last months with the kindness a lover ought to have bestowed. I beg you to come to my side before I depart this mortal coil.*

*"And call on me in the day of trouble; I will deliver you, and you will honor me."*

*Until then, I remain,*
*Your Sylvie*

---

*62 Great King Street, Edinburgh*
*May 11th*

*Dearest Louis,*

*I promised I would write when the end neared. I believe it to be imminent; it could be mere hours.*

*She calls for you constantly, but before you attend her, you must brace yourself for much physical change. She is thin, wasted by this cancer. Her face bears spots, her figure shows the signs of these tumors. It is a cruel, degrading disease.*

*I urge you to ease the conscience of a dying woman. I would not like you to have cause for regret when it is too late.*

*Jane has recalled your son from school; he is traveling home now.*

*I pray you will arrive in time.*

*With love,*
*Clarissa*

# Edinburgh

"Have you seen it?" Millais asks, as soon as Iris opens the door. He rests his topper on the stand. "Louis! Louis—where are you, sir? Have you read today's *Times*?"

"Seen what?" Louis asks. His cheeks are a little rosy—Millais rang the bell at the moment when Iris tipped into ecstasy, and they dressed hurriedly, giggling like a pair of flower sellers. His shirt studs are buttoned wrong.

"This," Millais says, stabbing at a newspaper. He begins to read, "'Your usual liberality'—blah blah—'their fidelity to a certain order of truth etc.—ought at once to have placed them above the level of mere contempt—'"

"What are you jabbering about?" Louis asks, but Iris can see that his interest is piqued, and he steps forward and takes the paper from Millais.

"*Ruskin*," Millais breathes. "He wrote to *The Times*—he has defended us. John Ruskin! And he has explained our principles perfectly."

Iris reads the article over Louis's shoulder, but she is only halfway through when he says, "It is good, really. It isn't glowing—not at all. But it avoids partisanship, and that may carry more."

"Isn't it marvelous? He wrote to me," Millais says, taking out a neatly pressed letter as if he were a butler presenting a pristine bowl of turtle soup. "He wanted to buy *The Return of the Dove* but it's sold. Oh, if only I'd waited! He inquired about your *Guigemar* too."

"You can tell him it isn't for sale," Louis says.

"But it's *Ruskin*," Millais says, aghast, and Iris hides a smile. Louis might as well have announced that he'd just cut and rolled the canvas into a hundred cigars. "This isn't a Mr. Boddington, or a city clerk. This is Ruskin, the greatest critic of our times."

"I know perfectly well who he is," Louis says. "And it isn't for sale." He seems to absorb the news. "But Ruskin, he really wanted to buy it?"

"He did," Millais says.

"Well, abuse is in the air too, let's not forget," Louis says, and Iris recalls his and Millais's feigned nonchalance when *Punch* published balloon-headed parodies of *Mariana* and *The Imprisonment* the week before, and the review in *The Times* that made Louis light the broadsheet with a match. *Cramped style, crude color, caricature.* Louis rattles the paper. "But surely this, *this* could be our tipping point, couldn't it? Our moment of stepping into greatness."

Millais nods. "I believe so."

"It is too wonderful," Iris says.

She follows the men into the sitting room. Louis leaves briefly to pay a child to bring them hot pies and brandy. Iris does not want to drink any longer; her head aches from the day before. She invited Rose, but she had agreed with Mrs. Salter that she would not leave the shop until a new apprentice was found, and Louis and Iris rowed to Richmond with Rossetti and Hunt. They brought two bottles of claret and Curaçao. It was a beautiful May afternoon, pink flowers on the riverbanks and the shadows of trout drifting under the surface. All the men were awful boatswains, and she took the oars for most of the way back with Louis's help, much to Rossetti's indignation. It was not, as Louis pointed out, an outrage sufficiently strong to drive him to take the paddles himself. But Louis's arm knocked against hers as she pulled the water back, and he glanced at her, his eyes brimming with affection.

It is late afternoon when the letter arrives. Millais has gone out for a stroll and Iris is on the sofa, sketching a bowl of strawberries in charcoal. She can't get the smooth roundedness of them right in her painting, the way the stalks should sit in relation to the rim of the bowl. Louis has told her to draw them repeatedly, so her hand can learn their shapes. She is using his tucked legs as a surface on which to lean her sketchbook.

The bell rings and Louis sighs. "I'm sorry to remove your bureau," he says, and he is only gone for a minute. When he returns, he sits next to her and does not look at her. He holds a letter.

"What is it?" she asks. "What's the matter?"

"It's from Sylvia," he says. "I don't usually open them, but I recognized Clarissa's hand on the envelope."

"Oh?" Iris tries to keep her voice neutral, to overlook the twist she felt at the name. "And what does she say?"

"She's—" Louis looks down at the paper. "It seems she's dying."

"Oh," she says again.

"She wants me to go to her. To say good-bye."

Iris toys with the charcoal, her palms blackening. "And will you?"

"I think—I think I must. She's requested me there. There's a steamer that leaves for Edinburgh"—his eyes flit to the clock—"soon, if I hurry. She's *dying*. I can't deny her that. She wants to reconcile."

"Reconcile?" Iris keeps her voice level.

"Not that way—or at least, even if she does, I have no interest in it. I should go, you know, put her mind at ease that I bear her no ill will. It would be cruel not to, wouldn't it? It would be cruel of me not to go, not to let her die with a clear conscience. And my son—I must comfort him too."

"I thought you said she feigned illness—"

"My sister wrote, and if you don't believe me—"

"It isn't that I don't believe *you*," Iris says. "I don't believe her."

Louis gives her the letter. "Read it for yourself."

"*My love, my strong knight, my Valentine—How can you care so little for me—a lover ought to have bestowed—reconcile with me—come to my side—your Sylvie—*"

Iris's hands are shaking. It is so simpering, so hysterical, so insincere. "It's a billet-doux—"

"That isn't a billet-doux," Louis says, taking it back. "It's the final missive of a dying woman."

"Of course," Iris says, briskly. "And do you care for her?"

"How can you ask that?" he asks, and Iris expects him to insist that no, the idea is absurd. But instead he says, "Of course I do."

She stares at a patch of wallpaper above his head, where the pattern is not quite aligned. Its annoyance has snagged on her constantly, and now she wants to tear the whole sheet down.

Louis tries to take her hand, but she shakes him off. She should be more sympathetic, more supportive; but her temper flares.

"I know you think—"

"Please, don't tell me what I think."

"You know I love you. I don't love her—how could I? But she's dying, and I care for her. I was married to her, she is—*was*—my wife." He looks at her. "I will be free then."

"Free?" Iris says, and her irritation ebbs. "For what?"

"It would make things more honest for us."

Iris does not dare frame the question directly. She imagines waking in the morning, untangling herself from the humid warmth of his limbs, and propping herself onto her elbows. *My dearest husband*, she would say, and her parents would forgive her the indiscretion of modeling, because the match is better, *far* better than the oily porter, and she loves Louis too—how she loves him! "More honest?"

"Well, I would no longer have a wife."

"And—what difference?" She picks up the charcoal, and then places it down again.

His face falls. "Oh, Iris—not that. I didn't mean for you to think—I meant—didn't I always say I don't agree with marriage? I meant, we'll *feel* free. There won't be any scandal." He pulls at his earlobe, that old sign of agitation, but his words are fists. "I wish you knew how I loved you—"

"Not enough."

"But I do! Too much—I want to be with you forever."

"You must see," she says, and her anger is back, a tight veil that she struggles against, and she articulates feelings she would have been mortified for him to know only two minutes before. "You must see how it is for me. My parents won't even bear the sight of me! You expect me to yield to you, and you won't give me the basic modesty of becoming your wife—but you did for *her*, for Sylvia—"

"But I've always been clear that I don't agree with marriage, regardless of Sylvia—who, I should add, is a person, not just an encumbrance between me and a second union—"

"Oh, to be guided by a mere principle! How easy it must be for you."

"It isn't easy at all," he says.

"How? How isn't it?" She stares at him. "You have everything you want! You cleave to your principles, and you are a man with the advantage of station! This—this *interaction* with me—it doesn't degrade you. In the eyes of the world, it makes you a rake, but it makes me a whore." He flinches, and she says it again, louder. "Yes, a whore! And what of *my* principles? What of the way I'm looked at, sneered at even by your charwoman? Your mere mistress—and if you discarded me I'd have nothing."

"I didn't mean—"

"No," Iris says, and she looks away from him. "I wouldn't *dare* to entangle you, to degrade you, to have you suffer the torments of an old wife when there's the thrill of sweet love."

"It was Rossetti who said that, not me."

"It may as well have been you," she says.

He reaches for her hand, but she turns away.

"I love you, Iris."

"But you'll never marry me."

Louis is silent, and it is enough.

The disappointment is a slap, a cool rankling, and she can bear it no longer. She has to quicken his departure, like the rapid pulling of a tooth. "When does the boat leave?" she demands.

"Can we—"

"When does it leave?" she says again, and he holds up his hands.

"Every evening at six."

She glances at the grandfather clock. "Well, you had better be on your way. Your services as Sylvia's *Valentine* are required." Her temper mists. "And perhaps when you return, you will find yourself gloriously untangled from me altogether—"

Now she has started she cannot stop. The threat sits in the air between them. As soon as the words have left her, she longs to take them back, but it is too late, she is too proud, and she stares at her reflection in the curved mirror, at this little world, newly shattered.

"Iris—no—" Louis says, aghast, but she swats him away. "You can't mean it."

"I'll find you a cab."

"I won't leave until—"

"Leave," she says, the final wrench. "Go—I will fetch you a cab—"

And before he can stop her, she has slammed shut the door, and is storming down the street, the straw slippery under her feet.

Imaginings swirl: Louis, in Venice, his hands tight against Sylvia's waist as they dance at a ball; him, rising against her, engendering a son—"My strong knight," she whispers, gripping his back—and now, Sylvia lying on her deathbed, as pretty as a cameo brooch, her hair spread on the pillow behind her. Louis at her side, summoned like an obedient lapdog, and he kisses her hand, easing her departure when he tells her that he loves her. Iris tries to stop the thoughts, but they pile on—more—Louis's lips on Sylvia's, the quick reawakening of his desire. Iris shakes her head because she knows she is being unfair, that she is jealous of a dying woman. He should go. He *must* go. But it isn't the fact of him going to her side that stabs at her. He loved Sylvia enough to marry her, and he will not allow Iris the same dignity.

"I love you!" Louis calls from the studio window as she turns the corner onto Charlotte Street. "Please, Iris."

But she does not answer. She can only just keep a lid on the sobs that she feels building within her.

# Cab

Summer has come early, and the heat is starting to rise, a thick pall that settles on Silas and makes him sweat under his collar. He takes off his patched blue coat, and his eyes drift to a cat that is clambering along the windowsill of the empty shop. Its spine is oddly curved and he wonders if it was a partial break or a birth deformity. A few months ago, he might have followed it and tried to trap it, pinned out the backbone on his slab, but he loses interest and returns to his contemplation of Louis's house. A little boy has come and gone with a letter. He dabs at his brow. It will be evening soon, and when it is cooler he will relax.

The door slams. He looks up and sees Iris hurrying down the pavement. She walks away from him, and he can see the rustle of her skirts against the cobbles, her dress already dusty.

A window opens, and Silas pulls himself back from the glass. "I love you! Please, Iris," he hears Louis call, and Silas's mouth tastes of lemons.

Iris will come to him—her chin tilted in the oil-light, just as it was at dawn in the painting. "You have helped me to love you," she will say. "How is it that I never noticed you properly before?"

He wonders if he should follow Iris, but she was not wearing a shawl or bonnet, and she wears them wherever she goes. He waits, expecting her to return quickly. And indeed, he is proud when he sees her a few minutes later: if he were a member of the constabulary, just think how useful he would be, how many crimes he would solve with his skills of observation! Behind her trots a cab, the bay horse frothing in the heat, sweat greasing its hide. The coachman has a curling ginger mustache, like the tusks of a sea cow, and Silas worries that Iris will climb into this hansom, that she will be alone with this man.

But it seems the cab is for Louis. He stands at the door with a small trunk, which he heaves onto the roof, and the driver lashes it down with ropes. The horse whickers and snorts.

"London Bridge Pier," he hears Louis say. "And make haste."

Louis tries to take Iris's hand, but she turns away from him, says something in a raised pitch, which Silas does not catch. Louis pleads a little, and then sighs as he climbs inside.

Silas's head aches from the grind of his teeth. Such relief: he knew she did not love Louis really. And with it, a thought is springing up. It is just a shoot—a green bud peeping through the soil—but he grasps hold of it—because *this* is his moment, and it is so perfect, so precisely *his* that he thinks it can only have occurred by design.

Everything is ready. Silas has prepared the cellar, bought twenty-eight stoppered vials of chloroform. He is ready for her visit. He remembers a French word, which he heard uttered in a salon from a strumpet visiting from Paris—a *séjour*. He is ready for her *séjour*. He must not tarry. What if her sister were to arrive just at the moment when he has everything arranged so precisely? It is exactly as he heard the surgeons discussing when he used to loiter around University College London: the body is laid out, the chloroform has been administered, and the incision must be made swiftly and cleanly at the right angle and with the correct pressure. Precision lies not only in accuracy but in the timing too.

As the cab turns the corner, and Louis holds his foolish hand out of the window, Iris stands there, cradling herself with her arms. She starts to cry.

*My life is dreary.* He will bring her joy and comfort.

She is all alone now. It is meant to be, and who is he to deny fate?

Silas runs for the first time in years. His legs dash, ungainly, angled, and he careers around swells and ladies, sweeps and costermongers. A woman spills a pyramid of oranges over the pavement and bellows after him. He races like he has seen the urchin race, and his heartbeat is percussive, his throat aching from the heat, sweat veining his back, salty beads dripping down his cheek.

He pictures her following the same route, her footsteps falling into the ghosts of his, but she is a lady, and he is sure she will not run, despite the urgency. He sees the angles of the buildings as if through her eyes. What will she make of it all? He turns into his alley. He has never noticed the green slime on the walls before, never felt how close and cramped the houses are, as if they might topple and compress him, never concerned himself with the dust heaps that slope against the bricks. Will she pass down here or will she wait at the entrance of the passage? It is narrow and fetid. He scans the ground for the spaniel, but a bone grubber must have taken it to sell to a glue factory. At least the dead-end alley is empty: there are no children in rags sheltering out of the wind, and the traffic at this time is deafening, with the iron grind of carriage wheels on the Strand, and the chatter of black clerks scurrying home after their office days are finished. Nobody will hear her cry out. Will someone glance up the passageway? But no—it is too dark—their eyes would not adjust in time, and he will be quick. Even now, he can barely see. The street outside with its white houses was blinding, and now in the darkness he sees green and yellow shapes whirl across his vision. She will experience the same and will not notice him crouching behind the doorpost.

Although he knows the answer, he wants to check one final time that everything is in order, and he ducks into his house. He lifts the deerskin that covers the trapdoor, and imagines carrying her through the shop, light and dainty in his arms. If she breaks an ankle as he ferries her down to the cellar, it will only hamper any attempt she might make to escape. He tries to calm the tremble in his hand. He touches the chloroform bottles on the dresser, strokes the thighbone he will use as a club. Soon he will have his companion.

All he needs is a letter-writer, and there are dozens on the Strand, often used by the clerks who don't have the education they pretend to.

He has prepared the words that will be written.

# Flea

**W**hat did he want?"

The snooty boy with the quill pauses.

Albie shoves closer. He stares at the neat squiggles on the advertising board. He wonders how those loops can form words, how anybody can understand them.

"What did he ask you to write?" he demands.

"What did who ask?"

"That man what just left. With the blue coat." Albie has been following Silas all afternoon, and watched as Louis clambered into the cab, ordering it to London Bridge Pier.

"What's it to you?" the boy sneers. He wears a tatty velvet jacket and a boater, the straw unraveling at the brim. The boy looks past Albie, calling out in his voice with its stretched vowels, "Letters written for fivepence! Fine letters for fivepence!" then lowered, "Shove off, wretch, or you'll put off my customers."

"Listen to me, cur," Albie hisses. "That man. What did you write for him?"

274

"Clear off," the boy says again, and Albie glares at him, as if he thinks he's any better because he's had his education. The boy has a portable desk in front of him, stacks of vellum and paper held tight by a paperweight and string, and a milk-bottle of ink. Albie seizes hold of the jar, uncorks it and sloshes a little ink onto the pavement. "Give me that!" the boy cries. "That's ten bob's worth—"

But Albie raises the bottle above his head. "I'll drop it, I will," he says. "Now tell me, what'd you write for him? I ain't afraid to smash this, neither—"

"You'll be sorry—you'll rue the day!"

"Just tell me what he wanted," Albie repeats, trying to keep his voice even, to guard against the urgency. He could smack this wretch about the chops. *Tell me*, he wills him. *Please just tell me.*

"He *won'id*," the boy says, imitating Albie's accent, "for me to write a letter."

"I know *that*," Albie says. "But what did it say? I ain't fooling around." He knocks another splash of ink onto the pavement.

The boy growls, but then relents. "It was a note from a girl asking her sister to meet him down some street. Down that alley"—he thumbs in the direction of Silas's shop—"and saying she was hurt, or something. That's all I know—that's it. Damned if I know what it means. Now give me that back, before I smack you."

Albie chews on his lip, trying to make sense of the jumble.

"What were the name of the girl he sent it to?"

"*Was* the name," the boy corrects with a sneer. "Besides, I couldn't say."

"Was it Iris?"

"Might've been. Now," the boy says, his accent unraveling, "I ain't teasing. Give me that bottle before I cry out *thief*, and hang the ten bob—"

And Albie thrusts the vial of ink at the boy and weaves off before he can give chase. His steps slow as he rounds a corner.

He thinks of Silas arranging this note and Iris, left alone—Louis must be going for a few days too, what with the trunk he carried.

Will Iris believe the trick of the letter? Albie's heart pitter-patters.

*You yellow coward, you weakling—you got her into this fine pickle—*

And his sister is safe now, in her new lodgings with the women's charity in Marylebone, with three pound notes tucked into her pinny. She's bought herself freedom from the rookery, started learning the duties of a housemaid. She's assured of work soon, and they'll find her a respectable position; Silas would have no way to find her—

He always told himself he would act when he was certain, and isn't he certain now?

*You're as good as a brother to me.*

Albie hops from one foot to the other, an icy shame spreading over him. He would like to kick himself, to beat the breath out of his body. How could he be so *tardy* in his warning—?

But it isn't too late. Iris is still safe. He has to warn her.

He can race quicker than that messenger. He can reach Iris first. And what then? They don't have enough evidence to lead to an arrest, but at least Albie will have done all he can, and she'll have her wits close and won't be harmed and won't that be something? Perhaps the feather he found—Bluebell's feather—that will incriminate the man.

He runs like he has never run before, as if powered by steam. The air is cold in his throat. The journey seems to take hours, and he uses his old shortcuts, the streets he could race around blindfolded. He is just a child, just a bricky street brat, and yet he feels a surge of power. He can warn her. He has watched Silas, bided his time—he has knowledge that nobody else has.

His legs feel strangely liquid, like hot iron bent under the hammer of a blacksmith. He thinks of Iris, her fingers stroking the rosette he made her, how she gave him sixpence when his sister was sick, the five pounds for his teeth. His mind is cluttered as he barrels toward Oxford Street, less than five minutes from Colville Place. He is distracted, his thoughts roaring in his ears, and this time he does not look, does not check for the shapes and the horses and the hiss of danger.

A clunk, a grind of iron on iron, a splintering of wood. The horse screams.

And in the moment of impact, as the hooves clatter his chest, as he is tossed like a rag doll under the churning wheels of the cart, in the quiet pause before the iron splits his skull as easily as an eggshell, before the little thread of his life is snipped short, he does not think of his sister. He does not think of love or his dreams or even Iris, really. He just thinks of her finger, one day in the doll shop, sliding down the seam of a miniature skirt and cracking the back of a flea. It made such a sound—such a *pop*—and the bead of blood was so pretty.

# Lumley Court

*14 Lumley Court*

*Dear Miss Iris,*

*We are not acquainted but I write on behalf of Miss Rose. She has suffered an accident. She was attacked when walking on the Strand. The villain has been apprehended. I have taken her into my abode—she passed me your address and begs you to come at once. You can find me on Lumley Court, at the end of the street. Her injury is not grievous, though a doctor has been summoned so do not trouble yourself on that account.*

*Sincerely,*
*Mr. T. Baker*

# The Cart

There is a commotion on Oxford Street. A cart is on its side. As Iris hurries down the road at a half-run, pushing past the craning passers-by, she tells herself not to look. She can hear screams, and a lady has fainted to much hysteria and scurrying. Looking will only distress her, but as if pulled by invisible strings, Iris cannot resist turning her head. In that short, snatched glance, she sees juddering hooves pawing at sky, bone showing on the horse's knee, red foam from its mouth pooling in the gutter. She sees the coachman trying to comfort the horse, lamenting that it will be shot—that the urchin didn't look. And she sees a little body, shrouded in cloth, but with muddy toes peeping out like tiny shells.

There is a girl with white-blond hair crouching over the boy. She wears a plain blue dress, freshly pressed and neat—Iris recognizes the fabric and the cut as identical to the garments she sewed for Clarissa's society for fallen women—and the girl shakes the body. She is weeping piteously, screaming at the man, "My brother—my brother—"

"He didn't look! He dashed out—" the coachman is shouting to a constable, and he cracks his whip at a child who is trying to make off with the wheel spoke.

Iris turns away, shaking her head as if to loosen the image. It seems that there is a contagion in the air. First Sylvia so close to death, Rose attacked, and now this urchin, knocked down just around the corner from her. She tries to bury her fears; it happens all the time. She has seen more dead bodies on the streets than she can recall. Some are burnt into her memory: a pure collector frozen on a doorstep, an old gentleman clutching his heart, a sobbing pauper gripping a gray baby. And yet, no matter how many she sees, they do not lose their power to shock her.

She wonders how badly Rose will be maimed, hopes that it is a broken arm and not her face that is shattered again, worse. She remembers her sister, stretching out her hand to Louis, swallowing any vestiges of jealousy she felt.

She will forgive him; when he climbed into the cab he said he would marry her, but she was too angry, too hurt to take him seriously. "I want you to *want* to, not because I've begged you," she'd said. When the letter arrived about Rose's injury, Iris's temper had cooled and she was gathering her cloak to follow Louis to the docks, to clear their argument before he left on the steamer. She will write to him instead, in Edinburgh.

The city hums around her, lives continuing, and all she wants is to hold her sister and Louis. Her breath rasps in her throat. A green-frocked girl shoves a pair of down-at-heel shoes at her ("Tuppence, miss"); a child grasps her arm and proffers a basket of mackerel that glint like silver combs, and Iris has to swerve to avoid knocking the fish into the dust.

Iris zigzags this way and that, slowing to a walk when the crowds thicken and the muck is too dense underfoot. The streets are winding, clogged, and every so often, she'll take a wrong turn down an alley and have to double back. As the stink from the Thames intensifies, a drunken gentleman topples out of Rules restaurant and grins at her, but she pushes on, closer to the river, to the Strand, where she is spun in the tumult of hurrying clerks, a colony of ants spilling from a disturbed nest. She wonders where this house can be—she expects it must be grand because the letter was written on a fine, thick card.

"Lumley Court—do you know it?" she asks a child, stooped under the weight of a basket of mottled soap.

"Oh, yes," he says, pointing to a decrepit tunnel. "There it is."

How peculiar, she thinks to herself, but perhaps Mr. Baker isn't as wealthy as his paper led her to believe. She thinks of Louis modeling for her painting, the handsome boyishness of him, his dark curly hair—she would shadow it with emerald.

She does not look twice at the alley as she runs down it, barely noticing that her shoulders have grazed the stone entranceway and stained her dress. She searches for a house—but the sun from the street has blinded her now that she stumbles into gloom, and the crack against the back of her head takes her unawares.

*Part*

# THREE

Ses sires l'ad mis'en prisun
En une tur de marbre bis,
Le jur ad mal e la nuit pis.


She was locked in a gray marble tower, where
the days were bad and the nights worse.

—MARIE DE FRANCE, "GUIGEMAR" (C. 11TH CENTURY)


My life is dreary,
He cometh not.

—ALFRED, LORD TENNYSON, "MARIANA" (1830)

# The *Séjour*

Iris is lying on the floor of Silas's cellar, and he reaches out to her. She is pale, white, her lips parted like a wound. He edges down her high-necked dress. There it is, just as he has seen it all those times. At the Great Exhibition, in the painting at the Royal Academy, in the streets when her shawl fluttered loose. A twist of skin over bone. The texture is pleasing, like the knotted wood of a hand-worn banister. He smiles: he has done it. Everyone who laughed at him, who mocked him—his mother, the boys in the pottery yard, Gideon—they would not have achieved what he has. To have her in his museum, here on a *séjour*.

She appeared in the alleyway with the daylight streaming behind her, and she ran right past him. Of course, it was difficult to bring the bone against her head, but he always knew it would be, and where would the satisfaction lie if it were easy? It was like making a plate: if it didn't need two firings and the throwers and the turners and the glazers, then where was the joy in turning over the smooth porcelain?

He timed it perfectly. She staggered a little and moaned, but he had the chloroform-soaked cloth and he clamped it to her face. She was so stunned that she barely struggled; she flailed, groaned, but passed into sleep so easily and so pliantly that he was sure she wanted it. His letter was in her fist, and it relieved him. That was the greatest risk he took: that she'd leave it behind and Louis would know where to look for her.

He stares at her again, and he feels a sudden sadness. He does not understand it. It is a bitter taste that lurks at the back of his throat, and no amount of swallowing will rid him of it. He sighs, and then lifts her onto the chair. He wraps her legs and wrists tightly with strong bandages, knots the fabric more times than he needs, and then he sits back.

He will leave her to adjust to the situation on her own. Later, he will bring her food and they will talk. They will begin to learn one another's habits and stories. When he trusts her more, he will untie her hands and they will dine together. She will tell him about her life in the doll shop, and they will laugh over her awful tales about Louis. ("That swine—I know it is undainty to use such language but I pray heaven will forgive me! Thank goodness you have freed me from his clutches—")

He smiles, his black mood soon forgotten. And by the time he is in the shop, his Lepidoptera cabinet pulled over the trapdoor, he is laughing, a loud, hammering guffaw that he feels could propel him anywhere. He can do anything, *anything* he wants, and he tears up to his chamber and back down to the shop with the energy and mindless glee of a bedlamite.

# Quiet

When Iris opens her eyes, it makes no difference. She is in a coal blackness that she has never seen before, a silence she has never heard. It is a darkness that admits no moonlight, no faint yellow from a gaslight across the street. It is a quiet that does not carry the lilt of a drunk, the distant mew of a baby or whinny of a horse. It is thick, syrupy, and heavy, like being bundled into a roll of dark velvet.

When she commands her hands to her face, she finds that they are bound tight. She wills her fists harder, but they do not shift at all; and the bindings chafe her wrists. Her legs, too, are stiff and secured, her feet swollen from where the blood has pooled. She is giddy. Her head hurts.

She tries to moan, but there is something covering her mouth and the sound is muffled, her breath ricocheting warm against her cheek. She gasps, but the cloth sticks to her lips. She spits, writhes.

She feels a creeping sense of panic that winds her. Where is she? What has happened? For a joyful second, she attempts to square it away: it is Louis who has done this for a prank—but she knows it isn't, and she feels queasy, flattened, beaten by waves of fear.

She is barely conscious of what she does, just of sudden surges of pain: her feet, which she bangs against the floor, her fingers, which she writhes and twists. She rocks the chair until it tips over. She hits the ground sideways, and pain sings through her ribs and hips. Her arm is trapped under her, her elbow digs into her stomach. Her face is packed tight against the earth, and the back of her throat tastes musty, of the tannin of wine. The more she squirms and knocks against her confines, the greater her terror.

*Ngggghhhh*, she tries, choking on the soft wad of cotton. *Ngggghhhh*.

She can't breathe—she gasps for air, but each lungful feels as if it reaches only the fronts of her teeth. Nothing. The dull pulse of her breathing intensifies, her limbs as chilled and stiff as china. She retreats into the sheer giddying physicality of fear. It makes her bowels ache with the need to release them.

The shackles bite; and then she understands.

*Silas*.

The bindings searing her flesh are his fingers on her wrist. That grip—how she fought against it! The earth is his clasp, his damp smell. The gag is his mouth on hers, as limp and cold as an icy flannel. He lured her here with the letter, and she danced for it, like a dog drawn by a lump of rotten meat.

Her thoughts turn monstrous, and she tries to rein them in. Silas's hands on her, air choked out. What will he do when he comes for her? Or will he just leave her to die, a rat ensnared in an upturned pail?

She is alive. She is breathing, steadier now. She thinks of her fingers, spread against the wallpaper, the blue veins ferrying blood; she dredges comfort from the knock of her heartbeat.

But all the while she shakes.

# Caramel Truffles

Silas hurries through the streets, a green paper bag in his hands. He knows that he is being irrational, that the butterfly cabinet is heavy and there is no way she could have escaped the restraints, but he worries that his jewel will find a way of slipping between his fingers. He will come in the door, hear silence, and it will have been nothing but a dream. He will be alone once more. The solitude is a lash. He has always pretended that he enjoys it: he has no choice in it, so why rue what has come to pass? But the loneliness of his shop, the cool expanse of bedclothes next to him, the only conversations his own mutterings and the knocking of his thoughts—he has felt hollowed out.

And now he has his magnificent creature. When she sees he has brought her favorite sweets, from her favorite vendor, any distress will fall away. How can it not? She is a lady, schooled in gratitude.

He opens the door and listens. If he cranes his ear to the floor, he can hear a faint noise, a straining, but it could be a cat or a child in a nearby building.

He pushes away the Lepidoptera cabinet, lifts the trapdoor, and the whimpering intensifies. He considers shushing her, reassuring her that he is her savior, her comforter. He does not pause to examine how he sees her and himself—is she his prisoner, his guest, his maiden, or his specimen? And is he in turn captor, host, rescuer, or collector? Really, the only thing that really matters is that she is *here*, with him.

He holds the oil lamp in his hand, and the paper bag in his teeth, as he descends, and when he reaches the bottom step of the ladder, he turns and sees that she has knocked the chair onto the floor. Her eyes are wild, the whites threaded with red.

"I don't want to hurt you," he says, but she cowers when he approaches. He sets her upright. "I have a gift for you."

She stares at him, and he fiddles with his sleeve. The look of fear on her face! He cannot understand it. There is nothing extraordinary in what he has done. It has happened to thousands, to millions of women across the stretch of time. She herself appeared in a painting of one such lady.

He whisks the green bag from behind him, and that glare is as sharp as a blade. "Toffee dipped in chocolate," he says, but her expression does not change. He tries another tactic. "If you are good, I'll remove your bindings."

He coughs. He is not used to this power. It is not unpleasant, but it leaves him uncertain what to do with his hands.

He unties her gag. She works her jaw, and does not say anything. She does not scream.

"I can feed you the chocolates," he says, but he wishes that he did not have to suggest it. It is uncouth to be fed food like this, as if she were a baby, or a dog.

"Let me go," she says, and her voice is so surprising, so pleading, that he almost drops the bag. "Please—let me go. I won't tell anyone about you—I won't say anything—but I beg you, *please*, let me go."

"They're from your favorite vendor," he says, trying to change the subject and hoping that she will not notice.

"What do you want from me? If it's money, Louis will pay whatever you ask. You must let me go—"

"Toffee centers," he says, holding one out. "A penny for a dozen of them."

"I don't care about the chocolates!" she shouts, and then her eyes do that wild dance again. "Please, let me go."

"I only want to be your friend."

"And then you'll release me?" She seizes on this as a hound would fall on a dropped steak. She gabbles. "Of course I'm your friend—just please, let me go and I'll show you—"

"I need you to prove your friendship by writing a letter."

"A letter?"

"Telling that"—he levels his voice—"man you mentioned, that you are safe and not to worry."

"But I'm not!"

"But you are," he says, with equal conviction. "You *are* safe with me."

She starts to rock on the chair again, back and forth, back and forth. "I don't know what you want," she says. "I'll be your friend—I'll do anything—just—"

"I want you to write the letter," he insists, and then as his tone sounds unnatural and too high, he tries to say it in a more commanding way, "You will write the letter."

But she shakes her head. "Please let me go," she repeats. "I'll do anything."

He feels a rush of distaste. "I told you. I told you I would when I know you're my friend."

"I am—I *am*—just tell me what I need to do to prove it—"

"I brought you your chocolates," he says, sickening at her repeated laments, and he holds out a truffle on a flattened palm as he would to a horse.

She rears her head and bites his finger with a strength and a sharpness that he could never have expected. He wrenches his fist free, knocking her teeth at the same time. He nurses the digit. She might have broken the bone.

What follows is worse. Her screams fill the cellar, a piercing baying that echoes back and round, and he wants to clamp his hands over his ears, to hit her hard against the skull. It is not a faint wail, like he imagined coming from her lips, but full and throaty and bestial, punctured only by strained gasps for more air.

"Stop it!" he says, scrambling for the bottle in his pocket, and he pours the contents onto the rag, and she screams and screams. It feels like hours until it takes effect. She flounders and bucks until all she can do is snuffle until—finally—silence, and she slumps forward.

# Collarbone

$S$ ilas's eyes glow yellow in the reflection of the lamp.

*What did you do to me?* she wants to ask, but behind the gag, she can barely make a sound. She does not understand it, but the handkerchief seems to send her into a thick sleep, impossible to resist, as if he is some kind of magician. What could he do to her when she can't fight or scream?

"If you won't behave, then I won't let you speak."

No speaking, no walking, no eating except from his hand—and worse, her bladder is full. She fights against it, longing to try and break free. She must master herself, not let the fringes of terror descend. Despite everything, she feels a twinge at her lack of composure, at the rawness of her screams, at the way she challenged him. She has always been taught to button her passions, not to shout, to respect the opinions of men. Her emotions have always simmered more than they should, and now they boil over. She could suffocate in her anger.

But Rose will find her lodgings empty tomorrow, and Louis will return from Edinburgh soon. She told him about Silas seizing hold of her—and won't he realize that their argument was just a tiff? He will come here and rescue her. He *will*.

She stares at the walls of the cellar. They are low and damp, and small crystals have formed in places. The light quivers and dips, and Silas's gaze is searing. He does not stop looking, and she thinks it will shrivel and wither her, burn her to a crisp.

*I must gaze on this for days until I've learned it by rote.*

She is merely modeling; the ache is from sitting still, holding a pose. The eye watching her is that of an artist—of Louis, his look one of desire and love. Two dark pools she could drown in; a color she could never mix. And soon he will tell her she can move—

She glances, minnow-fast, at Silas, and registers the hunger in his gaze, his leer a drop of black paint spreading through water, infecting her and everything with it. She tries to recall Louis, tapping his brush against the easel, learning her by heart. *My Queen*—

A thought occurs to her, and she follows Silas's eyeline. He does not stare at her face or her breasts, but at her neck, at her collarbone, which—she realizes now—is exposed, the dress cut open.

Iris bucks in the chair. Everything begins to align: why he singled her out when she has ignored every attempt he has made to engage her. She thinks of that butterfly wing trapped under glass—and the other thing Silas had with him. The skeleton and a pelt of a puppy, he said. And Louis said that he made the creatures for their paintings. What is he—a collector? A morbid collector—an assembler of bones, of dead things—and her cry ricochets off the walls. Her bladder, held tight until now, loosens. She feels the warm liquid pool and drip off the chair.

# Blackberrying

Silas is in his shop, a newspaper in hand. He is perched on the edge of a barrel. Ten crows float in it, unseen behind the rusted tin. They used to sit in glass bottles in his cellar, but he decanted them when he moved all of his specimens into the shop. They are little more than a headstone to his past desire.

His room is higgledy-piggledy, objects heaped on objects. Gone is the quiet order, the clean dressers and the neatly labeled jars. Instead, the shop reflects the rupture of his mind. There is dust everywhere—he sneezes—and there is a stink too. One of the flasks has cracked, and the fluid has leaked onto the floor, leaving the dove hearts to rot. He runs his hand over the jag of glass, over the edge of an object he can no longer identify—a bone of some description?—and finds his fingers furred with grime.

He hears a faint noise from downstairs, and he thinks of that smell, the ammoniac reek of urine. It horrified him. His beautiful, his composed, his *ladylike* Queen, gibbering and biting like a caged beast, and then wetting herself over the floor. He turned and left, scrambled up the rungs, willing himself away from her. He imagines her bladder within her, wet and pink like the inside of a peach, and then apart from her, dried out and white like a crisp pig's ear.

He scans the newspaper, wishing he could read faster. He can only relax when he reaches the frivolous soap and perfume advertisements: there is nothing on Iris's disappearance.

He needs to escape this place and its clutter and disarray, and he puts on his hat. He has to get away from *her*, if only for a short while. The cellar never felt small with his silent bottled companions, but she seems to grow monstrously, filling the room with her squawking and the smell of her waste. At least she is sitting and he doesn't have to contend with her height too. A doubt occurs to him for the first time: she is different from how he thought her. And might that mean that she behaves differently too—that she fails to love him, that she continues as she is now, obstinate and ill-mannered?

He sets off on his walk. It is midmorning, and the omnibuses rattle with workers. He chides himself: she has been there perhaps twelve, fourteen hours and he is worrying over her behavior. Of course she is confused, of course she will take a little time to adjust. He just needs to be patient, forgiving of her foibles. And the night *did* pass quickly, with somebody at his side.

He watches Rose in the doll shop, for no reason except to settle his mind, and then follows her when she takes a stroll at noon. She walks to Iris's lodgings. The matron opens the door. He can imagine their conversation, the matron stating that Iris did not return the evening before; he takes in the crease of Rose's ruined brow, the worry that shows itself in gestures that are too abrupt. Rose knocks on Louis's door, hammers it, but there is no answer, and she steps back into the street. Silas wonders how much Iris might have told Rose about him, and regrets again seizing her wrist at the Royal Academy. He feels nauseated at his lack of control, his lack of knowledge. She *must* write him the letter—she *must*.

He leaves Rose, and wanders through the winding alleys toward Hyde Park. He has a blister and he limps; he flags an omnibus. He tries to remember how Flick smelled. Clean, surely, not like Iris. He remembers the white purity of her, but there is a piece missing between her cramming blackberries into her mouth and then lying still and cold in the meadow. He has always had these flashes, but he has shut them away, lidded the jar precisely and firmly. It was her father who did off with her, and Silas found the body. Or the body was merely his own imagining, a vivid dream, and she escaped the factory and her father's beatings to London.

He has worn other memories of those days as smooth as sanded porcelain. Flick's expression as he handed her the hothouse fruits and told her that she could find more if she followed him. He didn't have a plan then, not really. He was young and inexpert, and he just wanted to spend the evening with her, for her to love him.

She didn't walk with him. She would never have done so, would never have endured the taunts of the other children for his sake. He could see the fresh budding of her breasts through her shift, and he wondered if they looked like the dugs of a pregnant hound, or prettier, like a kitten's wet nose. Then she hung back from the others, and followed him deeper into the countryside where the brambles were thickest.

"Is this it?" she said, looking at the scraggy bush. The blackberries gleamed like rubies, but she glanced around her, her face wrinkling. "I thought you said there was apples and plums and them peaches, not just blackberries—there's a scrub of *these* near my cottage, if I wanted 'em."

Silas fidgeted. "I thought—"

"Liar," she says. "You bought them other fruits from the market."

"I didn't," he insisted, but he found himself growing angry. He'd made all of this effort! He'd tried so hard, and spent so much money.

"Where d'you nick the tin from for it?"

"I didn't," he said. "I don't thieve. I only wanted to show you—"

"I should tell your mam," she said, and she started stuffing the blackberries into her mouth, greedy, her hands thrusting like the hammers and anvils in the factory. "Why d'you look like that?"

"Like what?"

"Like—" She pulled a face like she was a halfwit, and he hated her. "Go home."

"But this is my place," he said. "I took you here. I want to show you my collection. I saved money for us—we can go to London—"

"Scram," she said, as if she were wafting away a cat, and then she hurled a blackberry at him. She laughed as it burst against his shirt, and then she threw another, and he took hold of her hand.

"Let go," she said, but he held on harder.

"I want to show you my things." He pulled her to a shaded copse where he had laid out his treasures—the ram and the field mouse and the fox skulls, all in a tidy row—but he couldn't fathom why she didn't want to see them. She was trying to jerk free of his grip and scratch him, and he had to hit her across the cheek to calm her down. She kicked the ram specimen as she fought, splitting the skull in two.

And then she was lying on the meadow, her face bruised with berry juice.

He feels a rush of anger, even now, at the cruelty of her words, her mockery. Didn't they race through the countryside together, didn't the sun light on her hair?

No.

He will not think of it. Instead, he stares at the grand building in front of him—the Crystal Palace, with his puppies inside. All those brats from the factory who mocked him with their sneering clay-dusted faces will likely be dead of potter's rot by now. Gideon, too, has failed to achieve renown, and Silas has scanned *The Lancet* anxiously for years. Perhaps he is dead too, of a disease contracted from a workhouse hospital.

The Great Exhibition glitters in the sun, its tiers and domed roof looking like the elaborate cakes he has seen in the confectionery shops either side of the doll emporium. Its smooth geometry pleases him.

The crowds are vast, shifting, and Silas elbows between winding lizards of schoolchildren and travelers—a woman has walked from Cornwall, she says loudly to anyone who will listen—and through the turnstiles, showing his season ticket. He takes his time today, loitering over the great black cogs of industrial machines—engines, printing presses, boilers—the press is clanging and whirring, steam puffing, and the smell of coal thickens the air. Now that he isn't worrying over whether Iris will appear, he finds he is calmer, more appreciative.

He wanders up and down the aisles, astonished by the variety. The museum seems to contain everything ever invented or built or formed—an expanding coffin, the Koh-i-Noor diamond, a vase made of mutton fat, velocipedes and carriages. He pauses at the pieces that interest him most. The German Customs Union has submitted a collection of taxidermy frogs being shaved with bibs around their chins, and a litter of kittens sitting at a table drinking tea. He notes that the stitching is roughly done, and the small limbs protrude at unnatural angles.

He saves his own exhibit until the end, a boiled sweet in his sleeve that will taste even more delicious from the anticipation of waiting. The conjoined puppies—one pair stuffed, the other its skeleton articulated—are there on their dual mountings, his name underneath them.

"*Silas Reed.*"

That is him, and this is his work.

If only Iris had come to him. If only she had come when he

invited her to his shop, when he asked her to the Exhibition. Things could have been so different. If only Flick hadn't teased him but had walked next to him and taken his hand in hers. He merely wanted to be their friend. And really, they only have themselves to blame.

# Robe

Iris's tears dampen the gag. Her cheek pricks from the salt, and her thighs itch and sting. She has soiled herself too—she could not help it, and when she moves, she feels it slide against her buttocks. She is hungry and thirsty, but the idea of eating out of Silas's hand is too much to bear. Her situation is so desolate, so utterly pitiful, that she wonders if she will ever escape this cavern.

"Write me a letter," he says, again and again. "That's all I want. Just a letter."

He uses it as currency, a shilling traded for a spinning top, a guinea for a china doll.

If she writes him this letter, he'll untie her hands and let her eat unaided.

If she writes him this letter, he'll let her roam the cellar without restraints.

If she writes him this letter, he'll let her into the shop.

If she writes him this letter, he'll—he'll—he'll—and still she stays tight-lipped, shakes her head.

Because she knows it is all lies. She pins so many hopes on Louis that it aches. If she loses this chance, she has nothing.

She digs her fingers into her palms. *Stop crying,* she tells herself. *Stop it.* She will not sit here weeping. She will do all she can to survive, even if it means eating and drinking from his hands like a beast. She will keep herself alive.

She distracts herself by thinking of Louis's painting and the careful knot in the Queen's robe, the exactitude of the brush-strokes. Just a little patch at a time, a touch more; green-blue shadow on a wet white ground, all of these dabs creating the illusion of a real person, a real scene, when actually it was nothing but pigment and sable. The tie that only Guigemar could unbind. She tries to remember the vivid colors. Here it is all brown, black, yellow, as if emerald and crimson and ultramarine exist only in her imagination.

At least Silas left the lamp, and she can see how the cloth of her restraints falls. She examines the chair: her calves, tied to the chair legs above the cross-bar. The two scrolled arms, where she is fastened just below the elbow. The way the wood tapers, thinning out where it meets the seat.

She contorts her body, wriggling the binding down to the skinnier part of the chair arm. It takes hours. In minuscule increments, the fabric starts to loosen, and she bends her hand back on itself, prizing the knot between her fingers. If they can grip a pencil and move it across the page, surely they have the power to unfasten her? And right enough, the restraint starts to slip, a little at a time, until she has teased her right wrist loose.

She will be free. She will not die here. She will hear again Louis's voice, the pitch often tipping halfway to a joke: *We are here to rescue you from King Mériaduc.*

She flexes her fingers—her arm is patterned with the imprint of the bandages—and pulls off the gag. She runs her tongue over her lips. Her mouth tastes sour and dense. The air is fresher.

Untying her left hand is the work of a moment, and her legs swiftly follow. She tries to stand, but her limbs buckle underneath her. She is a jelly, prized from its mold before it is set. She stands more slowly, rotating her foot and then her leg. The pain is so acute it is difficult not to cry out.

She knows it is hopeless, but she climbs the ladder rungs and pushes against the door. She might as well be trying to knock over the Royal Academy.

Instead, she plots what she will do. She picks up the lamp. It is heavy, and she swings it experimentally, imagining it colliding with Silas's head. It will stun him, and then she will escape. She rocks it too hard, and then curses when the sudden rush of air causes the wick to stammer and die.

She fumbles for the chair, repositions herself in it, and drapes the bindings over her arms and legs so that she still looks tied up. The lantern is in her right hand, on the side facing away from the ladder, so she hopes he will not notice it at first.

She hears the scraping of the weighted item that holds down the door, and her heart rackets. It is as if he knows, as if he has allotted exactly the right amount of time for her to break free. As if it is nothing more than a game.

His footsteps on the rungs reverberate around the little cell. Light filters down like a flash of sun between clouds. He does not speak, and he is carrying an object. A chair. He grips it awkwardly, and he even falls the last few steps, cursing under his breath.

In the moment before he steadies himself, she raises the lamp. He ducks, and it glances his ear, so she wields it again, and he is knocked sideways, and stumbles to the floor.

She throws herself at the ladder—the trapdoor is open—and her hands are slippery on the rungs. The metal is hard, cold, welcome, and she starts to pull herself over the edge, into a strange, untidy room, but there is something stopping her.

He has grasped hold of her foot. She kicks, flails, and she thinks, *You will not be the master of me, you will not defeat me*—and jerks her ankle free. She is half in the shop, just lifting her legs up, but the hand is on her ankle again, firmer this time, as tight as a manacle.

"Help!" she shouts. "Help! I've been attacked! Help! Help! He'll kill me—he'll—"

She loses her footing, and with a roar of anger, of utter desperation, she falls back into the cell.

This might be her only chance, and she must do it. She must escape. She moves to stand, ready to fight and claw and thrash—but he is above her, and the handkerchief is in his hand.

She feels a ringing in her ears—what did he hit her with? His fist?—and she is flat against the ground. The rag nears.

"No," she begs. "Please don't—I'll sit down—I'll be good— please—"

"I don't believe you," he says, and he grips her hair. The handkerchief is around her mouth, pushed hard against her nose. She tries to focus on staying awake. She holds her breath. She writhes, keeps her mind active, but the world shimmers before her, miragelike.

It fades.

# A Companion

*He'll kill me.*

Silas watches her as she sleeps. How can she think that of him? It explains her erratic behavior, and her fear, at least. He must make her understand that his intentions are nothing but honorable, that all he wants is to be her friend. How beautiful she is—the sockets of her closed eyes, that clavicle. He feels a pulling in his crotch. *What a fine truncheon.*

He remembers the girl in the rookery and her falseness, the hollow timbre of her voice, the dye of her hair. The smell of that fleapit—it was almost as bad as the stench of Iris soiling herself.

After returning from the Great Exhibition, he visited a carpenter to ask him to cut a hole in the seat of a chair. It was meant to be a gift. He imagined Iris's joy at the surprise of it. But instead, when he carried it down to the cellar, she had beaten him: and how did she find a way to break free? He nurses his wounds—cranium, ulna, and digit. What a vicious beast she can be; even her features look vaguely simian in this light.

She sits, lolling forward in her new chair, a tin bucket underneath her. He has lifted her petticoats, but he did not touch her, even though he longed to look. He loosened her bindings a little, just out of kindness: the flesh was mottled and slightly bruised, like the skin of a week-old corpse. He took his lavender oil and dabbed it around her temples and her skirts, and now he breathes it in. The smell of waste is muted by the scent. So sweet, and so pretty!

Her mouth stirs. A skein of dribble hangs from it. A choking sound, and her eyelids flicker. His prisoner, his pet awakes!

She looks about her, and a groan escapes her.

"I moved you to your new chair," he says. "There's no use crying out—nobody will hear you."

She is silent, chewing her lips.

"I just want to be your friend. I wish—"

"You're going to kill me." Her voice trembles. "You're going to turn me into one of your specimens. You want my collarbone—"

Silas bends down so that his face is level with hers. "No," he says. "You don't understand—I never would. How can you think that? I want to be your friend. I want you to love me."

She shakes her head.

"What is it?" he asks.

"Love you?" she scoffs, and her mouth is pulled into a sneer, just like his mother's. "I will never. I despise you! I hate you—I—"

"You don't mean it—you will learn to. You'll see—"

She lifts her jaw and spits out each word: "I. Will. Never."

"But you will."

"You repulse me."

Silas did not expect this level of vitriol. He slows the anger in his chest, his frustration at her obstinacy. She is worse than the wayward ox that dragged the coal for the kilns, always stumbling, tripping, never going in the right direction. But the foreman broke it in, scored its back with whippings until its gamboling became a slow trudge, its skull bowed.

He waits for her to speak, and at last she does. She does not look at him.

"Why do you do it?" she asks.

"Do what?"

"Collect—kill these creatures, take away their lives?"

He shakes his head. She does not understand. He doesn't end their lives but preserves their memory; totems that will last all of time, pelts that would have grayed then rotted in alleys. And what's more, they *mean* something to him. Why does everything need to have a function in this modern age? Can't joy be enough? He is about to articulate this when she abuts his thoughts.

"I want food," she says, in the tone of a princess commanding a serf.

He will taunt her first, just as a jest. "I'm not sure about that."

She doesn't rise to it, so he sighs.

"You bit me before, didn't you?" He holds out his finger, red and swollen, four sickled gashes made by her incisors.

"I won't. I won't this time—I'm so hungry and so thirsty." She raises her eyes to him, and she is beautiful.

"Very well, very well," he says, giving in sooner than he intended. He chuckles: she knows how to get her way.

He takes out a tin surgical dish, kidney-shaped. He won't risk his hand again. He picks up the dirt-speckled chocolate bonbons that were thrown across the cellar before. He places them on the tray and holds it against her mouth. She turns her head onto one side and snatches one sideways. She eats them all.

"Water," she says, and he fumbles for a bottle in his coat, pours the liquid into the tray, and she laps it like a cat. Dust floats in the dish.

"Better?" he asks, but she is silent.

He must make her love him.

"I mean it," he says. "I just want to be your friend."

He waits, and wonders if she is asleep.

"I've been"—he mouths the word first, because he has never said it aloud before—"lonely. I've been—I've been so lonely."

There is no answer.

"When I was a child, nobody wanted to be my friend. I never had one. I wished someone would want to be, but they all despised me. They laughed at me. And I thought I had one once, a surgeon, but he mocked me and—"

He tells her everything. He talks and talks, until his throat is hoarse. Gideon, his mother, the skulls he sold to the factory wives; he spills his life into the room, his words and worries embedding themselves in the fabric of the cellar. He tells her how sad he has been, how hard he has worked, how his curiosities have been an escape.

Still, she is silent.

# Darkness

Time passes. Iris could not say how many days or how many nights. Silas brings her food and water. Part of her begins to look forward to the scraping against the ceiling, the whine of the trapdoor hinges, and to his footsteps on the ladder rungs. She hates herself for it, pounds her feet against the ground as if in revolt at her own mind, but in his company, she does not feel that she is going mad.

Because it is all black, black, black, endless black, until she thinks that she might suffocate. There is no pigment dark enough, no brush thick enough, to describe it. Her thoughts grow ragged-edged and unreal. She starts to imagine her sister sitting in the corner, her head bowed over her sewing, the hiss of her needle. A rat scratching becomes the *scrape-scrape* of Millais's palette knife against the canvas. The press of her bindings becomes Louis's caress on her arm, his whisper in her ear. She does not move, and the stiffness is pain. She wets herself and shits into a bucket. She is an anchoress bricked into an abbey. A medieval maiden trapped in a tower. A conspirator in a jail. A doll in a box. A dog in a cage.

*By Jove, I'll need to find a stupendously beautiful creature for it!*
*What a fine creature she is!*

She eats, conserving her strength. She does not try to escape again because first she must contrive a plan that will not fail: she must be measured, calm, and patient. Silas must trust her first. He must make a mistake, forget something. He must let his guard slip. She was too hasty before. She should have waited, or hit him harder with the lantern. She bucks in the chair at her own stupidity. It could have been her only chance.

She wonders if Louis has returned. A thousand scenarios track through her mind. He falls in love with Sylvia again, who recovered, and stays in Edinburgh. His steamer is delayed, or sinks. He returns home and thinks she has abandoned him, as she said she would.

Or—

Or—

He arrives at Colville Place, hears the quiet hum of the house, feels the chill of the rooms. He calls her name, and his voice echoes back.

He shoulders his cloak (if only she had left the letter!) and walks to her lodgings on Charlotte Street.

She hasn't been seen for over a week, the matron tells him. (Has it been a week? Or has it only been a couple of days? Time is slippery.) She has taken nothing from her room, nothing to suggest a journey. He is disquieted.

He visits Rose—Iris can hear the chime of the bell, smell that sickly sweetness, feel that patchy carpet under his boots—and she has heard nothing either. She is disturbed too, because Iris wasn't there for their walk, and she thought that Iris and Louis had gone away together on a whim.

He remembers Silas now—of course he does! He remembers the

bauble and the hand on her arm, Iris's unease and fear, and he comes at once to the shop.

He shoves past Silas, knocking him squarely on the chin.

She hears another man's tread upstairs, and she screams for him, again and again and again.

He pushes aside the heavy object blocking the door.

She sees it open, and Louis is there, calling her name, holding her, pulling her free of her restraints—

# Madame

$S$ilas is sitting in his armchair when he hears the snap of the trap. He folds *The Lancet* and *The Times* carefully and tucks them into the journal rack he made out of whittled bone and badger hide. He cracks each of his knuckles in turn.

Usually he would ask Albie for specimens, but he hasn't seen the wretch in weeks, and when he went to rap on his window as a reminder of their *agreement*, he almost scared a different child senseless. Perhaps he's gone away, moved to a new brothel, and can do without Silas's generosity. It's easier this way, as he wouldn't want the little imp sniffing around while he has her here on a *séjour*. Silas already worries he suspects too much.

There is a plump white mouse lying in the jaw of the trap. Its eyes are blank and staring, two red rubies, but its belly writhes. Silas prods it with a toothpick. How perplexing!

It is then that he understands—the stomach is quickening with baby mice. He has only ever seen this once before, but on a hound. Is there a name for them? Mouslings? Mouselets?

He prizes the mouse free. It is a good specimen. The cracked spine does not matter; he wants it for its pelt, and the fur is unpunctured.

Silas sits at his workbench, lays out his tools in a neat row—three pared scalpels, elbow scissors, a fleshing tool, and skin scraper—and pins down its four feet. He cuts the quivering belly, picturing himself as a surgeon.

"Naughty mouse," he says. "Let's ease out your bastards."

Each baby writhes in a sac. He splits the membranes, watching as each creature tugs free and begins to nose its way over the bureau. Six stumbling mouselets. They are raw and pink, their eyes faintly bruised like the fly in a maggot. He laughs a little at one, nudging his scalpel with its translucent snout.

Then he grows bored and squishes them with a mallet, one by one.

He concentrates on the mother mouse, working carefully around the points where the muscle attaches to the fur—ears, tail, forelegs—and when he has the limp, salted pelt in his hand, he decides to leave it to dry before stuffing it. This way the creature is less likely to turn moldy.

He remembers Louis and the damned rotten dove. That is what started all this—handing Iris to him—

As he runs a moistened finger inside the mouse's coat, he realizes that this is the first time he has thought of Iris all morning. She is starting to tire him, with her fearful eyes and the stench of her waste in the bucket. It is foul, inhuman. It didn't even occur to him that she might make such *smells*.

There is a knocking at the door.

Silas flinches at the sound, resolves to ignore it. There have been a few customers whose footsteps he has heard in the alley, but the *"Closed"* sign has been enough to deter them even from ringing or knocking.

The hammering grows louder, more insistent, and Silas tucks his quivering hands underneath his thighs. He hears the faint pulse of the bell in the cellar; Iris will hear it too. This is no ordinary visitor. He imagines Louis there, led by Albie—

"Mr. Reed—I command you to open this door," a man says, stern and commanding, but Silas does not move.

Another voice. "Open the door, you bastard—"

He would recognize that yowl anywhere—it is Madame from the Dolphin. What can she want now? Surely this is not still the nonsense about that dead harlot? It hasn't even been in the newspapers, so it can hardly be important. This is not the time—he thinks of Iris in the cellar, the pitch of her scream—how tightly did he fasten that gag? A pellet of sweat gathers on his brow.

"Open up!" the man's voice says, and the door bucks on its hinges. They will beat down the door if he doesn't answer it. He wonders who the man is, concludes it must be a heavy from the tavern.

Silas scours his dressers for the sharp blade that he uses on the larger specimens. He will assuage any of their fears, respond to their questions. And if the heavy wants any nonsense—well, he's a fair enough match for any bludger—

"What is it?" Silas asks, cracking open the door.

But to his surprise, it is not a heavy with Madame, but a tall peeler, dressed in a long navy coat and varnished leather hat. A truncheon, lamp, and rattle sit at his waist. His silver badges and buckles gleam like herrings.

Silas feels the knife slip in his palm, and he tries to tuck it down the back of his trousers.

"Sorry to disturb you, sir," the constable says, and Madame's eyes are narrowed, two serpentine slits.

"You bastard—I know you did it—" she says, lunging forward, but the peeler stills her with his hand.

"Please, ma'am—control yourself."

"Did what?" Silas says, forcing levity into his voice. "If there's any inquiry I can assist with, please let me know—"

The constable's mouth moves under his sprawling mustache, and at first Silas can only focus on the movement of it, a small, twitching mammal on his slab—

"What?" he says, blinking.

"I asked if you are familiar with Jane Simmond?"

"Bluebell," Madame barks. "Bluebell. Of course you knew her, you yellow—"

"I knew her, in the way that others in the tavern knew her. She was often there, hustling."

He sees by the tapping of the policeman's foot that he is already impatient with Madame, keen to dismiss her as a hysteric. Silas knows what he must do. He must address him man to man.

"I didn't know her myself, except by sight," Silas continues. "She was ill-mannered. I heard tell of her death, but in truth I'd forgotten about it." He arranges his face into a perplexed expression. "But really, I thought there was nothing suspicious—I heard she was out of her wits on opium or gin, and slipped—so I can't fathom why you are here."

The constable nods. "That's what we were led to believe, but—" He beckons toward Madame.

"I know it was you," she spits. "I know it was, and I won't let it rest—"

Silas buries his chin into his neck, feigns a look of surprise. "I can't think, if her death was an accident, what on earth *I* could have to do with it."

The policeman glances him an apology. "I must ask: where were you on the night?"

"Here, I should imagine," Silas says, crossing one foot over the other in a casual stance, but his leg is shaking and he feels hot. The knife is starting to slip, and he longs to rid himself of these people—

He hears her, a quiet, insistent mew.

His heart is sore. Men have surely died of lesser shocks. They must leave—he has to get them away from here—

"Sir?" the constable asks, peering closer at him. Silas feigns a smile.

"Sorry. I didn't quite—"

"I asked you what happened on that afternoon when you quarreled. Tell me from your arrival at the Dolphin, and then afterward."

He went to the rookery—that false girl with her counterfeit tresses—and then returned to the Dolphin, and nothing after that until he waited at Colville Place. More: Louis and Iris entwined, and a smell—the scent of Bluebell's perfume. He has to steady himself on the door frame. But he must not think of it. He just has to stop them from hearing Iris's bleating.

"What did you do that afternoon?" the constable prompts.

"I visited the Dolphin, and she was a little rude, I admit," Silas says, and he hears the words pour from his mouth, and cannot believe how silky they are, how convincing, how educated, when everything in his mind is disorder. "But I put it down to her being in her cups. She was rolling in her seat. She had some gentleman with her. An elderly fellow. Really, I did not think of it at all. I mentioned to Madame here—"

Madame snarls at him.

"That I was concerned she was over-soused on gin—"

"He was livid! The anger was a heat off him—"

The peeler holds out his hand, and silences her, and Silas keeps talking. If he fills the void with words, then the sound will mask the squalling that he hears at his very core—

"And after that, well, I came back here."

"Was anyone with you?" the man asks.

"I live alone. Surely there can be no suspicion?"

The peeler stops. "What the devil is that noise?"

"What noise?" Silas asks, and a coolness creeps over him. His throat is dry and he clears it.

"That sound. You must hear it too?"

"Oh, *that*. It drives me wild," he says. "The brats living in there"—he points at the derelict building behind him, where he has seen nobody pass for weeks—"they keep a kitten in a cage. The cruelty of it is quite upsetting."

"I see," the policeman says, and he shrugs. "Urchins."

And as he veers into conversational small talk about London's housing problem, Silas can scarcely credit that the constable has given up the thread about Bluebell entirely, and believed him so readily about Iris's cries. The policeman trusts him and sees nothing suspicious.

"Was there anything else?" Silas asks, daring to push the conversation to a close, and then, "I'm sure you're grieving, Madame. I know we haven't always seen eye to eye, but really, dragging me into this mire when it's clear it was nothing but a tragic accident—"

"You bastard! You—" and Madame hurls herself at him, her fingers on his hair, pinching and scratching, and Silas does not respond, just bears her lashes until he feels the constable pulling her free, rebuking her.

"Really, Madame—"

"I don't blame her," Silas says. "It's the gin. It can pickle a brain to hysteria if taken too often."

The peeler rolls his eyes, and says, "Enough, ma'am—and thank you for allowing us to trouble you—" and Silas closes the door, and presses his back against it, breathing hard.

# Guigemar

*Dear Guigemar,*

*Our love affair has soured. I have little to say except farewell. You are not to worry about me. I ask only that you do not try to find me or correspond with me.*

*Yours,*
*Iris*

# Beast

I ris closes her eyes. The floor is cold against her cheek, and she has tipped over the chair again in her frenzy. The bucket has fallen onto its side along with the seat. Some of the contents leach into the ground, some into her skirts. It is all hopeless. All for nothing. She tried so hard. She tried and tried and tried, a deep throaty wail in her lungs that was muffled by the gag—again and again she cried out, stamping and rocking the chair beneath her. She heard the shout of a woman—it was faint but it was something—and the vibration of the door closing.

And now she hears his footsteps across the ceiling.

The heavy item is pulled back, and the trapdoor opens. She blinks against the brightness of his lamp. She can smell herself. Piss and sweat. It appalls her. She remembers washing herself each morning from the pail, squeezing the coal-warmed water from the sponge and dribbling it under her arms, between her legs.

"Write me the letter," he says, once he has set her upright and removed her gag, and he is agitated, his fists white. But he is here, and that is something. It must have been over a day since he last came. Her throat is dry from thirst, her stomach barks for food. Her tongue sits heavy in her mouth.

She thinks, *Silas's hand on my clavicle—*

She thinks, *The rats that squabble on the floor—*

She thinks, *Escape. Escape. Escape. If I escape, I will find Louis and believe him when he says he loves me, and embrace Rose and pay for an education for Albie—*

Silas holds out a paper and quill. "All I need you to do is write to him. If only you weren't so disobedient!"

She tries to speak, but her thirst makes her croak. "I—will do it."

"What?" His eyes snap on her, in surprise and disbelief.

"I will pen your—your blasted letter."

"Iris, dearest. Don't use such foul language—"

And she grits her teeth. "I will do it, but only if you loosen my bindings and bring me food and water."

He pauses for a moment, and she can tell by his sneer that he's considering teasing her. But he sighs and does as she asks, presenting her with the metal dish. She will not look at him as she laps at the cloudy liquid—and she feels a sudden hatred for Louis. Where is he? Why hasn't he come?

When he unloops her right arm from the restraints, his clammy palm brushing hers, she cries out. She rotates the wrist, the joint clicking.

He gives her a pen, but when she tries to write, her hand will not grip it. She sighs, and then in a burst of temper hurls it across the room.

"Shhh, shhh," he soothes her, picking it up again. "Is my patience not boundless? Take your time."

And he recites the words that she must write, the lies that must spill from the nib.

When she is finished, he snatches the paper from her.

She hopes the reference to Guigemar will be enough. She only ever calls him Guigemar as a jest, so he will be startled by it, puzzled. From there, she hopes, he will understand that it is a signal to him that she is trapped, that, like the Queen in his painting, he must rescue her. It is her only chance, a gamble. But what if he believes the letter, believes she no longer wants to hear from him?

Iris coughs, and her chest smarts. This damp room, with its dripping ceiling and dank walls—how she longs to escape, to free her limbs, to run—to see daylight and the green expanse of Hyde Park—

"D-ear—" Silas reads, and then he stops. He peers closer. He raps the paper, creasing it in front of her face. Iris flinches.

"What is this?" he demands. "Gu-Gug-e-mar?"

"It's what I call him. I never call him Louis. If I wrote 'Louis' he would know it wasn't me."

"You're lying."

"I'm not," she insists. "I'm not. I call him that—Guigemar. It's my name for him—"

"You're lying," he says again, and he is shouting now. He crumples the letter. "You're a liar. You're a little liar. You're nothing but a filthy beast, an animal. I just wanted to love you and I've tried—"

"I'm an animal? Me?" Iris screams, her temper matching his. "I'm not the monster who locked me up here, who tricked me—"

"You wanted me to—"

"Wanted you to? You're a deluded—a deluded devil of a man! I hate you. I hate you with every ounce of my being, every last breath in my body. You're pathetic. It's little wonder you have no companions, that you're all alone—"

"Silence!" he shouts.

"It's why your mother loathed you. She saw what a wicked, ugly soul you had—" The words flow out of her, unstoppable, a black tide of vitriol that she has bottled for the last—how long? Week?

Fortnight? A mere few days? And where is Louis? Why doesn't he come?

"Silence!" he bellows again, and she sees him scrabbling in his pocket, and she knows what is coming next—the rag. She does not want it, but still the words pour—she knows she should be quiet, because she fears him too, but her temper is up.

"I won't love you, never. I'll do nothing but hate you—hate you even more than your mother did—" She hawks, turns over a lump of phlegm, arcs her neck, and spits in his face, relishing the sight of it sliding down his cheek.

After that, he rocks the chair, knocks her to the ground, and his hands are on her throat. She tries to splutter, to cry out, to moan, but she can't. The only sound she makes is that of a choking cat.

# Glass Eyes

It has been two days since Silas visited Iris. He awoke as if from a reverie—his fingers on her throat, the *chk-chk-chk* as she reached for air—and he stumbled back. He pulled her chair upright, her broken rasp for breath a rebuke in his ears. "I'm sorry, I'm sorry," he muttered, "but you shouldn't have—you shouldn't have angered me—" She retched then, and he mopped the yellow string of vomit with such tenderness. "There, there, see how I care for you," he said, and replaced the gag, and faltered from her, up the rungs of the ladder. Her eyes were wild and bloodshot, flitting from side to side. And her whimper! He crammed her letter into the dresser drawer, determined not to see it again.

Silas has not forgotten her look and the sound she made. It has been enough to keep him away from her for two days. Besides, he has been busy: scanning the newspapers each morning, trying to scout out Albie, and preparing the mouse. It is what he is working on now, stuffing the crown with cotton, matching up the black beads to the eye sockets, nudging the cloth into the corners of its limbs.

The work calms him. Before long, the mouse starts to fill out, to resemble itself when he pulled it from the trap.

He tries not to worry about Bluebell. There have been no more inquiries, no articles in the newspaper. After all, they have no evidence except the crazed suspicions of a hysteric. Madame must have had something meaty to dangle over that peeler—perhaps he was one of the Dolphin's less salubrious regulars—to overcome the clear skepticism that he betrayed in a single glance. The constable can't have been serious in his questioning. If they really suspected Silas, they would have ransacked his shop, dragged him off to the cells.

Silas holds his concentration, twisting the wire down into the tail. He's sure he won't hear anything more about Bluebell. But what would have happened if the constable wasn't satisfied with his story about the trapped kitten? What if he pushed in, saw the knife behind Silas's back, and found her in the cellar? Silas has been so careful to cover his tracks, to sweep behind him for footsteps, but it only takes a foolish lapse like that, a prying voice at the door, for everything to be ruined. And won't Louis return soon and find Iris missing?

He mops his brow and positions the mouse upright. It is not his finest work, but he tries to stitch the incision closed. His hands will not do as he commands, and he jabs at the fur, digging too far, his needlework ragged and uneven. He sighs. What is happening to him? Usually each piece is an improvement on the one before.

In order to mollify the souring turn of his mind, to reassure himself that he is being too critical of his own abilities, he hurries upstairs, to where the mice are laid out on the shelves. He counts them: thirteen. A baker's dozen. He picks up the creature he made most recently, brown fur with the pink feather. He examines the stitching, admires its neat zigzags. How finely made it was! And the first mouse he ever stuffed—smaller than the others, holding a plate with the patch of ginger pelt glued to its scalp. That was made at the beginning when he was inexpert, and her body bags a little, her head overfilled and the fur stretched.

Perhaps his new mouse is not as badly made as he thought. He returns to his desk and picks it up—but it *is* all wrong. The wire has not reached to the ends of the paws, and the stuffing is unevenly dispersed. The trip upstairs has done little to calm him.

*You liar, devil of a man, Starey Silas, lopsided gait*—all these people have mocked him, hated him, bullied him—he slams his fist onto the table, yanks back his chair, and resolves to visit her.

# Currant Bun

Hands on her collarbone, breath on her neck—Louis? Silas? Or merely her imagination? Louis rises before her, a desperate mirage—his hair curling at the nape, his smile. He tells her that Guinevere has built a palace for her, and he leads her through the house to a yawning bright studio, each wall made up of thousands of panes of glass, a raised dais for her models to sprawl on—but then the floor falls away and she finds herself in black dankness, and Louis's face shifts into Silas's—she begs him to come back, not to leave her, but it is too late. There is a hand pawing at her clavicle, and it is the marble hand from the British Museum, with its grasping stone fingers—

"Louis," she croaks. "My darling—my darling." And then, "Water." The glass is wet against her lips. She drinks and drinks. It spills down her front, chilling her. There is a currant bun too, shiny with sugar glaze, which Silas balls into smaller pieces and feeds to her.

"More," she says, even though her stomach seizes, because she doesn't know how long he will leave her next time. What if he stops coming and leaves her to starve? What if he is detained somewhere, or killed? Nobody would know about her trapped here. "More—"

Another bun, eaten greedily.

"I was so lonely before you came," Silas says, and her head thunders.

"Please let me go," she says. She has lost count of how many times she has said these words. "Please let me go. I won't tell anyone about you—I'll pretend I went away—"

"Liar," he says, but his voice is not unkind.

"Please," she begs, and the tears drip off her nose and chin. "Please, Silas. I'm a girl, a person like you, not a specimen, not an animal—please—"

"I wanted you to be my friend," he says. "I wanted it so much, and you ignored me."

"I'm sorry," she says, through her sobs and her rattling cough. Her body feels damp with fever. She must keep him close to her, make sure he visits her again soon with food and water. "You're my friend. You are, aren't you?"

"I don't believe you."

"I'm telling the truth," she presses, and then, "Will you ever let me go? Will you?"

Silence.

"I'd visit you—I'd still be your friend—we could go and see the Exhibition together—"

"But you didn't before."

"I know you now! I know you—if you'd only let me go, you'd see how I wanted to be your friend, how I meant it, how—" On she prattles, her words echoing each other, repeating, ever repeating, *friend, friend, friend*, and he sits there, clasping hold of himself with his arms.

"Tell me about yourself," he says.

"I'll tell you next time," she says. *Please let there be a next time.* "If you bring me a hot pie and some milk and beef tea—"

Her words are cut short by the wheeze of a bell in the corner of the room. Silas leaps to his feet.

Iris starts to scream, but her throat croaks and the sound is scratchy, far from the clear shrieks from a few days ago. Before she can gulp for more air, he has the handkerchief with the strange liquid on it and he holds it to her face.

She rears and rams him with her head, trying to shake free, to raise her voice over the piece of fabric braced over her nose and mouth.

The bell rings again, and she struggles and struggles.

*Stay awake, Iris*, she tells herself. *Do not let the world fade. This is another chance—another glimmer. Do not let the world fade—the roar of crowds at Queen Victoria's marriage—the horsehair mattress— the boy under the cart and his sister's distress—a dab of color on the canvas—a brush poised, needle-fine—the iris Rose brought—the niche below Louis's shoulder, carved out for her head to rest on—Louis Louis Louis Louis—*

# Bell Pull

The ringing of the bell startled Silas from his reverie. He believed Iris for a moment, trusted that she truly wanted to be his friend, *was* his friend, and he genuinely toyed with the idea of releasing her. He could, after all. He could bask in the knowledge of his own generosity and her gratitude to him. In time, *she* could comfort *him* by bringing him food, sitting with him while he worked on his specimens. He could open the shop again—because it is not long until the landlord will demand the overdue rent, and then what will happen?

But when her screams filled the cellar, he knew that she was dissembling. If he released her, she would call the constable, and everything would unravel.

He stares at her for a moment, head rolled forward. The bell peals again, more insistent, and the knocking is unremitting. If it is Madame and the peeler back again, and they burst in before he has a chance to leave Iris, they will see the trapdoor open—his hands slide on the rungs in his impatience to climb into the shop. He hauls the cabinet over the cellar entrance, hastens to unbolt the main door. It can only be Madame. Nobody else is this persistent.

"What is it?" Silas demands.

But it isn't Madame on the threshold.

It is that bastard, Louis. Rose stands next to him, as ugly as a purple-skinned sow.

Silas flinches, readying himself for the punch, for the end.

But the man does not hurl him to one side, does not barrel into the shop and run down to Iris. Silas grips the door frame. That means that Louis cannot know—if he did, wouldn't he have the constable with him, or at least a gang of his friends, determined to take the law into their own hands? Silas must act as normally as he can, avoid chasing him away or rousing any form of suspicion. He tries to distort his mouth into a smile, but he merely grimaces, baring his teeth in a slight snarl.

"Can I—be of service?" Silas asks. His voice is unsteady, the forced joviality grating. How long does he have until Iris revives from the chloroform? Five minutes? If Louis hears her struggle, he won't be appeased by the kitten story—his heart flits, a canary knocking against the walls of its cage. "Are you here for another specimen? Another dove, perhaps, or a cat?"

He thinks his guilt must be written all over his face.

"Where is Iris?" Louis demands, and Rose narrows her good eye at him.

Silas cringes, but he reminds himself that they know nothing. Their suspicions have no foundation.

"I beg your pardon?" Silas says.

"Is she here?" Louis demands. "Do you have her?"

"She told Louis you seized her wrist," Rose says, over him. "And you came to her lodgings, and now she's left without a trace. Where is she?"

*She's left.* Not *she's been snatched* or *she's disappeared.* Silas treasures this hint of their true belief, but still, he can scarcely breathe. "Oh, she's inside, of course—having tea," he says, through the treacle of his fear. He barks a false laugh.

Louis looks one way, then another. He runs a hand through his curls, and Silas wishes he had his poniard with him, could press Louis against the wall and hammer each breath out of him. What a fool, what a pup!

"You're very welcome to step inside," Silas says, "though heaven knows what you're expecting to find."

He glances behind him, sees his knife on the dresser where he left it.

Louis peers into the gloom, as if afraid that crossing the threshold will be the beginning of a descent to lunacy. Silas expects him to refuse, but instead Louis says, "Well, if you wouldn't object—" and Louis and Rose shove past him.

"Go on—why don't you search the bureau drawers for her too?" Silas says, subduing the panic that grips him. "Come out, dearest!"

He slips the knife into his pocket.

Louis says nothing, just peers around the exhibits and then—the indignity of it—starts to climb the stairs to Silas's chamber.

"I must insist that this quite oversteps—" but Louis ignores him. The pocked wench scowls, and he finds himself mesmerized by a crater on her cheek, wondering whether her skin would still retain that dimpled quality if it were pulled free of her skull and spread flat.

"What can you mean, that she's left?" Silas asks, and a thought occurs to him. He turns his back to Rose, and rifles through a drawer, tears a slip of paper and puts it in his pocket.

"Gone," Louis says. "No note, no word, nothing." Silas is relieved to see him downstairs again, an expression of sheepish unease on his face.

"You didn't find her hiding under my bed?"

"It isn't at all amusing," Rose snaps. "My sister is missing and we will find her. It isn't regular—"

"Damned right it isn't amusing," Louis says, and his face is even paler than usual. "If you think you can make light of it, when you—when Albie warned me about you—and Iris—you attacked her, unsettled her. And then mere weeks after you accosted her, I return from Edinburgh to find she has vanished entirely—it is most out of character."

Silas recalls the averted kiss, the final stamp of hostility as Louis's cab creaked along the straw-strewn road.

"Can there have been any cause for it? A *quarrel*, perhaps?"

"That is beside the point," Louis says, but Silas reads the wavering in his voice. "And Albie—he said you were watching her—"

"Albie?" Silas asks, and he plucks at a strand of hair. Albie the loose end, the imp—it would take just a breath from the boy to betray him, for it all to be ruined, and could Albie have confided what he knows to Louis, risked his sister?

"Albie was killed," Louis says, quite flatly.

"Killed?" Silas repeats.

"By a cart. His sister came to me. I've employed her as my house-maid, and she told me all about Albie's loathing of you—"

That vile urchin—an outright traitor when Silas showed him nothing but kindness! He mustn't dwell on it: instead, he must concentrate on evicting them from his shop. He must enact his plan, sketchy though it is. And if it doesn't work or Iris wakes— He runs his finger along the edge of the blade, feeling the slice against his thumb. He will conquer by surprise, slit that man from gizzard to groin, and cut Rose's throat in an instant.

"Disappearing is in her character, after all," he begins.

"What do you know of her character?" Louis snaps.

"She didn't tell you?"

"Didn't tell me what?" Louis steps forward, and Rose continues her glare, her eye as piercing as a carriage lamp.

"A lady's business—well," Silas says, with the same teasing tone as if he were withholding a secret. The thrust of his heart will give him no rest. "Well—it would be indelicate."

"How dare you," Louis says, but he lets Silas speak.

"I'm not quite sure how to say this—but, well"—Silas bites down on his lip—"we were—romantically involved. *Venereally* involved—"

"You were not—" Louis says.

"Liar!" Rose says. "I'd know—"

"Oh, Rose. She carried on under your nose."

"You're a villain—a monster—"

Silas feels his control ebbing. "When she worked at Mrs. Salter's—didn't I come to the shop to find her?" He marvels for a second over his own memory. Sometimes it has the haze of a pea-souper, other times it is pin-sharp. "You remember that—"

"When was this?" Louis demands, turning to Rose. "What does he mean?"

"I—I was angry at her. As if my sister could associate with some-one as foul, as rotten as him."

Silas's fingers close over the handle of the blade. But he steadies his gaze on a hare floating in a jar, and takes a breath—

"It is true we were not involved long—I cared for her—she in-vited me to the Royal Academy Private View, said her portrait was hung there—and what's this nonsense about me seizing her, attack-ing her?"

"You grabbed her wrist," Louis says. "And wouldn't let go."

Silas scoffs. "I did no such thing. She invited me, we conversed civilly—unless this was a story she concocted to gain your pity, your attention—"

"Liar," Louis says, but his voice falters. "I don't believe you—that Iris would lie—"

"It was vexing."

"What have you done to her?" Louis demands again.

He reaches into his pocket—how long until Iris wakes? They must be gone—

"Nothing—truly—I've done nothing at all. She has a habit—a habit of disappearing. I'm sure you didn't quarrel, but well—if you did. She left her sister easily enough, didn't she?"

"That was different," Rose attempts, but he speaks over her.

"And she discarded me as carelessly as an apple core. See for yourself."

He takes the letter from his pocket, torn off where it began "*To Guigemar.*" Silas could recite it by heart.

"*Our love affair has soured. I have little to say except farewell. You are not to worry about me. I ask only that you do not try to find me or correspond with me. Yours, Iris.*"

Louis snatches it and Rose cranes over his shoulder.

"Where did you get this?" Louis demands.

"She sent it to me—isn't it in her hand?"

And Louis covers his face. "By God, I can't believe it."

"It isn't true," Rose says. "I don't know what trickery he used to get this—"

"I—really don't believe it," Louis says, but he sounds like a deflated bellows. "I won't let her go, damn it! I won't give up—"

"Now, if you don't mind, I have business to attend to—"

Louis lunges forward, his fist raised, but Rose stops him, a gentle hand that has the same effect as if he were checked by a prizefighter. He sags, a slow emptying of air, and allows Rose to lead him from the shop. "This isn't the end—you haven't heard the last of it—" he says, but his words have lost their bite.

Silas slams the door shut.

There is a sudden hammering.

"I don't believe you—not a jot—" Louis shouts. "I'll get to the bottom of it—if you've hurt her, you'll be sorry—I love her—" and Silas realizes that the man is sobbing.

"Come. There's nothing to be gained," Rose says, and the door judders with a final kick.

There is a moment of sweet silence before Iris's mewls begin again.

# Pigeon

When Iris and Rose were children, a bird seller used to call out his wares on the pavement outside their house. He wore a buff waistcoat and a cocked hat, and he wielded wooden cages containing pigeons and greenfinches, their feathers painted in the colors of exotic birds.

"Canaries a bob, parrots two bob," he cried, and Iris lingered there each morning, transfixed by the gummed wings of the creatures, their listless squawks, the way they would stand poised as if to fly, but only thump the edges of the cage.

She could not bear to see the birds in their confinement, and she and Rose told him so, her sister with wide-eyed supplication, Iris by stamping her feet and demanding he release them. He wafted the twins away, cuffed Iris about the head, and said she'd make a poor hawker if she weren't willing to do brown and think up such dodges.

"One as sweet as a strawberry, and the other a sour red currant," he said of them.

"You shouldn't like it if it was *you* stuck in that cage," Iris spat back.

"Oh, please let them go," Rose begged.

Every time they passed him, Iris's anger grew, until it was as hot as a fire iron. One day, she was in disgrace for some reason—it could have been dirtying her pinny, or sitting tight-lipped at dinner and refusing to eat a dish of brown-boiled vegetables, or laughing in church, or singeing her eyebrows on a candle to see what happened—and she whispered to Rose to divert him.

"What are you intending—?" she tried, looking at Iris fearfully.

"Just—distract him."

As Rose gabbled about pigeons and asked whether humans could learn to fly, and the man chortled and said, "Mankind fly? We'll sooner stroll on the moon," Iris grabbed one of the cages. She tried to undo the latch, but it was held fast. The birdman was still prattling, so she snapped three of the wooden bars, which were little wider than matches. "Fly," she urged the painted pigeon, but it only stared at her, perplexed, and coo-cooed.

"*Go*," she pleaded, giving the cage a shake, but the bird would not move.

The seller noticed Iris, and moved to grab her just as the creature hopped free.

She imagined it would soar into the sky, a brightly colored pigeon like a miniature peacock. She pictured it settling among the dull grays of its species, the rapture with which it would be greeted. It hadn't occurred to her that the paint glued its feathers together, preventing it from spreading its wings. It waddled into the street, its neck jerking with each step.

"No," she cried, but it was too late—it was minced under the wheel of a dog cart.

She hated herself then. She'd meant so well. Rose wept as the birdman struck Iris with the leather of his shoe, and he chased her parents for two shillings too.

Iris doesn't know what prompted her to think of this. Other thoughts and imaginings cram into her mind.

Louis, the beat of his body against hers as they lay on the rooftop together, her skirts around her waist, his trousers bunched at his knees. There in broad daylight, tupping under the sky. Unabashed, brazen. *I love you I love you I love you* whispered into the conch of her ear.

He has not come. There has been no rescue, no Louis racing down the ladder and undoing her restraints. She is helpless, ignorant of any flurry that could be going on around her, the release that could be mere minutes away.

*My life is dreary. He cometh not.*

She imagines him finding her in this room. Dirty, stinking, feverish, and soiled, the real face of imprisonment: little more than a pig in a trough—not the idealized face in his painting, pale and clean, turned toward the light.

She longs for the scrape of the trapdoor, but it does not come. She hears Silas overhead, pacing up and down, and his detachedness terrifies her. She needs him to be frenzied and affectionate, to have him reassure her that he does not want to hurt her, that he only wants to be her friend.

*Visit me*, she wills him, *talk to me. Give me food.*

What she means is, *Do not leave me here to die.*

Terror claws at her.

The bird.

Its gummed feathers.

Now it is her in the cage, and there is no child to snap the wooden bars.

It is then that a thought occurs to her. A distant idea.

# The Royal Academy

Silas wakes after noon. A newspaper is on the bed. If Iris hadn't forged that false *Guigemar* on the letter, he wouldn't have noticed the wording in the bottom left-hand corner. It has been a mere day since Louis visited, and he has wasted no time in placing an advertisement. Perhaps Silas's insinuations provoked him to it.

Silas picks up the broadsheet, the print contorting in his grasp. He stumbled over the words first of all, but now he could recite them with his eyes shut.

*My Queen,*

*I will not cease looking for you; I love you and I know you love me in return, that our quarrel was little more than a tiff. I will find you, and I will marry you, if you will accept such a shabby prospect—please, write to me—I cannot do without you.*

*Your Guigemar*

It is so infernally sentimental. So *unoriginal*, so grotesque—Louis has no concept of love, of the patience required, the planning, the care—Silas stands and stares at the costumed mice on the shelf. He feels a dryness in his mouth, a deep pain as if he has been split open like kindling.

He cannot blink away his recollections any longer. There is the pottery mouse. Small, snuff-colored and holding a plate.

The beady face was Flick's, clay-dusted, dented by her father's fist. She, not smiling, but snarling, afraid, underneath him. *Liar*, she said, *Liar*, and she kicked at his prized specimen in her haste to escape. It was the ram with its curling horns—he can remember it vividly—and she split it in two, and that was what really pushed him into the roiling pitch of heat and anger and lashing fists. Before he knew what was happening, she was below him, his hands on her neck, her face purpling and swelling and that nought of her lips—*he had done it*. He joined in the hunt for her, visiting her body twice, tracing his fingers over her skin as it bruised and decayed. He wanted to explore the pillars of her bones, but the search frightened him, and he buried her one night in the woodland, watched only by the sickle of the moon and a fox, which ran from him. The leaves of the trees seemed to curl away in horror, the owls hooting the secret of it into the air, beetles scuttling to unseen places.

He puts down the Flick mouse. Next to it sits the only male mouse, dressed in the habiliment of a medical student: tiny glazed cap, flannel jacket and apron. The creature's pink paw clutches a needle for a scalpel.

It is Gideon.

It was a blustery night, speckled with rain, and Gideon was so late leaving the university that Silas wondered if he had missed him. He waited, a blade in his hand and resentment thick in his heart.

He runs his finger across the mice and sucks on his teeth. He recalls Iris as the Queen in the painting, regal.

He cleans himself for the first time in weeks, scrubbing at his armpits and genitals with a cloth, teasing away the human smells with his clean scent. When he is dressed, he takes a scalpel from the dresser drawer, the sharpest one, which he uses for the initial incision in his creatures, and he leaves his house.

He turns into the din of the Strand. An omnibus is disgorging black-whiskered lackeys and working women, a herd of bobbing mushrooms with their broad-tipped bonnets. The masses part before him. All his life, he has been mocked and slighted and it has made him *miserable* and so, so alone.

He marches across Trafalgar Square, and he does not even flinch when he knocks into a hot-potato seller whose orange coals spark and hiss onto the pavement.

There is a man at the entrance of the Royal Academy and Silas will not be stopped. He does not cringe at the sight of two companions, taking the steps arm in arm, does not turn away when he sees a girl whisper in a man's ear. The knife is in his pocket—he feels its promise—and he cuts a straight course through the maze of grand, painting-papered rooms to the West Room.

There she is.

She was so sweet then, so clean, so pure. When he was last here at the exhibition preview, he was so hopeful. He felt it rising, a hot-air balloon of desire and certainty that she would love him. He thought he would always be happy if he could see her each day, hold her collarbone, speak with her. He pictured her face turned to his, joyful at her captivity, just like in the painting. He would trust her enough to let her roam the cellar, and he would heap food at her feet: silver goblets filled with wine, fresh loaves, porcelain bowls crammed with strawberries and figs, and she would look always dainty, pristine, her hair falling down her back, her skin soft and pure, her skirts smoothed.

But the small, perfect world he was promised is unraveling by the day. She has revealed herself to be a soiled beast, her skin rubbed pink and raw from her gag. Her language, foul and base; her temper, intolerable. What's more, the constable or Louis could return. They could be at his shop now, heeding her cries, lifting the butterfly cabinet and cutting her free. He rubs his chin.

He peers closer at the Queen's face, sees a hint of a brush-stroke on her cheek, the daub of light in her eye, the inside of her mouth a lurid, unnatural green. Close up, the painting reveals itself as nothing more than a feint. It is a trick, just like that wench's deceitful red hair. He cannot endure falseness; it is the worst thing of all.

His hand is shaking as he draws out the knife. He waits for the crowds to thin, for a particularly raucous conversation to reach its pitch in the corner. He presses the blade into the edge of the canvas. It is as hard as wood, but the scalpel is sharp, and it punctures the canvas with a snap. The painting is not large; it is the length of his arm.

In a smooth, tugging motion, he pulls the knife across it. The sound is throaty. The paint chips, the threads fray. The Queen is severed at the waist, the window cut in two. He smiles, tucks away the blade, and he enjoys the clip of his footsteps across the parquet, down the steps, across the courtyard, and into the clamor of the street.

# Water

Iris's legs are as useless as if Silas had clipped her knee tendons. She imagines a pair of glinting surgical scissors in his hand. *Snip, snip.*

The moment she hears him leave, she tries to inch herself onto her toes, a hunchback pushed forward by the chair. But she cries out at the pain of it—the muscles in her legs are so stiff and wasted—and rocks backward again.

She pants into her gag, and her breath is so foul, so putrid, the skin around her cheeks so sore, that it gives her strength to try again. She must escape; she must breathe fresh air, smell something other than her waste, see something other than this black void—and in her second attempt she manages to shuffle the chair to the wall. She rests her forehead against the cold, damp stone, bites hard on her lip at the cramping of her muscles.

*I am alive*, she thinks.

At first, she is anxious not to maim herself as she rocks the armrest into the wall. A scrape of wood on stone, a stuttering of two textures colliding. She catches her forearm, gasps, feels the warm running of blood. She does not care. She takes a perverse joy from this: she can endure anything.

Pain stabs at her legs, her arms, her head with its slow pulsing headache, but she hurls herself at the wall again and again and again. Sometimes she is sure she hears a slight splintering, but when she tries to rotate her wrist, the wood does not give. She just needs one arm free, and then she can untie herself. Just one arm—

Sometimes she closes her eyes and tells herself it is hopeless, and she feels herself tugged as if by an invisible current, weighed down by the pitifulness of her situation. She will never escape him, never be free. She coughs until her throat is raw. The world swims with giddiness, and she feels so sick, so feverish, that she is tempted to fall asleep.

But she will fight it. She *will*. She *must*.

Her arm is cut, her legs burn, and she counts the number of times she tips herself at the wall. Twelve, thirteen, fourteen.

She imagines that her limbs are nothing but china, her soiled, torn dress the smart habiliment of a porcelain doll. She wears stiff satin with a frothy lace trim, and her feet are black with tiny painted buttons. The pain is nothing more than the accidental pricks of Rose's needle as she stitches the skirt closed over her cloth body.

"Dead or alive?" she asks Rose, who conceals a smile.

"Sister, must you always play this game?"

"Her eyes are a little blurred. I think—"

Dead or alive—is she—

She roars, and the strength in her legs surprises her as she throws herself at the wall one final time and then—at last—the most glorious sound. The wood snaps.

She feels it at once: the sudden release of the binding. Pain crackles through her wrist, up her arm, and for a moment the work and the agony flatten her. But there is a solace in carrying on beyond the limit of what she thought she could bear. She works her fingers into the other three knots, stretches her wrists, her ankles. Soon she will try and stand.

She hears Silas pacing. The ceiling creaks. His footsteps pause above the trapdoor.

If he comes down, he will see the broken chair arm, the restraints lying at her feet, and she has no plan prepared. She is weak, helpless. He will tie her up again, tighter, in a different way to prevent her from smashing herself free once more, and she will never escape—

She hears the object being pulled back and she could scream and curse and rail. The door opens, and the cellar walls are lit, as yellow as gangrene. Her arm is scratched, bloody, her clothes soiled and stained. She hears the clank of the lamp, the scratch of his boot, and he will be here soon—

She tries to shout at him, to swear, but she is so thirsty she cannot form the words. Her throat will not obey her. She barely recognizes the monstrous gargle that comes from within her—

*Do not come down*, she urges him in her head. *Do not*—

And then—she can hardly believe it—he closes the door, and his footsteps recede.

When she pulls herself out of the chair, her legs falter. She remembers when she tried to move after posing with her feet tucked under her for an hour, and how Louis had laughed. She tilted as if drunk, and fell sideways onto the sofa. He holds her now, coaxing her upward, propping her as she adds weight to her limbs, a touch at a time. Rose whispers encouragement. *Try again, sister.*

Her only weapon is the chair-arm. She searches the floor for anything—even a mere shard of glass—but he has been too careful. She remembers then the bell that rang in the corner; could she prize the wire loose? She isn't sure how it will help, but it might be something. She must try, at least.

She runs her fingers along the stone roof of the cell, one row at a time. It is damp, slimy, and the crystals crumble in her hand.

She lights on cool metal. The bell is domed with a little hammer beside it. Spider's webs catch on her. She fumbles for the bell and teases it free, carefully so that it does not drop and make a noise. It is the hammer that is linked to the wire, but the cable is taut and will not give. She saws it back and forth, pulls at it with all her weight, then slips and falls. She tries once more. There is a distant thud, a crack, a hiss of unspooling metal, and Iris inches the cable through, bit by bit, flinching at every sound. There are no footsteps above, no shouts. He must be asleep or out.

She wonders again what she will do with the wire, but it reassures her that she has something else if the chair-arm breaks. Could she tie him up? Garrotte him? This time, she will be unafraid of maiming him. When she swings the wood, she will put her weight behind it. She practices, whipping it through the air.

All she needs is for Silas to appear.

She waits and waits and waits.

She sleeps in the one-armed chair, her eyelids sinking of their own accord. She tries to conserve her strength by sitting still, walking every so often in case her muscles seize, but she feels weaker by the minute, and the mistiness starts to return. Thirst. Hunger.

She has never experienced thirst like this. It hollows her out, gnaws at her insides, makes her head feel swollen with the sharp pain of it. She dreams of water, of dipping her brush into a jar of murky liquid and then drinking it all down—

She blinks, and tries to concentrate on her body. On her breath.

She is alive.

Why doesn't he come?

She licks moisture from the wall until her stomach convulses.

There is nothing for her to vomit. She considers biting her arm and sucking the blood, but what good will that do, and surely that will only loosen her grip on the world even more?

She is swimming in a clear lake, and she dives down, opens her mouth, and lets the cool water flow in. She seizes hold of a stone, but it is the china head of a doll, stained by the paint water she knocked over it. When she looks again, it is the skull of a girl, *her* skull, and the lake bed is dense with them. Rows of dolls, rows of painted women, rows of skulls. Dead, dead, all dead—

Where is he? How much longer until she has nothing left in her?

She has fought all she can, and now she is gutted.

Louis's face looms out of the blackness, and she feels his breath on her cheek.

"We should go inside," he says, nuzzling her earlobe.

"Let's stay here," she says, and he pours the sun-warmed port into her mouth until she splutters. It stains her dress, and he kisses her and kisses her, until she feels nothing.

The darkness is so soft and so warm, a goose-down counterpane. She settles into it, into Louis, and she is with him at last.

# Needle

S ilas glues the tiny pieces of wood together. They are the same size as four matchsticks. He lifts the final edge—there—the outline of a golden square.

He picks up the white mouse, dressed in a plain blue dress, neatly stitched. Like many of the surgeons whose conversations he has overheard, Silas is as comfortable with a needle as with a scalpel. He used to listen to them brag about their ability to darn socks, the sewing practice they undertook on their daughters' doll's clothes, their talk of the annual surgical embroidery prize.

"Aren't you a beauty, my Queen," he says to the rodent, stroking the soft fur of her head and securing her on a stand. He dangles a fly from the frame to represent the dove Iris grasped for in the painting, and props it in front of the mouse.

He regards the finished piece. It isn't perfect, but it will do. In the evening, he will carry it upstairs to join the other mice.

He hasn't heard Iris for over a day. There have been no whinnies, no poundings, nothing at all. The silence chills and comforts him in equal measure.

And how still, how eerie it is without any noise, without anyone to talk to! In truth, it is a relief. No baying, none of the interminable screeching, none of her cunning facility with words that made him consider releasing her. No; it is better this way, even if he did not intend it. Soon, he will be able to move all his jars and specimens back down to the cellar.

He dusts the bell jars, polishes the bones with oil and a cloth, re-arranges the stuffed pelts. He picks up a snippet of *The Lancet*, reads about the way the clavicle knits to other bones, about its articulation with the manubrium of the sternum and the sternoclavicular joint. There is a knocking, and Silas calls, "Who is it?"

"Mabel," somebody replies. "About a butterfly brooch for my mistress—"

He opens the door, and a servant stands before him.

"Your bell, sir. It seems to be broken. And your sign says to knock and ring." He looks where she points: there is an empty socket in the wall and the ringer is upended in the dirt. He curses.

"Can I come in, sir?"

He smiles, assumes his customer mask. "I've been away, I'm afraid, and the shop is chaos. *Chaos.* But if you return in two days, everything will be quite as it was."

When she leaves, Silas inspects the bell. It must be this sudden heat, melting the fastenings. He will go to the cellar, see how he can fix it.

He pushes back the Lepidoptera cabinet, shines his light down. Iris is slumped forward in the chair.

He presses his handkerchief to his nose and descends the ladder one-handed. He tries not to inhale.

At the base, he turns and she is there.

Her skin is whiter than it ever was in life. Sweat has gathered on it, like the damp on pork rind. She tried, he knows that. She tried harder, kicked harder, than Bluebell, than Flick, than any of the others.

He loves the fall of her hair. He pulls a strand of it through his hand. It is as soft as fur. Gold mixed with auburn mixed with brown. He tugs it. It is a little matted, but he will tease each knot free with a lover's care.

It reminds him of that first fox he found, its red pelt, the downy belly hairs as white as alumina. The powerful strength of the jaw-bone, putty-colored, and its interlinked teeth. It was once so full of movement, and then its skeleton was a mere monument to its former self.

It is then that the tears boil up in his throat, and he pours out all the emotion and worry and fear and love he has kept at bay over the last ten days. Ten days was all she stayed with him for! Ten days to trap this beautiful mouse, this sweetling. A new wave of sobs; they come from a deep well within him. For something this stunning not to exist any longer!

"I'm sorry," he says, again and again.

Her eyes are hidden by the fall of her hair and he covers his face and weeps.

# The Butterfly Cabinet

When he pulls her hair, she imagines that he is merely tugging a doll's curls, stitched from the shorn locks of a South German peasant. Her lips are carmine pigment. Her limbs are cold, fired porcelain. Her eyes are glossy green marbles. She is stiff on Mrs. Salter's shelf, a metal stand pinning her in place. His hands—his greasy hands—he is just a boisterous child, toying with her, and she will not flinch—

He doesn't seem to have noticed the missing chair-arm, the restraints draped loosely, the wire that hangs from her palm. His odor has changed, become chemical and clean. He smells of Mrs. Salter's medicine drawer with its crushed pills and lotions and syrups, all promising eternal youth and health. He smells of turpentine and freshly cleaned brushes.

Her vision falters, and she knows her only chance is surprise. He must continue to believe she is dead. She is sure that he must hear the gasp of her heart, her shallow inhalations.

When he starts to sob, a shred of pity only galvanizes her loathing.

She despises him with a force that almost makes her cry out, but she must stay still. *Queenie, do not move—*

*I could be mistaken for a memento-mori daguerreotype. If my image were taken, I wouldn't even blur—*

He crouches and covers his face with his hands.

But the air feels mud-thick, and when she tries to lift her arm, it will not obey her. It hangs by her side, as if it belongs to somebody else, as dead as if it had been tucked underneath her for hours, slowly numbing. She must do it little by little—a slow building of color—a twitch of her finger, and then the turn of her wrist.

Louis sits at one side, her sister at the other. She imagines seeing them again outside their shimmering presence in the cellar walls, seeing them as they are. Seeing them *truly.* Her sister, the mistress of a shop, penciling sales in her ledger, an apprentice at her side; Louis, painting next to her, the corners of his mouth twisting into an imagined joke, and the strength of his hands as he draws his brush across the canvas—and her painting, finished in the Academy, on the line or just above or below it—

With the final kicks of a drowning woman toward air, she lifts her arm and it is easy. Her body arcs as she slams the chair-arm across Silas's head. It is a clean smack—she can feel the vibration of his skull up her shoulder. The world takes on sudden flashes, a rough score of a palette knife, the abrupt violence of hurled paint on a finished piece. Silas flounders, turns, and she raises the wood once more, pounds it across his brow. It arms her with more hatred, more anger, until she is trembling with it, drunk on it. There is blood then—a shock of pure madder.

He howls, and his hands thrash the floor, grappling for her legs. She reaches for her bucket, brimming with waste, and she empties it over his head. He is fearfully close, and she beats him again with the arm of the chair, all while the world spins and dips around her. She hears the crack of bone—his ribs most likely—and the splintering of wood. She steadies herself on the wall, and the cellar swims.

The rungs of the ladder are before her, deliciously cold. But her progress is slow, hampered by fatigue and by her skirts, bunching and catching against her feet. The wire is wrapped around her wrist. She is only aware that she has cut her palm by the sight of blood. She stops, the world racketing around her, shapes looming from nowhere, and her fingers slip.

Silas is groaning, groping toward her. She sways with exhaustion and dizziness. This is her last chance, she tells herself. She will live—she *must* live.

She regains her grip and moves slower, more carefully. She can hear him below her, but she tries to shut it out. She must not fall. One more step, her petticoats kicked out of the way. Then another. And another. She is half in the shop.

The sun is sudden, pure. A slant of light, so bright she feels she could snag it between her fingers. She narrows her eyes against it. She can hear the distant hum of carriages on the Strand. Normal people going about their normal lives. The air, too, is cleaner, and pickled animals stare at her from their clouded jars. She moves to pull herself into the room.

She feels it again. His hand on her ankle; she turns and sees the oily crease of his hair below her. She kicks him, but it is not enough and she is fading. The wire; she remembers the wire, and she lashes it across his knuckles. A cry—she could not say whose.

The shackle around her foot is released.

It is enough time for her to lift herself onto the floor of the shop. The light! She wants to drink it in, to savor every last drop. But she hears him below, the hollow smack of boot on ladder, and she pushes the trapdoor. It slams shut, the edges misaligned. Already, the corner is lifting, his hand pressing it upward. She looks around her, but she does not have the strength to move the cabinet. She cannot even stand; she sits in a pool of her torn soiled skirts, her cheeks raw from the cut of the gag, her arm scabbed from the rocking of the chair against the wall.

She crawls to the other side of the cabinet—it is heavy mahogany and glass—and leans on it. The dresser shifts slightly, and she throws her weight behind it. It swings, hovers as if on a string, and then crashes downward. The dust billows, the wood cracks, and fractured glass and butterfly wings sprawl across the shop.

It is only when she knows that he is trapped that she keels forward. She pulls herself toward the door, the world blurring and bending and twisting around her. There are shards of glass in her fist, blood on her knees, her skirts ruched up. She falls into the passageway outside.

She flounders, and rights herself.

She can smell frying food and the eggy stink of the Thames and pipe smoke and wood fires and rotten vegetables and a thousand other things besides. The cinder heaps are as dry as dust, and the churn from the carriages makes her cough. Through it all, the sun shines, slipping between the tall buildings. It is all beautiful, all hers. The peace of a stilled moment.

She thinks there is nothing left within her.

And yet.

And yet, she stumbles forward. Toward the melee and the hiss and the hurrying clerks.

But most of all: the sight of it. She could gaze on it for days, years, and never tire of it. The chipped brick of a building, the outstretched arm of a boy calling out letters, the fading perspective of the Strand as she bursts onto it. She wishes she had her easel and paints, Louis at her side, showing her how to use the colors—the black of a topper, the unmixed emerald of a whisking carriage, and a girl with loose red hair—running.

*London*

*May 1852*

# THE PAINTING

R*oyal Academy: Second Notice. Our Critic Among Paintings—* excerpt of review in the *Illustrated London News*, 22 May 1852:

I have, in past years, rapped my pen over the palette of the Pre-Raphaelite Brotherhood, but this year I must be less severe in my censure. Indeed, upon entering the East Room, you find your eye immediately drawn to a medium-sized canvas a little below the line, and showing such a dignified feeling that I spent the most joyful hour regarding it. While it shows some defects in delivery, and no doubt the artist has room for technical improvement, her response to Nature is pleasing.

In common with the work of the so-called PRB, it is painted in lurid colors with an interest in light, and with an evenness of focus that attaches equal significance to each object. The issue with this approach is, of course, that little things are copied with great attention; great things paid little heed. A mouse escapes the grip of a cat, a vase is filled with irises and roses, all yet to bloom fully, and a blond maid sits in the background and helps herself to a bowl of strawberries while her mistress's eyes are averted. These unnecessary details detract from the true intimacy at the heart of this work, namely the embracing lovers. They turn toward each other as if on the brink of laughter, and are arranged with such a stark naturalness, such a sweetness, that the scene is prevented from tipping into a sickly sentimentality.

A convex mirror is discernible on the wall, portraying a broader dimension outside the scope of the painting. An overused trope in modern art, here the mirror's inclusion justifies its purpose by the doubling of its subjects. In the reflection, an almost-identical figure to the central woman sits at a desk, her focus absorbed by a brass cash register. This is well done, and her disfigured face hints at the passing of time and decay, with the register as a modern scales, symbolizing metaphysical judgment and the counting out of days.

The white-haired maid, meanwhile, finds her double in the similar features of a small boy in blue breeches, caught in a pyramid of light from the window. He reaches his hand toward the viewer, as if beckoning him into the frame, or perhaps begging for a coin.

This simple, though cluttered, painting may not take its cue from poetry or Shakespeare, but its quaint and honest rendering of a domestic scene has left this critic—scurril-knave and mocker that he so often is—filled with an admiration for the natural loveliness therein.

# AUTHOR'S NOTE

At the time this novel is set, Lizzie spelled her surname "Siddall," but Rossetti later persuaded her to change it to "Siddal," as it sounded more elegant.

# ACKNOWLEDGMENTS

Thank you—

To Maddy—champion, powerhouse, friend, and the best agent there is. For the teas, and later the fizz; for your belief in me; for your expert guidance and calm. To all at the Madeleine Milburn Agency: Anna Hogarty, Giles Milburn, Hayley Steed, and Alice Sutherland-Hawes.

To my superb editor Sophie Jonathan, whose hawk eyes and insights have made this book what is—thank you, a thousand times over. To my U.S. editor, Emily Bestler, for the invaluable suggestions, commentary, and enthusiasm. I am so grateful to both of you.

To those at Picador, including Camilla Elworthy, goddess among publicists, and Paul Baggaley, Lara Borlenghi, Katie Bowden, Gill Fitzgerald-Kelly, and Katie Tooke. To those at Simon & Schuster in the U.S., particularly Lara Jones and Libby McGuire.

To my workshop group in London, the best and most talented of friends: Megan Davis, Richard O'Halloran, Sophie Kirkwood, Campaspe Lloyd-Jacob, and Tom Watson. Extra special thanks to Emily Ruth Ford, whose editing, support, and friendship mean everything to me.

To Lydia Matthews and Diana Parker, who have read everything I've written for the last decade, and encouraged me through every setback. To Lucy Clarke, Alessandra Crawford, Elizabeth Day, Chris McQuitty, Julia Murday, Ed Parry-Smith, Emma Sharp, Nayela Wickramasuriya, and Elizabeth Wignall for literary guidance and cheering pep talks, particularly in early drafts of this novel. I am lucky to call you my friends.

To my English teachers: Paul Cheetham, Pippa Donald, Rob Harrison, Joe McKee, and Betty Thompson. To Fiona Stafford, my tutor at Somerville College, who nurtured my love of Victorian fiction, and encouraged me to write my undergraduate thesis on clutter in 1850s literature, which first sparked my interest in collectors, the Pre-Raphaelite Brotherhood, and The Great Exhibition.

To everyone at UEA who supported me, pushed me, taught me. To my tutors Giles Foden, Philip Langeskov, Laura Joyce, Rebecca Stott, and especially Joe Dunthorne; and to the workshop group which read the opening chapters of this novel and told me to keep writing.

To the Malcolm Bradbury and Ian Watt foundations, whose scholarships gave me time to write. To the Caledonia Novel Award and Wendy Bough, for the most wonderful news at a crucial time, for introducing me to my agent, and for the subsequent support and friendship.

To Josh Bennett, Terry Blundell, Dan Reeve and Viktor Wynd for expertise on topics ranging from medieval romance to taxidermy to oil painting. Any errors are my own.

And . . .

To everyone in my family. To my Aunty Dinah, the best of road-trip companions, who will always tell it how it is. To my brothers and sister, Peter, Hector, and Laura, for years of love and rivalry and fun. To my Grandma and Grandpa, Enid and Arthur Bourne, who were proud of me before I'd achieved anything, who taught me so much. I always promised you my first novel, and I wish we could have shared this. I miss you.

To Jonny. For everything.

To my parents, who have always encouraged me to reach beyond what I thought I was capable, who hugged me when I failed, and then told me to try again. For reading and loving every word I ever sent you (however terrible), and for always, always being there. Thank you.